On a Night Like This

Lindsey Kelk

HarperCollins*Publishers*

HarperCollins*Publishers* Ltd
1 London Bridge Street,
London SE1 9GF

www.harpercollins.co.uk

HarperCollins*Publishers*
1st Floor, Watermarque Building, Ringsend Road
Dublin 4, Ireland

First published by HarperCollins*Publishers* 2021

1

A catalogue record for this book is available from the British Library

ISBN: 978-0-00-840777-3 (HB)
ISBN: 978-0-00-840778-0 (TPB, Export, Airside, IE-only)
ISBN: 978-0-00-850568-4 (TPB, AU, NZ-only)
ISBN: 978-0-00-849675-3 (PB, US, CA-only)

This novel is entirely a work of fiction.
The names, characters and incidents portrayed in it are
the work of the author's imagination. Any resemblance to
actual persons, living or dead, events or localities is
entirely coincidental.

Typeset in Melior by Palimpsest Book Production Ltd, Falkirk, Stirlingshire

Printed and Bound in the UK using 100% Renewable Electricity at CPI Group (UK) Ltd

MIX
Paper from
responsible sources
FSC™ C007454

This book is produced from independently certified FSC™ paper
to ensure responsible forest management.

For more information visit: www.harpercollins.co.uk/green

For Juliette and Orlander,
who lent their names to this book
and deserve so much more.
Thank you.

CHAPTER ONE

'Once upon a time, in a faraway kingdom, there was a woman called Francesca who couldn't be on time to save her life,' Jess announced as I blew through the door of Suzette's Café on Wednesday morning.

'I'm so sorry,' I said, giving her a quick hug before starting to unravel my many winter layers. After an unseasonably mild October, November was not messing around in Sheffield. 'You know I hate being late but Stew said he'd drop me off but his dad called and he had to run and I missed the bus and—'

'Fran.' My best friend pushed a cup of coffee towards me, along with a white paper bag. 'It's fine, relax, I'm joking. Sit down, I ordered for you because I'm so nice.' I dumped my tote bag on the table and smiled as she opened her own bag and inhaled. 'What does she put in these bloody muffins? How are they so good?'

'Best not to ask,' I advised, glancing over to the counter where Suzette was fixing tinsel to the shelves with a threatening-looking staple gun. 'Something we're not supposed to be eating any more, like white sugar or stem cells or crack.'

'All very moreish in their own way,' she replied, breaking off a chunk of muffin before fixing me with a look. 'Are you all right? You two aren't fighting again, are you?'

'I'm fine,' I said, waving away her concerns with the end of my scarf. My hair frizzed up around me in a static halo as I pulled off my bobble hat. 'Just feeling a bit *meh*, that's all.' Jess narrowed her eyes to let me know she didn't quite believe me but wasn't going to force the issue. 'Seriously, I'm so sorry. Are you in a rush?' I asked. 'Or can you stay for a bit?'

She shook her head as she pulled a neon-pink travel mug out of her own tote bag, unscrewed the top and poured her giant coffee inside. 'I've got to run,' she said, the tip of her tongue poking out the corner of her mouth as she poured. 'There are a million meetings today and for some reason, they need me in every bloody one of them. I swear, if I wasn't there, the place would burn to the ground in twenty-four hours.'

Jess was a very cool marketing director who did very cool things at a very cool brewery and, while she complained about her job constantly, I knew she loved it down to her bones.

'No worries,' I repeated. 'Everything's fine.'

'Shall I come round tonight?' she suggested gently. 'Stew's got football practice, hasn't he?'

I nodded, extremely happy with that plan. 'Sounds grand, I'll make dinner. Is there anything you're not eating right now?'

'No, it's too close to Christmas for that,' she replied, screwing the lid back on her cup and dropping it in her bag. 'They've already got the Quality Street open at work, I'll bring you a big purple one.' She scooted around the table to give me a kiss on the cheek. 'What's on your agenda for today?'

'Sitting here and waiting for literally anything to happen?'

'We don't wait for things to happen,' Jess said, white paper muffin bag in one hand, car keys in the other. 'We make them happen!'

'You sound like an Instagram post,' I called after her. 'If you tell me to live, laugh and love, you're not allowed round for tea.'

'More like nap, nom and Netflix,' she shouted back, already halfway out the door. 'See you tonight.'

It had been almost a month since I'd finished my last temping job – a thrilling adventure through the world of data entry for a logistics company in Rotherham – and so far, not a single one of the agencies I was signed up with could find me a new one. Apparently I was 'over-qualified' for almost everything and even though I would have happily wiped Satan's bottom for minimum wage if it meant getting out of the house for eight hours a day, they couldn't find me a thing. All the shops had hired their seasonal staff already and no one else was recruiting this close to Christmas.

Peering through the window of the café, I watched as the shops and businesses turned on their lights, the high street springing to life, the post office, the off-licence, the beauty salon, the bookshop. Everyone else's day was starting while I drank my coffee, ate my muffin and pulled my computer out of my backpack. Everyone had somewhere to go and something to do except for me.

Hands hovering over the ancient laptop as it clicked

and whirred into life, I stared at the two rings I wore every day, the only jewellery I ever wore, really. On my left hand, my engagement ring from Stew, a dainty diamond affair shaped like a flower, that had belonged to his beloved Nana Beryl before it was passed down to me with the most serious of strings attached. And on the third finger of my right hand, my mum's gold wedding band. She'd be so disappointed, I thought, twisting it around and around and around. Susan Cooper hadn't spent so much as a day out of work, a fact she had been fiercely proud of, and the thought of letting her down when she wasn't here any more felt like the worst possible failure.

'Don't wait for things to happen,' I whispered, attempting to stoke a fire that had all but burned out. 'Make them happen.'

With some uncertainty, I slipped my earbuds into my ears and dialled a number I had not dialled in months.

'Vine & Walsh, Rose speaking.'

'Rose, it's Fran, Fran Cooper,' I said, straightening my shoulders and taking a deep, steadying breath. 'How are you?'

'I'm well, thank you, how are you?' The silky southern accent on the other end of the phone sounded surprised to hear from me, which was fair, given that I hadn't been in touch for the best part of a year.

'Really well but still looking for work.' I tapped my fingers against the edge of the table, heart in my mouth. 'I was wondering if you might have anything for me?'

'I'll happily take a look,' Rose replied. 'But I'm fairly certain we don't have anything in your area, unless you've changed your mind about taking work outside South Yorkshire?'

4

And that was the reason I hadn't been in touch for the best part of a year. Vine & Walsh was an executive recruitment firm, not just your average temp agency, and every time I spoke with Rose, she told me about one incredible job after another and I had to turn each and every one of them down. In my wildest professional fantasies, I was totally jet set. I dreamed of travelling, seeing the world, of waking up to find I was the kind of woman who could pack two weeks-worth of clothes in a carry on and could go from conference room B to the bar to an all-night karaoke party with nothing more than a swipe of red lipstick and a change of earrings, but after we moved back to Sheffield, Stew and I had both agreed we wouldn't travel for work. Admittedly, that deal was made three years ago when we were living in London and there were a lot more jobs to choose from, but a deal is a deal and it was made for a reason, so I kept my ambitions local.

'Sorry, no,' I said as my heart sank slowly back towards my feet. 'Just thought it was worth checking in.'

As Rose let out a quiet, frustrated sigh, a new email from one of the local temp agencies appeared in my inbox. A vet in Brincliffe needed an office manager to do a two-week holiday cover starting Christmas Eve. Utterly depressing and still the best offer I'd had in months.

'There is one thing, and you'd be perfect for it,' Rose said, a note of possibility in her voice. 'It would mean you'd have to travel, but it's very short term and the money is amazing. I need a personal assistant for a very, very – let me say this again – *very* high-profile client.'

I looked out of the window at the stone-clad buildings

opposite, almost the exact same shade of grey as the sky above them.

'How short term and how much money?'

'Not even a week, it's five days. All your expenses would be covered, and the salary is very generous. *Extremely* generous. And the money isn't even the best part.'

I wound the cord from my earbuds around my finger and squeezed it tightly. Curiosity might have killed the cat but perhaps I could get away with only being lightly maimed.

'OK,' I said, breathing out slowly. 'What's the catch?'

Rose gave a slightly maniacal laugh down the line. 'Don't let this put you off, but I can't say. Fran, it is *VV VIP*. You'll have to sign a non-disclosure agreement before I can even send the job description over, and I'll need you down in London to interview ASAP, but if I were you, I would seriously consider this one. It could be a huge break. This is a life-changing opportunity.'

A powerful rush of adrenaline shot through my body and I glanced at my cup to make sure it was definitely full of coffee and not rocket fuel.

'It's been a while since I did any top-level stuff,' I admitted, clenching hard. 'The last couple of years I've mostly been at smaller, local companies. Are you sure I'd be a good fit?'

'Positive. It's a PA role, not a corporate job, so you're not going to be making PowerPoints and pivot tables, no one's expecting you to be up on EU regulations or lack thereof. Plus you've got all the extras they're looking for, multiple languages, first aid qualifications, and the sailing experience is just *mwah*, chef's kiss. Puts you right over the edge.'

Ahh yes, the summer I'd spent working in the café on the Newcastle to Amsterdam ferry after my A levels. Truly invaluable sailing experience. Thankfully, I really did have a degree in French and Italian, even if I hadn't used either for anything more advanced than ordering a lasagne from Nonna's on Ecclesall Road in the last three years.

'I can't tell you anything else until you sign the NDA but, Fran, I cannot stress enough what a one-of-a-kind opportunity this is. If they'd let me, I'd quit and do it myself.'

'If it's that amazing, why hasn't it been filled already?' I asked, suddenly wary. Rose was altogether too excited for my liking and I knew from personal experience nothing in life was ever too good to be true.

'It came up quite last minute,' she replied with no small degree of hesitancy. 'And the person in charge of hiring on their end is quite particular. She knows what she doesn't want even if she doesn't seem to have a very clear picture of what she does want.'

So it was a she. I wondered who it could be. You heard all kinds of stories in the temp community. A friend of mine in London once did a stint at a fancy estate agents for a fortnight and ended up selling a house to George and Amal. Well, she was fairly sure she saw the back of George's head from her car when she went to drop off the spare keys, but when I thought about a choice between scheduling appointments for Gavin the epileptic guinea pig or potentially spotting the back of George Clooney's head, it wasn't going to be too difficult a decision to make.

'I'm going to call them right now,' Rose said, the sound of her keyboard clacking decisively in the background. 'Don't go anywhere, I'll bell you back in a sec.'

'OK, sounds good,' I confirmed. 'I'll be right here.'

She hung up, leaving me staring at my laptop screen, slightly out of breath and, I realized as I caught sight of my reflection in the window of the café, absolutely beaming. It was so long since I'd been excited about a job prospect, I'd forgotten how good it felt. The prickling nerves, the anticipation. I didn't have the interview yet, but I was already planning my first day outfit. And it was just five days, Stew wouldn't mind my being away for five days. Before, in my old assistant jobs, I was away all the time, traipsing up and down the country, nipping off to deeply exotic locations like Belgium for a convention or a trade show. I was practically never home. But it had been so long since I'd been anywhere, and things were so much better than they were last time. He wouldn't mind. He definitely wouldn't mind.

Leaning back in my chair, I stared past my reflection, out into the street. The pub on the corner was already busy with old boy regulars, and next door, the Be Beautiful salon was packed to the rafters with shadowy figures moving around behind the frosted windows. The door opened and the owner herself stepped out onto the street, vape pen in hand. I slouched down in my chair and wrapped both hands around my coffee mug. Lifting it to my mouth was as close as I would come to an upper body workout today.

Bryony looked beautiful, of course: blonde hair wrapped around her head in a braid crown, makeup perfectly applied and, even from across the road, I could see her perfect nails shone a rich ruby red. My own hair was full of half a can of dry shampoo, my makeup non-existent, and my nails were short and bare. Not painting them was the only way I could guarantee I wouldn't chip them. You weren't supposed to like your partner's ex, I reminded myself as I continued to watch her with my standard level of morbid fascination, and at least Bryony had the decency to be deeply unpleasant whenever we were forced to interact, which was all too often since she was still Stew's sister's best friend. It would have been much worse if she was a wonderful person and I was just a jealous arse, pouting over the fact a woman much more beautiful than me had also once been engaged to Stew Bingham. But Stew didn't care about things like elaborate hair and shiny nails, I reminded myself, reflexively touching my diamond ring. Stew cared about me.

It was a fact that might have been more reassuring if the door hadn't opened for a second time, my fiancé walking right out of the salon behind Bryony. He was wearing the Bingham & Son overalls he'd left the house in that morning, and had an adorable smudge of some-thing on his snub nose. Sinking lower, I pressed myself against the wall as I tried to come up with a reasonable explanation as to what he might be doing in the Be Beautiful salon, when he was supposed to be fitting a cast-iron claw-foot bath with his dad. Eyelash exten-sions? Colouring that flash of grey that had recently appeared at his temples? Or simply engaging in a good old-fashioned affair? Before my brain could completely spin off out of control, my phone vibrated into life with Rose's name and number lighting up the screen.

'Hello?' I answered, eyes still fixed on the scene outside the salon.

'Fran-it's-Rose-I've-got-good-news,' she said all at once, without pausing for breath,

'Good news as in I've got the interview good news?'

'Exactly like that! I'm sending everything over to you right now, you just need to whizz the NDA back to me and I'll send you a train ticket for tomorrow morning.'

'Tomorrow as in the day after today?' I asked, my heart pounding against my ribs. One eye on Stew, one on my phone. 'You didn't say I'd have to interview tomorrow?'

'And if you're successful, you'll start the job tomorrow as well,' Rose confirmed. 'Fran, don't turn this down. It's a once in a lifetime opportunity.'

'Once in a lifetime doesn't automatically translate into a good thing,' I replied, newly formed doubts beginning to take root in the back of my mind. 'Lots of bad things only happen once in a lifetime.'

'The interview is with a Sarah Pierce – don't worry about writing it down, I'll email the details – and I'm quite certain it's just a formality,' Rose said, talking over me excitedly. 'They love your CV, and from the sounds of it, they're desperate. You're a shoo-in.'

Charming.

'So, you'll sign the NDA and send it back right away?'

'Yes.'

'And you can be in London tomorrow?'

'I can.'

I peered out of the window to see Stew and Bryony still standing outside the salon, grinning at each other as it began to rain. Perfectly normal behaviour that didn't ring any alarm bells in the slightest. She held out her vape pen and Stew leaned forward to take a cheeky toke, his cough blooming in the chilly air as she pulled it away, laughing.

'Then I think that covers it,' Rose cut through my miserable thoughts and brought me back to earth with a bump. 'Any questions?'

I closed my eyes and pinched the bridge of my nose, focusing on work and pushing what was clearly happening right under my nose as far away as possible. I'd always been good at that.

'No, I don't think so,' I replied confidently. 'This is amazing, thank you so much.'

'I'm sending all the info over now,' she sang down the line, her voice full of cheer. 'Call me if you have any problems at all, any questions, any issues with the job.'

'I will,' I promised as I ended the call, knowing that I wouldn't. I didn't have problems, that was part of my charm.

Fran Cooper, dependable, reliable and one hundred percent guaranteed to make your life easier. That was my brand. As I watched Stew wander off down the street with a great big smile on his face, I realized the only person I ever made things difficult for, was myself.

CHAPTER TWO

'What are these and why aren't we burning them right this very second?'

Jess held a pair of pink flowered culottes aloft with a horrified expression on her face.

'They're Stew's mum's,' I said, snatching them out of her hand and tossing them back into the ironing pile that lived on the spare bed. 'I had to borrow them last Sunday after Mandy's youngest decided to hurl his pudding across the room and I got doused in custard.'

'What I wouldn't give to get doused in custard,' she sighed as she flopped onto her back. 'And now I'm hungry. What have you got for pudding?'

'I haven't got anything for pudding,' I told her, holding a smart black blouse up to the light to check it was in fact still black and hadn't been washed into a sad state of charcoal grey by our archaic washing machine, before putting it in my suitcase. 'In fact, I haven't even got anything for dinner, I was busy getting ready for tomorrow and I forgot. Pizza?'

'Can't beat pizza.' She took the sensible black blouse

out of my suitcase and dropped it down the back of the bed. 'You really don't have any clue who you'll be working for?'

'Haven't the foggiest,' I replied, reaching across her to pick up the blouse and put it right back in the suitcase. 'I tried Google, but there are about a million Sarah Pierces, I gave up after an hour. It's all very intense though, I've never had to sign an NDA for an interview before. And the job requirements list is a lot.'

'The no jewellery rule seems a bit much, but I do support the proper manicure and pedicure regulations – I can't bear manky feet.' Jess had not signed an NDA but she had sneaked a peek at my phone when I was in the toilet, so she knew just as much about my potential new job as I did.

'Hopefully they'll accept my DIY job, or I'll be out on my arse before I've even started,' I said, peering down at my newly polished pink toes. 'Fingers crossed it's not a foot fetishist.'

Jess pulled an ancient bottle of sunscreen out from the pocket of my suitcase, took a sniff and gagged, before throwing it in the bin. It had been a while since the suitcase had seen any action.

'I reckon it's Oprah,' she guessed. 'Or Mark Zuckerberg. Or Paul Hollywood.'

'Why Paul Hollywood?'

'Strikes me as someone who would enjoy the power,' she reasoned. 'I bet he goes through assistants like I go through hot dinners. To be honest with you, Fran, I don't know how you do it. I've seen too many people treat their assistants like absolute shit.'

I held my hand out for the pair of socks she had stuffed down the front of her shirt and tucked into her bra. 'Is this a good time to point out we only met because I was covering for your assistant?'

'Proves my point entirely,' Jess said, jiggling her boobs until the socks fell out. 'I'm a monster and you're a masochist. I thought you were looking into teacher training?'

I froze, socks in hand.

'Did Stew tell you that?'

She nodded slowly. 'He mentioned it at the pub quiz last week. Should he not have?'

'No, he shouldn't,' I bristled. 'Teacher training is his idea, not mine. Or, more specifically, it's his mum's idea. After twelve years, she's decided she doesn't like telling people I'm a temp, apparently. Can you imagine me as a teacher?'

Jess laughed so hard and so sharp, she started to cough and had to pause to wipe tears from the corners of her eyes. 'Sorry, but no, absolutely not.'

I shook out a black jumper with slightly more force than necessary.

'I love kids, don't get me wrong, but I couldn't cope with them all day long. My class wasn't that badly behaved and we gave my French teacher a nervous breakdown. He just stopped coming in one day, then we saw him at the duck pond in the next village over wearing a tracksuit with a massive beard. That would be me within a week.'

'And you could not pull off a beard,' Jess said.

'Not with my colouring,' I agreed. 'Shall we order the pizza? Large pepperoni and a medium whatever you want.'

She stuck out her tongue and gagged. 'Why are we getting pepperoni when we both hate it?'

'Because Stew loves it and I'm trying to butter him up.' I tossed a white T-shirt at my packing pile with a grimace. 'He's not going to be happy when I break the news about me going away.'

Jess clucked her tongue and shrugged.

'The only things that make Stew happy are the Blades winning and his mum. He'll get over it.'

I bit my lip and grabbed an assortment of clean underwear out of the chest of drawers, dumping it all into the suitcase. Even though I knew she was right, I still felt an unwelcome pang of disloyalty when I didn't rush to his defence. Jess would always be Team Fran, even though the rest of the world thought Stew was the greatest thing since sliced bread. One of the problems with moving back to your boyfriend's home-town, living within a five-minute radius of the rest of his family, was that he would always be the golden boy and I would always be the outsider. Most of the time it didn't bother me, but every once in a while something happened to remind me I didn't quite belong. Something like seeing him chatting to his child-hood sweetheart when he was supposed to be somewhere else entirely.

'Are you sure everything is OK with you two?' Jess asked, taking the pile of knickers out of my suitcase and rolling each pair before neatly putting them back.

It was the perfect opening. I could tell her what I'd seen outside the salon: she'd make grumbling noises, call Bryony a cow, then reassure me that nothing was going on and I didn't need to worry. But I couldn't do it. We shared almost everything, but when it came to me and Stew, I couldn't help but censor myself, even with my best friend. Voicing your fears only made them real. It was all so much safer and more manageable when it was just in my head.

'Everything is fine,' I said with as much authority as I could muster. 'It's just the working away thing, he's going to be annoyed. And what if I don't get the job and I've created drama for nothing? Do you think I should cancel my interview?'

'Fran,' Jess met the look of uncertainty on my face with a fierce expression of determination. 'You're going to go to London, you're going to get this job and it's going to be amazing. I saw how much they're offering for five days' work, you'd have to be certifiable not to go for it.'

'You're too nice to me,' I said with a smile, pretending not to notice as she slipped a black thong in my suitcase, hiding it underneath my more utilitarian underwear. Little did she know, it was a gym thong not a sex thong, making it the least alluring piece of underwear in the entire world.

'No, I'm not,' she stated. 'I'm just nice enough. You are kind and thoughtful and practically perfect in every way.'

'You know, I don't think Mary Poppins was all that pleasant,' I said. 'Have you ever read the books?'

'I think we both know I have not,' she replied. 'Since when was Mary Poppins based on a book?'

'Since forever,' I said, planting my hands on my hips and staring into the suitcase. Trousers, check. Shirts, check. Pants and bras and socks, check, check, check. Was that everything? I really wanted to be fully packed and ready to go before Stew got back from football practice.

'It's going to be fine,' she said gently, giving my hand a squeeze. 'What's the worst that could happen?'

'The last time you said that we ended up in lockdown for a year.'

'That reminds me, I promised I'd take some banana bread into work this week,' she muttered as she held up two nearly identical, worse-for-wear, nude bras. Or at least they used to be nude. If the fabric matched the skin tone of anyone on earth in their current state, I imagined that person might want to see a doctor sooner rather than later.

'These are the saddest bras I've ever seen in my entire life,' Jess declared, draping one of them over her head, the cups hanging down over her ears, as she twirled the other in the air like a lasso. 'They're begging to be put out of their misery, Fran. There's about as much support left in them as a ham sandwich.'

'The colour is a bit off, that's all. They're perfectly serviceable bras,' I replied, grabbing them back and stuffing them into my suitcase. 'Not everyone's under-wear drawer is made up of peekaboo leopard print push-ups and black silk suspenders.'

'One, the world would be a sunnier place if it was, and two, you can't have a peekaboo push-up bra, the padding gets in the way of the hole for the nip.' She eyed my fresh five-pack of white high-waisted briefs and blanched. 'And underwear can be serviceable without looking like you stole it from your nan. I'm going to get you some for Christmas. By January, you'll have a knicker drawer to rival Meghan Markle.'

'Is she a well-known lingerie connoisseur?'

'Just strikes me as someone who would have really nice pants,' Jess shrugged, fiddling with a tiny silver hoop in her left ear. 'Just trust me. Text me your size, and I'll get you something nice, totally tasteful.'

'Sounds like more of a gift for Stew than for me,' I clucked.

'I don't have a boyfriend, and my underwear game is top-notch,' she huffed. 'You know what they say, dress for the job you want.'

'And what job is that?'

'Beyoncé. She's bound to need someone to fill in at some point.'

I laughed as I closed up my suitcase, as ready as I'd ever be.

'Stew wouldn't notice if I wandered in wearing nipple tassels and a crotchless thong,' I said. 'He's not fussed about that stuff, you know?'

A flicker of concern crossed her face before she smoothed her expression and met mine with a smile. 'You two will work it out. You always do.'

'Yeah,' I agreed, giving my greying bras one last look before turning out the bedroom light and leading her back downstairs. 'We always do.'

Even though I was more than half asleep when the key turned in the lock, I snapped to my senses straight away. The TV was off, Netflix had given up on me hours ago, and when I blinked at the clock on the mantelpiece, the time was almost midnight.

'You're still up.'

Stew walked in, bleary eyed and clutching the door to keep himself steady.

'Sort of,' I replied, rolling out of my hedgehog ball and folding my arms across my chest. Immediately, I uncrossed them. Too much aggression and too much of a cliché. 'I thought you'd be home earlier, I was getting worried.'

'Phone died, I was so busy today I forgot to charge it before practice. The lads wanted to get a pint after all. Sorry.'

'You don't have to apologize for going out,' I said, even though I was glad he had. 'I just wish you'd texted me. Chris and Kaush have got my number, I was halfway to thinking you were dead in a ditch.'

He rubbed his hand over his face and winced. 'Yeah, they didn't go to the pub, it was some of the other lads. Like I said, I'm sorry.'

'Well, you missed out on a good pizza,' I said lightly. Some of the other lads? Which other lads? 'Did you get my text before your phone died?'

'No?'

'Right.' I sat up and wrapped his nana's blanket around me. Almost everything in the house belonged to Stew's nana because it was Stew's nana's house. He'd inherited it three years earlier which was why we'd moved back up to Sheffield in the first place. Well, one of the reasons we'd moved back up to Sheffield. 'I got an interview today.'

'Fran,' he groaned, stretching out my name as long as he could without running out of breath. 'I'm so knackered. Can we talk about it tomorrow?'

'Not really because the interview is tomorrow.'

He started treading down the heels of his trainers, still clinging to the doorframe to keep him upright.

'And it's in London.'

'Why would the interview be in London?' he asked, looking perplexed.

'Because the job is in London?' I replied with a weak smile. 'But it's just five days, I'd be back on Tuesday, and the money is amazing and—'

19

His confusion shifted into something sour.

'Why are you chasing another assistant job? I thought we'd decided you were going to apply for the teacher training at Hallam?'

'I don't think *we* have decided that yet,' I said. 'And anyway, that wouldn't be until next September – you can't just start a teacher training course when you feel like it.'

'Yeah, but our Mandy's said she'd get you in at her school to help out for a bit,' he replied. 'Get some experience under your belt.'

All of a sudden, all those cartoons where steam comes out of the character's ears started to make sense.

'And why would Mandy do that?' I asked. My voice was dangerously calm but Stew was too drunk or too disinterested to pick up on the signs. 'I haven't talked to Mandy about teaching. I haven't talked to anyone about teaching, because I don't want to be a teacher.'

'Fran, I'm knackered, I can't talk about this now.' He kicked his shoes close to their spot under the stairs and turned back into the hallway. 'We'll talk about it in the morning.'

'But I have to leave in the morning,' I said, following him into the hall as he trudged up the stairs. 'First thing, we won't have time to talk.'

'I'm going to have a shower, I feel like shite,' he called back down. 'Talk to me after.'

I returned to the living room, folded my blanket, and put the remote back beside the TV before my eyes wandered over to the framed photos that hung above the settee. They had been here longer than we had. Each and every picture was a Stew Bingham original, specially chosen for his biggest fan, Nana Beryl. It broke my heart that he barely touched his camera these days, but I'd long since learned there was no point trying to convince Stew to do anything he didn't really want to do, and he'd been quite clear about hanging up his camera.

I landed on one photo in particular, a candid shot of me, laughing so hard you could see tears rolling down my cheeks. I remembered the day so clearly, just the two of us hanging out on Primrose Hill years before, and for the life of me, I couldn't remember what he'd said to make me laugh, but whatever it was, I was in hysterics. We used to laugh a lot more back then. Just like we used to hold hands and kiss in the street, just like he would give me piggyback rides to the bus stop when my heels were hurting. If I tried to jump on his back now, at least one of us was likely to break a hip.

But it was normal for long-term relationships to struggle sometimes, I reasoned. You had ups and you had downs; sometimes the downs lasted a little bit longer than the ups, but it wasn't as though things were actually *bad* between us, not the way they were for other people. You couldn't even call it a rough patch really, more of a quiet patch. A nothing-much-to-say-to-each-other patch.

I was never any good when I wasn't working; I was someone who needed to keep busy and all this extra time to myself was dangerous. It was starting to feel as though the walls were closing in on me and I needed to give them a short, sharp shove. Five days in London would be just the trick and I knew that even if he wasn't happy about it, Stew would understand. Eventually. After popping two ibuprofen, I finished all the little tasks I took care of every night. Nana Beryl would be proud, I thought, as I wiped down the kitchen tops and hung the dishcloth over the mixer tap to dry out overnight.

When I finally made my way upstairs, I saw the bathroom light was still on. Leaving lights on, forgetting to turn the TV off, not quite turning a tap all the way, these were all Stew's specialties, and evidence, according to his father, that he simply wouldn't be able to cope without me. Wearily, I tugged the cord and stepped softly down the hallway, avoiding the two creaking floorboards, to find him tucked up in our bed, duvet clutched under his chin, eyes closed.

'Stew?'

'Mmm?'

'I need to talk to you about this job.'

The room was pitch black, his white noise machine hissing away beneath his bedside table.

'In the morning, Fran,' Stew yawned, rolling over onto his side, presenting me with his back. 'I'm shattered.'

I stared at the lump under the covers. He knew I wanted to talk. He knew this was important to me.

'OK, but I have to leave in the morning,' I said. 'So there won't be a lot of time.'

'We'll be quick then,' he said into his pillow, pulling the duvet over his head. 'G'night.'

The way I saw it, I had two choices.

The first was to scream at the top of my lungs, break something expensive, and possibly beat Stew to death with a shoe. The second was to close my eyes, count to ten, and bury my rage so deep down inside that I forgot all about it until it resurfaced in ten years and I went on a mad spree at the supermarket, pushing over the pastry cases and hurling packets of ham at poor unsuspecting shoppers. It wasn't much of a choice.

Besides, I didn't want to argue, not really. I just wanted him to listen to me.

Outside, I heard a car pass in front of the house, its tyres slick from the rain, and watched its headlights slip through the gap between the curtains and dance across our popcorn ceiling. I pulled my pyjamas out from underneath my pillow as Stew began to snore.

'Goodnight, Stew,' I whispered as I closed the door behind me and tiptoed across the creaky landing to the spare room.

CHAPTER THREE

'Stew?' I called, as I stumbled into the kitchen next morning. He wasn't in our bedroom, he wasn't in the bathroom, and there was no trace of him in the living room. Instead of my fiancé, I found a note on the kitchen table.

Gone to Bryony's to fix her sink, CU tonight

I stared at it, turning the scrap of paper over in my hands and holding it up to the light, looking for a secret message, some acrostic code or something written in invisible ink as I sank into one of the chairs that slotted underneath the Formica table. But just like Stew, it was what it was.

'Right,' I said to absolutely no one. 'That's that then.'

Picking up the pen he had left on the table, I crossed out his straightforward printing and wrote my own message underneath, my early morning letters looping gracelessly against each other.

~~Gone to Bryony's to fix her sink, CU tonight~~

Even though I loved Sheffield, I did miss London.

My train was late, the tube was packed, and I'd almost been run over three times but I didn't care. She was gritty and grimy and perfect to me. While there was a lot to be said for the comfort of a routine, I had a London-shaped hole in my heart that could only be filled by her particular brand of predictable unpredictability. She might not be my soulmate, but there was nowhere quite like London town for a quick and dirty fling.

'Watch where you're going, you wanker,' screeched a motorcycle courier as I stepped into the street at the exact same moment his bike tore around the corner.

'Sorry!' I called cheerfully, skipping back onto the pavement, giving him a wave as he replied with a very different hand gesture.

Reassured my beloved hadn't changed in the slightest, I trotted on happily to my destination. It was good to be back.

Dead on the dot of twelve, I was standing in front of the address Rose had sent me the day before, the Tower of London glaring at me from across the street, old and imposing and swarming with tourists wearing sweat-shirts with 'Oxford' emblazoned on the front, just in case you were wondering whether or not they'd been to Oxford. The office was snugged in between a huge glass-fronted co-working space and an ancient bookshop with a crumbling brick facade. Just a narrow sliver of a building with a glossy red door, no buzzer, no knocker, and only a small brass plaque that confirmed I was in the right place.

After checking the sneaky middle buttons of my white shirt and gently tapping the false eyelashes that seemed like such a good idea when I was doing my makeup that morning, I checked my watch once more to make sure. It was time. I rapped hard on the door, flickers of excitement sparking in my arms and legs, my entire body humming with a dangerous cocktail of adrenaline and the caffeine from three extremely large coffees.

'Come in.'

I opened the door. Inside the tiny, low-ceilinged room was a desk, and behind the desk, sat a woman.

'Hi,' I said with big smile and bright eyes. 'I'm Francesca Cooper?'

She looked me up and down, glanced at her computer screen, and made a small, confirmatory noise as if to let me know that yes, I was, in case I was the one who wasn't sure.

'Sarah Pierce,' she replied. 'Come in.'

Parking my suitcase by the door, I sat in the only available seat on my side of the desk and searched the room for clues. The office was extremely small and her large, modern desk looked extremely out of place, taking up more than its fair share of space. The floors were dark wood, the walls were whitewashed, ancient-looking beams supported the very low ceiling and all I could smell was coffee. A small window at the back of the room was the only source of natural light, and behind the desk, a narrow staircase wound around itself, disappearing into the ceiling. It felt old in the way that only London ever did, as though it had always been here. I wondered how many different people had walked into this room in the centuries since it was built, and how many of them had been forced to pee in a

Costa Coffee cup, due to the absolute state of the train toilet.

'We'll keep this brief because I don't have a lot of time,' Sarah said. She was all business, just the way I liked it. 'Obviously, I've got your CV and you answered the questionnaire quite well, so this meeting is to see whether or not you personally meet my requirements.'

I gave a terse smile and nodded sharply to show I understood. Understood that I was great on paper and if I didn't get the job, it was entirely because I was shit in person.

'Believe me when I say we've seen half of London for this job,' she went on. 'It might seem simple, but if you want to do it right, there's a lot to learn, and fast.'

Just like fishtail braids and blowjobs, and I was really only good at one of those things.

'I am always up for a challenge,' I said, flipping my perfect fishtail braid over my shoulder. Hadn't Rose said the face-to-face was just a formality? It certainly didn't feel like a formality. It felt like Sarah Pierce was looking for reasons not to employ me.

Her forehead creased into deep furrows as she picked up a piece of paper from her desk, and I immediately recognized the font. It was my CV. I pressed my clammy palms against the leg of my smart black trousers and cleared my throat. Once upon a time, I'd enjoyed the challenge of an interview – it was like trying to act against someone, only you hadn't seen the script and you had to guess all the right lines. But today I was more nervous than I was prepared to admit. I really, *really* wanted this job. I needed it. I had something to prove.

'I'm very capable,' I added, silently trying to communicate that she could absolutely trust me, that I respected her, and that I also really liked her top. 'I pick up new skills very quickly and I'm extremely reliable.'

'Yes, it says all that here,' she replied, giving absolutely no indication she believed me. 'The things I need to know aren't on your CV. Tell me, Fran, are you capable of discretion and do you have common sense?'

'Oh yes. Me to a T.'

There was no need for her to know about the time I tried to iron my shirt collar with my hair straighteners. While I was wearing it.

'Did you know the "T" stands for tittle?' I asked, my right leg bouncing up and down. Sarah arched her left eyebrow without moving any of her other features. 'And tittle is an old English word for the tiniest amount? I love words, I love language. Reading is one of my favourite things. You can't go wrong with a book, can you? Unless the book isn't very good, I suppose, but you can always learn something from a book, even a bad one. I didn't love *Fifty Shades of Grey* but I doubt there's anyone who read that and came away without learning anything, even if it was only about contract law.'

She stared across the desk, cool, calm and even.

'Anything else you'd like to share?'

I opened my mouth and then closed it again, shaking my head instead. Silence was, after all, golden.

'Good,' Sarah said, pushing aside my CV and clicking at something I couldn't see on her computer screen. 'Let's get down to it. The NDA you signed gives us legal protection against leaks, but I'd rather not have to sue anyone else out of existence. Quite frankly, it's a lot of paperwork and I'm busy enough as it is.'

I pressed my palm down on my knee, trying to calm my jitters. This was starting to sound less and less like your average assistant job. Who exactly had they sued out of existence? I felt a sudden longing for one of Suzette's morning muffins, slightly concerned I might be getting into something out of my depth.

'I've already run a background check and everything came up clean. Either you're very good at keeping out of trouble or very good at keeping trouble away from you. Which is it?'

'The first one?' I replied as I rubbed at the gold band on my right hand. 'Sorry, you ran a background check? On me?'

'Standard procedure,' Sarah said, as though it was a perfectly normal thing to tell someone. 'Don't worry, we didn't find anything incriminating.'

Make that two morning muffins and a vanilla slice chaser. Was this an interview for a temp position or was I being vetted to join MI5? I *was* good at languages and very much enjoyed listening in on other people's conversations, but I was a shit poker player and couldn't be in the sun for more than ten minutes before I turned into a lobster, and they both seemed like factors that would get in the way of my obtaining double '0' status. When was James Bond *not* titting around on a beach somewhere?

'You're not very active on social media, are you?'

'More of a lurker than a poster,' I replied, wondering if she had found that photo of the two sheep doing it as funny as I had when I posted it in 2016. 'Could we talk more about this background check?'

'No.'

Well, that answered that question.

'If you saw a celebrity on the street or at a restaurant would you ask them for a selfie?'

I sat back in my chair, horrified. 'Oh my god, absolutely not.'

I couldn't even tap a woman on the shoulder to say her tag was showing without breaking out in a rash.

'Let's say your employer asked you to do something you weren't comfortable with,' Sarah said with careful diplomacy. 'How would you feel about that?'

I was *definitely* being recruited as a spy. Time to cue up some YouTube poker tutorials and crack out the factor 50 sunscreen.

'It would depend,' I replied slowly, visions of me racing a speedboat through the Venice canals and immediately crashing into a gondola roaring through my head. 'As long as it wasn't illegal and didn't put anyone in danger, I'd deal with it.'

'What if it was something you found,' she waved one hand around in the air as she searched for the right word. 'Distasteful?'

'It's not my job to decide what is and isn't distasteful, it's my job to do my job,' I replied, thinking back to the time my first boss insisted I sign his wife up to Weight Watchers a month after she gave birth, 'as a laugh'. 'An assistant is there to assist, to make their client's job, their life, easier. That's what I'm good at.' I lifted my chin and looked her in the eye. It felt as though there should be a light wind blowing my hair back, a spotlight on my face, and a golden eagle swooping into frame. 'I'm a great assistant because I know that what I want and what I think doesn't matter. All that counts is making sure the client's goals are met.'

'And what if someone offered you money in exchange for information, or access.' She pressed her lips together so tightly, they all but disappeared. 'Or photos.'

Sarah pinned me to my chair with her gaze and I tried to imagine what kind of idiot might have met this woman and actively decided to piss her off.

'No,' I replied, utterly serious. 'That's terrible. I would never do something like that in professional circumstances or otherwise.'

Sarah Pierce leaned back in her chair, the corners of her mouth inching upwards into an almost smile until she very nearly looked happy.

'And the strange thing is, I actually believe you,' she said, tenting her fingers in front of her. 'One last question. What, to you, defines a good assistant?'

At last, I thought happily, an easy one.

'A good assistant is someone with good time management skills, good communication skills, and the ability to balance a lot of very different tasks at the same time,' I replied with well-earned confidence. 'But the difference between a good assistant and a brilliant assistant is the ability to anticipate potential problems before they arise. You've got to be prepared for whatever comes at you when the job turns out to be equal parts assistant, therapist, and best friend, but still know your boundaries. And you should always have mints. I've basically got stock in Tic Tacs.'

'Congratulations,' she said. 'You've got the job.'

A feeling that used to be familiar shot through me. Was it excitement? Happiness? There was an outside chance it was pride, but it had been so long since I'd encountered that particular emotion, it was too difficult to tell.

'And now I can tell you who you'll be working for,' she added, rattling her short, neat nails on the desk in a drumroll. 'You are officially the new personal assistant to Juliette.'

She held up her hands, fingers stretched out wide like shooting stars as I stared back at her blankly.

'Juliette who?'

'*Juliette*,' Sarah repeated. '*The* Juliette.'

My mouth dried up, my throat tightened, and I quickly scrolled through all the possible mononymous Juliettes on the planet.

And there she was.

'You mean Juliette, the singer, Juliette?' I asked.

'If there's one thing I could advise you to learn very quickly,' Sarah stood and smoothed down her red silk shirt before starting up the spiral staircase. 'It's that there is only one Juliette.'

CHAPTER FOUR

'Oh wow, it's gorgeous,' I breathed as I hauled my heavy suitcase up the final step of the narrow spiral staircase. The cramped, claustrophobic office bloomed into a huge, modern loft with the most impressive and presumably expensive view of the Thames I had ever seen.

'Yes,' Sarah replied, marching across the room without taking her eyes off her phone. 'It is.'

The living area flowed seamlessly into the kitchen, where sparkling stainless-steel surfaces clashed tastefully against the exposed brick, and bright green potted plants shone with all the confidence of too much money. It was pure interior design porn, straight from the *Architectural Digest* centrefold spread of my dreams, and I had to wipe my chin to make sure I wasn't drooling. If this was the accommodation Rose had mentioned on the phone, I really needed to look into squatter's rights, as soon as possible.

'Really, it's stunning,' I said, still taking in all the beautiful custom features. Farmhouse sink, be still my heart. 'Is it your flat?'

Sarah opened a built-in fridge and took out two Fiji waters while I pleaded with all known deities for her to say no.

'This? Oh, no,' she loosened the lid of the first bottle and handed it to me. 'It's just a space. It's helpful to have a secure spot near the marina for meetings and such.'

I nodded, as though it made perfect sense to me to keep a stunning multimillion-pound, river-view apartment in London to use as 'a space'. I loved mine and Stew's little house, but I'd have loved it even more if the couple who had just moved in across the road didn't consider clothing, body hair removal, *and* closing the curtains optional.

'So.' I breathed in the heady scent of whatever fancy candle was burning on the counter. 'I'm working for Juliette.'

I couldn't quite believe it. I had hit the temp jackpot, smashed it open and was rolling around in its innards like Scrooge McDuck.

Sarah unscrewed the lid from her bottle of water, took a careful sip, and replaced the lid right away. 'Are you a fan?'

'I'm not *not* a fan,' I replied carefully. 'But I'm not obsessed with her or anything.'

'If you were, you wouldn't be here,' she replied bluntly. 'Obviously the background check went through your Spotify playlists and iTunes library.'

'Obviously,' I muttered in agreement, making a mental note to change every password I'd ever made in my entire life.

She beckoned me over to a rack of clothes hanging on the far side of the room. 'We need to kit you out

34

with a few things. Juliette likes her team in black and white. Did the agency tell you that?'

'They did.' I wheeled my suitcase around in front of me and patted the pop-up handle. 'I think I have everything.'

'I'm sure you think you do,' she replied pleasantly as she tore through the rack, pulling out various shirts, T-shirts, and silk tops, and tossing them on the back of the settee. 'But better to be safe than sorry. You'll be accompanying Juliette to an important event, and as her representative, it's important you portray a certain image, especially given the occasion.'

I bobbed my head up and down like a nodding dog. Juliette would hear no complaints from me if she wanted to dress me up like a designer dolly. Sarah held up a particularly gorgeous black cashmere jumper and squinted as she sized up both me and the sweater.

'She's performing at the Crystal Ball on Saturday night.'

'Is that a big event?' I asked, my heart in my mouth as she wavered on whether or not to add the jumper to her pile. 'I'm afraid I'm not familiar.'

'Not entirely surprising given your most recent Spotify Wrapped list,' Sarah replied, tossing the jumper onto the settee and insulting my musical taste in one fell swoop. 'The Crystal Ball is the most exclusive, most opulent event of the social calendar. There are only 1,000 tickets issued each year, and attendees are hand-picked and screened by the Crystal Committee before they are invited to buy a ticket.'

I screwed up my face in confusion. 'You have to wait to get invited and you still have to pay for the ticket?'

Sarah nodded. '$50,000 a piece.'

'Bloody hell, I hope the goodie bag is decent,' I whistled. 'Are there really 1,000 people prepared to pay that much to attend a party?'

'Last year, more than 65,000 people applied for tickets.'

'That's too many people with too much money,' I replied as Sarah smiled. 'Who are they?'

'Celebrities, politicians, businessmen, and other obscenely rich or powerful people. The Crystal Ball isn't just a party, it's The Party. To be invited is to be anointed.' She met my eyes with a warning look. 'Everything from this moment on should be considered confidential. You cannot tell anyone who you're working for, where you're going, or what you're doing. Not friends, not family, not anyone. Got it?'

'It is got,' I replied, smothering my increasing giddiness for the sake of professionalism. Celebrities! Balls! Secret missions! It sounded just close enough to being a spy to still be glamorous and mysterious but without the trickier gambling and murder parts! 'Have you been before or is this your first time? And will I be expected to dress up because I thought I'd packed pretty well, but I'm not sure I have anything ball-worthy in my case.'

'Firstly, I won't be going to the ball, I'm tied up with another issue right now,' Sarah answered. A shadow of something passed over her face, but my super assistant Spidey-senses tingled and I knew not to ask for more details unless she offered more details. 'And secondly, neither will you. You'll be backstage with Juliette, who is performing then leaving. This is a job, not a jolly, please don't forget that.'

'Oh, of course, absolutely, one hundred percent. I'm

not really a ball person anyway, not that keen on crowds or big parties. Not that I've ever been to a ball, of course . . .'

'What size jeans do you wear?' she said loudly.

'A twelve-ish,' I replied, hoping it was still true. It had been a long time since I'd shopped for jeans and that was very much a conscious choice.

She opened a built-in cupboard and pulled out a stack of jet-black designer jeans, all with the price tags still attached, and peeled three pairs from the bottom of the pile. 'Take these,' she said, stashing the others back where she'd found them. 'They're stretchy, they should fit.'

'I have got black trousers with me, I think they'll be OK,' I said, running a hand over my hips, concerned that 'should' wasn't enough of a reassurance. There was nothing worse than jeans that didn't fit, for your comfort levels or self-esteem.

'I'm sure they are but Juliette likes things done a certain way.' Sarah held the jeans just out of reach and pursed her lips. 'How do I put this? If you aren't comfortable realizing someone else's vision as to how things should be done, you might not be the right person for this job and it's better we find that out now.'

'Lots of jobs expect you to wear a uniform,' I replied, accepting the jeans with a gracious smile. 'I understand completely.'

'Good.' She turned her appraising eye on my appearance, working her way up from the tips of my black leather heels to the top of my braided blonde head. 'Your hair is fine, she prefers it pulled back rather than loose, and it's no perfume and no jewellery, so you'll have to take off your rings.'

I rubbed my thumb against the back of my engagement ring with reticence. Taking it off felt strange at the best of times; taking it off when we were in the middle of an argument felt dangerously like a dare.

'While we're being honest about things,' I said, sliding both rings off my fingers and feeling so strangely naked as I slipped them into my pocket. 'I should probably mention I haven't assisted a celebrity before. My previous experience was more corporate.'

'I know.'

Of course she did. She probably knew my favourite Disney film, when I lost my virginity, and how many times a day I checked Britney Spears's Instagram. Not that I was obsessed or anything, I just liked to make sure she was OK.

'I suppose I'm wondering if there are any specific or particular duties to this role that weren't on the job description?' I said. 'Anything off the record that I really ought to know about.'

'Francesca.'

'Call me Fran,' I offered with a friendly smile.

'Francesca,' she repeated without a smile of any kind. 'I chose you for this job because I believe you're capable of it and the only specific or particular duty you need worry about, is doing as you're asked. The bulk of your duties will be incredibly boring. Getting coffee, checking emails, making sure she gets to the places she needs to be on time. Juliette is going through something of a difficult time and she needs a reliable, responsible adult in the room.'

'I'm a reliable, responsible adult,' I replied, half-statement, half-question.

'I need you to keep a close eye on her, keep her

38

company, make sure she doesn't do anything self-destructive. That sort of behaviour happens when people get bored. The boat is clean and I need someone on board to make sure it stays that way.'

'You want me to clean the boat?' I asked, confused. 'That wasn't in the job description at all and, truth be told, I'm not sure that's really in my skill-set. I mean, I can run a hoover around, but anything more than that and . . .'

Sarah inhaled deeply and closed her eyes, waiting for me to catch up.

'Oh,' I said.

Sarah exhaled slowly through her nose.

'You don't mean that kind of clean?' I said.

Sarah shook her head.

'You mean the other kind of clean.' I tapped my nose and sniffed theatrically.

'She really is going to love you,' Sarah sighed as she scanned the pile of clothing on the settee. 'I think we have everything you'll need. Put these in your suitcase and meet me downstairs. Your car is waiting.'

'My car?' I asked. I shoved all the beautiful clothes into my already crammed case, only managing to zip it through sheer force of will. 'Where are we going?'

'I'm staying here,' she replied as I followed her back to the spiral staircase, humping my even heavier case all the way back down. '*You're* going to the airport.'

'I am?'

She nodded. 'You're booked on a flight to Naples that leaves in forty-five minutes.'

'Naples, Italy?'

'Certainly not Naples, Florida,' she replied with an absolutely filthy look.

'No, of course not,' I scoffed, making a mental note of the fact that there was a Naples in Florida and wondering what it might have done to deserve such scorn.

Outside the office, a gleaming black Bentley filled the narrow street, waiting for us with a rumbling engine.

'The flight should land by four and a driver will be waiting for you. Call me as soon as you arrive at the docks, that's where you'll rendezvous with Juliette,' Sarah instructed. 'From there, you'll sail to Panarea, arriving in time for the ball on Saturday.'

Charter flight? Docks? Yacht?

And then it hit me. My invaluable sailing experience.

'I know my CV mentioned I've done some sailing, but it was a long time ago and probably more of a passive experience than your hands-on, knot-tying, ahoy-ye-matey stuff,' I said, the words tumbling out of my mouth before I could stop them. 'In fact, if I were to be entirely honest, I wouldn't call myself a sailing expert. Or proficient. Or in any way, shape or form capable of sailing a boat at all. Not even a dinghy. I once sank a lilo in Tenerife.'

'Then I'll tell the captain not to put you in charge of the engine room,' Sarah replied flatly. 'Is that all?'

'Yes?'

'Thank God. Here.' She handed me an iPhone, identical to the one tucked away in my handbag, as a driver in a smart black suit exited the driver's side of the car and silently took my suitcase from my hands. 'Your travel details and trip itinerary are in your email, and all my numbers are already programmed in. The passcode is your date of birth.'

40

'Naturally,' I whispered before giving her what I hoped was a look of confident, professional competence. 'Thank you for this opportunity, I'm excited to get stuck in.'

'One of your eyelashes fell off halfway through the interview,' Sarah said. 'Just so you know.'

'Fantastic,' I replied, ducking my head and gently yanking off the remaining strip lash, cheeks burning.

The driver stalked around to my side of the car, opening the door before my sweaty mitts could make contact with his spotless paintwork.

'Thank you,' I said as I crammed myself inside but he didn't reply. The car's interior smelled like expensive aftershave and money. Even as I fastened my seat belt, I could feel myself tensing every muscle in my body at once. Cream leather seats seemed like a terrible risk. What kind of person would choose to live so close to the edge?

Sarah tapped on the window, her eyes burning into mine as I kept my finger on the button to lower it until she could poke her head inside.

'I know you won't let me down,' she said, taking a step backwards onto the pavement before I could respond.

The car accelerated away from the kerb, pushing me back against the buttery back seat as an icy breeze blew in through the still-open window, but the chill in my bones had nothing to do with the weather. I was a good assistant, and I knew I could do this, so why did Sarah's words sound so much like a threat?

My window whirred into life, the driver sealing me inside the car as we locked eyes in his rear-view mirror, my new iPhone hot in my cold, sweaty palms.

41

'Should have you at the airport in twenty minutes,' he said, before turning his gaze back to the road ahead.

'Great,' I replied. 'Sounds perfect.'

And as we picked up speed and the streets of London and my flush of anxiety faded away into a blur, it all started to sink in.

I'd got the job.

I was on my way to Italy.

The adventure had begun.

CHAPTER FIVE

After biting each and every one of my nails down to stubs I gave myself permission to text Jess before my flight took off, just in case I hadn't been hired to be Juliette's personal assistant but had accidentally somehow become involved in a human trafficking ring. Without giving away any details that would lead to my great-grandchildren still paying off my legal battles, I told her I'd got the job and turned on my location services, gently but firmly suggesting she add me to her Find My Friends app. Just in case.

The flight passed quickly enough, nervous excitement speeding up the clock while I stared at the window and wondered what the next few days might hold. What would Juliette be like? Would I like her? Would she like me? I'd worked for so many different kinds of people, but never a celebrity. I assumed there would be considerably less photocopying and marginally more sycophancy, but the truth was every single person I'd ever worked for enjoyed having their ego fluffed up at least a little bit. It was hard to find someone who didn't.

When we arrived in Naples, another man in another smart black suit was waiting for me in the airport, my name on an iPad, glinting in the bright Italian sunshine. The air was cold, but the sky was sharp with brilliant sunshine and, as I followed him out to his car, I took a surreptitious photo of his number plate and sent another, slightly stronger worded text to Jess along with a second Find My Friends request, given that her response to the first was 'ha-ha, very funny'.

'We are almost there,' the Italian driver announced in English, turning off the main road and driving into the port proper. There were dozens of ships lined up on the water, stacked up side-by-side like huge floating hotels. As we drove on the boats began to get smaller, sleeker, and sexier. I felt my spine stiffen as I pressed my nose against the car window. These were the kind of boats you saw in the newspapers, setting the scene for paparazzi shots of supermodels and billionaires, and usually accompanied by articles full of words like 'cavorting' and 'carousing'. That or they belonged to the bad guy in a movie. The good guy never had a yacht, it was always the villain. A red flag flashed briefly in front of my eyes. *That's because nothing good happens at sea*, a little voice whispered in my ear. *Jaws*, bad. *Titanic*, bad. The remake of *Overboard*, terrible. Even all the stressful stuff in *The Little Mermaid* happened at sea. If Ariel had stayed away from ships, she wouldn't have ended up a child bride who never got to see her father or sisters again, and Prince Eric wouldn't have had to sneak out while his sixteen-year-old wife was asleep and eat fish and chips under cover of darkness. I assumed.

Despite my reservations, when we pulled to a stop

and the passenger door of the car opened from the outside, I clambered out of the car instead of hiding behind the front seat, and looked up into the face of the most beautiful man I had ever seen in my entire life.

'Miss Cooper?'

He held out a hand and I froze, forgetting my manners, my name, and how to breathe. It was absurd how handsome he was. Offensive, even. He was a Ken doll come to life, all hazel eyes, tanned skin and an extremely obvious bulge in the front of his very tight white trousers. Just before I began to turn blue, I remembered to breathe in and raised my hand to meet his, swooning at his firm grip and the warmth of his skin, hard-earned callouses rubbing against the tender tips of my fingers. He was a good few inches taller than my five foot four, and the highlights in his sandy brown hair simply screamed piña coladas and getting caught in the rain.

'I'm Lenny.' He spoke with a faint Australian accent, still shaking my hand slowly. His jaw was so square, I could have used it as a bottle opener. 'I'll be your chief steward.'

'Hello,' I stuttered as I released his hand, perfectly happy for him to be whatever he wanted to be. 'Please call me Fran.'

'Fran.'

Lenny's front teeth teased his bottom lip with my name as he enunciated slowly and clearly, and I felt myself ovulate from both ovaries at the same time. He took my suitcase from the driver before he looked over his shoulder, nodding down the docks.

'There she is,' he said. 'What do you think?'

Whatever I had been expecting, this was not it. Three hundred and fifty sleek feet of glass and steel

45

and whatever else yachts were made of because I had literally no idea; all I knew was that it was beautiful. It towered over the boats moored on either side, looking like Stew's MacBook had shagged a whale, and against all the odds, they had made an extremely beautiful baby. It was awesome in the truest sense of the word, and the closer I got, the louder it screamed 'not for the likes of you'.

'It's gorgeous,' I said, almost lost for words. 'I don't think we're going to need a bigger boat.'

'Jaws wouldn't dare,' Lenny laughed. 'Welcome to *The Songbird*.'

'Miss Cooper, I'm Captain Mark Shaughnessy.' An older gentleman with steel grey hair and a movie star smile welcomed me onto the deck, politely looking away as I fastened the middle button of my shirt which had worked itself open at some point in the last few minutes, presumably giving Lenny a great look at my delightful white T-shirt bra. 'Captain Mark, if it's easier. Welcome aboard.'

I noted his perfectly fitted navy trousers, his sparkling white short-sleeved shirt and counted four gold bars on the epaulettes as I shook his hand. He had a distinct air of 'firm but fair', which was extremely reassuring, and eyes so blue I had to wonder if he was wearing contacts.

'Thank you,' I replied, trying not to look as over-whelmed as I felt.

'Lenny will be your main point of contact on board, but if there are any issues at all, you can reach me at any time. Lenny, would you like to give Miss Cooper the grand tour?'

'Absolutely,' Lenny replied as the captain gave me the briefest of acknowledging nods and disappeared inside the boat. 'Shoes off.'

I leaned over, braid flopping over my face as I removed my sensible black heels. Sarah had prepared me for this. No shoes allowed on deck unless they were the hideously ugly deck shoes I had packed away in my suitcase. It seemed unfair to create something so glamorous and beautiful then expect people to tramp around it in the shoe equivalent of an anorak, but then again, the things rich people did rarely made sense to the rest of us.

'Like the captain said, if you need anything, I'm your guy. If you can't find me, pick up any of the phones on board and press star, you'll be connected to me directly, day or night.'

'Connected?' I asked, working my way down from his obscenely symmetrical face to his broad shoulders and tightly muscled back. It seemed to me a shirt that tight was not the most practical option for day-to-day wear, but what did I know? The last thing I wanted was to body-shame the man. And if every single one of the strained seams exploded at once, that was on him. I would just have to do my best to look away.

'The whole crew is linked to this system,' he replied, tapping an almost invisible headset in his ear. 'You'll get someone twenty-four-seven.'

I added the information to my mental notebook.

'Right,' Lenny planted his hands on his hips. 'How shall we do this? Top to bottom or bottom to top?'

'Bottom to top sounds good,' I said, stumbling over every single word. 'I like the bottom.'

He grinned as I died inside. I was not a good flirt, I

never had been. Stew and I met at university before 'clever bants' and 'good chat' were necessary. All it took to get a boyfriend back then was half a dozen alcopops, flexible standards, and the right Kings of Leon track playing in the student union.

'Let's start in the galley,' Lenny suggested. 'Good to take a look around before Chef starts on dinner.'

'There's a chef?' I asked, delighted.

'There are two,' he replied, glancing at me out of the corner of his eye. 'Didn't someone tell me you have sailing experience?'

'I have worked on a boat,' I replied confidently. This was a fact and a matter of public record. 'But it wasn't quite like this.'

Lenny grinned and a perfect dimple appeared in his left cheek. 'That's because there isn't anything quite like this. Francesca Cooper, prepare to be dazzled.'

As if I wasn't already? I thought as I followed him happily inside the yacht.

'Let me get this straight. There are two swimming pools, two hot tubs *and* a cold plunge pool, all on this one boat?'

'Two swimming pools, a cold plunge pool, *three* hot tubs, and she's a yacht, not a boat,' Lenny corrected as we stepped out of the lift. The lift on the yacht. 'The third hot tub is on the deck of the master suite.'

'Sure, why not?' I replied. We'd been touring the boat for almost half an hour and it felt as though we hadn't even seen the half of it. I trotted after him down a marble-lined hallway until he stopped in front of a pair of grand double doors.

'Speaking of the master suite . . .' Lenny gestured to the two gilded handles but didn't actually make contact.

They had been polished to the point of reflection, and even a single fingerprint would have been an affront.

'She's in there right now?' I whispered, heart pounding as I pointed towards the doors.

'What? Fuck, no!' he replied with bellowing laughter. An interesting response. 'You think we'd be running around on a tour if *she* was on board? Not likely. But we're still not going in. Your key will unlock her room but that's in case of emergencies. Never go in unless you're invited. Trust me, she wouldn't like it.'

'You've worked with her before, then?' I asked.

Lenny nodded. 'This is not my first, second or third rodeo with Ms Juliette. We see her fairly regularly, or at least, we crew for her fairly regularly. Whether or not I actually *see* her while she's on board depends on her mood.' Before I could ask any more questions, he turned to open a more modest door to his left. 'And this suite, is yours.'

He flung the door open with what turned out to be an entirely reasonable amount of drama.

'Welcome to your home for the next few days,' he said, ushering me inside with one well-muscled arm. 'I need to get back to my team and make sure everything is ready for departure. Anything you need, you can buzz me from one of the phones, remember?'

'I remember,' I replied, gazing around at the suite in quiet awe. As much as I enjoyed looking at Lenny, I very much needed him to leave. I needed some private time with the beautiful room to roll around naked on the plush carpets.

'Then I'll leave you to get settled,' he said, hopefully not reading my mind. 'And I hope you know what you're letting yourself in for.'

49

'Getting her coffee, making sure she arrives at a party on time, and telling her how nice she looks?' I smiled before telling him the same thing I'd told myself all the way here. 'Besides, how much trouble can she get into on a boat?'

Lenny sucked the air in through his teeth. 'Is this your first time working with someone like her?' he asked, a strange look on his handsome face.

'I've been an assistant for over a decade and no matter what people do for a living, most of them aren't that different,' I replied, artfully evading the question.

'Perhaps,' he said with a doubtful sniff. 'But Juliette isn't most people, you'll see.'

Rolling my eyes as I locked the door behind him and his ominous warning, I leaned against the solid wood and attempted to take it all in.

My room was gorgeous, with a huge bed in the middle of the suite, positioned so its resident could wake up and stare straight out of the sliding glass walls and into the ocean. That was if they didn't feel like staring at themselves in the mirror mounted on the ceiling, which I truly didn't. Every time I turned around, I was presented with another Instagrammable moment, and if Sarah hadn't been quite so clear about her position on social media, my fifty-four followers would already be enjoying a rare burst of interiors and sea views. Skipping across the suite to the overstuffed sofa, I wondered why it was turned away from the windows until I found a tiny remote control that summoned a flat screen TV down from the glossy ceiling. After watching it glide up and down four, maybe five times, I replaced the remote exactly where I'd found it and ventured off to investigate the bathroom.

And oh my god, the bathroom.

The high-sided soaking tub was big enough to fit five people, and the shower wasn't really a shower at all but a small studio apartment that flooded on purpose. As I sat down on one of two in-built marble benches inside the shower stall, fully dressed, it dawned on me that this room was not designed with the business traveller in mind. *The Songbird* was a wink and a nudge from top to bottom, seduction made manifest. I was sat in a shower in the world's most expensive shag pad. This room, this entire yacht, was made for the kind of sex kitten who wore Agent Provocateur underwear on the reg and slept in nothing but Chanel No 5, not a woman who exclusively bought her knickers in packs of five and slept in their socks because their fiancé refused to turn the heating on until December.

'I'm so sorry,' I said, tapping a bitten-down nail against the custom rose-gold fixtures. 'I feel like I've let you down.'

The shower was too polite to agree with me, but we both knew the truth.

Pulling open a door back in the bedroom, I saw someone had already unpacked my clothes while Lenny and I were touring the yacht, leaving me with nothing to do but remember why I was here in the first place.

Juliette.

I gave myself a good mental shake and walked back to the desk, spotting several items I had not brought with me, a black Moleskine notebook, a fresh box of black Pilot pens, a tiny black Swiss Army knife, a black leather wallet containing a slew of credit cards and stacks of Euros, plus a shiny new laptop. Beside them, was a large ring binder, with the words 'The Bible' debossed into the black leather in a cool, sans-serif font.

'Slightly sacrilegious but OK,' I muttered, settling into the leather swivel seat and opening it up, ready to replace my real life worries with work worries. Just the way I liked it.

The first page was fairly standard, emergency contact details, the same itinerary Sarah had already emailed to my phone and *The Songbird*'s incredibly cryptic WiFi password, songbird1. What genius would ever be able to hack that? But when I turned to the next page, there was a distinct change in tone.

While on duty, the assistant's personal electronic devices, including but not limited to phone, tablet, computers, cameras, must be locked in the provided safe. While on duty, the assistant must only use the provided phone and provided laptop. Both phone and laptop have keystroke tracking technology installed and all usage will be recorded and reviewed. Neither laptop nor phone are to be used for personal reasons. Any personal usage will be considered cause for immediate dismissal.

I chewed on the inside of my cheek, gently stroking my poor personal phone. OK, this felt a little bit paranoid, but if I really forced myself, I could understand it. Privacy and discretion were important, Sarah had been clear about that. Not to mention the fact it only said I couldn't use my phone while I was on duty, and I couldn't be expected to be on duty all the time.

I turned the page.

While on board The Songbird, the assistant is considered to be on duty twenty-four hours a day, seven days a week.

Well, shut my mouth.

The list went on.

The assistant will refrain from asking Juliette any personal questions. The assistant will answer any and all of Juliette's questions to the best of their ability. The assistant will join Juliette for all activities Juliette deems fit, including but not limited to eating meals, exercise, shopping trips, entertainment, professional obligations, personal care appointments and sleeping—

Sleeping? I had to *sleep* with her? I looked up from the ring binder and swallowed hard at the sight of my shocked reflection.

Flipping randomly through the binder, I landed on a section labelled 'exercise'.

Assistant will walk Juliette for one hour per day and administer post-walk stretches (instructions and diagrams below). Juliette is not to engage in high impact exercise that could damage her voice. Please consult with her trainer for a further list of allowed activities.

'Why do these feel like things that should have been mentioned before I flew to Italy?' I whispered, running my finger down the page in search of Juliette's trainer's contact details, but the nine-digit US number had been crossed out, one thick black line.

Turning the pages, I scanned the instructions in the other sections and at the bottom of each was the name and number of someone else to contact for further information, three hairdressers, a stylist, personal chef, Pilates instructor, vocal coach, dietician, driver, four different kinds of doctor, an aesthetician, a nurse practitioner, a holistic practitioner, a tarot card reader, and a witch.

Every single phone number had been crossed out.

'I'm sure there's a perfectly good explanation,' I told myself, closing the ring binder and ignoring my racing pulse. 'Maybe she's downsizing and realized an on-call witch doesn't spark that much joy.'

Staring out the window at the sea, I took a deep breath in. I'd been so busy losing my mind over *The Songbird*'s incredible amenities, I'd forgotten the facts. *I* was one of those amenities.

Lenny wasn't wrong. Juliette *wasn't* like most people, she was a megastar. Even someone as useless with music as I was knew most of her songs off by heart, because they were always playing somewhere. But beyond that I really didn't know anything about her. Was there a brief Hollywood marriage that ended badly, or was that someone else? A scandal with a prince? I knew it wasn't Juliette who had hit the car with the umbrella, but there was definitely something I was forgetting. Jess, a living pop culture encyclopaedia, would know but I couldn't ask her, not unless I wanted Sarah to sue me senseless.

Looking at the long, long list of instructions it seemed very obvious to me that Juliette didn't need an executive assistant, she needed a glorified babysitter, and seeing as I'd been sacked from that particular job when I was fourteen after my two-year-old cousin rolled off the settee and into the dog, things did not bode well.

'If only I'd watched more *Below Deck*,' I whispered. 'Then I'd know what to do when things go tits up on a boat.'

As much as it pained me to admit it even to myself, I was going to need help. I was going to need Lenny. But before I could pick up the phone, I felt a strange shaking sensation, as though I'd been pushed onto an ice rink even though I was still in my chair, safe and steady but not quite stable. I glanced out of the window and saw the boats on either side of us pulling away from *The Songbird*, only it wasn't the other boats that were moving, it was us.

We'd undocked.

My luxury cabin slowly transformed into a gilded cage as an unwelcome sense of dread settled around my shoulders. There was no way out now.

Standing uncertainly, I wobbled my way across the room as *The Songbird* dipped and surged out of the harbour, the low hum of the engines vibrating through the soles of my bare feet. I needed to get out of the room, quite certain I'd feel better on the deck. A bit of fresh air, another look at Lenny and, if I could find my way back to the galley, perhaps half a packet of Hobnobs to soothe my frayed nerves.

But the biscuits were not to be. As I rushed out the door, I collided with an absolute Amazon. Almost six feet and swimming in scent, the glossy skinned goddess took a short step back as I gripped the door frame with both hands in an attempt to stay upright.

'Oof, sorry,' I said, my stomach lurching as the boat shifted under my already unsteady legs.

The woman glared down at me. She had a tumble of white-blonde hair piled up on top of her head and a pair of comically oversized sunglasses covering most of her face, which she slid up, taking me in with perfect almond-shaped eyes, before dropping them back into place. It was all of three seconds, maybe five, but I felt as though she'd stared straight into my soul and knew all my deepest, darkest secrets. She knew I'd carved equations into the lid of my calculator to pass my Maths GCSE, that I'd once put two Chocolate Oranges through the self-checkout but only paid for one, and that I'd snuck out to see the last *Star Wars* film without telling anyone the day it came out, then pretended I hadn't seen it when Stew and I went together, three days later.

There was only one person she could be.

'Hello,' I said, trying and failing to keep the tremor out of my voice. 'I'm Fran Cooper.'

'Good for you,' she replied in a low, rich voice. 'I'm Juliette.'

CHAPTER SIX

Most assistant jobs ended up being more or less the same, whether you happened to be working for a multinational tech corporation or a family-owned box company run by idiots. I knew this because I'd done both.

But Juliette was not most people and this was not most jobs.

'So . . .' Juliette pulled her tortoiseshell sunglasses out of her hair and hooked one of the arms over her lower lip. 'You're the best she could come up with, are you?'

'Looks like it,' I replied with my head held high. Breaking in a new boss was a lot like breaking in a horse, you couldn't show fear or they would never respect you. Also, many of them were appreciative of sugar lumps and I personally didn't think riding them was a very good idea.

Behind Juliette, I saw a legion of mini-Lennys wearing *Songbird* crew uniforms and laden with stiff paper bags. Some of the names I recognized and some I didn't, but each and every one of them looked as though they would destroy my credit card inside fifteen minutes.

'We'll take tea in my suite,' the boss called to no one in particular, never once taking her eyes off me. 'Best you and I set some ground rules before we go any further.'

If only we'd set the ground rules while we were on actual ground, I thought, following her inside her suite and stooping to pick up her sunglasses when she tossed them at an armchair and missed by a good three feet.

'I'm sure Sarah has given you a thorough grilling and had you sign your soul away,' Juliette said, peeling off her luxe layers. A leather jacket, silk scarf and cashmere cardigan were all dumped on the back of a chair where they hovered for a moment before slipping into a sexy, extravagant pile on the floor. 'But all that really tells us is you're not going to kill me in my sleep.'

I laughed as I followed her into her room, picking up the clothes, still carrying her sunglasses, but she did not reciprocate, and I gulped as it dawned on me it was likely a very real thing she had to worry about.

'If we're going to spend a week together, I need to know what your deal is.' She chucked a neon-pink handbag on the sofa with the same lack of concern she'd shown all her other belongings, only the telltale inter-locking silver Cs on the clasp giving away its worth. 'So, who are you?'

'I'm Fran, Fran Cooper,' I said again, looking around the room as she opened every drawer in the dresser and pulled out half a dozen different jumpers until she settled on the right one.

Juliette's suite was twice the size of mine and even more absurd. Everything was either crystal or silver or silk, several of the walls were mirrored, just in case you wanted to look at yourself all the time, and every item of soft furnishing upholstered in heavy cream brocade. It was the least practical room I had ever seen in my entire life; all I could see were potential spills, stains, and fingerprints. Through an open archway, I spotted a bed, or at least I assumed it was the bed. It could easily fit ten people under the covers, so either Juliette had installed a wrestling ring in her room and popped a nice duvet on top, or this was yet more evidence I had almost certainly boarded a sex boat of my own free will. What if the Crystal Ball was a swingers' party? Visions of *Eyes Wide Shut* shenanigans swam in front of my eyes, with me sitting in the corner, taking minutes on my laptop and trying not to cry.

'Fran Cooper,' Juliette repeated as she admired her hair in a mirror, seemingly happier with her messy-on-purpose bun than she was with me. 'Is a name, not a person.'

She walked over to a sliding glass wall, opened it, and stepped out onto a terrace, gesturing for me to follow. Even though it was bitterly cold on the water and the sun was already low in the sky, hidden heat lamps above us kept the terrace toasty and I already felt a little too warm in my trousers and long sleeves. Juliette draped herself over a chair and nodded at the seat opposite. I sat carefully and crossed my legs at the ankles.

'Fran,' she said, inclining her head towards me, the chair holding her long limbs like a beautiful picture in an elegant frame. 'Tell me about yourself.'

In my experience, when the boss asked you to tell them about yourself, they didn't really want to know the innermost workings of your mind, just enough to make them feel like they'd made the effort, but not so much that they might actually have to think of you as an actual human being. Anything controversial needed to stay on the shelf, and that included religion, politics, football club affiliations, and whether or not you thought Kate Winslet could have made a little bit more room on that wardrobe door at the end of *Titanic*.

'What's there to tell?' I replied, fighting off the feeling I was on a bad date with someone well out of my league. The full lips, the deep brown skin, the solid, straight eyebrows that slashed decisively over each almond eye. It was a lot. 'I'm thirty-two and I'm from a little village outside Sheffield. Oh, and I did languages at university, French and Italian, so I'm really happy to be back in Italy, it's been a while.'

The sliding glass doors opened once more as two crew members appeared with afternoon tea. Two teapots, two tiny jugs of milk, and two three-tier platters of delicious-looking food. Juliette gave them a tight smile as they arranged it all on the table between us in complete silence.

'Thank you so much,' I said, eyeing the delicate pastries, the perfectly sliced sandwiches, and the fresh scones, my mouth watering. Other than half the Mars Bar I'd found in my handbag and shoved down my throat on the plane, I'd been too anxious to eat all day.

With the table set, the stewards retreated back inside, vanishing as quickly as they had arrived.

'What are you thinking?' Juliette asked, watching me watch them back out of her suite and close the door behind them without a word.

I reached for the third finger of my right hand and rubbed the indentation where my mother's ring should have been. 'Are they always that quiet?'

To my surprise, she picked up one of the teapots and

filled my cup before hers. It was a pretty big gesture from a woman who, according to the Juliette bible, required her assistant to hand-feed her as necessary.

'I've found when people are around me, they're either completely silent or they can't stop talking,' she said, picking up the milk jug and waiting for the go-ahead before tipping it into my tea. 'And if I had to choose, I'd take peace and quiet over a gobshite any day.'

I spluttered into my cup and grabbed a napkin to dab at my mouth. Juliette smiled, raising her cup towards me in a toast before relaxing back into her chair and gazing out to sea.

While she concentrated on the horizon, I concentrated on her, and the longer I looked, the harder it became to believe we were the same species. We were probably around the same age, she was a little bit taller and I was a little bit softer, but it was her face that really set her apart from the rest of us mammals. My skin had freckles and pores and a slender silver scar on my forehead from the time I attempted a one-woman performance of *Starlight Express* at the year seven talent show. Juliette's face was a masterpiece. Her skin was smooth and even, without even a suggestion of texture. A wrinkle wouldn't dare. Her wide mouth, strong nose and enormous eyes balanced each other out perfectly and her eyebrows were sisters, not twins, albeit the best-looking sisters on the planet. She had the Bella and Gigi Hadid of eyebrows. Even though Juliette glowed with the kind of youth and vitality that did not come cheap after the age of twenty-five, there was still something warm about her, something that invited me in, although, perhaps, only to the gate and not onto the grounds.

'What I'm looking for, is a happy medium,' she said,

picking a crumb off one of the scones, her face melting with bliss as she dropped it in her mouth. 'My ideal assistant is someone who isn't afraid to speak their mind but knows the difference between having something to say and saying something for the sake of it.'

'I think I know when to talk and when to listen,' I replied, waiting for her to eat the rest of the scone, but she didn't even glance at it. It was the kind of restraint I hoped to never know. 'And nobody has ever called me a gobshite. Not to my face, anyway.'

'People so rarely say it to your face,' she said with a wry smile. 'But don't worry, I will.'

And I fully believed her.

'I'm serious though, I want to know something about you. Everyone always knows so much about me, or at least they think they do, it's hardly fair.'

'Well, like I said, my name is Fran, I'm thirty-two, I live in Sheffield and when I'm not working, I like to read and watch films and . . .' I wondered how many versions of me she'd seen through the years and held out my hands, hoping my offering was enough. 'Oh, I'm engaged?'

'Where's your engagement ring?' she asked, inspecting my bare ring finger.

'Sarah said you didn't like jewellery,' I explained, thinking of the antique diamond tucked away inside my wallet and locked up in the safe along with my mum's wedding ring, my passport, phone and my laptop. 'I took it off.'

Juliette clucked her tongue in disgust. 'Well, that's absurd. What else did Sarah tell you I didn't like?'

'Is this a test?' I asked, looking all around. Surely it wasn't paranoia if you knew someone had run a

62

background check on you. 'Is she going to jump out from behind the settee and throw me overboard if I tell you?'

'Sarah is a brilliant manager and she likes things done a certain way.' Juliette wrapped her hands around her teacup and looked me straight in the eye. 'We don't always agree on what that way should be.'

'And how do you like things done?'

She sipped her tea and shrugged. 'Quickly, easily, and without anyone losing an eye.'

'Is that something I should be worried about?' I asked, blinking to make sure both of mine were intact.

'Long story, paintball accident, and that girl should have been wearing goggles anyway,' she said, setting down her cup. 'My point is, I don't care if you wear an engagement ring or not. I care about you not being an arse. Do you have any idea how weird it is, to have someone hanging around, waiting for you to need something?'

'Then why have an assistant in the first place?' I asked. 'Why not tell Sarah you didn't need me?'

Juliette laughed and kicked one leg up onto the railing that ran around the outside of the terrace. 'Because you're here for her benefit, not mine. You're basically an adult babysitter, babysitting another adult.'

'I've never thought about it that way at all,' I lied instantly. 'The way I look at it, I'm here to make your life easier.'

As the yacht took a turn, the last rays of the setting sun sliced across the table between us and shone right into Juliette's face. I pulled the pair of sunglasses I'd picked up from the floor out of my pocket and passed them across the table. She accepted them with narrowed eyes and half a smile.

'You're thirty-two, you're from Sheffield, you're

engaged, and you have a degree,' she said. 'Fine. But why are you here? Every assistant I've ever known has had an agenda.'

It wasn't the first time I'd been asked why I wanted to be an assistant, but it was the first time I'd been asked by the person I was supposed to be assisting.

'No agenda, I'm just here to do my job,' I replied. 'Cards on the table, all my other jobs were more in the corporate realm? This isn't exactly something I had planned.'

'Interesting,' Juliette clacked her fingernails against the frame of her sunglasses as she processed the information. 'But you've been doing it for a long time?'

'Best part of ten years,' I confirmed with a nod.

'Don't assistants usually move up to a proper job at some point?'

'Most of them,' I agreed, reaching for my ring again only to remember it wasn't there. For the want of something to fiddle with, I pulled my braid over my shoulder and began twisting the end.

'But not you?'

'When I graduated, the first job I was offered was assistant to the marketing manager at this online travel company,' I explained, thinking back to the fresh-faced Fran of what felt like a million years ago. 'I thought I'd stay for a year or so then maybe move up the company, work out what I really wanted to do, but then my boss was headhunted by a bigger company and she wanted me to go with her. The money was so good and I had so many student loans, I couldn't really say no. After a year or so, she went on maternity leave and I moved up to working for the CEO. Then he was offered a job in New York and wanted me to go with him but instead I joined an agency that specialized in placing executive assistants. So, no, I never planned on being an assistant for ever, but I'm good at it. I never had a passion for anything in particular, and the idea of getting stuck in a career I didn't care about just seemed so miserable. Admittedly, not every posting is a winner, but I get to meet new people, help them when they need me, and I'm always learning new things.'

'Why didn't you go to New York?' she asked, leaning in as though she might be genuinely curious.

'My boyfriend, fiancé now, lost his grandmother and she left us her house up in Sheffield,' I replied, launching into the same approved version of events I'd told so many people over the last three years. 'We decided it would be nice to be near family, so we moved back up north and I started temping.'

'And how exactly did you end up on this dinghy with me?'

'Still not entirely sure,' I replied with a smile. 'I know this isn't the kind of job little girls grow up dreaming about, but I really do love it.'

I held Juliette's gaze for as long as I could, before I looked away to watch the sun disappear beyond the horizon, everything behind us shifting from ambiguous shades of grey to solid black.

'You're not like the others, you know,' she said after a while.

'Is that a compliment?'

She picked up the teapot and refilled my cup. 'It most certainly is.'

'Are you excited about the ball?' I asked as I felt the yacht pick up speed, powering ahead into the night. 'Sarah says it's a very big deal.'

'You've never heard of the Crystal Ball?' She looked

surprised when I shook my head. 'Where *did* she find you?' Juliette breathed. 'Yes, I think so, I've never been before, but everyone says it's incredible. I was invited once but couldn't go – I had a thing in Australia on the same night, so the organisers blacklisted me – you know how these things are.'

'Sounds a bit like my future mother-in-law,' I replied. 'Miss her Boxing Day buffet once and you'll never see another invitation.'

'Someone else has taken over the organizing committee this year, so it looks like I'm in favour again, even if it is as a performer and not a guest. Instead of partying, I'll be flying across the room in a giant plastic bubble, literally singing for my supper. I have to suffer my punishment, I suppose.'

'Pretty nice punishment,' I said, a hand covering my full mouth. 'I hope it pays well.'

She pouted and poked a foot through the railing, her shoe hanging from her toes and dangling perilously over the water below. 'It doesn't pay at all because it's for charity, but no one turns down the Crystal Ball. Plus, Bey told me they spent a million on the firework display last year, and I *love* fireworks.'

'Really?' I didn't acknowledge the namedrop but I did file it away for future reference.

'They're my favourite thing,' she nodded. 'They always remind me of being little, watching the displays, all bundled up in my hat and scarf and a sparkler. Everyone's happy on bonfire night.'

I smiled at the thought of little Juliette oohing and ahhing at Catherine wheels, a miniature sparkler in her hand. 'I know what you mean,' I said, picking up the teapot and topping her off.

We sat in companionable silence, drinking tea and watching the outline of Italy melt away until an unseen mobile phone pinged loudly. Juliette flipped her legs off the railing and onto the floor, arching, cat-like, to pull a tiny flip phone out of the back pocket of her jeans. She read the message and sucked her bottom lip into her mouth, chewing on it thoughtfully.

'Everything OK?' I asked.

She stood and slid the glass door open wordlessly, leaving me alone on the terrace, but the look on her face was enough to answer my question. I placed our teacups back on their saucers, neatly folded the napkins and followed her inside. I had an excellent radar for disaster and could tell to within a one percent margin of error when the proverbial shit was about to hit the proverbial fan. Given the set of Juliette's jaw and the two hard lines carved between her eyebrows, I was fairly certain someone somewhere was about to hurl an entire sack full of faeces at my new boss.

'I'm going to take a nap,' she announced, still staring at her miniature phone and practically vibrating with rage. Whatever was in that text was not good news and whatever she was about to do, it was not sleep.

'Anything I can do to help?' I asked.

Juliette looked up at me with dark, flat eyes, all her easy smiles and warm looks gone.

'Yes,' she said, marching over to the suite doors and holding one open. 'You can leave.'

CHAPTER SEVEN

'OH MY GOD YOU'RE IN ITALY?'

I held my phone as far away from my ear as I could, which wasn't actually very far since I was hiding in the back of my wardrobe, wincing as Jess screeched down the line.

'Tell me everything. Do not leave out a single detail. I thought the job was in London?'

'The interview was in London,' I explained, stretching out one leg and then the other. It really was an absurdly roomy wardrobe. 'But it turned out the job itself is in Italy.'

'Who are you working for?'

'I can't tell you.'

'Tell me immediately.'

NDA aside, it wouldn't be fair to ask Jess, a woman who could tell you the shoe size of every member of Little Mix, past and present, to keep a secret of this magnitude.

'I can't,' I replied. 'You saw the contract, I can't say a word. All I can tell you is I'm assisting a celebrity while they perform at a charity event. And I'm on a yacht.'

Jess screamed at the top of her voice. 'Oh my god, you're with Juliette.'

'What? How did you know?' I pulled a spare blanket over my head in case there were hidden microphones as well as hidden cameras in the cabin. 'I mean, no, I'm not. I have confirmed nothing and cannot be held responsible in a court of law.'

'The Crystal Ball always takes place on the last Saturday in November,' she replied. 'Everyone knows Juliette is the headliner, and everyone knows she hates flying so she always travels by yacht. It is, isn't it? You're Juliette's assistant?'

'And you're basically Sherlock Holmes,' I said, confirming without confirming. 'You're wasted at that brewery.'

'Logic, my dear Francesca,' she crowed. 'Have you met her yet? Did you like her? What was she wearing? Did she really ghost Harry Styles after he proposed at the top of the Eiffel Tower?'

'I have, I did, she was wearing jeans and a T-shirt, and yes, that was the first thing she told me the moment we met, right before we got matching tattoos and braided each other's hair.'

'It's the first thing I'd tell someone if it were me,' she replied. 'What's she like?'

I pulled the blanket from off my head, red-faced and sweaty. What *was* she like? 'I haven't quite got a handle on her yet,' I confessed. 'I've only spent an hour with her. So far so not-a-demon.'

'You might think you're joking, but some of the stories that go around about her,' Jess whistled, which I took to be Not A Good Sign. 'Even if we go by the believe half of what you see and none of what you hear rule, she'd be a top tier, gold medal diva. Always has nice hair though.'

'Well, she didn't come across as especially monstrous; if anything, she seemed a bit lonely,' I said, squeezing the phone between my shoulder and my ear so I could examine my sharply filed down nails. 'Not that it matters. I'm just going to treat it like any other job. Come in, do my thing, go home.'

'Speaking of home, what did Stew have to say about you nipping off to Italy?'

I turned over my hands and stretched out my ringless fingers. 'Nothing,' I replied. 'He hasn't said anything.'

Hadn't said anything, hadn't texted anything, hadn't sent a WhatsApp, a DM or a voice note. I was officially on the receiving end of the patented Stewart Bingham Silent Treatment. Trademarked and copyrighted the year he was born, but I refused to give in and call him first. I needed this.

'I can't believe you're going to the Crystal Ball,' Jess said with a dreamy sigh. She really was a master of knowing when to change the subject, one of my absolute favourite things about her. 'I heard they put on a breakfast buffet at dawn and Gordon Ramsey mans the omelette station himself. And a couple of years ago, Rihanna set up a karaoke machine in the toilets and Leonardo DiCaprio and Bradley Cooper did a duet of "Anything for Love". And last year, I heard Ivanka and Jared showed up with tickets but got turned away because *you know*.'

'I thought it was all super top secret? What happens at the Crystal Ball stays at the Crystal Ball?' I replied, pushing my unhelpful thoughts and feelings back in their Stew-shaped box and locking it up tight. 'How is all this getting out?'

'There's no such thing as a secret in the twenty-first century,' she replied happily. 'Like, someone posted the karaoke photo on one of those Instagram gossip accounts, and it *was* quite blurry but it was definitely Leo. I think. One person said it looked like Boris Johnson, but I don't think there was enough hair.'

'If you can't tell the difference between Boris Johnson and Leonardo DiCaprio, you shouldn't be allowed on the internet,' I said, turning up my nose in disgust. 'I hate those accounts, people can say anything they like with literally nothing to back it up and everyone believes them.'

'It's hard to know what to believe these days, everything is information overload,' Jess reasoned. 'But what we do know is you are on a yacht with Juliette on your way to the Crystal Ball and I'm going to need all the gossip, all the photos, and you're definitely going to have to steal something for me. Last year, they had their own specially printed loo roll and I know that's true because I saw it on TikTok with my own eyes.'

'If you swear to keep this to yourself, I'll do my best,' I promised. 'But bear in mind, I'm not going to the actual ball, I'm just Juliette's helper monkey. Her manager was very clear about the fact I will not be attending the party.'

Jess's disappointment transmitted itself loud and clear from a living room in Sheffield, all the way to the inside of a wardrobe on a yacht in Italy. 'I don't want to be a dick, Fran, but this is no time to be Little Miss Follow-the-Rules. I love you completely, but if you don't find a way to go to that party, I don't think I'll ever be able to forgive you.'

'That's because it's way more your thing than mine. What am I supposed to say to Leonardo DiCaprio while we're in line for a Gordon Ramsey omelette?'

'Ask him why all his girlfriends are under twenty-six,' Jess replied immediately. 'And why he likes dinosaurs so much. He bloody loves them apparently, collects fossils.'

'Can't wait to work that into conversation,' I said, completely incapable of unknowing that fact for the rest of my life. 'If I run into any other celebs, I'll text you for icebreakers.'

'No, you won't, phones are forbidden,' she said. 'But I'll see if I can find any confirmed guests online and send you some just in case. Now, get back to making Juliette our best friend so we can go and visit her in LA. I just Google mapped her house and she's got a guest house with two pools.'

Outside the wardrobe, I heard another phone chirping, soft but insistent.

'I have to go,' I told my friend. 'I'll talk to you later.'

'Tell Juliette I said hi!' she called as I hung up one phone and crawled quickly across the floor like a particularly motivated baby to answer the other.

'Hello?'

'Juliette has asked that cocktails be served on the aft deck before dinner,' Lenny's voice came down the line, smooth and certain.

'OK, thanks,' I replied. 'Remind me, where's the aft deck?'

'I'll come and get you,' he said, the warmth from his voice radiating down the line and making me

72

shiver. 'Do you need anyone to help you with hair and makeup?'

'For dinner?' I asked, incredulous. 'I don't know, do I?'

'Forget I said anything,' Lenny replied, as though that was even a faint possibility. 'I'll see you in a while.'

Replacing the handset, I leaned back against the wall and wondered what the appropriate look might be for dinner on the aft deck of a super yacht with one of the world's most famous women.

'Can't believe they didn't teach us any of this in school,' I said, grunting as I rose to my feet, eyes fixed on my makeup bag. 'This stuff would have been so much more useful than bloody trigonometry.'

One shower, two failed updos and a very poor attempt at a cat's eye later, I opened the door to my suite to find Lenny waiting, a confused expression crossing his offensively symmetrical face at the sight of me.

'Why are you wearing a coat?' he asked.

'Because it's cold?' I replied, pulling the padded parka closely around me. 'And we're going outside?'

'You don't need a coat,' he said, rolling his eyes. 'Take it off.'

Reluctantly, I hung my coat back in the closet by the door, stepping out of the cabin in my black jeans and soft white jumper. After spending half an hour scouring YouTube for a cocktail-hour-on-a-yacht fashion tutorial, I checked the Juliette bible and was extremely relieved to discover I was supposed to wear my normal clothes and didn't have to fashion a cocktail dress out of the duvet cover.

'Only because you asked so nicely,' I said, flashing him a frown.

'I'm doing you a favour, you looked ridiculous. Follow me.' Bristling at his familiar brand of Handsome Man Arrogance, I did as I was told, but only because I really didn't have another option. 'How was your meeting with the boss?'

'It was fine,' I replied, turning left and right as Lenny navigated the labyrinthine corridors of *The Songbird* with ease. 'No drama.'

'Not yet.' He jogged down a grand circular staircase and I followed, taking the marble steps one at a time in my new deck shoes. They really didn't go with my outfit, but I suspected they really didn't go with any outfits and that was part of their lack of charm. 'Don't get taken in by her. She'll chew you up and spit you out if you fall for it.'

I would have laughed, but when he looked back over his shoulder I could see he was completely serious. 'She's my boss, not my boyfriend,' I replied. 'And I'm not a baby, I think I know what I'm doing.'

'So did the assistant before you,' he smirked as he pushed a heavy door open and led me out onto the deck. 'And the one before her and the one before him. Where are they now?'

The salty smack of sea air hit hard, making me forget all about Lenny and his not-so-cryptic warnings. All around the yacht, the stars were reflected in the sea and the whole world seemed wrapped in deep blue velvet, plush and promising. Less than forty-eight hours earlier, I'd been hacking at my shins with a blunt Gillette Venus because I couldn't be bothered to get out of the bath to find a new razor blade. It was almost too much.

'How long before I stop feeling like I'm about to fall over all the time?' I asked, bracing my legs in a half-squat and holding my arms out to recover my balance as the ship listed to one side.

'I've a feeling you could be waiting a while,' he deadpanned. 'We've dropped anchor for the evening which should help. We set sail again in the morning, should arrive off the coast of Panarea after lunch.'

As I walked along the deck, I tugged at the collar of my jumper, the warm wool rubbing against my sensitive skin the way it always did when I was too hot. 'Hang on, it's November, why isn't it cold?' I asked, looking all around and seeing nothing but sea and night sky.

'Hidden heat lamps,' Lenny answered. 'Now you can say thank you for me telling you to lose the coat.'

Or not, I thought, pushing up my sleeves and marvelling at the fact that even weather didn't exist if you were rich enough.

Juliette was lying on what looked like an outdoor bed at the far end of the deck, a barely-there floral spaghetti slip dress clinging to her body, nothing on her feet and her white blonde hair hanging loose. She was magnetic and I felt myself flush a deep and unforgiving red whenever she cast a smile in my direction.

'Fran, at last,' she exhaled my name and reached out to dip her hand into one of several bowls of snacks on the low table beside her. 'Lenny, we'll take two gin and tonics. Big ones. Put them in washing-up bowls if you have to.'

'Right away.' He gazed back at her with the same smile he'd bestowed on me when I first boarded, one I realized I hadn't seen since. It was clearly far too good to waste on the staff.

'I like your jumper,' Juliette said as I seated myself

on a marshmallow-soft sectional across from her. To me, the furniture looked as though it belonged in someone's super cool living room rather than the deck of a yacht, but I'd already established I had very little clue about what belonged on a yacht. The only thing I knew for sure was that I didn't. 'Is gin all right? Do you want something else? Sorry, I should have asked,' she scrunched up her lovely face and gently slapped a hand against her forehead. 'Lenny, wait!'

'No, it's fine, I love gin,' I insisted as Lenny turned to rush back. 'Only, I don't usually drink while I'm working, so just water is fine for me.'

'She'll have a gin,' Juliette corrected, overriding my order. She raised a challenging eyebrow and I held up my hands in submission as Lenny departed once more, this time without a smile.

'I'm technically on the clock, aren't I?' I said, perched on the very edge of the sofa. 'I don't think Sarah would like me drinking on the job.'

'Seems like it's after hours to me,' Juliette replied. 'I'm not going to need an assistant tonight. The only way you can assist me is by helping me get bladdered.'

I clenched my teeth together in a grim smile. 'Not to make myself unpopular, but my instructions say—'

Juliette sat up and crossed her legs, flashing her knickers without concern. 'Your instructions say I'm not supposed to drink forty-eight hours before I perform,' she finished for me. 'But these are exceptional circumstances. I'm sure there's something in there about exceptional circumstances.'

'Not that I recall. What are the exceptional circumstances?'

'Welcoming you to the team, celebrating our first night

76

on board,' she replied, counting off the reasons on her fingers. 'The fact I've had an unutterably shit day, and what else, oh, it's Thursday. Thursday is the new Friday, you know.'

'I have heard that,' I said, inching back into my seat and remembering my own words at the interview. My job was to make hers easier. Sometimes I had to be an assistant, sometimes I was a therapist, sometimes I had to be their best friend, even if it was only for one night. 'But be warned, I'm probably going to disappoint you. I'm not much of a drinker at the best of times. Sarah should have specified "able to hold their ale" in the job description.'

'I'm amazed she didn't do a blood panel and send your DNA off for testing,' she muttered, tossing another handful of sweets into her mouth. 'Actually, are you absolutely sure she didn't?'

'I'm not sure of anything any more,' I admitted, wondering what she'd done with the water bottle I drank from.

'I was going to do one but then Barack told me they pass all your DNA on to the FBI and I thought, no thank you very much. Although Sheryl Sandberg said they're not allowed to use it unless they have reasonable suspicion, but you just don't know, do you?'

She gave me a wink and I smiled, relaxing by a fraction of a percent. Every time she caught my eye, I felt my heart leap in my chest.

'Perhaps I can help with the unutterably shit day part,' I said, reminding myself why I was there. 'What was so terrible? Is there anything I can do?'

A muffled ringing sound interrupted her before she could answer. It was my phone. My forbidden *personal* phone. I'd stuck it in my back pocket, meaning to lock it in the safe before Lenny arrived, then got distracted when I found another TV that popped out of the ceiling, and completely forgot it was there.

'Gosh, I'm sorry,' I said, jumping to my feet. 'I shouldn't have this with me, let me take it back to my cabin.'

'Answer it if it's important,' Juliette said as if she didn't care either way, already rooting through a big bowl of crisps. 'Just be finished by the time your drink gets here or I'll likely down them both.'

'I'll be two seconds,' I promised, looking at the name on the screen, hitting accept and holding my breath.

'You went to London?' Stew barked.

I pulled the sleeve of my jumper down over my fingers, and looked over the side of the yacht into the water below.

'Yes. But, funny story, it turned out the job included some travel so—'

'I can't believe you went to London without clearing it with me first,' he cut in. 'I thought we agreed we'd talk about it?'

'We did, then you went to sleep,' I reminded him. 'And I told you I had to leave this morning, but you were gone when I woke up. When were we supposed to talk?'

'Yeah, I went to do a favour for a friend.'

'Bryony,' I corrected. 'You went to do a favour for Bryony.'

'We talked about you taking jobs away,' Stew said, ignoring my extremely salient point. I heard the familiar sounds of our kitchen in the background, the click of the kettle, the turn of the tap. 'We agreed you weren't going to travel.'

78

Closing my eyes, I pressed a hand against my fore-head, hoping it might warm up my brain and release the right words, ones that would stop the argument before it started and make this all OK.

'We did. but that was a long time ago and this was an amazing opportunity,' I replied. It was very hard to be diplomatic and non-confrontational, when you were also really quite annoyed and also trying to maintain some semblance of professionalism in front of your new boss. I looked back over my shoulder and saw Juliette watching me from the settee, not even trying to pretend she wasn't. 'And this is very much a one-off, not a regular thing.'

'You say that now,' he grunted.

'Stew, it's been three years.' I sighed and pinched the bridge of my nose. 'I'm sure you can cope for a few days on your own without—'

'Without what?'

I gripped the railing of the boat as I realized what I'd almost said, holding on so tightly, my knuckles turned white.

'Without me,' I finished, stunned at myself. 'I was going to say, I'm sure you can cope for five days without me.'

Ten silent seconds ticked by. We never talked about what had happened the last time I'd gone away with work, not ever. We didn't speak of it, we didn't reference it, we didn't even hint at it. The past was in the past and the best thing for both of us was for it to stay there. So why had I come so close to speaking it to life?

'We agreed you wouldn't leave again,' Stew repeated and I knew he wasn't going to let this go easily. I'd been a fool to myself if I thought he would. 'When exactly are you back?'

'Tuesday,' I said, twisting my hand around the railing. 'I'll be back Tuesday.'

'Good. I told our Mandy we'd go round for dinner Thursday night to talk about this teacher idea,' he replied. 'So, make sure you are.'

And then he hung up.

I kept the phone pressed against my ear for a moment more, taking an extra beat to compose myself. One breath in, one breath out, pack it all away and deal with it later. Clearing my throat, I slid my phone back into my pocket and turned to face Juliette with an apologetic smile.

'Well,' she said, holding out her hands for a fish-bowl-sized gin and tonic from one of the stewards who was not Lenny. 'That sounded fun.'

'It was nothing, just domestic strife.' I sat back on the sofa and took an enormous swig of my extremely strong drink. 'Please pretend it didn't happen.'

'The phone call from your fiancé or the domestic strife?' she asked, with one eye on me, the other on my rapidly disappearing drink. 'Assuming it was your fiancé?'

'It was,' I confirmed. 'And both, if you don't mind. It really was nothing.'

Juliette slid her feet up underneath her, tucking the edges of her dress around her shins. 'How did you two meet?' she asked.

Under normal circumstances, I avoided all personal chat on the job, but there was something about the look on her face and the way her brown eyes glowed in the dark that made me feel like I could talk to her about anything, even the fact I once had a sex dream about Keir Starmer so vivid, I couldn't so much as look at the *Guardian* for months.

'At university,' I said, smiling at the memory. It was still a happy one, even now. 'We were both in our third year, at some terrible first week back thing. I think there were three members of S Club 7 performing at the student union.'

'Makes perfect sense,' she grinned back at me and I felt warm all over. 'Who wouldn't be seduced by half-price alcopops and the undulating beat of "Don't Stop Moving"?'

'It was even more romantic than that,' I said. 'His friend was getting off with my housemate, so we thought we might as well.'

'Move over Romeo and Juliet,' Juliette replied with a throaty laugh, raising her glass to mine and clinking the two giant drinks together. 'I wonder how many people out there have ended up with someone they snogged for the sake of it.'

'I'd like to believe most people are living the most incredible love stories of all time, but I imagine it's actually quite a lot,' I said, thinking over my pre-Stew affairs. None of them could exactly be called a fairy tale. Drunken dance floor snogs mostly, with the odd, awkward, friend-of-a-friend set-up thrown in for good measure.

She pushed a small white bowl towards me. It was full of Skittles. I took a couple out of politeness and held them in my hand, not sure they would go especially well with a gin and tonic. 'You've been together a long time then?'

'A very long time.' I nodded, popping a green Skittle into my mouth and taking another swig. To my surprise, it was a match made in heaven. 'Twelve years.'

'I can't even imagine it.' Juliette pushed an errant strand of hair out of her eyes only for the sea breeze to

81

blow it right back again. 'I'm not very good at long-term relationships. Or relationships in general, if we're being entirely honest.'

'Really?' I hadn't meant to sound so surprised, but she smiled at my reaction. 'It's just, I would have thought people were falling over themselves to go out with you.'

She cocked her head to one side, the expression tightening on her face.

'It's difficult,' she said, looking skyward. 'Can't go on the apps, can't go to a bar. Meeting people at all is difficult enough, let alone people who will put up with all my nonsense. I know I shouldn't complain, but it's hard to have a relationship when your other half wants to go to Nando's but you can't because it'll be all over the *Daily Mail* inside half an hour.'

'That is a high price to pay for fame,' I said gravely. No number of platinum records could separate me from half a medium chicken and a spicy rice. 'No blind dates? No set-ups?'

'It's not really a blind date when one of you was on the front page of the *Sun* because your nip slipped out of your Oscar gown,' Juliette replied. 'And set-ups never work for me. It's not the same without that moment, that chemistry. That split second when your eyes meet and your heart stops and they transform from a stranger into someone, right in front of you. That moment is everything.'

'You know, you should write love songs for a living,' I told her, my own heart beating just a little bit faster. 'You totally had me going there.'

She cupped both hands around her glass and drank. 'In my experience, relationships are mostly not worth the hassle, but they do make for good material.'

'So, there's no one?' I asked, curling into my seat.

Juliette opened her mouth as if she were about to say something, but instead she gave a resigned sigh and began twisting the hem of her dress around her finger. 'No,' she said, the shadow of the same expression I'd seen right before she kicked me out of her room threatening her features. 'There's no one.'

It was such an obvious lie. The only way it could have been more obvious would have been if she had a neon sign flashing over her head that said 'I'm lying' and a tattoo of the person's name in the middle of her forehead. But if she didn't want to talk about it, she didn't want to talk about it.

'Could be worse,' I assured her. 'You could be me and Stew.'

She looked up at me from under her eyelashes. 'Things are that bad?'

'We're very much at the "arguing over who took the bins out last" stage,' I replied. 'Totally fine, really. We argue, it blows over, we go back to business as usual. Not exactly the kind of affair people write love songs about.'

'As someone who literally writes love songs for a living, I can tell you ninety-seven percent of them are based on utter bollocks,' Juliette declared, the darkness suddenly lifting and leaving nothing but her usual light loveliness. 'Cheaters always cheat, players always lose, and you can't build anything that lasts on big, loud, messy love. It's not real. I want a love that is so sure of itself, it doesn't have to shout.'

I smiled at her across the table, shaking my head gently.

'That's beautiful,' I said. 'Is it from one of your songs?'

'No, but it's good, isn't it?' she said with bright eyes. 'Get your phone back out and write that bugger down. We could have a hit on our hands here.'

'See?' I pulled out my phone and tapped her words into my Notes app. 'You did need an assistant tonight, this is me, assisting.'

'God, you're right.' Juliette leaned back against the sofa, gin and tonic in hand. 'Whatever did I do without you, Fran Cooper?'

'I do not know,' I replied. 'I honestly do not know.'

CHAPTER EIGHT

Friday was not the worst day of my life.

'Aren't you coming in?'

Juliette popped her head out of the pool on the main deck, where I had set up a mini outdoor office. Her hair was slicked back and half her face was obscured by her giant sunglasses, but what I could see of it was smiling.

'I'm waiting for Sarah to call,' I said, holding up my work phone as evidence.

'That phone's waterproof,' she replied as she pushed off the edge, slicing backwards through the water. 'You could swim and wait at the same time.'

I turned it over in my hands looking for confirmation. 'It is?'

'Sarah switched all the work phones to waterproof ones after I "accidentally" drowned five of them,' she called back. 'Don't make me swim on my own, Fran, get in the bloody pool.'

'Never really been much of a swimmer,' I demurred, pulling my black cardigan closely around me. Even though I was wearing my regulation black one-piece under my clothes, cannonballing into a pool with the boss didn't feel particularly professional to me. And then there was the fact that no one other than Stew had seen me in any state of undress since they did away with the communal changing rooms in Primark, and even he usually turned the lights out first.

'Hot tub then?' Juliette swam towards the steps and rose up out of the water, tossing her hair around like something from a Herbal Essences advert, before thoroughly destroying the dream by reaching back to pull her bikini bottoms out of her bum.

'Stew hates hot tubs,' I said as I dutifully followed her across the deck. 'We went to Center Parcs with his sister and her kids once and we were just getting relaxed when this bat came flying out of nowhere and scared him half to death. Haven't been in a hot tub since.'

She eased herself into the water, stretching her arms out along the side and resting her head against the back of the sunken tub. 'No bats here,' she said, the steam rising up around her in the crisp November air. 'And no reason why you shouldn't get in.'

I looked at the phone and then back at the hot tub. It did look inviting. And the number of opportunities I would have to sit in hot tubs on yachts with pop stars in my life were probably limited.

'Get in the sodding hot tub, Fran, it's an order.' Juliette tipped her head back, long hair fanning out all around her. 'You're stressing me out.'

'Fine, fine, I'm getting in,' I breathed, slipping out of my cardigan as quickly as possible. Juliette said nothing, her eyes still hidden behind her huge, mirrored sunglasses. It seemed impossible to straighten your shoulders, suck in your stomach, stick out your arse and walk all at the same time, but I did my best, certain that she was watching me behind the dark lenses. Juliette's body was perfect to me, all soft curves and glowing skin. Next to her, I felt like an undercooked fish that had been left out on the side for too long.

'I love that suit,' she said, once I was safely hidden under the warm, bubbling water. 'Who is it by?'

'I'm not sure, Sarah gave it to me,' I replied, cupping a hand over my eyes and noting the difference between asking 'who is it by?' rather than 'where is it from?'. Subtle but not insignificant. 'I didn't realize I would need one.'

'Looks like it was made for you.' She sank lower and lower until only her face was above the water. 'But then anything would look amazing with your boobs.'

'Really?' I rearranged the simple straps of my suit and considered my extremely average 36Bs. 'I've always thought they're a bit small to fill out a swimming costume.'

'That's because we're never happy with what we've got.' Juliette sighed as she reached one arm out of the hot tub, patting along the deck until she found a large, colourful cocktail with several umbrellas sticking out of it. 'I super appreciate the body positivity movement, but I think that I'm too old for it to take. Ever since I was born, people have been telling me how I need to lose weight and be as thin as possible and now, over-night I'm supposed to what? Feel *good* about myself? It's madness, I tell you. I wouldn't know where to start.'

'Your body is incredible,' I insisted, and having stayed up half the night reading up on my new boss and looking at roughly one thousand paparazzi photos of her taken from every conceivable angle, I spoke with complete authority. 'You should feel better than good about your-self.'

'Well, yes, we all *should*,' she replied. 'But I'm not allowed. Not according to those lovely magazines that like to circle the parts they don't consider up to scratch. And pretty much every single person on the internet.'

'Ahh, that well-respected critical body,' I pulled my legs away when our toes touched, scooting them off to the side to avoid any future transgressions. 'You're gorgeous. If you can't feel good about yourself, what hope do the rest of us have?'

She lowered her sunglasses and looked at me with smiling eyes. 'I think you just hit the nail on the head. Look at us, brilliant at complimenting each other, but entirely incapable of thinking good things about ourselves.'

She wasn't wrong. What a shit nail.

'Do you think there are any men having this same conversation right now?' I asked, fondly squidging my outer thighs under the water.

'Yes but only three, and they're all watching a Chris Hemsworth movie.'

'I can't imagine The Rock makes many men feel good about their bodies either,' I said, looking up at the pale blue sky and powder puff clouds above us. 'It's got to be a nightmare staying in shape like that.'

'Oh, it is,' she agreed. 'He's always walking around with a bag of grilled chicken, it's disgusting. You can't take him anywhere. Literally, we were asked to leave The Ivy once when he wouldn't put it away.'

'I wouldn't mind grilling his chicken,' I replied. I meant it both literally and figuratively. Couldn't cook for shit but I would one hundred percent dust off the

George Foreman Grill for Dwayne. 'Stew turned *Baywatch* off halfway through, and I don't think it was because of the plot.'

'Are you sure it wasn't because of the plot? Because that was not the best movie I ever saw.'

I smiled and reached for my phone, keeping it away from the water just in case it wasn't quite as waterproof as Juliette seemed to think it was. Sarah had scheduled a daily catch-up but so far, no call.

'You do that a lot, you know,' Juliette said, pushing her sunglasses up on top of her head.

'Check my phone?' I replied, pushing it away.

'No, I meant how you answer a question about yourself with a story about Stew.' She pulled up her legs and wrapped her arms around her knees. 'Stew didn't like the film, so you turned it off. Stew was attacked by a bat, so you don't go in hot tubs.'

'Oh.' I fiddled with the strap of my swimsuit again and realized it was twisted at the back, under the clasp. No matter how much I stretched and arched, it would not come straight. Juliette reached for her cocktail again while I continued my contortionist routine.

'Only an observation,' she said.

'I think it's because we've been together for so long. We're basically one person now, his stories *are* my stories,' I said, giving up on the strap. It would just have to stay twisted. 'I'm sure he does the same about me. He's probably moaning to his brother right now, about how I'm always nagging him to replace the toilet roll and shut drawers properly. Honestly, why is it so impossible for a grown man to close a drawer? Drives me mad.'

She picked up her cocktail and held it out towards

me. I leaned forward and took a small sip through the straw. It was predictably delicious.

'I guess that happens in long relationships,' she replied. 'I wouldn't know.'

I shielded my eyes from the sun with my hand and smiled. 'This is the part where a friend would say "you'll meet the right man one day".'

'Followed by the part where I would kick that friend in the tit, so best not to,' she tilted her head gently to one side and matched my expression. 'But who knows what's going to happen?'

'Me,' I replied, glancing at the clock on the screen of my phone. 'You're due at the salon in ten minutes.'

Juliette groaned and slid all the way under the water, as though I'd just told her she needed to go inside and do her homework. According to the itinerary, her pre-performance prep included a mani-pedi, full body tanning, a massage and a cut and colour, all of which would take place in the salon, in the spa, on the yacht. To think I once spent three Euro extra on a lilo because it had a cupholder, and Stew said I was being extravagant.

'I don't make the rules, I only enforce them,' I said as I climbed carefully but quickly out of the hot tub. There was no way to do it with grace. 'Come on, you don't want to be late.'

'Why?' she asked. 'Have they got another appointment after me?'

'No,' I replied, holding out her obscenely fluffy robe. 'But they're expecting you and you don't want to be rude.'

'Jesus Christ,' Juliette muttered as she climbed out of the hot tub. 'Your fiancé is either brave or stupid. I wouldn't dare leave a drawer open in your house.'

Squinting as I held out her robe, I wondered which it was.

'Here,' she said, holding out her sunglasses. 'You're going to get a headache if you carry on like that.'

'Thanks,' I said, slightly stunned by the offering.

'You're welcome,' she replied as she wandered off across the deck, dripping on the polished woodwork as went. 'No big deal.'

But, as I slid them over my eyes, relaxing as the sepia film soothed the too-bright light of the pool deck, I couldn't help but feel as though it was.

'How is she?' Sarah asked. 'What's happening? What's her emotional state?'

'Absolutely fine,' I confirmed from my cabin, having safely delivered my charge to the spa only to find three missed calls from Sarah demanding we Zoom immediately. 'Juliette's fine.'

She stared at me with such intensity through the screen of my laptop, I froze, afraid the slightest blink or intake of breath might cause her to have a stroke. 'That's it? She's *fine*?'

'Everything's been great,' I replied, pushing my new sunglasses up on top of my head. 'She seems happy enough to me. In good spirits, I'd say.'

'And what about the crew?' Sarah pressed her fingers against a tiny vein that throbbed in her pixelated forehead.

'I've barely seen them,' I admitted. 'It's mostly Lenny, the chief steward. He's . . . not a problem.'

'OK, good.' Her eyes flicked back and forth between me and what I assumed was another computer, one hand occasionally shooting out to tap something manically on a keyboard. 'And no one has been lurking in the background or taking photos or anything?'

'Absolutely not. It's practically a ghost ship, we barely see anyone. If it weren't for Lenny popping up every couple of hours to make sure everything is OK, I might think this was a modern day *Black Pearl*.'

'I don't get that reference and please don't explain it to me,' she said. 'You've got all your instructions for tomorrow?'

Holding up a printed, laminated piece of paper from the desk, I nodded.

'Crystal Ball itinerary. We dock at lunch, the hotel is sending golf carts to collect us, Juliette has her sound-check at five thirty, makeup will be waiting in her suite – the stylist has already delivered wardrobe, by the way – Juliette performs at half past eleven, thirty minutes onstage, we stay overnight at the hotel, then it's back on the boat Sunday morning. I've confirmed and double-checked everything, carts, hotel, makeup, security, crew, all of it.'

'Good. Make sure you remind the organisers of the event that there aren't going to be any meet and greets,' Sarah said, still typing furiously with one hand. 'She's performing and she's leaving, that's it. She won't be attending the gala, she won't be mingling, and we have an absolutely zero tolerance policy on selfies. She's singing and that's that.'

'Got it,' I replied, wondering if the policy on selfies extended to me as well.

'She can get stressed out the night before a perform-ance, so make sure she goes to bed at a decent time tonight, and since I'm sure she's still drinking even though she shouldn't be, no more than one glass of champagne,' Sarah went on. 'She's got meds if she needs them, dosage amounts are on the bottle and in the bible, all the pills are locked up in your safe.'

I nodded, glancing at the black leather ring binder. I'd had to give a boss's Pekinese worming medicine once so I was pretty sure I could convince an anxious performer to take her Xanax. I made a mental note to ask Lenny for some cubes of cheese in case I had to pull the old hidden tablet trick. Hopefully I wouldn't have to clamp Juliette's mouth shut and massage her throat while reassuring her that she was a good girl.

'Any questions?' Sarah asked.

'Not really,' I said, wiping some crumbled mascara away from under my eye. 'Only I've noticed she's not eating much. Little bites here or there, but she's hardly touched any of her meals. She seems to be mostly subsisting on Skittles and gin.'

For the first time since I'd answered the call, Sarah's shoulders dropped from around her ears and her face broke into an almost-smile. 'Is that all? That's fine. She doesn't eat, not really. Probably worried about fitting into her dress tomorrow. Not a concern, Fran.'

'Perhaps her anxiety would be better if she was eating better,' I suggested, more concerned than ever. 'I could ask Chef if he can make her a green juice or a smoothie, something like that?'

I almost jumped out of my skin as Sarah threw her head back with laughter so violent, I was truly worried it would snap off her shoulders and roll away across the room.

'Oh, that's a good one. If you are going to give her a green juice, please film it and send it to me,' she gasped, wiping at her weepy eyes. 'On your work phone,

93

obviously, don't leave yourself open to a lawsuit. Gosh, thank you, I needed that. I'll schedule her for a vitamin infusion and a colonic when she gets back.'

The very thought of it made me clench. Surely eating an apple every now and then was better than being stuck with needles and having a hosepipe shoved up your bum?

We went through the itinerary one more time before Sarah ended the call, leaving me gazing out of the window of my cabin as we sliced through the sea. The sky had turned overcast and rain was threatening to fall, but inside, my room was toasty and warm.

I'd adapted to yacht life very quickly. My bed was always made, my clothes were always clean and freshly pressed and every time I turned around, something magical had been delivered by the invisible stewards; a steaming pot of coffee, a pillowy soft sandwich, platters of tropical fruit and, on one very special occasion, a freshly baked chocolate chip cookie the size of my head. It was like being in the fanciest hotel ever, only the hotel was moving and there were more staff than guests. The only bad part was having to remember that I was one of the staff, not one of the guests.

Scanning the ceiling one more time for hidden cameras, I pulled my forbidden phone out from underneath my pillow and saw a text from Jess.

Well?? What's happening??

Grinning, I sent back a kissy face emoji and promised to fill her in properly as soon as I could. There were still no messages from Stew and nothing of great importance in my inbox other than a marketing email from Marks and Spencer. A week ago, festive Percy Pigs would easily have been the most exciting part of my entire day. Not that it wasn't exciting now, Percy Pigs were life, but I was on a yacht, in Italy, with one of the nicest, coolest, kindest women I'd ever met. A week from now I'd be back at home, in the rain, staring down the barrel of a PGCE with the most miserable fiancé who had ever lived and all of this would be nothing but a memory.

'Might as well make it a good one,' I resolved, sighing as I stared out to sea.

CHAPTER NINE

At the front of the boat, on the second highest deck, was the Grand Dining Room. Double height windows ran all the way around the room, a glass ceiling let the stars shine down on its occupants and as I stepped inside, I felt as though I was cruising through the night sky itself. My black jeans and white silk shirt felt criminally casual for such a dramatic setting and I wondered if there was time to go back to my room and change into another human being. The dining table was one enormous slab of polished rose quartz and around it were twelve chairs, all made from the same rose-gold and pink velvet, but each one of them was ever so slightly different. The back wall was mirrored to add to the illusion of open space and, above the table, a low-hanging chandelier shimmied as the boat breathed with the waves.

'I hate this room.'

Juliette arrived with a scowl. A black dress set off her freshly coloured white blonde hair, flowing all the way down to her toes and moving with her body as she walked around the table.

'Sorry, Lenny, I thought I'd asked Sarah to say we didn't want to use this room any more.'

'I assumed that was an error. You've always loved entertaining in this room in the past.'

He sounded innocent enough but there was a catch in his voice on the word 'entertaining' and the slightest hint of a smirk that I did not care for.

'It wasn't an error,' Juliette replied. 'I don't want to use this room again.'

'It really is gorgeous in here,' I said, still hovering in the doorway and attempting to defuse the situation before she had him banished to the brig. 'Stunning, really.'

But Juliette did not agree.

'It's too much,' she muttered before flinging open a concealed cupboard to reveal a full bar. Bottles and bottles of chilled champagne, every spirit known to man, and endless rows of crystal stemware hung from shelves that ran almost all the way up to the ceiling. 'It's so fake, can't you feel it? This room was designed by a man to impress a woman.'

'Well, someone should tell him it worked,' I replied, tucking my hands safely under my armpits. 'Although I daren't touch anything.'

'You can touch a drink because I'm opening a bottle.' Juliette pulled a magnum of champagne out of the bar, grabbed two flutes, and closed the mirrored door with a swish of her hip. My entire body seized up as the crystal chimed inside. I didn't use that much force to close the dishwasher – something about this room had really pissed her off.

'I'm serious, I can't eat in here,' she declared. 'Lenny, can we eat in my room? Or on the deck? Literally anywhere else on this boat.'

'The weather's forecast to turn rough, so I wouldn't recommend the deck,' he replied. 'I can have a table set up in your room, shouldn't take more than a few minutes.'

'Fine.' With an expert's touch, she turned the cage that protected the champagne cork and tossed it to the floor. 'What's on the menu?'

Lenny smiled and took a half bow. 'Chef has prepared some of his specialities in honour of the Crystal Ball, starting off with an *amuse-bouche* of—'

The cork popped out of the bottle, firing across the room and missing the chandelier by half a hair's breadth. I didn't realize I was holding my breath until the cork rolled to a stop in front of my feet.

'OK, sorry again, but no,' Juliette said without missing a beat. 'You're going to list seventeen courses and their respective wine pairings when all I really want is some McCain oven chips and a Findus crispy pancake. This was all supposed to be in the notes. I don't want any big fancy feasts.'

A fleeting look of panic crossed Lenny's face. 'I don't think we have any of whatever they are, but I can ask Chef to—'

She sighed sadly, cutting him off. 'No, I know you don't, I'm not even sure they still exist. Fran, do Findus crispy pancakes still exist?'

'I can find out,' I replied, immediately tapping at my work phone. As someone raised in a 'you get what you're given' household, the combination of Juliette's frustrated demands and the look on Lenny's face were enough to make me break out in a rash. Not to mention the fact I was far more interested in a seventeen-course menu with wine pairings than oven chips and a soggy-bottomed chicken and mushroom abomination.

'I really am sorry, please apologize to Chef for me, but I can't eat all that tonight. My stomach is in knots.'

Soothed, I assumed, by the giant swig of champagne she then took straight from the giant bottle.

'She has got a big day tomorrow,' I said. 'Maybe a heavy meal isn't the best idea. Could Chef make us something lighter instead? Maybe a pizza?'

'Ooh, yes!' Juliette gave a thumbs-up as she continued to chug the vintage Dom Perignon. 'I could absolutely go for a pizza.'

'I'm sure that will be possible,' Lenny replied, all the colour drained from his face, the smirk nowhere to be seen. 'Or I could send the helicopter out to collect from Naples?'

'We are *not* sending a helicopter out for pizza,' I declared before looking at Juliette, who was gathering the two crystal champagne flutes and a second bottle of fizz in her arms. 'Are we?'

'I don't care where it comes from as long as I don't have to eat it in here,' she replied, gaily dancing out of the dining room. 'Thank you, Lenny!'

'Not at all,' he said, before turning to hiss in my ear, 'a little notice on any menu changes would be nice in future.'

'Did it look like I got any notice?' I replied as Juliette disappeared down the corridor. 'If you send me the menus ahead of time, I'll get her to look at them, but clearly, I can't make any promises. And she did say she'd submitted these requests before she even arrived.'

'Those requests never mean anything, she always says one thing then does another – how was I supposed to know she meant them this time?' His top lip curled up in disgust and it became abundantly clear that he wasn't nearly as handsome as I'd first thought. No matter what was on the outside, I didn't go for the inside at all. 'Chef's going to go ballistic.'

'Then Chef might be in the wrong job,' I suggested archly before dashing out of the dining room to chase down my charge and, more importantly, the two bottles of champagne I somehow had to stop her from drinking.

Chef may not have taken Juliette's pizza request kindly, but even if he had licked every slice out of spite, it was still the most delicious pizza I'd eaten in my entire life. The thought of going home and settling down to a two topping, two medium meal deal made my heart and my tastebuds weep. Sitting on the floor of Juliette's cabin, I polished off my third generous slice while Juliette continued to pick the tomatoes from her first.

'Can I ask you something?' I said, stealthily moving the third bottle of champagne that had arrived with the pizza out of her reach. She drank the stuff like water, and it didn't even seem to touch the edges. Somehow I'd managed to put away two glasses without really trying. Who knew Dom Perignon went so well with a thin crust pepperoni?

'You can ask, but that doesn't mean I'll answer,' she replied.

'How come you prefer to travel by boat?' I sat up to help a stubborn bit of crust work its way down my gullet. 'It's not exactly efficient, time-wise, and I can't imagine it's very cost effective. So why bother?'

'It's extremely cost effective when your friend lets you borrow their boat for free.'

I did a double take as I thumped my chest to help the pizza on its way.

'*The Songbird* doesn't belong to you?'

She raised her eyebrows and laughed at the look of surprise on my face. 'I know I'm not hurting for cash, but do you really think I have yacht money?'

'I just assumed,' I said, glancing around the cabin with fresh eyes. 'It seems as though you're really at home here. Everything seems very "you".'

'It does feel like I spend more time here than I do in my actual house these days, but no, *The Songbird* isn't mine.' She picked a piece of pepperoni off her pizza with her newly long and sparkly red nails, considered it from every angle and then dropped it in her mouth. 'The current owner is a fan. He renamed her for me, which was very sweet, but even if I had a spare half billion dollars hanging around, I wouldn't be buying myself a yacht. They're boys' toys. Extremely expensive and elaborate penis extensions. Trust me, you could count on one hand the number of female billionaires who have spunked their money up the wall on a yacht.'

'You have some nice friends,' I said, trying to imagine how to begin a conversation that might end in the offer of a free yacht. 'My best friend wouldn't even lend me her car to drive to Ikea.'

'Just because someone is a Russian oligarch doesn't mean he can't be your pal,' Juliette said with a flashy smile. 'Not that I ever see him, he's always jetting around somewhere with his latest wife. Lending me the boat is some sort of weird flex that I don't entirely understand and honestly, don't care to question. He likes telling his friends I borrow his boat, I like to let him. I know they say there's no such thing as a good billionaire, but

101

I've had just as many shitty experiences with normal people as I have with the obscenely rich. In my experience, the richer they are, the more up front they are about being a cock. There's something quite reassuring about that.'

'I suppose so,' I replied, frowning at the thought. 'Wouldn't it be nicer not to have to deal with any arseholes though, rich or otherwise?'

She leaned forward and patted my hand. 'Oh, Fran,' she said sweetly. 'Never change.'

I chewed my pizza thoughtfully, wondering whether or not I could get away with opening the top button of my jeans without her noticing. Three slices of gourmet pizza were still three slices of pizza, and I wasn't nearly done yet.

'Since you're all questions, let's play a game,' Juliette suggested, letting her almost empty glass fall on its side as she clapped her hands together. 'Truth or dare.'

My hand shot out to catch the glass before the dregs of her drink could stain the carpet. 'I don't think that's a good idea,' I replied, squeezing all my features into one long, uncertain sausage. 'Dares, champagne and open water don't feel like a good mix to me.'

'Great, I'll go first then. Dare.'

'I dare you to finish that slice of pizza and enjoy an early night. How's that?' I fixed her with the most forceful glare I could muster, a vain attempt to replicate her power over Lenny, but the effect was somewhat lessened by an aggressive hiccup that appeared out of nowhere.

Juliette uncurled her body in one smooth motion, lying flat on the floor with one leg kicked over the other, the skirt of her silk dress fluttering to the ground around her. 'Fine, you go first.'

'You're going to make me do this, aren't you?' I said, looking sadly at the rest of the pizza. She was supposed to be having an early night and I was supposed to be tucked up in bed, watching one of the TVs that popped out of the ceiling, and eating leftovers until my new jeans no longer buttoned up at all. This was a blow.

'Yes, so the sooner you give in, the easier it will be.'

'All right then,' I said with a resigned sigh. Sometimes the quickest route was through. 'I choose truth.'

Juliette knitted her eyebrows together as she attempted to come up with a suitably traumatising question.

'Got one,' she said finally. 'Have you ever cheated on your fiancé?'

I opened my mouth to say something and then stopped myself, reaching around the bed for the hidden bottle of champagne, tearing off the foil to reveal the cork.

Juliette gasped. 'Christ alive, you have? I wouldn't have thought you capable. So scandaloso, Francesca.'

'I have not,' I replied, fumbling with the cage. 'I have never and I would never.'

'So . . . he cheated?'

The cork popped out of the bottle, shooting off into the bathroom, hundreds of pounds worth of vintage champagne spilling down the sleeve of my white silk shirt.

'Shit,' I muttered, trying to keep the spill off the carpet and away from her bed. 'Shit shit shit.'

'It's all right, it's nothing,' she insisted, leaping up to grab a clean linen napkin from the cart that had delivered our dinner and pressing it gently against the damp patch. 'Do you want to talk about it?'

I shook my head as I took the napkin from her hand and watched the champagne from my shirt darken the pale pink fabric. 'I'm sure Lenny will be ecstatic if I balls up the carpet.'

'Lenny can piss off,' she replied as she pressed another napkin into the thick white pile. 'I've never met another human who fancies himself as much as that man, and I've had dinner with Kanye twice.'

Pushing aside the many, many questions that statement brought up, I knelt beside her as we cleaned up the wet spot together. 'He's not exactly who I thought he was,' I admitted. Juliette turned her head, her hair falling in front of her face.

'I'm sure he isn't. But who is?'

It was an excellent question.

'Let's start this game over,' she said, sitting back on her heels. 'I dare you to chug your glass of champagne.'

She filled my glass all the way up to the brim as I winced, my pizza-filled stomach turning at the thought.

'I've had more than enough,' I replied, noting how the edges of the room had already become a little fuzzy. 'I told you I'm not a big drinker.'

'If you don't, I will,' she warned.

'No,' I shook my head, putting my literal and figurative feet down. 'We both need a big glass of water and an early night. No more champagne.'

'I was hoping you'd say that,' she replied as she tipped the entire glass back in one gulp. Wiping her hand across her mouth, she beamed at me with slightly glassy eyes and reached for the bottle to refill. 'Your turn, or I'll do it again.'

What other option did I have? The more I drank, the less was left for her. It wasn't perfect logic and I already knew I'd regret it in the morning but I really couldn't see another choice.

'This is the last glass for both of us,' I said, reluctantly clinking my glass against hers. 'We finish this one and then it's straight to bed.'

'Aye-aye, captain,' Juliette confirmed with a sharp salute, grinning as I drank.

'All you're going to do, is knock on the door, ask a very simple question, and while he is answering said question,' Juliette reached out one arm to steady herself against the wall as we staggered down the narrow hallway of the upper deck. 'You're going to nick his hat.'

A brisk wind from an open window blew her long hair into her face, her eyes wide with excitement as she bounced up and down on the spot, only slightly hampered by the fact she was now wearing a bright blue beaded ballgown, roughly the size of a Fiat 500. I wasn't quite sure why, but my plan to put us both to bed after one more glass had not been as effective as I'd hoped it would be.

'Isn't it illegal to take a captain's hat?' I asked, punctuating my question with a sharp stab of a hiccup. 'What if he makes me walk the plank?'

'That's policemen,' she slurred, shoving me towards the door. 'He's not Jack Sparrow, his name is Mark and he's from Slough and there isn't a plank. As far as I know.'

'But I don't want to,' I whined, her hands digging into my shoulder blades. 'Do another dare, I dare you to do me another dare.'

'No.' She pulled away from me, attempting to focus

105

both of her eyes on the same spot at once. 'I dared the dare and now you've got to do the dare. That's the law of the sea. Maritime law. I'm an expert. Is your phone recording?'

I looked down at the iPhone hanging from my neck from Juliette's Gucci phone pouch.

'Yes but I'm going to get the sack for this,' I replied, waving a hand in front of the camera and seeing it appear on the screen. 'I'm not supposed to use my own phone.'

'But you can't use your work phone because then Sarah will see it,' Juliette said, tapping her temple as though she was a genius. 'This way, she'll never know.'

'But why do we need to film it at all?' I protested.

'Because,' she leaned in and covered her mouth with her hand, dropping her voice to an extremely loud whisper, 'I said so.'

I watched my boss as she swayed from side to side, her glamorous ballgown accessorized with a pair of neon-pink cowboy boots and a very fetching, twirly moustache I'd drawn on with eyeliner one bottle of champagne earlier.

'You've got to do it,' she ordered with one last shove towards the door. 'And don't forget to say the thing.'

Raising a wobbly arm, she knocked on the door to the bridge for me, before scurrying around the corner, the train of her dress lagging behind, and giggling to herself, entirely audible from her rubbish hiding place.

Captain Mark opened the door, movie star blue eyes widening in surprise.

'Ms Cooper?'

He seemed somewhat perplexed, which was fair, given that I was wearing nothing but a coconut shell bra and a mermaid tail we'd fashioned out of a pair of curtains.

'Is everything all right?'

'Everything is so good,' I flicked my wrist to make sure he knew I really meant it and almost toppled over. I did not know my own strength. 'Perfect, actually. Better than perfect. Can things be better than perfect? I don't know, they're brilliant though.'

'That's an interesting outfit,' he said, trying very hard to keep his gaze away from my coconuts.

'Oh yes,' I replied, prodding the shells I'd superglued onto my second best bra. 'We were doing a live re-enactment of *The Little Mermaid* but Chef didn't have any scallop shells big enough so, you know, coconuts.'

I slapped myself in the tit and winced.

'Which reminds me, he's going to want that lobster back.'

Captain Mark's eyes flitted to the corner where Juliette was doubled over laughing. 'Is there something I can help you with?' he asked.

Taking a deep breath in, I felt the boat give under my feet and reached out for the wall to steady myself. Either the boat was moving or my head was spinning, but either way, I needed to get this over with before I threw up.

'I'm really sorry but I have to do this so maybe you could just go along with it,' I said, accessorizing my stage whisper with a theatrical wink. 'It's a dare, you see, and you know how it is. You have to do a dare when you're at sea, it's maritime law.'

'It absolutely isn't.'

'Probably just best to get it done, not to think about it too much,' I said, more to myself than him. 'It's just a dare, isn't it? No big deal.'

'Ms Cooper.' The captain was starting to look nervous. 'I think I know where this is going and I'd rather you didn't—'

Rather than let him finish his sentence, I reached out and ripped the hat from his head, turned as quickly as my tail would allow, and ran as fast as my fins could carry me.

'You didn't say the thing!' Juliette howled as I blitzed right by her. 'You've got to say the thing!'

'I'm the captain!' I screeched, slapping the hat on my head as I bolted for sweet freedom. 'I'm the captain now!'

CHAPTER TEN

Without the magical hidden heating of the lower decks, the observation deck of *The Songbird* was bitterly, bitterly cold. We were up as high as it was possible to be, hiding on the tiny platform directly above the bridge, and curled up inside the duvet Juliette had dragged out of her cabin.

'You look good in coconuts,' Juliette remarked as she handed me the bottle of Dom she had stuffed inside the duvet. 'You should wear them more often.'

'And you should grow a moustache,' I replied, straightening the captain's hat on my head. 'That's what's been missing from your look, I reckon.'

She laughed and curled up closer. 'If I didn't get waxed every week, I'd have one. Maybe I'll let it grow out, see what the *Daily Mail* has to say about that.'

Staring out into the endless blanket of black before us, I let out a heavy, happy sigh.

'What are you thinking about?' she asked, her voice thick and dreamy.

'How badly I need a wee,' I replied truthfully. 'But I don't want to break the seal.'

'These are the moments when I really wish I was a man. Imagine if you could just take a slash over the edge of the boat. You'd feel like a god.'

'I wouldn't want to have to deal with the rest of it though,' I said, sticking out my tongue at the thought. 'Penises are so unpredictable. One minute you're standing in the queue at Sainsbury's, minding your own business, and the next thing you know, you've got a boner. They're so disrespectful.'

'And ironically, having one generally grants you far more respect than not having one. Maybe I'd get taken seriously if I had a penis.' She raised her hand and made an L shape with her finger and forefinger. I did the same and pressed my hands against hers. Although I didn't say so, I was pleased to see my imaginary penis was slightly larger than Juliette's.

'You get taken seriously now, don't you?' I said. 'I mean, you *are* playing the Crystal Ball.'

'There's a difference between success and respect.' Juliette took the bottle from me for a small sip. 'It's better now than it was for me starting out, for women in general, I think, but it's still harder. You still have to prove yourself ten times over, there are still a lot of piles of shit to shovel. Humanity is happiest when people stay in their boxes. The box the industry chose for me isn't serious, so I can't be taken seriously unless a serious man says so.'

'I'm sorry,' I said quietly, my hair blowing all around my face as I thought about all the things I'd sniffed at and dismissed as 'not for me' without really thinking why.

'You don't have to apologize, it's not your fault,' she said, looking off into the distance. 'It's all of us. Everyone

110

does it, me included. Women have two options, either be a victim or be a hero. You can't just exist. Be the person they want you to be, or else. Do as you're told, or else. And the only shortcut to credibility is going through something truly terrible and sharing it with the world but, tell me, why should we have to do that?'

I sat with her words, waiting for them to straighten out in my head. Was I a victim or a hero? I certainly wasn't a hero, and I didn't like where that left me.

'It must be hard, balancing all of that with your actual career,' I replied. 'I don't think I could do it.'

'Singing and writing songs is all I've ever wanted to do,' Juliette said, her words pitching upwards as she spoke. 'I'm not stupid, I know how lucky I am, no one's sending me to the front of the sympathy line and nor should they. I'm not Biebs, I'm not going to write a song about how hard it is to be wealthy and successful because dear god, has there ever been a better way to lose sympathy? I told him it was a terrible idea, but he never listens. He doesn't have to, he's Teflon.'

'Typical,' I scoffed, my eyes bulging slightly out of my head. 'Classic Biebs.'

'But it would be nice to have one day where I don't have to worry about anyone's preconceived notions or expectations,' she said with a soft sigh. 'I really wish I didn't have to care so much about what other people think.'

'While I'm right there with you at the back of the sympathy line, I do hear what you're saying.' I said with a sniff. My nose was starting to run in the cold. 'Everyone's got an opinion on how you should live your life, no matter who you are.'

Even if you're me, I added silently.

'I'll toast to that,' she said, raising the bottle and clinking it against my invisible glass.

It felt so strange, to connect with someone whose life was so different from mine. Even more so, given the fact that someone was a celebrity, we were under a duvet on the deck of a yacht, and I was wearing a bra and a curtain, but still, it was nice. I felt my shoulder blades sliding down my back as she handed me the champagne. I took the tiniest sip then passed it back. I'd had more than enough.

'You're really easy to talk to,' Juliette said, sounding surprised. 'Do people ever tell you that?'

I waved away the compliment before it could take root. 'Good listening skills are part of my job.'

But Juliette shook her head. 'Have you not considered that you might be good at your job *because* you're a good listener, not the other way around? This is the most I've talked to anyone in months. Maybe years.'

'You know what?' I said, my heart swelling three sizes at once. 'Me too.'

Gentle waves lapped against the side of *The Songbird* and I smiled at nothing in particular. I turned to look at her perfectly etched profile and found her smiling back at me.

'Juliette?'

'If you're going to ask a question it counts as your turn.'

'Why didn't you bring one of your friends on this trip?'

She snorted and somehow she even managed to make that pretty. 'Well, Fran, I imagine it's because I don't really have any friends.'

'I'm sure you've got lots of friends,' I said quickly

112

and with too much enthusiasm, as though I was a primary school teacher, and she was a sad little six-year-old playing by herself at lunchtime. 'How could you not have friends?'

One of her hands emerged from the duvet and she scratched the tip of her nose gently. I noticed one of her nails was already chipped and made a mental note to get it fixed tomorrow.

'I'm not trying to make you feel sorry for me; friends just aren't really part of this package,' she explained. 'It's hard to keep in touch with people when you're moving around as much as I am. People tend not to have a lot of sympathy with you missing their baby's christening because you're playing a festival in Rio after the third time it happens. Again, no one's fault but mine.'

'Having a lot of friends is overrated,' I declared. My tongue was beginning to feel thick and fuzzy. 'Quality, not quantity, right?'

'Tell me about your friends,' she said, giving me an encouraging pat on the knee. 'I bet they're amazing, I bet you're like a South Yorkshire *Sex and the City*.'

'Well, I've got Jess,' I began, happily summoning a mental image of my best, best friend. 'We met a couple of years ago. I was covering for her assistant while she was on mat leave actually, but right from the first moment, it felt as though I've known her all my life. She's brilliant, you'd like her, she's the kind of person who would help you bury the body before asking any questions.'

Juliette laughed. 'I could use a Jess, definitely. Who else have you got?'

I opened my mouth but my mind went blank.

'I really like my spin instructor,' I said, hesitantly. 'Does he count?'

'What's his name?'

'Cody.'

'Is he a real-life person or a man on a screen?'

'Man on a screen.'

Juliette shook her head.

'Then it's just Jess,' I said, surprised at how hollow I felt as I said it.

'That's it? Really?'

'My mum used to say friends are something women have between boyfriends,' I said, blowing the words away before they could come back to haunt me. I rubbed the bare finger where her ring should have been. 'I've never been very good at the whole friend thing.'

'Christ,' she muttered. 'Your mum must be hard as nails.'

'She died ten years ago.' I spoke lightly, my big toe escaping from underneath the duvet. 'But yeah, she was not to be messed with, my mum.'

It was never really quiet on the yacht, the sounds of the engine and of the waves swelled to a pleasing background drone, but there was a kind of stillness and separation from the rest of the world that made my voice echo, even when my words barely registered above a whisper. Juliette's eyes opened wide and I saw the same expression on her face I'd seen on a hundred others before. It was the sort of thing that would never get any easier to say or hear. She leaned forward and quietly tucked the duvet around my bare foot.

'I'm sorry.'

'Thank you.' I pinched my blue toes through the warmth of the fabric, the cold already sharp in my bones. 'I thought she was right about the friend thing for a long time,' I said quietly. 'When I went to uni, I lost touch with almost everyone from school pretty much right away, then I lost touch with most of my uni friends when I started going out with Stew, and I didn't really try to make any real friends when we moved to London. You don't miss mates when you're twenty-one and in love, I didn't think I needed anyone but him.'

'Why did you leave London again?'

'Lots of reasons,' I replied, ready to roll off my well-prepared list of answers. 'Stew inherited a house from his nan, which was a big factor, obviously. He was still working as a photographer then and we couldn't afford to buy a house on just my salary.'

'You couldn't sell her house and buy in London?'

'Stew couldn't face it,' I replied, remembering the night I'd suggested exactly that. One of our first proper arguments. 'We always said we wanted to end up back there, the Peak District maybe, be closer to family. Plus the timing was right, Stew wasn't getting a lot of work as a photographer, and his dad suggested he come and work for him. My boss was moving to America . . . like I said, there are lots of reasons. Lots of really good reasons.'

'And because he had an affair.'

A simple statement that sliced right through me.

'It wasn't an affair, not really,' I whispered, forcing the words off my sticky tongue. It was so long since I'd talked about it, I hardly knew how. 'Just one of those things, some girl he met in the pub. I was working away a lot and he was lonely. I wasn't there for him and that was really hard.'

Juliette yanked the champagne bottle out of my hand

and gave me the same serious look she'd given Lenny several hours earlier. Somehow, the eyeliner moustache only managed to make it more terrifying.

'Absolutely not,' she declared. 'Absolutely bloody not.'

I blinked, taken aback by the anger on her face. 'Absolutely bloody not what?'

'You're not going to sit there and say it's your fault your partner putting his penis in another woman,' she replied. 'That's fucked up.'

A blast of wind swooped across the deck and chilled me right down to the coconuts. 'I'm not blaming myself,' I countered. 'But if I'd been there, if I hadn't been away quite so much, it might have been different. I'm not excusing it, I'm just saying I can see how it happened. From his perspective.'

'No. No, no, no, no,' she whirled around, full of fury, her dress filling the tiny deck and pushing me backwards against the railing. 'We cannot blame ourselves for betrayal, for cheating, for lying, for taking something private and precious and shattering it into a billion pieces and—'

'Are we still talking about Stew?' I asked, a little confused.

'Yes, yes, we are,' she answered, fire burning in her brown eyes. 'Does he still feel as guilty as you clearly do? After you somehow compelled him to bone someone else by simply doing your job? What sort of effort did he make to fix things?'

'He asked me to marry him,' I muttered, thinking of the other ring tucked away in my wallet, Nana Beryl's ring.

'Fran. A proposal shouldn't be an apology.'

I puffed out a breath of air and watched it appear as a cloud in front of my face before it melted away into nothing.

'What does your friend think? Jess, you said.'

'I don't really talk to Jess about Stew stuff,' I admitted. 'She's had loads of bad luck with relationships, some really awful stuff. I don't like to put our problems on her, doesn't feel fair.' I paused to adjust my coconuts and blink back whatever was happening behind my eyes. They certainly couldn't be tears. 'And she'd probably tell me to break up with him.'

'How's the sex? You must be getting something out of this?'

I pressed my hands against my face and groaned. 'What sex? It's been months.'

Juliette raised both eyebrows but said nothing.

'That doesn't matter,' I said, even though it was starting to feel as though I was mostly arguing with myself. 'You don't break up with someone you've been with for twelve years because one person made one mistake or because the sex isn't as exciting as it used to be. You don't break up with someone when . . . when . . .'

'When you're so unhappy you can't even talk to your best friend about it?' she suggested. 'Fran, listen to yourself. What would you tell Jess to do if this was her?'

'You don't understand.' I closed my eyes and sucked in a lungful of fresh air. 'We've been together for so long, we're basically one person. We're Stew and Fran, Fran and Stew. We're Frankenstew.'

She took my cold hand in her warm one. 'And that's a good thing?'

'I don't know,' I replied honestly. 'It's like he's all the good bits, the parts everyone likes. He's the arms and the legs and the really great hair and I'm the inside parts you need to keep you alive but no one wants to think about. Oh my god, I'm offal.'

'But that means you're the brains as well,' Juliette said as I choked back a threatening sob. 'You're running the whole show.'

And then I couldn't hold it in any more.

'We haven't got a brain,' I wailed. 'We're just a zombie, going on and on for no reason. We're a brainless offal zombie.'

Juliette snaked an arm between the railing and my back and pulled me in for a hug. 'People don't give offal its due,' she said, calmly stroking my back. 'If we didn't have kidneys, we'd . . . actually, I don't know what would happen. Remind me what kidneys do again?'

'They clean your blood and send all the poison out as piss,' I replied, fully weeping now. 'But I don't know how much longer I can keep cleaning all the piss.'

She held me tighter as I cried it out, stroking my hair and making soothing sounds that I couldn't quite make out.

'You're right,' she said. 'I don't think I do understand. Why would you want to stay with him if this is how you feel?'

'Because we've been together so long and I love him and it'll get better and . . .' I squeezed my eyes closed as I spoke, stymying my tears. 'I don't know which is more frightening, the thought of staying and things being like this forever or the thought of leaving and having no clue what I'm getting myself into.'

'Oh, Fran,' she sighed. 'I think you do know.'

She didn't understand. She couldn't.

'I can't. I can't leave him, I don't know who I am without him,' I whispered. 'And he was there when my mum died. She loved Stew so much.'

'That's it, isn't it? Juliette said. 'That's why you won't go?''

I took a deep breath in through my nose, determined to get myself under control. 'One of the last things she said to me was not to mess things up with him. I know if she was still here now, she'd tell me to make it work.'

Juliette gave me a sad half-smile. 'With all due respect to your mum, I don't believe that. She wouldn't want you to be unhappy, would she?'

I looked up at her, wiping my eyes with the edge of the duvet.

'I want to say no?' I replied. 'But I'm not entirely sure. You didn't know my mother.'

'But I do know you're allowed to be your own person, not just someone's daughter or someone's girlfriend,' she said, soft but sure. 'Who does Fran want to be? Where does Fran want to live? What does Fran want to do?'

'Fran wants a wee,' I replied, ducking under the duvet and pulling it up and around my head like a bonnet. 'And to stop addressing herself in the third person.'

Juliette grabbed the edges of the duvet around my face, brown eyes boring into my blue ones. 'Fran. I don't know much—'

'But I know I love you?' I finished hopefully.

She rolled her eyes and sighed. 'You have the musical taste of a sixty-year-old woman.'

'Thank you,' I whispered.

119

She pressed her fingers into my cheeks and squeezed until I felt my lips making a pouty fish face. 'What I was going to say was, I don't know much about relationships, but I do know about blaming yourself for something someone else did wrong and burying your needs so deep it's practically impossible to dig them back up. You've got to work out what you want and grab hold of it before it's too late.'

'What if Stew is what I want?' my fish face replied. 'He might not be perfect, but he isn't a bad man.'

Juliette shook her head.

'A lot of brilliant women have been crushed by not-bad men.'

I didn't reply for a minute. Instead, I thought back over all the times I'd given something up, turned down an invitation, cancelled plans, all to make Stew's life easier. And not just Stew's, I'd done it for everyone. Whether it was deciding what to have for dinner or turning down the opportunity to work in another country, I'd set myself up time and time again thinking an easy life would make me happier. But it hadn't. What did Fran want? Who did Fran want to be? I had no idea, I hadn't even let myself consider the question.

'Is it time to go in?' I asked, tired and confused and definitely ready for the rest of the pizza. If one of the stewards had taken the leftovers away, I would find out which one, hunt them down and kill them.

'It's time for another dare,' Juliette answered as she grabbed my hand and pulled me to my feet. 'Come on.'

We staggered along the boat to the highest point of the observation deck, both of us leaning into the curve of the railing. I rested my hips against the cold steel and held my arms out on either side.

'If you're about to do the *Titanic* bit, so help me god, I'll push you in myself,' she warned. I lowered my arms and turned back to face her, guilty as charged. 'I want you to call Stew.'

'Oh, no,' I replied, grabbing at the phone that was still hanging around my neck. 'Absolutely not.'

'I want you to call Stew,' she repeated. 'And I want you to tell him how you really feel.'

Shaking my head, I sniffed loudly. 'How can I tell him that when I don't even know? I can't call him now, it's too late.'

She held her watch up to my face.

'Fuck me, it's not even nine,' I breathed. 'I thought it was the middle of the night, I'm a disgrace.'

'Do it now before you overthink it,' she said, placing the phone in my hand. Obediently, I tapped in his number, white digits on a black screen, only some of them blurring double.

'But what am I going to say?' I asked, desperate for an answer.

But Stew picked up before Juliette even had a chance to reply.

'Fran?'

'Stewart,' I pulled back my shoulders and stood tall. I was a strong, powerful woman who happened to be wearing coconut shells she had glued onto a bra. I could do anything. 'It is I, Francesca.'

I pictured him sitting on the settee with his hand down his pyjama bottoms. A standard Friday night.

'I have something to tell you,' I said, reaching for the railing while Juliette dropped into an encouraging twerk, one arm in the air. 'And that is . . .'

'That is what?'

I slapped her on the back, manically gesturing for help as panic dried up my throat, all my words stolen by champagne.

'Fran?' He sounded testy. 'What do you want? Are you drunk?'

'Repeat after me,' Juliette hissed over the whipping wind. 'We can't go on together.'

'Stewart,' I said into the phone. 'We can't go on together.'

'With suspicious minds,' she sang, swivelling her hips under her ballgown.

'With suspicious minds?' I added, swaying my foot to her beat and completely forgetting why I had called him in the first place. 'And we can't build our dreams—'

'All right, I think I've got the point,' Stew interrupted my song with an annoyed grunt. 'What is going on? Where are you? How are you this rat-arsed when you're supposed to be working?'

I opened my mouth to answer but was cut off by the sound of a doorbell that was not ours.

'Stew!' a familiar voice called in the background. 'Hurry up, food's here.'

'I've got to go,' he said quickly. 'I'll call you back later.'

'Is that Bryony?' I asked, gripping the railing tightly as a spray of freezing cold saltwater slapped me in the face. 'Are you at Bryony's?'

Juliette stopped dancing. Stew said nothing.

'Stew?' I said. 'Answer me.'

'You and Elvis might be right,' he replied, finally. 'We can't go on like this and I don't think we should speak again until you get back. I've got some thinking to do.'

And then he ended the call.

'Fran,' Juliette said, pushing wet strands of hair out of her eyes, a look of concern on her face. 'Are you all right?'

'No,' I replied. 'I'm not.'

And then I pulled back my arm and hurled my phone, as hard as I could, as far as I could, into the Tyrrhenian Sea.

CHAPTER ELEVEN

'Fran! Are you hurt? Is anything broken?'

I opened my eyes to see Lenny crouching over me in a panic, his face looming close and closer.

'What are you doing?' I groaned, shoving him away as I sat upright, only to hit my head on something hard. I poked at it gingerly and looked for the offending weapon. Why was there a big silver bin in my room?

'I thought you were dead,' Lenny said as I attempted to stand up, his jaw set solid. 'What are you doing in here?'

'What am I doing in where?' I asked, extremely confused.

With a throbbing head, I shuffled around until I was halfway to vertical and took in my surroundings. Instead of my beautiful cabin, there were bright fluorescent lights, cold tiled floors, and shelves full of food stacked all the way up to the ceiling.

'Why am I in a store cupboard?'

'You tell me.' Lenny held out an arm to help me all the way up as I shook off the tea towels I'd repurposed as tiny blankets. 'The last time I saw you was at three a.m. when you and Juliette were trying to start one of the jet skis.'

'Jet skis?' My throat was dry and scratchy and my tongue felt like I'd used it to clean a lion's litter box.

'Jet skis,' he confirmed. 'You were both very determined, in spite of the fact they were chained up, the ramp was closed, and neither of you knows how to start a jet ski.'

'We were trying to find my phone,' I said, groaning as I pressed my fingers into my temples, flashes of the night before coming back in sharp, stilted fragments. 'I lost it.'

'You told me you were going to visit Ariel and all the other mermaids,' Lenny replied flatly.

'A girl can't do two things at once?' I asked with a wince. 'I'm so sorry.'

'No need to apologize, it looks like you're suffering quite enough as it is.' He cleared his throat to smother a laugh as I popped my left breast back into my coconut bikini before following him down a very narrow corridor and into the galley. 'Coffee?'

I nodded and more memories shook themselves loose. The champagne, the pizza, the captain's hat. My conversation with Stew. A flush of feeling coloured my cheeks. That wasn't even the worst part. I'd crossed a line I had never crossed before and it was something so much worse than getting off with the boss.

I'd fallen in friend with Juliette.

Like all great love stories, it happened slowly at first and then all at once, and under the influence of alcohol.

'In case you're interested, we arrived at our destination two hours ago. We can't take *The Songbird* any

125

closer than this, she's too big and the water is too shallow.' Lenny poured a huge mug of coffee and I grimaced as he handed it over without adding any milk or sugar. I was an unprofessional, hungover mess, he was right, I didn't deserve dairy. 'We'll go over on the tender when Juliette is ready.'

'Juliette.' Any colour that might have come back to my face drained away. 'Oh my god, where is she?'

'Isn't keeping tabs on madam your job?' he replied. 'It's still early for her, she doesn't usually surface until the afternoon when she's had a big night.'

'What time is it?' I asked, willing him to say something bright and early.

Lenny pointed at the large analogue clock on the galley wall. It was twenty to twelve.

'Fuck,' I drained the coffee mug in three big gulps. 'Fuck, fuck, fuck. Sarah is going to kill me. We're supposed to be on the island by twelve.'

'It's not Sarah you should worry about.' He held out his hand for the mug as I started for the door. 'Juliette's not your friend, don't forget that.'

'Seriously, what is your problem with her?' I asked, gasping when I saw my hair reflected in the mirror behind me. Why was it bright pink?

This time he didn't bother to hide his sneer. 'She's like every other guest on this yacht, a rich user and a nasty piece of work. I don't trust her, and neither should you.'

'No wonder she's so paranoid,' I said, sad that she was right about him. 'She's not stupid, you know, she knows you don't like her.'

'But she likes the yacht that she doesn't pay for. Although obviously we both know she's paying for it one way or another, if you get what I mean.'

'Wow,' I said, enunciating extremely clearly. 'That's really dark and even if that were the case, which I don't think it is, it would have nothing to do with you.'

'You'll learn how these things work when you've been here for a while,' he replied, straightening up until he towered over me. 'Not that you'll last. Her assistants never stick it out for more than a few months, and you are not an improvement on any of the others. The last one did pretty well, she was around for a while, but then she was gone, no explanation, just vanished like the rest of them. Juliette is rude, arrogant, and she only cares about herself.'

'Maybe she just needs someone to give her a break,' I shot back. Lenny had sparked a fire in my guts that made me want to defend Juliette in a way I would never have thought to defend myself. 'Maybe she just needs someone to be her friend, to be nice to her, have you considered that?'

He let out one loud bark of a laugh. 'What are you talking about? Everyone's nice to her, all the time.'

'Everyone's kissing her arse all the time,' I countered. 'There's a difference. She can tell when it's bullshit.'

'She hasn't got a clue what's going on,' he said, dismissing my anger in the way that only men do. 'You don't know her.'

'And neither do you,' I said, turning towards the door and marching out of the kitchen with my fins held high.

While I was furiously changing out of my mermaid ensemble and into yesterday's jeans and the first T-shirt I came across, I found a box of pink hair dye in my bathroom and I realized there was nothing I could do about that until I had a lot more time and possibly a bottle of Domestos. Once I was dressed in people clothes rather than mermaid drag, I let myself into Juliette's suite and closed the door behind me as quietly as I could. Showering would have to wait, we were already late and I couldn't risk Sarah finding out about any of this.

'Juliette?' I called softly. 'Are you awake?'

Her room was untouched. The bed hadn't been slept in, there were no dirty clothes anywhere and, after searching every inch of the bedroom, living room, dressing room, and bathroom, she was nowhere to be found.

'Fuuuuck,' I breathed, hands on my hips, work phone in my hand. My own phone was at the bottom of the sea and any messages from Stew were being played for the fishes. But that was another problem that would have to wait.

'One cock-up at a time,' I muttered to myself before raising my voice slightly. 'Juliette, where are you?'

After piecing together the evening as best I could, the last thing I remembered was going to the galley for a late-night snack. Evidently, I had remained at the scene of the crime, but Juliette had not. So where was she hiding? I glanced over to the terrace and saw the door was slightly ajar. My stomach lurched. Surely not surely not surely not.

'No,' I said loudly, turning away from the window and the possibility. 'Nope, no. She's in here somewhere.'

Looking back at my reflection in the mirrored wall opposite her bed, I balked at the pale, drawn cheeks, panicky eyes and patchy pink hair tied up in a topknot. Not my best look. Stepping closer to the glass, I raised a hand to my face to swipe at a tenacious smudge of mascara, when the yacht dipped sharply to one side.

'Shit!' Reaching out my hands to stop myself, I stumbled towards the wall, colliding face first with the mirror. But the moment I grazed the glass, the wall gave way, swinging backwards to reveal a secret room hidden behind it. Inside, nestled amongst a giant pile of powder-pink pillows, was Juliette.

'Juliette!' I exclaimed, throwing myself to the floor and shaking her by her narrow shoulders. She was still wearing the ballgown and the cowboy boots but the moustache had been half wiped away, leaving her with a fairly unflattering five o'clock shadow.

She breathed in and opened her eyes, staring at me like she'd seen a ghost.

'Oh my god, I thought you were dead,' I exclaimed, falling back on my heels and pressing both hands against my chest, breathing hard as she lifted her head, blinking at me with foggy confusion.

'I'm not dead,' she murmured, blinking slowly. 'At least I don't think I am.'

The lighting in the room was soft and low and every surface was padded. My first thought was tiny asylum but make it fashion until I realized the restraints built into the wall probably weren't meant for someone suffering a mental breakdown. Less red room of pain and more pink room of pleasure, but *still*.

Sex. Ship.

'Are you OK?' I asked, focusing on Juliette and not on the weird bench thing behind her that looked like a pommel horse but almost certainly wasn't. 'I can't believe how much we drank last night. I woke up in the *kitchen*. Actually, Lenny woke me up in the kitchen, and he was not amused—'

'I'm fine,' she replied, cutting me off sharply. She

looked up at me, eyebrows drawn together as though she was either trying to work out something very complicated, or she was incredibly constipated. Given how little fibre she ate, it really could have been either. 'What do you want?'

Someone did not appreciate being woken up when they were suffering.

'I wanted to make sure you were all right,' I said, finding my way to my feet and trying not to read too much into her change of tone. 'And to let you know we're here. We've arrived in Panarea, I mean.'

Juliette continued to stare at me as if I was speaking a foreign language.

'The original plan was to dock at twelve, but we don't have to be at the hotel for your soundcheck until five thirty so we can leave a bit later,' I kept on talking, waiting for her to smile or laugh or stick out her tongue. Literally anything other than the death stare she was giving me would have been better. 'I figure sooner rather than later is better? Get settled in, make sure you have everything you need—'

'I need a San Pellegrino,' she said, shifting her gaze to the wall behind me. 'An orange one.'

Something had changed. I wasn't sure what, but something was different. This wasn't the same woman who had decided I would look incredible with pink hair at two a.m. and given me a piggyback all the way to the ship's salon to steal the temporary tint to prove it.

I crossed her cabin to the mini fridge by her bed and rifled through the cans. 'There's no orange in here,' I called back. 'Just lemon.'

'I asked for orange, didn't I?' Juliette replied. I felt my shoulder blades snap towards each other and was glad to have my back to her. I was too hungover to disguise the dismay on my face.

'I'll go and see if there are any in the galley,' I suggested, slapping my hands on my thighs as I pushed myself up to stand. 'Can I get you anything else while I'm there? Coffee? Breakfast? Ibuprofen?'

'If you could just do as you're asked, that would be great,' she said, giving me a sour smile. 'And close the door. I don't want to be disturbed again.'

'And what would you like if they don't have any?' I asked, subtly scratching my suddenly itchy scalp. An allergic reaction really would top off my morning beautifully.

Juliette stretched out one long leg and touched the tips of her toes to the inside of the door.

'If they don't have any, you will go and get some,' she said, slowly and clearly.

And then she kicked the door closed. Juliette and the secret room disappeared and all that was left was my own shocked reflection staring back at me in the mirror.

'Juliette doesn't drink orange San Pellegrino,' Lenny grumbled as the tender rolled off *The Songbird*'s ramp and into the water eight long minutes later. 'It's not on her list, she only drinks lemon.'

'Maybe you should go back and tell her that,' I suggested, cupping a hand over my eyes to block out the low winter sun. My new sunglasses were still on my desk, along with everything other than my work phone and the handful of cash I'd grabbed on my way out of my cabin. Between the hangover and my less than delightful interaction with my boss, it was fair to say I wasn't really thinking about sunglasses when I left.

131

His face stretched into an unbecoming grin as he steered the boat towards the dock, bumping up and down on the waves and weaving in and out of all the other yachts that filled the bay. None of them were as striking as *The Songbird*, but I couldn't help but wonder who might be hiding in a pink padded safe room inside those cabins.

'Just so you know, I'm not the kind of guy who says I told you so.'

'Thanks, appreciated,' I replied, my voice flat and my words terse as I gripped the edge of my seat. The less I said, the less likely it was that I would puke over the side of the boat.

'But I did tell you so,' he went on, completely unable to stop himself. 'Last night, you're her best mate and today, you're the shit on her shoe. Classic Juliette.'

'Is there any chance we could slow down a bit?' I asked, breathing in and out very, very slowly.

'No,' he replied as he gunned the engine even harder. 'The shop is there, at the end of the harbour. Blue building, white awning. Can you see it?'

Squinting, I followed his gaze as we rose and fell, bouncing over the choppy waves. Every time we dropped, my stomach threatened to send back my black coffee, but the sea air soothed my headache, leaving me in the confusing state of feeling better and worse at the same time.

'Aren't you coming with me?' I asked as Lenny tossed a rope towards a dark-haired man waiting on the dock.

'I have to stay here in case we have to move. This is the busiest day this harbour sees all year, I can't leave the tender unattended.'

I staggered across the boat with awkward, stiff legs

as it bumped against the dock, testing my balance with every stride. The dark-haired man held out his hand and I grabbed hold so tightly, I was worried it might come off.

'Jump,' he shouted in Italian. 'It's not far.'

Don't fall in, don't fall in, don't fall in, I chanted inside my head as I propelled myself from the edge of the tender onto the dock, collapsing onto my helper in a pink-haired heap.

'I'd like to get back to *The Songbird* before sundown,' Lenny called as my dark-haired helper shook me loose, stalking away down the dock and muttering loudly to himself. 'Hurry up, if you don't mind?'

The sensation of solid ground beneath me was so wonderful, I almost fell to the floor and kissed it, but the look on Lenny's face suggested there wasn't time. 'I'm going, I'm going,' I said, making a grand show of scooting off down the dock. 'I'll be back before you've missed me.'

'We don't have that long,' he shouted, laughing at his own joke, to which I responded by smiling brightly and secretly giving him the finger behind my back.

Panarea harbour had a long jetty, jutting out into the sea in an L shape, and there were happy, busy sounds all around me, dock workers yelling back and forth as more boats approached, motors revving then cutting out. The Italian language curled around my ears like an old friend and I smiled as part of my brain I hadn't used in such a long time fired into action.

Travelling by boat was confusing. You knew where you were with air travel, literally and figuratively. You went through the airport, you stormed Duty Free, you sat on the plane, and then, as if by magic, you arrived wherever you were going, tired, emotional and full of Toblerone. The two days I'd spent at sea felt like a trick. I had no idea when one place turned into another, but here on dry land, the fact we were in Italy became real. It moved into focus, warm and golden and full of blue sky promises, the sun still low and glinting off the waves that ebbed and flowed on either side of me. The unfamiliar but unmistakeable smell of the sea carried on the breeze, ruffling my ridiculous pink hair and, even though it wasn't warm enough to be out in only jeans and a T-shirt, it wasn't nearly as cold as it had been at home. November in Italy was a very different kettle of fish to November in Sheffield.

The buildings that lined the dock were low and white-washed, with wooden shutters, open balconies, and big terraces. A line of ubiquitous Italian scooters marked the end of the jetty and the beginning of the harbour and I saw dozens of people moving about their business. Most of the tiny shops and restaurants were closed, tourist season long over on Panarea, but there was a tangible sense of excitement brought on by the Crystal Ball. Over by the sea wall, I saw a cluster of children, all of them pushing and shoving and shouting, desperate to see who was on board the armada of yachts moored off the coast.

I saw an old man sitting on a wooden chair outside the harbour bar, stick in hand, deep lines etched into his face, and gave him a benevolent smile as our eyes met. The stories he must have, the wisdom he must keep. I wondered who he was and how long he'd lived here and what he must make of the world today.

'Why is your hair pink?' he shouted out in Italian,

throwing in an aggressive hand gesture for good measure. 'It looks stupid.'

'*Grazie mille*,' I replied gratefully, ducking my head and hurrying on. He wasn't wrong. But no number of awkward looks and sideways glances could distract me from my mission. Juliette wanted orange San Pellegrino and orange San Pellegrino she would get. It wasn't *such* an irrational request, I decided, nodding to a fisherman, who took one look at me and burst out laughing. She had drunk at least twice as much as me and I felt like utter dogshit, plus she was probably anxious about performing. Who wouldn't want their favourite can of pop under those circumstances? When I multiplied performance anxiety by hangover dread, I could see how she had ended up in a mood. Besides, I was the person hired to keep her on the straight and narrow, and I had most certainly failed at that. She hadn't asked to be dragged into my personal drama. Well, maybe she had, but it was still my fault for allowing it to happen. Personal problems did not belong in professional settings. Especially when those personal problems had been made worse by calling my fiancé and performing Elvis while twatted, from the observation deck of a yacht while dressed like an off-brand Little Mermaid.

The pale blue sky was smeared with white wisps, clouds stretched so thin across the horizon they couldn't quite hold themselves together, and I knew exactly how they felt. Between Juliette, Stew, Sarah, Lenny and my hangover, I felt as though I was being pulled in a thousand different directions. Usually, I was so good at compartmentalizing but usually, I hadn't drunk enough champagne to drown an ox. At least there was one thing I didn't have to worry about. Assuming Sarah didn't fancy calling in a search and rescue team to dredge the bottom of the Tyrrhenian Sea for me to check my voice-mail, my phone was lost for ever. Unless I met a billionaire at the ball who thought it might be a laugh. I'd seen *Titanic*, I knew what was possible if you had enough time, enough money, and very little else to do with your life.

I arrived at the *Supermercato da Pina* and was immediately struck by a pure hit of grade A, childhood-holiday nostalgia. The bright white awning, the hand-painted sign above the open stable doors, the spinning racks of postcards standing sentry on either side, it was all so painfully, joyously familiar. Buckets and spades were stacked up against the wall outside, alongside a snorkel and mask set that hung off a piece of cardboard so faded I could barely make out any of the print, and a giant fridge full of ice cream hummed happily as I went inside.

'Good morning,' I said, stumbling over my pronunciation as I twisted my furry tongue around Italian words I used to know. 'Do you have any orange San Pellegrino?'

The sour-faced teenager behind the till gave me a disapproving glance in the way only teenagers can, then pointed to the back of the shop.

'*Grazie*,' I said, my mouth watering at the sight of orange fizzy sweets hanging in long strips from a hook on the wall, as she went back to staring at her phone.

I moved through a hodgepodge of wooden shelving units that looked so old, I was afraid the entire place would collapse if I so much as sneezed on them, until I came to a line of fridges backed up against the wall. I saw Fanta, Orangina, Coke, Pepsi, Sprite, 7-Up and every possible variation on a Red Bull, but there was no orange San Pellegrino.

'It's got to be here somewhere,' I whispered to a small black cat who was curled up underneath a rickety shelving tower, crammed full of over-priced Kellogg's Corn Flakes. It opened one eye, hissed, and went back to sleep. Even the cats of Panarea weren't having a bar of me.

'Where the fuck is the fucking San Pellegrino?' I said aloud as I searched the fridges again. Pressing my fingertips into my temples, I rolled my head from side to side, front to back, trying to ease the crick in my neck as I regrouped.

And there it was.

An entire case of San Pellegrino *Aranciata* sat right there above me, on top of the tallest fridge.

'You weren't going to tell me?' I asked the cat, who sat up, glared at me, and began lazily licking its front paw. 'Typical.'

Rising up onto my tiptoes, the case was just out of reach, my fingertips brushing against the edge of the outer plastic packaging. Even when I strained as far as I could, I could only just manage to tap the underneath of the cardboard box. I stuck my head back around the shelves to ask for help, but the girl at the till had vanished.

'Ladder,' I said to the cat. 'I need a ladder.'

But there was no ladder, no step-stool, absolutely no climbing apparatus to speak of. Ever the resourceful assistant, I dragged a heavy, solid box of cat food across the floor and positioned it in front of the fridge, pressed on it lightly with my left foot to see if it would take my weight. It gave a little, my foot pressing through the cardboard and onto the cans inside, but it didn't cave in and it didn't collapse. So far, so good. Shifting my full weight onto the box, I eased the case of orange pop off the top of the fridge and into my arms. Below me, the little black cat sat and watched, waiting for something terrible to happen.

'Sorry to disappoint,' I told it, pulling the case towards me. It was heavier than I'd anticipated and not an easy thing to manoeuvre. 'But I'm not planning to break my neck today.'

With the case of San Pellegrino cradled against my chest like an extremely heavy newborn baby, I stepped backwards, lowering my foot by fractions of an inch until I felt solid ground beneath me. It wasn't much, but I'd actually accomplished something and, with a hangover like mine, I couldn't have been more pleased if I'd invented a time machine and gone back in time and stopped myself from spending fourteen English pounds on a ticket to see *Cats* at the cinema.

I nudged the box of cat food out of the way with my foot, so that no one would trip over it and smash face first into a fridge full of Diet Coke, then stuck my tongue out at the cat, who immediately began cleaning his bum. Ecstatic at the thought of returning to *The Songbird* and presenting Juliette with twelve cans of her precious pop, I turned to march back to the till, victorious.

Of course, it had all been too easy.

The very moment I let down my guard, a tall human-shaped blur came tearing around the shelves and smacked straight into me, sending me flying backwards into the fridge.

The case of San Pellegrino fell to the floor and bounced off my foot. I yelled out in surprise and then pain as several cans popped open on impact, spraying me with a sticky shower of orange fizz. With a shriek far too big for its body, the tiny black cat leaped into the air and went straight for my attacker. The man's arms windmilled at the shelves as the cat darted away and disappeared out of harm's way.

'Watch out!' I cried, alarmed as he staggered backwards, towards the decrepit wooden shelves.

But he did not watch out.

Instead, he skidded in a pool of San Pellegrino, arms still grabbing at the air, and his entire body rolled backwards into a unit that was stacked right up to the ceiling. I watched in horror as the first set of shelves hit the second set of shelves, and the second set of shelves hit the third set of shelves, all of them falling like dominoes. The man hit the floor with a loud crack as dozens of bags of crisps sailed high into the air and landed on top of him, burying him in deep-fried potato goodness.

'Are you OK?' I asked, dropping to my knees and digging through the bags of crisps, searching for a hand, a face, anything to confirm he was still with us.

'*Ungh*,' he replied in a deep voice.

'Oh, thank god, you're not dead,' I breathed out, so relieved. Death by crisp and cat was no way to go, and I didn't trust myself to explain what had happened to the police without laughing.

A large hand emerged and pushed a packet of Ruffles away from his face. Dark eyes, dark hair, and a shadow of stubble that said he hadn't bothered to shave came into view. Wincing in pain or confusion or both, his eyes met mine and, without warning, everything stopped. The shop, the cat, the chaos all around us, it all disappeared and for one moment, there was just us, the only two people in the entire universe. At exactly the same moment, we both began to smile.

139

'Hello,' I said softly.

'Hi,' he whispered back.

'*Ma dai!*'

I looked up and saw the girl from the checkout standing in the shop's doorway, a large brown box in her arms. It fell to the floor with a heavy thud as the little black cat reappeared and wound itself around her legs.

'It's OK!' I shouted in Italian, waving my arms in the air to reassure her that we were both alive. 'I think he's going to be OK.'

'I don't care if he is OK, look at this place!' the girl replied, taking in the devastation. 'I went out for two minutes to collect a delivery and you destroyed my dad's shop?'

'I didn't destroy your dad's shop!' I exclaimed as the man tried to roll onto his side, still groaning and clutching his head. 'Technically, *he* bumped into *me* then fell over the cat So, I'm not sure anyone could be considered at fault in a legal sense—'

'I'm calling the police,' the girl muttered, fumbling for a phone in her pocket. 'My dad is going to kill me. Don't move.'

'Oh, but I have to.' I gathered the non-exploded cans of San Pellegrino, still struggling to take my eyes off my assailant, who stared back at me from the floor, dazed and confused. 'I'm sorry, I really have to go.'

'You cannot go!' The girl looked around wildly before grabbing a mop from beside the door and wielding it like a staff. If it weren't dripping dirty grey water all over the floor from where she'd pulled it out of the bucket, the whole thing would have been very *Game of Thrones*. 'You do not leave.'

'Look, I can't explain, but I have to go. I have to get this to someone who really needs it,' I said, as she began twirling the mop from hand to hand, advancing on me slowly. I stood up slowly, stepping around scattered bags of pasta and smashed jars of sauce with half a dozen cans of pop in my arms.

'You pay,' she replied with eerie calm. 'You pay for all of this.'

'Can't right now,' I told her, fumbling for the money in my pocket and dumping a small stack of Euros on the counter. I scribbled my name and phone number on a small white pad next to the till, keeping the cans securely on my person. 'This is all the money I have, and this is my phone number. I swear I'll come back and work it out, but I do have to get this back to the yacht and—'

'You cannot leave!' She held up the mop, braced herself, and charged, screaming a vibrant array of Italian swear words I'd never heard before in my general direction.

Panicked, I took one last look at the man on the floor, a jolt of something running through me as our eyes met again. I couldn't explain it and I wasn't sure I wanted to, it just was. Leaving him with one small smile, I ducked underneath the girl's mop, darted out of the door, and ran down the quayside as fast as I could, wailing as I went. Past the café, through the gang of kids, and around the line of Vespas, not even pausing to breathe.

By the time I reached the jetty, my chest was heaving with a stitch, I'd rolled my ankle twice, and I was almost positive that the moment I stopped running, I was going to vomit. But all that mattered to me, a semi-functioning adult woman, was getting these bloody cans of pop on that bloody boat. I stuttered to a stop at the end of the jetty, doubling over and panting heavily. The surge of adrenaline seemed to have kicked my headache into touch so that was something as hangover cures went, I would still have preferred two cans of Coke and a sausage sandwich.

Squinting at all the boats tied up on either side of the dock, I searched for Lenny and the tender, ignoring the stares and cackles from the local fisherman, very keen to complete my getaway.

But I couldn't find him.

I hobbled up and down the jetty, checking each and every boat, my heart still thudding in my ears. I couldn't see Lenny anywhere. Shifting my gaze to the horizon, I scanned the sea for *The Songbird*, but her sleek contours and towering decks weren't anywhere to be found off the coast of Panarea.

The tender was gone.

The Songbird was gone.

And I had been left behind.

CHAPTER TWELVE

'Sarah speaking?'

'Sarah, it's Fran. I've got a bit of a problem.'

I stood on the edge of the dock, work phone pressed against my ear, an unforgiving pain shooting through my ankle and panic burning in my chest.

'I'm on Panarea, picking up some things for Juliette,' I explained, glossing over the unnecessary details. 'And Lenny was supposed to meet me with the tender to go back to the boat, but I can't seem to find him and I don't have his number in my phone.'

'Ah, yes,' she replied. 'That's because they've gone.'

My heart hit the floor, landing right next to the sad little pile of dented San Pellegrinos.

'What do you mean "they've gone"?'

'They've gone,' she repeated, speaking more clearly for effect. 'Juliette has decided she doesn't want to perform tonight, so they left.'

'I-I don't understand,' I stammered. 'What do you mean?'

'What do you mean, what do I mean?'

'I mean, *what do you mean?* How can they be gone? How can she decide she doesn't want to perform? How could they leave me here?' I craned my neck to see past all the other yachts, looking for *The Songbird*. Surely they couldn't have got that far in the time it had taken to destroy a very small local supermarket.

'Fran, do you remember when you told me you could be calm in a crisis?' Sarah asked, the angry sound of fast fingers striking a keyboard clacking down the line. 'Juliette called me half an hour ago to say she wouldn't be performing. I called the captain and told him to get her out of there, Lenny said you weren't answering your phone, so they left without you.'

'Lenny didn't even try to call me!' I wailed. Calm in a crisis, my arse. I was stuck on a Sicilian island with pink hair, no money, and no passport. My head hurt, my ankle hurt, I was hungry and thirsty, and a deranged teenager with suspiciously impressive staff-wielding skills could be coming for me at any second. This was not how I had anticipated spending my Saturday, this one or any other, ever.

'I hate to be the one to remind you of this, but you're supposed to be on the boat, taking care of Juliette,' Sarah said, her voice cool and crisp, a sharp contrast to imminent breakdown. 'This is not the time for *you* to lose your temper with *me*.'

She was right.

A sudden pang of guilt sliced right through my panic.

I was supposed to be on the boat, making sure things were running smoothly. If I hadn't been hungover, if I'd been thinking clearly, I'd have sent someone else to the island to pick up the supplies. This was entirely my fault.

'What do you want me to do?' I asked, the weight of

failure dragging me down, numbing me to any other thoughts or feelings.

'Go to the hotel and wait for my instructions,' she replied. 'There's a chance she'll decide she wants to perform after all, so you need to carry on as normal. I haven't told the organisers she isn't coming yet, so don't say anything to anyone. If she doesn't change her mind, I'll arrange to get you out, but you're likely stuck there until tomorrow.'

'Tomorrow?' I looked at the sad stack of San Pellegrino cans by my feet and strongly considered booting them into the sea.

'Tomorrow,' she repeated, almost sounding as though she might feel a little bit sorry for me. 'Trust me, Francesca, there are worse places to be stranded over-night. I'm not placing all the blame on you, I know what she's like, but I'm in a difficult position right now and I'd appreciate it if you didn't make things even more trying.'

All at once, the adrenaline wore away, leaving me an empty, hollow shell. I sank down to the ground, squatting on the wooden jetty and trying not to cry. 'How do I get to the hotel?' I asked.

'If you look up the hill, you should see a big white building, flying the Italian flag.'

'I see it,' I said, standing back up as what I hoped was seawater seeped through my jeans and soaked my backside. 'It's got sort of a dome on top.'

'That's the one. That's where you're going, they'll take care of you.'

It was a lovely thought.

'The hill is quite high,' I said, popping the tab on one of Juliette's precious cans and drinking deeply.

'That's why the hotel has such great views.'

'Sort of looks more like a small mountain than a hill.'

'And such a suntrap if you wanted to get a bit of winter sun.'

'I'm going to have to walk there, aren't I?'

'Always good to get some exercise after a couple of days at sea,' she replied. 'I'll be in touch when I have an update.'

The phone beeped twice in my ear to let me know the call was over.

I looked up at the hill and tried to imagine it was just like the hills at home – Sheffield was full of them.

'Just imagine you're on your way to Suzette's for a coffee and a morning muffin,' I told myself. 'And try not to dwell on the fact you've failed at your job and been stranded on an island without so much as a spare pair of knickers.'

With a choked sob, I turned back around and limped along the jetty, one more time.

After what felt like hours but was really only thirty minutes, the steep, rough road gave way to a long, even driveway. I had arrived at the hotel. Melting from my hike, I staggered in off the street and smiled at the two attendants who flanked the double height, dark wood doors as they exchanged a quizzical look.

'Hello,' I said, a hobbling, filthy mess, clinging to my three now-empty cans of San Pellegrino. 'I'm here for the Crystal Ball.'

Without words or questions, they ushered me inside one of the most beautiful buildings I'd ever had the privilege in which to sweat and, as the doors opened, I almost broke down and wept.

From the outside, Hotel Panarea looked like a pretty white villa, much like all the others I'd passed on my long, arduous trek up the hill, but once I was inside, everything changed. The hotel had been built into the side of the hill and it was deceptively huge, the cavernous lobby full of elegant furnishings and even more elegant people. Chandeliers hung from the ceiling, winking at me every time the front doors opened to let in the low winter light, and the white walls were accented with panels of golden silk that cast a glow over everyone like a beauty filter come to life.

And then there was me, the rumpled, damp disaster, standing in the middle of so much beauty and opulence with three empty drinks cans and looking like something several cats had worked together to drag in.

'Excuse me, *signora*. May I be of assistance?'

A silver-haired gentleman in a midnight-blue suit appeared at my side, a mild expression on his distinguished face.

'*Sì*,' I replied, pulling back my shoulders and attempting to look like I belonged right where I was. My old boss always said the richest and most successful people weren't the ones who were perfectly put together and dripping in designer labels, but I assumed they didn't often arrive at luxury hotels on foot, with scraped back pink hair, sweat stains under the arms and a damp bottom either.

'I'm checking in,' I said confidently.

He gave me a very short, very polite smile, his eyes only briefly dancing over to the squad of impeccably dressed security guards that had gathered by the entrance.

'Please follow me,' he replied before turning to cross

the lobby and place himself safely behind a white marble check-in desk.

I trotted after him and an assistant placed a silver platter with a warm hand towel in front of me, only the slightest flicker of horror crossing his face before he regained his composure and added a second towel to the tray. I took them both gratefully and dabbed at my wrists, neck and temples, resisting the urge to bury my face in the flannel and scream until I passed out.

'Could you confirm the last name on the reservation?' asked the gentleman, Paul, according to the discreet silver name tag pinned to his lapel.

'There isn't one,' I replied in Italian. He looked up at me, half a smile on his face. 'I'm checking in on behalf of Juliette. I'm her assistant.'

Paul looked up at me from underneath his eyebrows. 'And the code word on the reservation?'

The code word. The code word I couldn't remember, which was printed in the itinerary that was on my desk in my cabin on *The Songbird*.

'The code word is . . .' I began, buying an extra moment with a bright smile. 'Moist.'

The one word no one on earth would willingly say to a complete stranger in a fancy location with zero context.

'*Sì, sì*, welcome to Hotel Panarea,' he switched to Italian without comment, and something in him seemed to relax. 'I hope you didn't have any trouble finding us.'

'None at all,' I replied, patting the pink bird's nest on top of my head.

'Everything is in order here and the suite is ready. Would you like to see it now or perhaps refresh yourself at the bar until the rest of your party arrives?'

'I think the suite,' I said politely, not sure if there was enough alcohol in the world to refresh me. 'Juliette is running behind, so probably best if I get things ready for her.'

'*Molto bene*. And your luggage?'

'Coming later,' I lied smoothly.

Paul dipped his head and took a large silver key from a hook on the wall.

'Please,' he said, holding it aloft. 'Would you follow me?'

The lift doors opened with a sigh on the third floor and Paul gestured for me to exit first before taking the lead down a long, carpeted corridor.

'You must be very busy today,' I said, looking out of the windows at the beautiful view. Sarah was right, it really was stunning.

'Yes, the busiest night of the year,' he replied, tapping the heavy silver key in the palm of his hand. 'But we are preparing for tonight all year long. The hotel is always at capacity for the Crystal Ball, it is quite the event, quite the sight to see. Lots to do, always.'

'I'm sure,' I said, not knowing how else to respond. I wasn't going to the ball. I was going in the shower and then I was going to bed, with a possible pitstop at the room service menu. A raging evening, to be sure.

'Here we are, the presidential suite.' Paul took a step back and waved his hand over a small silver square mounted on the wall. 'We have a biometric lock for the room for maximum security. If you would press your index finger against the silver pad, for me?'

I did as I was told and a tiny green LED sparked into life, acknowledging my fingerprint.

'If for any reason the biometric lock does not work,'

he handed me the silver key which was just as heavy as it looked, 'you can open it the old-fashioned way.'

The door swung open on its own and we both stepped inside the room. Only it wasn't a room, it was a palace. An extravagent, decadent palace filled with beautiful things meant for beautiful people.

'Fuck me,' I exclaimed, before clapping a hand over my mouth. 'Sorry, I don't know where that came from.'

'Not at all,' he replied, cheerful at my inelegant compliment. 'This is not an uncommon response.'

The first time I saw *The Songbird*, I thought it was the most luxurious thing that could possibly exist on this earth, but the presidential suite at Hotel Panarea made the yacht look like the least pleasant toilet cubicle in a well-frequented service station.

'Allow me to show you around,' Paul offered as he strode through the entry way, and into the sitting room proper, waving his hands at concealed televisions, state-of-the-art sound systems, Bluetooth hook-ups, a fully-stocked bar, three different seating areas, and a ridiculous number of gift baskets, piled high with food, drink, beauty products, and gadgets all for Juliette. Did she really need three Apple watches? Did anyone?

'Both of the bedrooms are masters,' Paul said, still talking even though I had stopped. 'Many of our more artistic guests prefer the feng shui of the Aeolian suite, but the Tyrrhenian is, to my taste, just as lovely and with a prettier view. It just comes down to the preferred facilities. The Aeolian has the infrared Himalayan salt sauna while the Tyrrhenian suite enjoys a four-person steam shower and six-person Jacuzzi tub.'

Yet more evidence that everything made for rich people was all about shagging.

'Shall I show you the kitchen area?' he offered.

'That's very kind, but I think I'll manage on my own,' I replied. I'd been following him from room to room for twenty minutes and I'd already forgotten literally everything he'd told me. 'I should get things ready for Juliette.'

'But of course.' He gave a polite nod and started back towards the entrance hall. I was standing in a hotel suite that had an entrance hall bigger than my first flat. 'If there is anything at all you need, my entire team is at your disposal. We look forward to receiving such an esteemed guest.'

I waited until I heard the lock click behind him before I collapsed into a human puddle in the middle of the sitting-room floor. There were two beds, five settees, seven armchairs, four barstools, and sixteen dining chairs to choose from, but the floor felt right. I belonged on the floor.

For the first time in my entire life, I'd failed.

My job was to take care of Juliette, to get her from the boat to the hotel and back again. Now I was at the hotel and she was god only knew where doing god only knew what, unsupervised and all alone. I had always been a master of tucking my feelings into boxes and storing them away in the psychological equivalent of that warehouse from the end of *Indiana Jones and the Raiders of the Lost Ark*, and I could not even begin to work out how this had happened, let alone how to fix it. Filtering through my feelings, I registered shame, guilt, and embarrassment, and the fact that I'd genuinely believed Juliette wanted to be my friend added an extra spicy dash of mortification to them all.

As if my emotional pain wasn't enough, my ankle

was still extremely tender and my feet throbbed from the uphill trek in new trainers. I kicked off the shoes, then poked my left big toe into the opening of the right sock and peeled it away from my foot, holding it up and letting it hang from the end of my toe. I was that sock. Damp, sweaty, utterly redundant, and deeply undesirable. Juliette had left me behind at the first opportunity. Stew was at his ex-girlfriend's house the moment I left the country. Without my personal phone, I couldn't even call Jess to commiserate and, quite frankly, even if I had been able to talk to her, I was too ashamed to put what had happened into words. I silently thanked all known deities that my mother wasn't around to see the state of me.

I was a failure. A complete failure. I stared up at the ceiling, unwelcome tears trickling down the sides of my face.

In my back pocket, my work phone buzzed through my bum cheek. I pulled it out to see Sarah's name on the screen.

'Hello?' I said, swiping her onto loudspeaker and resting the phone on my chest.

'A helicopter will collect you from the hotel's helipad tomorrow at seven a.m.,' she announced. 'Be there.'

'There's no way to get me out of here sooner?' I asked.

'Not unless you want to find a way to find a hydrofoil to take you back to Naples, a taxi from Naples to the airport, and a last-minute ticket from Italy to Stansted without your passport or your credit cards.'

She'd lost me at Stansted.

'Have you spoken to Juliette?'

'She wasn't feeling terribly chatty.'

'She's not coming?'

'She's not coming.'

I gnawed on my thumbnail, determined not to cry on the phone.

'While I attempt to unpick this mess, I'm asking you to stay put and stay quiet,' Sarah ordered. 'Please remember you're still under an NDA and if even a hint of a whisper of this gets out—'

'It won't,' I promised. 'I swear, it all stays with me. Sarah, I'm so sorry. I shouldn't have left *The Songbird*, it's all my fault.'

'You're not the first assistant she's out-manoeuvred and you won't be the last, but I do hope your replacement lasts longer than forty-eight hours, whoever the poor soul might be.'

There it was. For the first time in my life, I had been officially fired.

To Sarah, I was just one more disappointment in a long line of failures, but to me, this was oh-so new and oh-so shit. I squeezed my eyes tightly together and two more tears appeared, racing each other to see which could reach the ground the fastest. Perhaps Stew and his mum and his sister were right. Maybe I'd make a good teacher. The fact I had zero interest in the profession and a pathological fear of children might work in my favour. At least half my teachers clearly despised kids and I'd turned out OK.

'Call me when you're back on *The Songbird*,' Sarah said. 'Until then stay in your room, stay out of trouble, and don't speak to anyone.'

She ended the call without waiting for confirmation, leaving me alone on the floor where I belonged. Reaching down and around, I peeled off my other sock, then my still wet jeans, my formerly white T-shirt, my bra and my pants, tossing them all into a pile across the room. Just like Natalie Imbruglia in Jess's favourite karaoke song, I was cold and I was shamed, lying naked on the floor.

'You need a shower,' I told myself. 'You stink.'

But for whatever reason, I just couldn't find the energy to move.

My mother always used to say 'what you don't know can't hurt you' and in that moment, I couldn't think of a more accurate statement. I knew Stew had spent Friday night with Bryony, I knew my supposed new friend had abandoned me on Panarea, and I knew I wasn't half the assistant I thought I was. All three of those things stung like a motherfucker and I would have happily given up the knowledge if that was an option.

What was it Jess had told me? Don't wait for something to happen, make it happen. Well, fat lot of good that had done me. If I hadn't called Rose, I could be merrily handing out treats to Sheffield's goodest boys and girls at the vets in Brincliffe instead of being assaulted by devious Italian shop cats. This was what happened when I opened the door and poked my head outside the room. I'd ruined everything.

'Everything is such a mess,' I whispered to the ceiling. 'I just wish there was someone to tell me what to do.'

And at precisely that moment, the doorbell rang.

CHAPTER THIRTEEN

'Just a minute!' I yelled, praying whoever it was didn't have a key to the suite. I scrambled to my feet and grabbed a blue and gold blanket off the back of the nearest settee and wrapped it around my shoulders before sprinting across the room.

'Hello?' I said, swiping errant strands of pink hair away from my sweaty face as I cracked open the door.

A pretty redhead dressed all in black smiled back at me.

'Hi, I'm Rachel. I'm here to do Juliette's makeup?'

A sudden flashback to the itinerary on my desk on *The Songbird* hit me in the chops like a damp haddock. The makeup artist. I hadn't cancelled the makeup artist.

'Oh my god, I am so sorry,' I said, adding another failure to Fran's Fabulous Fuck-Up List. 'This is my fault entirely but we're not actually going to be needing you today.'

Her pleasant expression dissolved into confusion.

'I'm sorry, what?'

'There's been a slight, last-minute change in plan,' I said, trying to explain without explaining. 'I'm her assistant, Fran, and I should have contacted you before now, but the short version is, Juliette isn't going to need makeup after all.'

No lies or NDA-breaking admissions detected.

I held my breath as the redhead silently ran through an entire gamut of emotions, expressing them exclusively with her eyebrows, before settling on righteously pissed off.

'Are you kidding me? Is she in there?' she demanded, standing on her tiptoes to peer over my shoulder and into the suite. 'This is completely out of order. I flew in from London for this, I dragged a suitcase full of makeup on a ferry. Let me speak to her.'

I held the door open to show her the empty suite. 'She's not here. I'm really sorry you've had a wasted trip, I don't know how to apologize enough. You must be really frustrated.'

Rachel switched her attention to me, narrowing her eyes to give me the once-over.

'Why are you wearing a blanket?'

'Because I'm an idiot.'

'Are you really her assistant?'

'Yes. Or at least, I was. For two days.'

'A new record.' She thrust out her hand and reset her face. 'Let's start over. I'm Rachel Summers and I'm sure this isn't your fault, sorry I lost my rag.'

'Not at all,' I replied as she trotted into the suite, pulling a suitcase almost as big as she was in behind her. 'But I should have cancelled you earlier, that part is definitely my fault.'

'I can't wait to hear this story,' she said, considering all her options before selecting a seat. 'But just so we're clear, I'm still invoicing for the day.'

'Oh, yes, absolutely, you must.' I kicked my discarded clothes underneath the settee, out of sight. 'Can I get you anything? Tea, coffee, water?' I poked at the cellophane on one of the gift baskets. 'Ashwagandha tea with ceremonial grade matcha and guarana extract?'

Rachel's eyes rested on a bottle of vintage champagne chilling in an ice bucket on the coffee table 'Here's a suggestion,' she said. 'Why don't you go and put something on that isn't a blanket, and I'll open this.'

'What if I haven't got anything that isn't a blanket?' I asked cautiously. She picked up the bottle and nodded with approval at the label.

'All the more reason to crack a bottle. Surely there's a robe?'

'Surely there's a robe,' I agreed, scuttling off into the blue bedroom and fishing around in the wardrobes until I found exactly what I was looking for, a plush white dressing gown with the name of the hotel embroidered on the chest. Nothing could be that bad when you were wearing a hotel robe, it was an unwritten law of the universe. Sliding my feet into the matching slippers I found tucked away in a corner, I returned to the living room feeling fractionally more human.

'Come on then, what's the story?' Rachel handed me a glass of champagne and then settled on the settee closest to the window. 'What's she playing at?'

'I would love to tell you but I really can't.'

'NDA?'

'NDA.'

'If it makes any difference, I signed one too, so if you felt compelled to vent, please know I am the soul of discretion,' Rachel said with a wink as I sat in the armchair across from her, keeping the champagne as far away from my nose as possible. 'Keeping people's secrets is my second most valuable skill after applying liquid liner. But I understand, you don't have to tell me anything if you don't want to.'

I set the champagne down on the table, even the smell of it was too much, and exchanged it for a miniature bottle of water.

'Even if I could, I wouldn't know where to start,' I told her. 'She isn't here and she isn't coming. That's it, basically.'

Rachel looked flat out shocked.

'Wait, you mean she's not performing at the Crystal Ball? I just assumed she'd double-booked me.'

I shook my head but didn't say a word. You only had to mention the words 'chicken nuggets' and your phone bombarded you with adverts for air fryers; who knew who was listening in to this conversation?

'And you're left to clean up her mess?'

'I think that was literally my job description,' I said, before giving her the very short version of my very long day, redacting anything that felt like it could get me into trouble, leaving out some of the Juliette parts, adding in some of the Stew.

'This is all classic Juliette,' Rachel declared as I wrapped up. 'When she is good, she is very, very good but when she is bad, she's a dickhead.' She poked around in one of the gift baskets, pulling out various snacks and sweets until she found a box of fancy-looking shortbread biscuits. 'And your fiancé sounds like a cock. Sorry. Want one?'

'Should we be opening these?' I asked doubtfully. 'I mean, they're for Juliette.'

'A box of biscuits is the least you deserve after the

time you've had,' she said, tearing open the packaging while I took a delicate sip of precious, life-giving water. 'For what it's worth, which might not be much, I don't think this is your fault. You were doing your job, she's the one who has chosen not to do hers.'

'Well, when you look at it like that . . .' I said, wishing I could. 'Do you want me to see if I can get you booked on an earlier ferry out? Prove to myself I'm not completely useless?'

Rachel shook her head and chomped a shortbread finger. 'It's only a couple of hours, hardly worth it. I'm happy to hang out here until it's time to leave if you don't mind? I won't get in the way of, well, whatever you were doing in that blanket.'

'Not at all,' I said, surprisingly happy at the thought of company. 'Although at some point, I am going to have to have a shower.'

'I didn't like to say, but yes, I think that would be a really good idea.'

This time, when Rachel smiled, it was an open, infectious grin that seemed to come with no strings attached. She rested one arm along the back of the settee and pulled her legs up to stretch out, and I could almost imagine myself beginning to relax.

'The good news is, if I'm not doing Juliette, I'll have much more time to work on you,' she said, considering me with a more critical eye. 'Not that you need extra time, only Juliette always takes for ever, and everyone else ends up going out with the most basic look imaginable. Now we really have time to play.'

'Me?' I hacked out a laugh, spluttering through a mouthful of water all over my robe. 'Oh no, I'm not going to the ball.'

'But, Cinders,' she gasped, clutching at her imaginary pearls, 'you must!'

'No way,' I replied. 'I have a thrilling evening planned with the giant Jacuzzi in the bathroom and the rest of the Mars Bar in my handbag, then an early night in the world's biggest bed.'

'Under ordinary circumstances I would say bed, bath and Mars Bars is my dream threesome,' Rachel acknowledged. 'But this is the *Crystal Ball*. You can't not go to the Crystal Ball. Are you really going to sit up here and sulk about what some man might have already done when you could be having the time of your life instead?'

'Yes,' I replied. 'Absolutely.'

But Rachel wasn't taking no for an answer.

'You're going,' she declared. 'That's all there is to it. You'd have to be out of your mind to pass this up.'

'What if you're not necessarily out of your mind but not invited and under strict instructions to stay hidden in your hotel room?'

She looked back at me with a wicked smile.

'All the more reason to go.'

Rachel put down her glass and shuffled around the coffee table on her hands and knees until she was kneeling in front of me with a very serious look on her face.

'Fran, I know we just met but I'm afraid I'm going to have to stage an intervention,' she said, looking up at me with big, beseeching eyes. 'I've been a makeup artist for fifteen years and I have worked for all kinds of people, all over the world, and in all that time, I have never heard anyone talk about anything the way they talk about the Crystal Ball. You *have* to go.'

'But it's just a party,' I said, a tiny tingle of curiosity blooming underneath my sadness. 'Isn't it?

Rachel scoffed loudly. 'If Jay Gatsby and Taylor Swift got together with Anna Wintour and Elton John, *maybe* they could dream up something a fraction of what the Crystal Ball is supposed to be. Are you following me?'

'So, you think it might be a good time?' I asked.

She punctuated each of her words with a clap.

'It. Is. Going. To. Be. Incredible.'

I wrinkled my nose doubtfully. 'Well, you're here. Why don't you go?'

'Because I have to go home to my wonderful bloody husband and magical, ungrateful children who I love very much,' she muttered, before slumping onto her bum and pouring herself another glass of champagne. 'Trust me, I'd much rather be hanging out with the A-list than sleeping in bed with my five-year-old because my husband will definitely let him watch *The Rise of Skywalker* again while I'm out, even though it gives him nightmares every time.'

'Why does he want to watch it if it gives him night-mares?' I asked, confused.

'I see you don't have children or a husband,' she replied, downing half her drink. 'That's not the point. The point is, you've got to go. Do you want to wake up one day, years from now when you're a wizened old crone and think "Hmm, wonder what would have happened if I'd gone to the world's most exciting party instead of sitting on my arse and being sad in a hotel room"? And don't say "Ooh, I'm not supposed to", because you weren't supposed to be sitting here on your own wearing a blanket when I arrived, were you?'

She made a series of strong and fair points.

'It does look cool.' I glanced out of the window just in time to see a big wheel being erected on the lawn

161

below. In fact, there was a whole fairground down there, complete with something that looked suspiciously like the actual It's a Small World ride from Disneyland. 'But how would I even get in?'

'You would leave that to me,' she replied. 'Come on, woman. There are no cameras, no press, phones are forbidden. How would anyone ever know you were there? It's not like you're going to bump into someone you know, is it?'

That much was true. You don't see Chrissy Teigen at the Aldi in Highfield that often.

'And what's Juliette going to do? Sack you twice?'

I stared out of the window again, watching as all the people below set up the spectacular. It would be so me to sit up in my room while the world's shiniest people had the time of their lives downstairs because I was doing as I was told. All the fear and the shame and the sadness tied itself into a tight knot in my stomach. Where had doing as I was told got me in life? I was alone, lonely, and unemployed. Stew, Juliette, Sarah and all the rest of my messes would still be there in the morning, whether I spent the evening up here on my own or at a ridiculous party where I might get to use the toilet at the same time as Beyoncé.

The last few days had already given me so much to regret. Surely it was better to regret crashing to the ball than not going at all?

'OK,' I said, turning back to Rachel with a dizzy smile on my face. 'I'm in.'

'Yes, you are!' She clambered up from the floor and gave me a very quick hug. 'Now, let's find you something to wear. The stylist sent me pictures of all the gowns she'd pulled so I could match the makeup. Do you know where they are?'

'I haven't seen them, but they're definitely here some-where.' I jumped out of my seat with an unexpected burst of energy, leading her across the suite to the first bedroom. 'We had them sent ahead, they arrived yesterday.'

Rachel paused dramatically in front of a closed door.

'What do you think is behind door number one?' she asked.

I tried to suppress a smile as she flung open the door.

'An infrared Himalayan salt sauna?'

'Well, that's cheating because you clearly already knew that,' she grumbled, tapping her fingers against the wooden frame of the sauna. 'What's in the other one?'

She pointed to a mirrored wall, just like the one in Juliette's cabin. I gave it a gentle push and sure enough, it sprang out to reveal a dressing room, and inside the dressing room were three long racks full of dresses.

'Jackpot,' I breathed, following her inside as soft golden lights beamed into life.

'Look at these.' Rachel held up a floor-length column of neon-pink chainmail. 'Have you ever seen anything so wonderful?'

A cascade of yellow chiffon ruffles called out to me from the middle of the rack and I felt another wobble of excitement.

'How is this even a dress?' I asked, taking it off the rack with the utmost care and holding it up to the light. 'It weighs next to nothing.'

Using both arms, Rachel pulled a long, teal dress, covered from top to bottom in beading and feathers, from the rack.

'All designer stuff is the same,' she answered, straining with the effort of holding it off the floor. The dress was twice as tall as she was. 'Everything either weighs a whisper or a metric ton. There is no in-between.' She held the dress in front of her and checked it out in the huge tri-fold mirror that stood in the corner of the dressing room. 'God, I'm going to have to try this on, aren't I?'

'I think you are,' I confirmed. 'I'm going to try the yellow.'

'Nope,' Rachel countered, turning back to the rack of dresses. She considered each one with a Terminator-like level of determination on her face before yanking something out from the middle of the rack. 'This is the one for you.'

In her hands was a floor-length, powder-blue gown that nipped in at the waist before billowing out into layers and layers of tulle. Tiny little crystals were stitched into the fabric, glinting like the first stars in a twilight sky, and the bodice was all wrapped up with sparkling silver ribbons that came together in a bow at one shoulder before cascading down the back of the gown and trailing all the way down to the floor.

'You don't think it's too much?' I asked, mesmerized by the way the crystals sparkled under the ceiling lights.

'Fran, this might be the only occasion in your entire life where the words "too much" do not exist,' she replied, thrusting it into my arms. 'Or do you have another event coming up in your social calendar where you might wear twenty grand's worth of couture ball-gown?'

'Nothing in the diary at the moment.'

'Then let's see if it fits.'

164

'I'll go in the other room,' I offered as she began peeling off her clothes, jeans already unfastened.

'Now I *know* you don't have kids,' she cackled from inside her T-shirt. 'After two of them, no part of me is sacred, but I used to be like you, I totally get it.'

With a deep breath, I turned my back and shrugged off the hotel robe. Today was the day for me to put on my big girl pants, although only metaphorically speaking given that I didn't have any pants on at all.

'What do you think?'

I cranked my head as far as it would go over my shoulder to see Rachel beaming at me, drowning in a sea of greenish-blue beading. The deep V-neck slashed almost past her belly button and the heavily embellished fabric pooled around her feet. It was definitely a dress made for someone less blessed in the chest department than Rachel. And someone taller. And someone with more money than sense.

'That is a very nice dress,' I said, even though it was not.

She turned to frown at herself in the mirror. 'It looks like I borrowed my mum's favourite kaftan then got into a fist fight with a parrot,' she replied. 'I suppose not even Gucci gets it right every time. Let's see yours.'

I took the dress off its hanger and stepped into the bodice, careful not to tread on the tulle as I pulled it up over my arse. Rachel fastened the single shoulder strap and I looked up at my reflection in the mirror. My mouth fell open. When Jess went shopping, she was always searching for the outfit that would most clearly communicate who she was and who she wanted to be, the pair of shoes that told the world who she knew she was, deep inside. I, on the other hand, considered my clothes camouflage. Simple, neutral, don't look at me. This was something else entirely. I hadn't just put on a different dress, I'd stepped into a different life. Gone was the girl who wore beige bras and sensible cardigans, and in her place was a glamorous, confident, beautiful woman. She was the kind of person who didn't worry about things like how far she might end up walking before deciding which shoes to wear. The woman who wore this dress never ran all the way back home from the bus stop to make sure she'd turned the central heating off because the bill wasn't going to pay itself. A legion of friends hung on her every word, her boyfriends adored her, and it was someone else's job to make sure there was toilet paper in the bathroom before she sat down to pee.

'Look at you,' Rachel grinned. 'This is it, this is your dress.'

It fit, just. Juliette and I were close in size, if not in shape. The bodice was a touch on the snug side, but if we didn't tie the shoulder strap too tightly and I didn't bother with breathing, I was fairly sure I could get away with it.

'I don't think I dare move,' I said, resting my hands lightly on either side of my waist. 'I'm scared it'll rip.'

'It's stronger than it looks,' Rachel replied wisely. 'And it's perfect. You and this dress were meant to be.' She pulled my hair away from my face, lifting it up and back, sharpening my cheekbones.

I laughed, a short hysterical giggle I couldn't control, as I pulled away, my hair falling back down around my shoulders.

'I don't believe in all that,' I told her. 'Nothing's meant to be.'

'Call it what you want,' she said with a shrug. 'But something special is happening between you and that frock.'

I looked back at my reflection and straightened my shoulders as I met my own eyes. The dress deserved better than slouching. Rachel clapped her hands twice and started to unhook the fastening at my shoulder, my heart swooping low as it fell away from my body.

'No need for a face like that,' she said. 'It's time for you to take a shower and then you can put it back on.'

'Are you sure this is a good idea?' I asked as I stepped out of the dress and transformed back into regular old Fran, trying to look casual as she stood naked in front of the stranger. 'Sneaking into the ball, borrowing a designer dress? What if I get caught? Or worse, what if I spill something on it?'

'And what if you don't?' Rachel countered. 'What if you have an incredible time? What if you spend the entire evening laughing and dancing and smoking a joint in the toilets with Rihanna?'

'Do you think she'll be offended if I turn it down? Only, the one time I tried to smoke with Stew, I got obsessed with the idea of making a cheesecake and ended up putting Dairylea on Hobnobs. High or not, it was not a successful experiment.'

'I would still probably eat it,' she replied, hanging the dress back on the rack. 'Now, get in the shower, I'm going to order us something delicious from room service, and then we'll get started on your makeup before we run out of time.'

Pulling on my robe, I was overcome with a sudden rush of gratitude as she shuffled out of her hideous Gucci gown.

'You've been so kind,' I said, slipping the hotel robe over my arms. 'I don't really know how to thank you.'

'You don't have to,' she replied as she hopped up and down to squeeze into her jeans. 'A stranger did something very similar for me once upon a time and I realized there are moments in our lives where we all need someone to remind us we're allowed to be happy.'

I bit my lip and nodded, tears pricking the backs of my eyes even though I wasn't sure why.

'But seriously, get in the shower, I can smell you from here,' Rachel said, wrinkling her nose. 'We haven't got all night and the Crystal Ball isn't going to wait for you, you know.'

'I'll be as quick as I can,' I promised. 'When you call room service, can you order me a big Coke? A regular one, not a diet?'

'One full fat Coke, coming right up,' she replied, waving an invisible magic wand. "Your wish is my command.'

CHAPTER FOURTEEN

'I am a very good makeup artist,' Rachel declared, mascara wand in one hand, a tissue in the other. She took a step back and gestured for me to look in the mirror. 'You like?'

But she wasn't a makeup artist, she was a miracle worker. My skin glowed, my eyes shone, and my lips were full and plump. I looked like someone who got eight hours of sleep every night, an hour of exercise every day, and always drank enough water, rather than an habitual insomniac who wheezed walking up the hill and couldn't start her morning without three cups of tea at home and the promise of a giant coffee on the way to work.

'I've kept it simple,' she said, dropping bits and pieces into a clear plastic sandwich bag while I continued to stare at myself. Even my hair looked good. I'd twisted it up into a messy braided knot at the back of my head, with just the tiniest hint of pink left after my extremely thorough shower. 'Good skin, tiny bit of highlight, big eyes, nude lips. You don't want to be worrying about touch-ups all night.'

'Can you come home with me?' I asked. 'I can't believe I actually look this good.'

I stood up in my dress and marvelled at the full effect. Thanks to some incredibly clever engineering, you couldn't even tell I'd just put away an entire pizza and half a plate of chips. However much this dress cost, it was worth every penny.

'Believe it.' Rachel held up the sandwich bag for my inspection. 'This has everything you need for touch-ups. You've got lipstick, pressed powder, blotting papers, a couple of tissues plus a tampon and a Sharpie.'

Tearing my eyes away from the mirror, I took the bag and turned it over in my hands. 'Well, thank you, but I don't need the tampon and I am confused about the Sharpie.'

'*Someone* will need the tampon and you'll be there to save the day,' she replied. 'And a Sharpie is always a good idea. What if Taylor Swift wants your autograph? Now, where's your bag?'

'Oh, shit.' I gritted my teeth and sucked in the air. 'I don't have one.'

'Nothing handbag-like in those gift baskets?' Rachel suggested, looking around the dressing room for a viable alternative.

I shook my head. 'Not unless you count the actual baskets themselves and that might be a touch too Red Riding Hood for what we want.'

'I could draw a Louis Vuitton logo on the sandwich bag and you can tell people it's a repurposed LV by some wanky avant-garde designer they haven't heard of?'

'Let me check the gift baskets again,' I said, gathering my skirts and sprinting into the lounge. But before I made it all the way over to the dining table, I spotted something even better.

'Look!' I said, dashing back with a small silver cushion in my hand. 'It's perfect!'

'It's a cushion,' Rachel replied flatly, her expression only changing when I ran my fingernail around the seam, looking for the concealed zip. I removed the pillow pad, slid the sandwich back inside, and held my creation aloft.

'That's actually very good,' she admitted. 'If only we could have found a pair of shoes that fit.'

'I don't know,' I lifted up my skirts to reveal my freshly cleaned white trainers. 'These are more comfortable than heels. And thanks again for the spare pair of knickers.'

'I never leave home without them.' She stepped back, took one last admiring look at her work, and planted her hands on her hips. 'Francesca Cooper, are you ready to go to the ball?'

'Not in the slightest,' I replied, taking as deep a breath in as was possible, considering the dress's internal corsetry. 'But fuck it, why not?'

'You're going to have the most incredible time,' Rachel said, placing her hands on my shoulders and gently but firmly turning me around until I was facing the door. 'Eat everything, drink everything and remember it's ten extra points if you accidentally trip Mark Zuckerberg.'

'I *am* still quite mad about the "on this day" feature,' I replied as I started for the door. 'Wait, you still haven't told me how I'm supposed to get into the ball without an invitation. I'm assuming there's some sort of check on the door?'

'Oh, it's worse than that,' Rachel replied gaily, packing

away the last of her makeup brushes and zipping up her suitcase. 'There's a facial recognition thing at the entrance that does a biometrics scan, you know, where they scan your iris? So, you can come in and out.'

'Right,' I said, feeling a bit weak. 'That could be a bit of a problem.'

She rolled her eyes as we walked out of the dressing room, across the living room, and down the entrance hall together.

'I hate to be the one to point this out but you're a beautiful white woman wearing a stunning designer dress, and once you're inside the room, no one is going to bat an eyelid at you,' she said, one hand on the door handle. 'I mean, looking the way you do right now, you could probably rob an orphanage and get away with it. We're only trying to get you into a party. All I have to do is get you past the scanner and then you're away.'

'What will I tell people if they ask me who I am?'

'Lie,' she replied. 'Make up whatever you want. Who's going to fact check you? You could be absolutely anyone.'

I paused and gripped my cushion cover bag tightly. I could be absolutely anyone.

'OK,' I said, standing in the doorway in a 'borrowed' couture gown and someone else's knickers. 'I'm ready.'

The grand entrance to the Crystal Ball was in the lobby of the hotel, but when we stepped into the lift and the doors slid shut, Rachel pressed the button for the basement.

'I haven't worked the ball before,' she explained. 'But I did do makeup for someone who went to a wedding here. The actual ballroom is one level down, all the guests have to walk down this *über* dramatic staircase, but if we can find an entrance in the basement, we should be able to sneak you past the security checks.'

'I was literally just thinking I'd make a good spy,' I muttered, trying not to sweat on my dress. 'I was wrong. You're the junior James Bond here.'

'Definitely see myself as more of a Killing Eve-type,' she replied as the lift pinged and the doors opened. 'Stay back here and don't make a sound.'

Rachel skulked away with her suitcase, leaving me conspicuously alone. Shockingly enough, it was dark in the basement. The walls had been lined with heavy fabric that deadened the music on the other side and kept everything just this side of pitch black.

'I hope they let me get changed before they take us to prison,' I whispered. 'At least my makeup will look good in the mugshots.'

'Can I help you?' An American accent stopped me short and I froze in the dark, wrapping myself up in the black fabric.

'Yes, hi, I'm looking for someone and I think I got turned around,' I heard Rachel say. Holding my breath, I leaned as far forward as I dared and peeked around the corner to see her talking to a sturdy-looking man in a black suit and black tie. He held a tiny torch, which he was shining directly in her eyes and, as he pressed his finger against a black earpiece, his jacket rode up to reveal something shiny and gun-shaped strapped to his waist.

Oh good, I thought, realizing the gun-shaped thing was probably a gun. We're not going to prison, we're going to die.

'You can't be down here, it's guests and hotel staff

only,' the man said to a still-smiling Rachel. 'And I don't think you're either.'

'Got me there,' she laughed, her accent taking on a cut-glass edge. 'No, I'm a makeup artist, my client is a guest. She's inside already, but she forgot something and I need to get it to her. Would it be possible for me to slip in for just a moment?'

'No,' he replied. 'It would not.'

'Fine, I absolutely get it.' Rachel pulled a tampon out of the back pocket of her jeans, holding it out like a baton in a relay race. 'Do you think you could give it to her?'

The big, burly, armed security guard turned white as a sheet. The man was literally carrying a gun, but he was too scared to take hold of a tampon.

'Totally understand that I can't go in, so if I can give it to you to give to her, I know she'll be very grateful. Honestly, it'll be a disaster if she doesn't get it, she has terrible periods, so heavy, it's like someone turned on a tap. I tried to get her to switch to a menstrual cup, but she wouldn't have it, and I said to her, I said, Rebecca, they're so much better, much less mess. They *catch* the blood rather than soak it up and—'

'Enough, enough,' he said, holding out his hands, and I began to panic that if she didn't stop talking, he might find a way to make her. 'Her name is Rebecca? Rebecca what?'

'Rebecca de Winter,' Rachel replied with complete confidence. 'She's wearing a red dress, very pretty, dark hair. I'm sure you'll spot her right away.'

'I'll find her and bring her out to you. Wait there,' he ordered, looking over his shoulder before slipping through the black curtain and disappearing from sight.

'Fran!' Rachel hissed. 'Now!'

'Rebecca de Winter?' I asked, sidling around the corner, my heart thudding in my ears. 'Really?'

'I was watching the Netflix version on the plane on the way over,' she muttered. 'There's two hours of my life I'll never get back. It was the first thing that came to mind.'

'Thank god he's not a reader.'

'I had an inkling.' She straightened the bow on my shoulder and took a step back to check me over. 'Right, shoulders back, put a smile on your face, and look like you belong there, because you do.'

'What if I get caught?' I said, beginning to panic. 'What if that security guard comes back, shoots us both, and throws our bodies in the sea?'

Rachel gave me a delicate hug so as not to disturb my dress, then grabbed the handle of her suitcase. 'You're completely insane and I love that about you, but I also need to head back to the harbour for my ferry, and you ought to get in there before the clock strikes midnight,' she said.

'What happens at midnight?' I asked, suddenly very sad that she was leaving. 'Will I turn into a pumpkin?'

'I heard that's when Beyoncé is going to perform,' she whispered with bright eyes. 'Go on, go, before he comes back!'

With a deep breath and an uncertain nod, I pulled back the black curtain and stepped through to the other side.

The dimly lit space beyond the curtain was full of bizarre items, seemingly placed specifically to send me sprawling to my death. I held my hands out in front of me as my eyes adjusted to this new lack of light, stumbling against giant cages fit for pterodactyls, a martini glass big enough to keep a dolphin like a goldfish, and a spectacular pile of disco balls that were almost twice as tall as me. Across the room, the fabric wavered and a narrow sliver of light drew me forward, graciously highlighting each new obstacle as it came my way. Sidling around a life-size glass horse, I slipped my hand through the curtain and pulled it back, blinking as the darkness gave way to the light.

Just like that, I was in the Crystal Ball.

The walls glittered and shimmered with seamless iridescent panels and when I looked up, I saw that even the ceiling was draped in silver silk. Hidden lights were designed to make the room glow, giving all the guests the soft-focus sheen of an Instagram filter as they wandered around the ballroom greeting each other with cries of delight. The staircase Rachel had mentioned, also crystallized, dominated the far side of the room, and I watched in awe as couples descended, all the men wearing sharp tuxedos and the women wrapped up in such fabulous confections that even my extravagant gown seemed almost casual.

Out of the corner of my eye, I spotted the black suit, black tie security guard from the corridor wandering around, looking for a dark-haired woman in a red dress and I immediately turned in the opposite direction, walking away as quickly but as calmly as I could.

So this was it, the Crystal Ball, the world's most exciting party. I shuffled away from the curtain and attempted to blend into the crowd. This was the most sought-after invitation, the most exclusive gathering on the planet.

But what was I supposed to do now I was inside?

I'd attended a lot of mixers, a lot of industry dos in my old London job, and they were always awkward at best, especially if you were on your own. That's why people get so impossibly shitfaced at work parties and weddings; it just isn't natural to enjoy yourself in front of so many people you don't know. Dancing is intrinsically embarrassing for ninety-nine percent of humans and yet for some reason, we think it's a good idea for people to sit in a convention centre for eight hours, listening to the latest developments from the world of concrete manufacturing, then expect them to get out on the dance floor and bust some moves to a dodgy cover band, blasting out their best interpretation of 'Come on Eileen'. This didn't feel that much different to me, although admittedly, the attendees of the Crystal Ball were dressed very differently to the attendees of ConcreteCon 2018, and Hotel Panarea was a far cry from the Heathrow Radisson.

While most of the male attendees had opted for traditional black tuxes, and the women by and large played it safe with classic gowns, those who had chosen to be more creative with the dress code had truly gone for it. There were sequins and feathers and bustles and bodices to spare, in fact, I'd never seen such a vast array of bold fashion choices, and I'd been on a Friday night out in Newcastle more than once. I watched as one person strolled across the crystallized floor wearing what looked like a light-up igloo for a skirt with three minions scurrying along behind to make sure no harm came to the wearer or, more likely, the dress.

In the far corner, on an elevated platform that looked to have been carved out of ice, a string quartet played a Britney cover, and right in the centre of the room was a huge circular stage, currently hidden from view and draped with curtains made up of strings and strings of crystal beads. The stage where Juliette was supposed to perform. The air smelled like a mixture of Christmas trees and the nicest candle I had never owned, and I realized as I wandered aimlessly through the growing crowds of guests, I was smiling.

'Isn't it marvellous?'

I turned to see a beautiful older woman with jet-black hair fashioned into old Hollywood curls standing beside me. Her deep wine-coloured velvet gown looked so soft, I had to stop myself from reaching out to stroke it.

'It really is,' I replied with a polite smile, a flutter of nerves in my stomach.

'They've really outdone themselves this year,' she nodded towards a twenty-foot bar at the far end of the room, carved out of a solid block of ice. 'I think this might be David's best work yet.'

'Oh, yeah, David's killing it,' I agreed with absolutely no idea who David might be. 'I love your dress, it's very original.'

Another trick I learned from attending one too many conferences. When in doubt, compliment people.

'Oh, thank you,' she gushed as she gathered a handful of the heavy red fabric. It was tightly bound around her chest with strips of black leather before falling, tent-like, all the way to the floor where it gathered in an enormous pool. It looked as though she'd taken my nan's living room curtains, cut a slit in the top for her head, then fastened it to her top half with electrical tape and hoped for the best with the bottom. 'Stephen says it's not really a gown but a deconstructed concept of a gown. Perhaps

178

you saw it at the shows in Paris in the spring? It was originally a pale pink, but I called him and said, Stephen, I *must* have it for the Crystal Ball but you *must* change the colour. Can you imagine me? In pink? I don't know what he was thinking.'

'Classic Stephen,' I replied with an eye-roll, and the woman rewarded me with a wink.

'Forgive me,' she said, giving me a look that assured me she'd be frowning if she were physically able. 'I'm terrible with names. Have we met before?'

'I don't think so.' To my credit, my voice was only slightly squeaky. 'This is my first time at the ball.'

'How exciting! Who are you here with?'

'It's just me.' I fanned myself with my cushion cover clutch. 'I'm here on my own.'

'Excuse me, ladies.'

It was the security guard. With an audible gulp, I looked around for the quickest route of escape, but there wasn't one.

'Would either of you happen to be a Ms de Winter?'

Fuck. Fuck fuck fuckity fuck.

'Genevieve Orensen,' the woman replied, holding out her hand as the security guard looked at me, clearly unsure as to whether he was supposed to shake it, kiss it, or pull her into tango. 'And this is . . .'

'I'm—' Both of them looked at me expectantly as I realized giving my real name was a terrible idea. 'Francesca. Anne.' Why was I such a crappy liar when it actually mattered? Francesca Anne was my literal name. 'Francesca Anderson,' I finished finally. 'I'm Francesca Anderson.'

It was good enough.

'Have either of you seen Ms de Winter?' the guard

asked, not giving a fig about my clearly nonsense pseud-
onym.

'The name isn't familiar,' Genevieve replied. 'And I
know everyone. Except you, Francesca dear.'

'Oh, Genevieve,' I said, laughing too loudly. 'You're
always such a card.'

'Please enjoy your evening,' the guard said with a
small bow and a frustrated huff. Genevieve looked at
me, more than a little confused.

'Well, I must be off,' I said. 'Lovely to meet you—'

But before I could escape, a short, slender man with
altogether too much hair and a black silk fedora perched
precariously on top of it took the guard's place, scooping
up my companion's hand for a mealy-mouthed kiss.

'Genevieve, there you are, what an exceptional gown,'
he cooed. 'Stephen?'

Underneath her dense makeup, Genevieve's cheeks
turned pink. 'Andrew, you recognize it from Paris,' she
gushed. 'Have you met Francesca?'

'Not yet,' he said, turning his greedy eyes on to me.
I balked as he picked up my hand and pressed his dry
lips against it, forcing myself to smile in the name of
politeness. 'Andrew Jergens.'

'Francesca Anderson,' I said, withdrawing my hand
and subtly wiping it against the back of my skirt. 'Nice
to meet you.'

'Anderson, Anderson, Anderson.' He said my name
over and over while he stared up into my face. 'Are
you the one who just married Voss Anderson?'

'God, no,' I replied without thinking. 'Is that even a
real name?'

Andrew and Genevieve both burst out laughing.

'He won't like that one bit,' he replied before pulling an

obnoxiously large vape pen out of his pocket and taking a heavy drag. 'So tell us, Francesca Anderson, how did you come to be here this evening? I thought I knew every name on the guest list. You know I helped Carden put it together? We've tried to change things up a bit this year.'

'As long as you didn't invite any undesirables,' Genevieve replied, casting a filthy look around the room. 'I'm all for freshening the mix, but I do hope that's possible without lowering the tone. The polo was a hideous mess this year.'

'No lowering the tone here; if anything, we're raising it,' Andrew assured her. 'I have it on good authority a certain princess will be attending.'

'Meghan?' I asked excitedly.

'Um, no,' he replied shiftily.

'Kate?'

He shook his head and the fedora wobbled.

'Eugenie?' I guessed with fading enthusiasm. 'Beatrice?'

'Not British royalty,' Andrew said, clearing his throat. 'She's from somewhere in Eastern Europe, one of those countries that doesn't exist any more, and I haven't actually met her, but still, adds a certain something to have an HRH, don't you think?'

'Absolutely,' Genevieve agreed. 'My mother was very pally with the Queen Mother's chief lady-in-waiting's next-door neighbour and they really are just another class. But I'll tell you the same thing I told Artemis at the polo, I shan't rush back if they're going to insist on inviting all those Click-Clock children, shoving their phones in everyone's faces. It's bloody rude.'

'You don't have to worry about that here,' Andrew assured her with a condescending pat on the shoulder. 'You know all phones are banned inside the ballroom.'

On cue, they both burst out laughing at a joke I had somehow missed.

'Have you heard any rumours about who might be performing?' he asked. 'I asked Carden, but he wouldn't spill.'

'No idea. I've heard everyone from Madonna to me,' Genevieve said, gesturing for us all to lean in and share a secret, even though she didn't bother to lower her extremely loud voice. 'But you know Juliette is no longer on the bill.'

'Oh really?' I asked with what I hoped was an appropriate amount of surprise. 'Do you know why?'

'Apparently, she walked in, told them she wanted a million dollars to play, and when they refused, she walked right back out,' she replied, eyes as wide as saucers.

'Not what I heard,' Andrew said. 'My source told me she's in rehab. They were hoping to keep the whole thing quiet, but she relapsed last week and the facility won't let her out.'

'Oh, that's terrible.' The older woman arched her eyebrow. 'But I can't say I'm exactly surprised.'

He nodded, spurred on by the colour in Genevieve's cheeks. 'She checked herself in at a clinic in Arizona thinking it would be a jolly, but by all accounts, the doctors think she's completely mad and won't let her leave.'

'I don't think that's true,' I said, suddenly feeling even grubbier than I had when I arrived at the hotel. Juliette wasn't exactly top of my Christmas card list, but I couldn't just stand there and listen while complete strangers spread lies about her.

'My source is very close to Juliette's camp,' Andrew

replied, disinterested. He took a swig from his glass and looked away. 'I have it on very good authority.'

'Regardless of the excuse, I think it's for the best. I've heard she's terrible,' Genevieve said, clearly very keen to slag off Juliette. 'Rude, unreliable, and you know she can't sing live any more. Completely destroyed her voice with drugs. Has to mime all the time, can barely speak.'

Andrew nodded and raised his glass to hers. 'That's meth for you. I heard she's bald. Always wears a wig, never seen in public without one.'

I coughed, champagne spluttering up into my nose and burning my eyes.

'Simply put, she's a terror,' he concluded. 'And my cousin told me she only got her first record deal because she was very comfortable on her knees, if you know what I mean.'

That was it, I'd heard enough. I had as much right as anyone else in the room to be angry at Juliette but that was the final straw.

'And how exactly would your cousin know?' I interrupted. 'Does he *own* the record label?'

'No,' he replied coolly. 'But his cousin's husband works in the label's legal department and—'

'This is ridiculous,' I said, abandoning my still-full glass on a passing tray. 'Even if half your theories were anywhere near true, she'd be dead in a ditch. Why would anyone book a bald junkie to play the Crystal Ball if they can't even sing?'

Andrew raised the vape pen to his lips and sucked so hard I thought-slash-hoped he would choke on it.

'Francesca Anderson,' he said, looking me over from head to toe. 'I really don't recall your name from the guest list.'

183

'Well, I'm going to leave you to enjoy your evening,' I said, changing my tone and smiling broadly at their suspicious faces. 'It's been lovely to chat, have a great ball.'

But it hadn't been lovely, it had been stressful and confusing and unpleasant. Why were people so happy to believe such terrible things about each other? How was their evening improved by talking such incredible shit about someone else? They were already at the most exclusive event, wearing the most extravagant clothes, drinking the most expensive champagne, but they still felt the need to stick the boot in someone who wasn't even here.

I marched across the ballroom, following a steady stream of people towards an open door with the sole intention of getting as far away from Andrew and Genevieve as possible. On the other side of the door was a terrace, almost as long as the ballroom itself, dotted with sofas and armchairs and other assorted items of furniture that didn't really look as though they belonged outside. But as I'd learned on *The Songbird*, 'outside' wasn't really a concept rich people had to worry about.

Blowing a stray bit of hair away from my face, I wandered over to the edge of the terrace and rested against the marble balustrades. Through the darkness, I could see all the yachts moored offshore, their little lights blinking to remind me the real world still existed. Or at least something real-world adjacent.

Everyone was right, the Crystal Ball was an experience, but I had experienced enough. If even half the people in attendance were like Andrew and Genevieve, I didn't need to stay one minute longer. I would take a quick turn around the room, secure some snacks, then leg it back to my room for a swim around the six-person Jacuzzi. Jess would be deeply disappointed in me but that was on Jess. I was beginning to think there was a slim chance I didn't need to live every moment of my life to satisfy other people.

I turned my back on the bay, looking back towards the hotel and the crowds of people swarming out of the ballroom for a quiet moment or, more likely, a cheeky cig. None of their happy, shining faces were familiar except for one. But it wasn't an actor or a singer or the daughter of a disgraced former president of the United States.

It was him, the man from the supermarket.

And for a single moment, everything stopped.

CHAPTER FIFTEEN

A warm, sweet shock pinned me in place as my lips curved into a smile.

'Hello,' I said.

'Hi,' he replied.

And then I completely forgot how to make any other words. That split second when they transform from a stranger into someone. Wasn't that how Juliette had put it?

Even though the terrace was lined with heat lamps, a crisp, cool breeze still came in off the water and as it blew past me to ruffle his hair, it smelled sweet, like sea salt and secrets.

'You're here,' he said.

'And you didn't die,' I replied, truly a master of flirtatious banter.

'Nothing but a bruised behind and a dented ego.' There was happy confusion all over his face and my ears prickled at an American accent I hadn't noticed before.

'Was everything all right in the shop? The girl was

so angry,' I said, still marvelling at the perfection of his face. 'I felt horrible for leaving, but I had an emergency I had to take care of.'

'I remember, some kind of soda emergency, right?' he replied. 'Don't worry about the girl, I took care of her.'

I gasped and lowered my voice. 'You killed her?'

'No!' He laughed loudly enough for several strangers to turn around to see what they were missing. 'I meant I paid for the damages.'

He was taller than me, but not so tall that it would be the first thing you'd tell people about him, not when you could wax lyrical about his eyes for months on end. They were dark brown, sloping downwards at the corners ever so slightly, and when he smiled, his entire face came alive. He was smiling now, a wide, curving grin so gorgeous, it deserved its own fan club.

'Did you get the sodas to whoever needed them so urgently?'

'If we could agree to never speak about the sodas ever again, I would be eternally grateful,' I replied. 'You really paid for all the damage? I'm so sorry I had to run out, I feel awful.'

'We can't have that,' he replied gently. 'And for real, don't worry. It's just money.'

A sudden flush of self-awareness forced me to break eye contact and engage in a very important staring match with the floor.

'I'm Evan,' announced the most magnetic man I had ever met, holding out his hand.

I took it in mine and fought the urge to lick it.

'Francesca,' I replied, a warmth radiating from my hand, all over my body.

I had never, in my entire life, felt anything like this.

There had been a million crushes before I met Stew, most of them unrequited and all of them disappointing. Falling for someone who didn't even know I was alive had been a real talent of mine and I was extremely familiar with the thrill of unexpected eye contact or an accidental touch that went absolutely nowhere but could sustain me for days. But I couldn't remember ever feeling such instant and overwhelming desire for another human being. I wanted to climb onto his back, sniff his head, then have him lie on top of me while he read everything he'd ever posted on Facebook aloud. It was as though I'd had all the wind knocked out of me and replaced with something lighter than air and, any second now, I fully expected to float away.

'Are you OK?' Evan said when I didn't let go of his hand long after the socially acceptable period of time had lapsed.

'I'm not sure,' I admitted. 'Is it me or is it warm out here?'

He slipped one finger under his tight white collar and pulled it away from his neck. His eyes followed mine as I looked around to make sure there were still other people on the terrace. They could all have vanished into thin air and I wouldn't have noticed.

'Francesca.' He said my name in a voice that made me weak, the frequency corresponding directly with my ovaries. 'Maybe we should get a drink.'

But I couldn't move. Instead of nodding, smiling, following him to the bar for a drink, accepting his proposal, marrying in the little church near my nana's old house and having three kids, two we planned and one who was a surprise albeit a welcome one, I stayed exactly where I was. Something like shame washed over me, drowning my desire with an unwelcome truth.

'I have a boyfriend,' I whispered.

It was an answer to a question he hadn't asked yet. His face fell, leaving nothing but the ghost of a smile that I was sure would haunt me for ever. I was not one for dramatics. I'd always been the practical one, the sensible person who thought ahead, packed a snack and made everyone go for a wee before they left the house, but there was something about this man that made me feel like I could be someone else entirely. Except with just four words, whoever she might be, I'd sent her away for good.

'You have a boyfriend,' Evan repeated, as though he needed to hear it out loud again to convince himself. 'Of course you do.'

'I'm sorry,' I said. And I meant it.

'Don't be,' he said as he took a big step backwards, sticking his hands deep into his pockets. 'I would be more shocked if you didn't. Anyway, you seemed pretty stressed back at the store so I wanted to make sure things were OK. I hope you and your boyfriend have a wonderful evening.'

With that, he turned and walked away.

I watched him melt into the crowd, his black tux and dark hair mingling with all the other black tuxes and dark hair until I couldn't work out which one was him, and my heart sank into the soles of my trainers, through the island of Panarea, and down to the bottom of the Aeolian sea.

There were only three things I had ever been absolutely certain of in my life. One, Facebook would bring about the end of civilisation; two, tea should never

189

be made in a microwave; and three, one day I would marry Stewart Bingham. Now I had a fourth certainty to add to that list, that I would never, ever forget the look on Evan's face when he saw me standing on the terrace.

And what that meant for my certainty about marrying Stew, I did not know.

'Christ,' I whispered, grabbing for the bannister beside me, trying to ground myself in reality. There was nothing like re-evaluating everything you'd ever believed on a Saturday night before you'd had so much as a sniff of a drink.

'Francesca?'

Pulling myself together, I looked up to see Andrew, the curly-haired man in the hat, standing a few feet away and staring right at me. He was surrounded by a gaggle of other men, all of them crowded around one another, giggling and muttering to each other. I slapped on my best please-leave-me-alone smile and nodded. Truly the last person I wanted to talk to.

'Come here,' he ordered. 'I've got something to share with you regarding the whereabouts of Ms Juliette.'

Curiosity really did always get the better of me, even when I didn't even care that much, but this time, I actually did care. How could he know where she was when I didn't? The group parted as I walked towards them, all five men huddled around the glowing phone in Andrew's hand.

'I thought there were no phones allowed in here?' I said with what Jess referred to as my 'big Head Girl energy'.

The whole group guffawed as they pulled out their numerous illicit mobile devices.

'Send me those, will you, Andy?' one of the men said, slapping his porky fingers against the screen of his massive phone. 'Even if they're deepfakes, they're good enough for me.'

'These photos are definitely not fake,' Andrew crowed. 'Came to me from a very reliable source. I'm going to flog them to Carden.'

His face was flushed and his eyes unfocused as he swiped at the screen, already well on his way to being completely and utterly shitfaced. Someone was not going to make it to the dawn breakfast buffet. One less omelette for Gordon to make.

'What are you talking about?' I asked. 'Who's Carden?'

'Clive Carden.' A man with a face like a frog gave me a filthy look. 'You don't know who Clive Carden is?'

I replied with a not terribly apologetic shrug.

'He's a great man,' Andrew snorted. 'He's a philandrop – a philantop – you know what I mean.'

'I can't tell if you're trying to say philanderer or philanthropist,' I replied honestly. 'Are you talking about the man who owns all the newspapers?'

'I'd say he prefers the term media mogul,' he said, a shade of suspicion crossing his face. 'Who also happens to be the head of the Crystal Ball Foundation and if you weren't on my guest list and you weren't on his guest list, whose guest list were you on?'

'Are you going to show me these photos or not?' I asked, hitting him with my best 'May I speak to the manager?' tone. Sometimes we had no choice but to use the only weapons available to us.

He thrust his phone in front of my nose and even though I closed my eyes very quickly, I wasn't quick enough. It was a photo of a woman. A naked woman

191

in a small, pink room, surrounded by pillows. And the naked woman was Juliette.

This random man had naked photos of Juliette on his phone.

'Where did you get these?' I demanded, knocking the phone away from my face.

'Where does anybody get them?' he muttered. He scrolled through a whole gallery of photos, smirking as his audience moved in closer for another grubby look. 'Someone leaked them.'

'What do you mean "someone leaked them"?' I asked, very much wishing I could wash out my eyes. 'You're saying these are private photos someone shared?'

All five of them burst out laughing, loud, flabby guffaws that echoed around the balcony and rang out over the bay.

'Not that private,' Andrew replied. 'If she didn't want people to see them, she shouldn't have taken them in the first place.'

'Bloody glad she did.' The froggy man pawed at the phone to get a better look. 'Never thought that much of her before now, but yes, I would definitely give her a go.'

'Stop it,' I cried, a dangerous cocktail of adrenaline and righteous anger rushing through my veins. 'Stop looking at them, this is extremely gross.'

'This one isn't.' Andrew swiped to the next image and they all cocked their heads to the left at the same time to get a better look. 'And you calm down, babes, phones get hacked, photos get leaked, it happens all the time.'

Babes? He was lucky I didn't kick his balls off his body right then and there.

'If she hadn't decided she was too good to show up tonight, whoever leaked these photos might have thought twice about it,' declared another man in the group; this one had his hair slicked and his dead eyes were almost completely black. 'And everyone knows, only sluts send nudes.'

My entire being pulsated with white-hot rage.

Before I could second-guess myself, I grabbed the offending phone out of Andrew's hand and, for the second time in as many days, launched a very expensive piece of technology into the sea.

'What did you just do?' Andy screeched at the top of his surprisingly high voice. 'That's my fucking phone!'

'I'm getting good at that,' I whispered, panting slightly as I leaned over the edge to see if there was any trace of the offending article, but there was absolutely, positively, nothing. Just pitch-black peace.

'Who the fuck do you think you are?' Froggy exploded as the others began to make similar angry noises. 'You can't just chuck someone else's phone off a balcony.'

As the red mist cleared from my eyes, I realized I was alone on the terrace of a hotel, surrounded by five furious men.

'Who is she anyway?' the one with the dead eyes asked the others. 'I've never seen her before.'

'Not this again,' I groaned. Being rich must be a lot like coming from a small town. Everyone knew everyone and outsiders are not looked upon kindly. 'Look, I'm sorry I threw your phone into the sea just like I'm sure you're sorry you had those photos in the first place.'

'I think you should go and find Andrew's phone for

him,' Dead Eyes said, suddenly overtaken with an eerie calm. I blinked at the placid fury on his face.

'But Andrew's phone is down there,' I said, pointing over the edge of the terrace.

'Precisely,' growled Frog Face.

They began to crowd around me, glowering with neutered menace as they approached. I could see the newspaper report in my head, 'Sheffield Woman Found Dead at Charity Do. Local police confirmed Fran Cooper, 32, was wearing trainers with a ballgown and someone else's pants. Related story on page 5, Cooper's grand-mother rolls over in grave.'

'Come on,' I protested as the world's worst *Reservoir Dogs* tribute act inched towards me, each daring the other to go a little bit further with every step. 'You're hardly going to throw me off the terrace, in front of hundreds of witnesses?'

But as they all exchanged questioning glances, it did seem as though that was exactly their plan.

'Oh, for fuck's sake,' I said, considering my options and the state of my updo. Even I knew it was no good getting into a scrap with your hair down. 'I haven't been in a fight since year seven, but I sent Donna Maria Bowers home with a black eye that day and I'm fairly certain I can do it again if I have to.'

'Francesca, there you are!'

Evan stepped between me and the five men, their menacing expressions suddenly turning sheepish.

'Making friends?' he asked, quirking one eyebrow upwards.

'You know me,' I replied with just the tiniest tremor in my voice. 'Just such a people person.'

'I'm calling security!' Andrew threatened, as Evan

offered me his arm and I slid my hand through it, relief flooding through me. 'She threw my phone off the terrace!'

'I know, I saw that,' Evan said with a huge grin. 'And I thought it was kind of amazing.'

'I could have taken them, you know,' I said as we hustled away as fast as my trainers would carry me. 'I didn't need you to save me.'

'Oh, I wasn't saving you from them,' he replied. 'I was saving *them* from *you*. You, Francesca, are a badass.'

I was a badass, I thought happily as we crossed the terrace back into the ballroom. I could live with that.

CHAPTER SIXTEEN

'You don't really think they were going to push me off the balcony, do you?' I asked as we walked briskly down a narrow corridor, lit with a ceiling of stars, arms still linked and my heart keeping double time. Whether it was from Evan's body next to mine or the fact I'd come within seconds of being chucked over the edge of a cliff, I wasn't sure, but I didn't care. Maybe it was both. Two things could be true at the same time.

'I definitely get the feeling all those guys tortured more than one class hamster back in the day, but no, I don't think they were going to hurt you. I think they were trying to scare you, which is still a dick move,' he replied. 'And I'm sorry if I overstepped, but I saw what was happening and I couldn't stand by and watch. I really hate those guys.'

'You didn't overstep,' I assured him, my fingers resting lightly on what felt like a nicely developed bicep under his tux. 'Who are they anyway?'

Evan made a distasteful noise in the back of his throat. 'Assholes?'

A loud laugh rattled out of me and it felt so good.

'A bunch of tragic cases who used Daddy's money to buy into successful companies because they wouldn't know an original idea if it bit them on the ass,' he clarified. 'But assholes is more concise.'

'I should have known when I saw the fedora,' I replied. 'He's so clearly one of those men who thinks wearing a hat is equivalent to having a personality.'

The tunnel opened up into another room, much more intimate than the ballroom, with walls draped in gunmetal grey silks and black velvet-covered tables dotted all around. It was filled with yet more people in outfits that cost more than ten times the average mortgage payment. And there was me thinking the ballroom was the entire event. Oh, sweet, naïve Fran. I chose a table in a dark corner, Evan pulled out my chair, and I sank into it, trying not to show surprise at the random act of chivalry. It wasn't something I was used to.

'They shouldn't get away with it,' he said, his perfect nostrils flaring as he spoke, clearly still annoyed. 'They think they run this thing but that was so far out of line. I'm going to find someone from security and—'

'No!' My hand shot out to pull him back. 'I mean, it's all right, you don't have to do that. I don't want to make a fuss.' The last thing I needed was a chat with an armed security guard in possession of a guest list.

'They were threatening you, Francesca. I think that warrants a fuss.'

He was right, it did, but I'd already been threatened with an unexpected dip in the sea and I really didn't want to end my weekend in a cell. I clearly wasn't dressed for it.

'I think us laughing at them did more damage than

security ever could,' I told him. 'And I *did* throw his phone over the edge.'

Evan's face semi-relaxed into a frustrated smile, and my heart soared. 'Not that I don't fully support your actions, but can I ask why?'

'He was showing photos he should never have had in the first place,' I said, flashing back to an extremely unwanted memory. 'Naked photos that were clearly not sent to him by the subject.'

'Nudes?' Evan looked down at my hand still on his arm and I snatched it back. Hands to yourself, Francesca. 'Who was it?'

'Juliette.'

'The singer, Juliette?'

'There is only one Juliette,' I replied wearily.

Resting my elbows on the table, I pressed my finger-tips into my temples. Maybe if I pushed hard enough, I'd find the reset button for my brain.

'How'd they get them?'

I turned my palms upwards and frowned. 'Your guess is as good as mine.'

'Could have hacked her phone, I guess, they're all tech bros. Or they could have bribed someone for them, you never know. Do you know her?'

'That's debatable. God. If they'd just left their phones in their rooms like we did, I wouldn't be thinking about this right now.'

Evan reached inside the breast pocket of his tuxedo and pulled out his handset.

'Everyone was *very* clear about not bringing phones into the ball,' I groaned as he put it away. 'Am I the only person here who did as she was told?'

'Yes,' he replied. 'Almost certainly.'

198

'Classic Fran,' I said with a sigh. 'Follows all the rules and still gets it wrong.'

'Hey.' He smiled, warmth flooding his eyes and smothering my panic with his calm assuredness. 'I'm sure it's not that big of a deal. She's probably been through a million bigger scandals than this, and you know how fast things come and go online these days, it'll be old news by Monday.'

'That doesn't make it OK though,' I said, sitting upright. 'Just because shitty things have already happened to her doesn't mean she should be all right with more shitty things. And please don't say she shouldn't have taken them if she didn't want anyone to see them because I'll have to punch you and I really don't want to.'

'I would never say that,' he said, looking chastened. 'I'm not perfect, but I do know sharing nudes goes under the "bad" column. It always feels skeezy when they get leaked.'

'But you still look at them?'

'We all looked at that Chris Evans pic, and don't tell me you didn't,' he answered. 'But yes. I don't feel good about it and I would never actively seek them out, but I have seen them.'

'Maybe this is one of those things we know is wrong but don't really worry about until it happens to someone we know,' I said, fully aware I'd seen more than one naked celebrity in my time and really hadn't stopped to think about it before now. 'But this arsehole was talking about selling them to Clive Carden.' The look of alarm that took over Evan's face did not fill me with confidence. 'Do you know him?'

'Do I know Clive Carden?' Evan asked, laughing as he spoke. 'Yeah, yeah, I do.'

'Of course. Everyone knows everyone here,' I replied, thinking about Juliette, alone on that yacht, blissfully unaware that at least six people not of her choosing had just seen her vagina. 'It's illegal, isn't it? For him to try to sell the photos?'

'I don't know,' he answered with a grim look, 'but I am sorry. This isn't how you should be spending your first Crystal Ball.'

'How did you know this is my first?' I reached a hand up to my head, scraping a bit of fringe back behind my ear and feeling altogether too aware of myself. 'Did you see my shoes?'

'I did not but I'm sure I would love them,' he said as I shuffled them away under my skirt. 'You kind of gave yourself away by not having your phone. Everyone has their phone and takes photos, they just don't post them. It's kind of an unspoken agreement. Besides, if you'd been here before, we would have met before, and there's no way on this earth I could have forgotten.'

A tickle of anticipation forced a smile onto my face. 'I don't know about that. You did hit your head this morning.'

'True.' He grinned and my stomach flipped. 'But I am very sure this is our first time.'

My cheeks flamed as I stared at my cushion cover clutch bag, saying nothing.

'Your boyfriend must be looking for you,' Evan said, clearing his throat. 'I guess I should go.'

'But my boyfriend isn't here,' I said quickly. 'I'm here on my own.'

His eyes lit up, warm, brown and liquid. 'Really?'

I gave a cautious nod. 'Would you believe me if I said it's a long story?'

He covered my hand with his and it felt as if I'd licked my fingers and stuck them into a plug socket. An unanticipated jolt caused by an incredibly reckless act.

'Yes,' Evan replied, his voice and his eyes soft. 'I would believe anything you told me.'

My heart pounded, my knees went weak, and various other parts of my body reacted in ways I hadn't felt in so long, it really did feel like the first time.

'I am going to get a drink,' I announced, wondering if the bartender might be so kind as to hose me down with soda water if I asked nicely. 'Can I get you anything?'

Evan pulled at his collar again then straightened his perfectly tied bow tie. 'I'd better come with you,' he said. 'Just in case you run into any more trouble.'

'I thought we agreed I can take care of myself?'

'Oh, I know you absolutely can,' he said, holding out his arm and leaning into a shallow bow. 'But I also want you to know, you don't have to.'

'Be still, my beating heart,' I whispered before sliding my arm through his and venturing off to find the bar.

'What's happening in here?' I asked, while we waited for the bartender to pour one glass of champagne for him and one Diet Coke for me. Ball or no ball, it was still far too soon for me to consider alcohol. Several tall tables lined the edge of the room, each one bearing an iPad on a stand. 'Is this room sponsored by Netflix or something?'

'The Netflix and Chill room is downstairs,' Evan said, raising his eyebrow as I laughed. 'You think I'm kidding?'

I thanked the waiter for my drink and gulped down the first mouthful.

'It's a silent auction,' he said. 'Wanna take a look?'

'Why not?' I replied, walking beside him across the room with one eye on the door, just in case we were joined by any security guards or angry fedora wearers.

He picked up a tablet and an animated Crystal Ball logo appeared on the screen, followed by a long list of available lots. Swarovski-studded jet skis, a platinum iPhone, a litter box decorated by Banksy . . . it was like an Argos catalogue for people with no taste and too much money.

'You tap on the item you're interested in, type in your name and the amount you want to bid,' Evan explained, summoning the entry for a diamond-encrusted Cartier dog collar. 'Then you wait for someone with shares in Facebook to outbid you by a million bucks.'

I started to laugh but the sound got stuck in my throat when he tapped on a helicopter ride around Barbados with Rihanna, and I saw someone had already bid a quarter of a million dollars.

'Someone really wants to meet Rihanna,' I said, my eyes open so wide I was afraid they might fall out.

'Everybody wants to meet Rihanna,' he replied. 'But I'm going to pass on this one. I hate helicopters.' I almost laughed and then remembered how much a ticket to the ball cost. Evan probably rode around in helicopters like I took the bus. 'I nearly fell out of one on the way to my best friend's bar mitzvah,' he said, staring off into the distance while I concentrated on looking as sympathetic as possible.

Part of me had to have known he was wealthy, he

was at the Crystal Ball, he'd told me he paid off the girl in the shop, and he had not rented that tuxedo from Moss Bros, but I hadn't really thought about it until now.

How rich was he?

Who was he?

'Anything catch your eye?'

'There's just so much to choose from,' I said, turning my attention back to billionaire's eBay when he caught me staring. The only thing that had caught my eye was Evan.

'How about this?' He tapped on one of the lots and Elton John's 'Rocketman' began to play. 'Two round trip tickets to the moon on Elon Musk's private spaceship?'

I frowned. 'Would I have to go *with* Elon Musk?'

'Most likely.'

'Then I will pass,' I said, returning to the list. 'Besides, I wouldn't have thought that would work out so well for someone who's scared of helicopters.'

'The irony of me,' he said with a smile. 'Hates to fly, but grew up wanting to be an astronaut.'

'You'd better put your name down then,' I replied, wondering if he would. The current bid was already at one hundred thousand dollars and against my better judgement, I was curious to know what kind of game I was playing here.

'Elon, though,' he replied with a grimace. 'I'll wait.'

'How about this?' I suggested, choosing the next high value item on the list. 'A luxury shopping spree in New York with a personal stylist and insider guide to the city. That sounds incredible.'

His whole face lit up at once. 'We don't need to win that one, I can be your New York guide, I live in Manhattan.'

'I've never been,' I replied as I gazed at the screen of the tablet, fingers lightly touching the glass. 'Always wanted to go but never made it.'

'You've never been to New York?'

I looked up to see disbelief all over Evan's face, and then I realized. I wasn't the only one who was making assumptions about the other person, only I had a feeling his were much further off the mark than mine.

'It's another long story,' I said, although it wasn't, not really. I just didn't want to talk to him about Stew or any of the myriad life choices I'd made that I was starting to regret. This was my fantasy night and I very much wanted it to remain that way. 'Is that where you're from, New York?' I asked.

'Opposite coast. I was born in California but I grew up in New York, lived in Manhattan since I was six. I can't believe you've never been.'

'I know, it feels as though everyone else in the world has,' I said, readying my next question before he could ask me anything. There was so much more I wanted to know about him, like his middle name, what he did for a living, his inside leg measurement, and how it would feel to weave my hands into his thick hair and pull him towards me and—

'I think we should bid on this,' he said, grabbing the iPad and tapping away while I attempted to compose myself. 'If it's your first Crystal Ball, you have to bid on *something*.'

'First and last,' I corrected.

He pursed his lips then entered a ridiculous number with an obscene number of zeroes and I began to feel faint. I had some money in my savings account, but that wouldn't even stretch to a luxury shopping trip in old York, let alone the new one. 'I didn't expect this evening to be so complicated,' I confessed. 'Someone should write some kind of guide for newcomers. Which rules you're actually supposed to follow, which ones are optional, where the toilets are, all the important stuff. It really would make things a lot easier.'

'You've just given me the greatest idea,' Evan declared. 'I have a proposal.'

My heart stopped as I wrestled the words 'I do' back into my mouth.

'I don't like to brag, but I'm kind of a Crystal Ball expert,' he said, eyebrows raised knowingly.

'Is that right?' I asked, smiling in spite of myself.

'Yeah, I mean, it's not my first rodeo. And they did have a rodeo-themed ball like ten years back, but Don Jr got kicked in the balls by one of the bulls so they banned them.'

'And no one got a photo of *that*?'

He shook his head and leaned in towards me until his lips were just inches away from my face. 'You're right, the ball can be pretty confusing to figure out if you're on your own and you don't know the ropes. If this really is your first and last Crystal Ball, you really should make the most of it.'

'I should?' I squeaked at the thought of what that could mean before clearing my throat. 'I mean, yes, I suppose I should.'

'I'm here on my own. You're here on your own. It doesn't make any sense that we should spend the entire night by ourselves.' He was so close I could smell his aftershave, something warm, spicy and expensive. 'What would you say if I were to offer my services as your escort for the evening?'

Escort. He wanted to be my escort. But did he mean the kind of escort they talked about in *Downton Abbey*, or the kind of escort that cost extra if you wanted them to stay the whole night? Maybe he wasn't a rich kid, maybe he was a male prostitute, trying to scam *me* out of *my* millions. It was a strangely reassuring idea. Better to be grifted by a pro than to develop a ridiculous, instantaneous crush at thirty-bloody-two.

'I would say . . .' I swallowed hard as he bit his lip and gazed into my eyes. Then, over his shoulder, I saw the security guard stride into the room. Was he still looking for Rebecca de Winter, or was he looking for me? 'I would say that I need to use the toilet,' I corrected hurriedly. 'Do you know where it is?'

'Not the response I was expecting, but it's not a no,' Evan replied, giving me a thumbs up. 'There's a ladies' lounge right over there.'

'Thanks,' I said with a tight smile, grabbing my bag from the table and walking quickly away from Evan and the guard, and towards the safety.

Of course, the toilets couldn't just be toilets. Oh no, they had to be golden thrones, hidden away inside a luxuriously decorated lounge with semi-opaque rose quartz walls and soft pink sofas positioned in front of giant gilt-framed mirrors, perfectly positioned for forbidden selfies. Evan was telling the truth about the phone thing, I really was the only person at the ball without one, and I made polite noises as I edged around a group of women arranging themselves on top of each other for maximum photographic impact, long, lithe limbs stretching up and out to ensure their best angles.

Passing into the bathroom proper, I bustled myself

backwards into a roomy stall, only slightly put off by the silent, blurry outlines of people walking by, visible through the crystal walls.

'Right,' I said as I placed my clutch back on the handy shelf on the back of the door, before fighting with my layers of tulle to make sure they were safely out of the toilet water danger zone. 'Here's the deal. You're here, you're in the most beautiful dress you have ever worn in your life, and a very handsome, very kind, very funny man really wants to spend the evening with you. You can either say sod it, have a lovely time, let someone else take the lead for once and worry about the real world tomorrow, or you can go back upstairs, feel sorry for yourself, order room service and for ever wonder what might have happened if you'd stayed here with the handsome man and said sod it.'

Room service aside, it really wasn't much of a contest.

Only I really didn't know anything about Evan. Just because he was absurdly good looking and seemed all chivalrous didn't mean he wasn't planning to throw me down a deep hole and turn me into a three-course meal and a skin suit. This is *exactly* the kind of event Patrick Bateman would be into.

Stew wouldn't like it, that went without saying, but Stew knew I wouldn't like him having dinner with his ex and it hadn't stopped him. And Evan wasn't suggesting we elope, just that we spend a couple of hours together at a party. Even if we did fancy each other, we were both grown-ups, we could control ourselves. People met other people who set them off every single day, and you didn't see them rutting in the streets. Very often. I wasn't going to rip my (borrowed) knickers off just because some fit American came along and gave me a look that made my heart *and* ovaries explode.

'But you *do* still have a fiancé,' I reminded myself. 'This is just harmless flirting.'

I rubbed my hands together and thought about my engagement ring, tucked away in my wallet, in the safe on *The Songbird* and sailing far away from me somewhere on the sea. Would Evan even have approached me if I'd been wearing it? And would the answer to that question make me feel better or worse?

Emerging from the stall, I turned on a rose-gold tap at the rose-gold sink and washed my hands slowly and thoroughly. At the basin beside mine was a tall, gorgeous woman with a golden puff of natural curls and eyelashes so long, you could have used them as feather dusters. She smiled at me in the mirror and I returned the gesture.

'I love your dress,' I said, sticking to tried and tested conversation starters. 'It's gorgeous.'

'Thank you,' she replied, giving me a little shimmy. 'Yours too. Like something out of a fairy tale.'

'It certainly doesn't feel real,' I told her, drying my hands on a soft, pink towel.

She raised her chin and gnawed on her bottom lip, as though she was debating whether or not to say something.

'You're here with Evan?' she asked.

There it was.

'No, I wouldn't say I'm "with" him,' I replied, alarm bells ringing loud and clear. 'We just met. Well, we met this morning, sort of and we just met again. What I'm trying to say is, we're not here together-together, if that's what you mean.'

She smiled into the mirror, showing off her absolutely perfect teeth. 'I was only going to tell you to enjoy him,' she said as she accepted a small fluffy towel from an attendant who appeared out of nowhere. 'Enjoy your evening, I mean.'

The attendant reached across me to turn off her still running tap as I stared at the woman's reflection, watching as she sauntered away to join a gaggle of other beautiful women and cover them in extravagant kisses.

'What was that supposed to mean?' I muttered as they disappeared through the door and passed right in front of me, one amorphous, multi-limbed blob on the other side of the crystal wall.

'I think this is what it means,' the attendant replied, making an O shape with her thumb and forefinger on one hand and poking the forefinger of the other in and out of the hole rapidly.

'Yeah, that's what I thought too,' I said as she nodded, cleaning up the basins with a smile on her face.

Evan was still waiting at our table when I returned and I watched his face light up as I walked towards him, his dark eyes sparkling. Every time I saw him was like the first time. The spark, the rush, the pull. It was a lot to process for a woman whose most erotically charged experience in the last five years was two consecutive nights at Magic Mike Live where I'd accidentally karate chopped one of the dancers in the nuts when he tried to give me a lap dance, earning myself a lifetime ban.

'You came back,' he said happily.

'I did,' I replied, picking up my Diet Coke and downing it quickly. The security guard was nowhere to be seen.

'And did you think about my suggestion?'

'Yes,' I said. 'And I don't know if it's a good idea.'

'Oh, I'm sure it's a terrible idea,' Evan replied cheerfully. 'But before you say no, how about some ground rules; first names only, no personal questions, just one night of good, clean fun. At the end of the night, we'll go our separate ways, no harm, no foul. It'll be like *Strangers on a Train*, only we're not on a train and we won't kill anyone.'

'It's still early, so let's not make any rash promises,' I said, checking the room for blonds in fedoras.

'And this goes without saying, but I will say it anyway. We're talking a strictly PG interaction, Boy Scout's honour.'

'Were you a boy scout?' I asked, equally doubtful and disappointed.

'No,' he replied with a wolfish wink. 'But I think I've got the gist of it. I won't even try to go past first base.'

'Sorry to be extra British, but I've never really understood the bases,' I confessed. 'Just so we're entirely clear, what is first base exactly?'

'Full penetration,' Evan answered without hesitation, and I laughed so loud and so hard, several heads turned to see what was so funny.

'No, I swear, entirely honourable behaviour,' he said as I smothered the sound with my hands. 'Even your grandmother would be disappointed by our lack of physical contact. I'll be a perfect gentleman and you call all the shots.'

As indecent proposals went, it was incredibly decent.

'So.' Evan sipped his champagne. 'What do you think? Are you ready for an adventure?'

'What do I think?' I repeated the question out loud to myself.

I thought Stew would hate it and I thought I was at risk of doing something incredibly out of character and spectacularly stupid with someone I didn't even know. I thought the sensible thing would be to go back upstairs, take off this dress, and eat the cold chips that were waiting for me in my room while looking for a new job online.

But I was so tired of doing the sensible thing.

Smiling, I raised my glass to Evan's and clinked.

'I think I'm in.'

CHAPTER SEVENTEEN

'Every year the ball is a little different,' Evan explained as he led me out of the silent auction and through a starlit tunnel. 'But the basics are the same. You're always going to have the carnival with the crystal Ferris wheel, that's iconic, there's always dancing in the ballroom, and they never change the most important part.'

'And what's the most important part?' I asked, my arm nestled in the crook of his elbow as we emerged into another room where my question was answered.

'The food,' he replied. 'The most important part is the food.'

Be still my beating heart.

They say men fall in love through their eyes and women through their ears, but as far as I was concerned, all right-minded people could be seduced through their stomachs. It wasn't just food, it was mountains of food. It was Stew's mum's Boxing Day buffet after a full Hollywood glow up. There were so many different stations, groaning with silver serving dishes, platters and tureens, not to mention an actual ice cream van parked in the corner of the room complete with a man in a white paper hat, handing out perfectly scooped cones to the partygoers.

'What do you think?' Evan asked. 'Hot, cold? Sweet, savoury? Whatever you want, it's yours.'

'The cheese,' I murmured, dropping his arm as I was drawn across the room in a dairy-fuelled daze. 'Look at the cheese.'

Now, I had been known to put together a pretty nice cheeseboard in my time. Four, sometimes even five different cheeses from the deli on Sharrow Vale Road, a selection of Carr's crackers, and even a few nuts and grapes if I was feeling fancy, but this was something else. They must have milked every cow in Christendom and come up with a different cheese for each day of the year. Christmas had come early, and Christmas was made of cheese.

'You're a cheese gal,' Evan said. 'Duly noted.'

'When I was little, my mum used to slice up a tomato, give me chunks of cheese and call it a salad,' I told him as I gazed longingly at my first love. 'It would still be my last meal, if I had to choose.'

'You're telling me, if you were on death row, you'd ask for a plate of cheese and a tomato and you'd be happy?'

'Throw in a crusty baguette and I'd turn on the chair myself,' I confirmed.

'You prefer savoury over sweet?'

'I believe in equal opportunities,' I replied, swooning at the sight of an untouched wheel of Brie. 'Just because cheese is incredible, doesn't mean ice cream can't change your life. And don't get me started on baked goods. I can't be left alone with a plate of brownies.'

The server behind the cheese counter began slicing tiny slivers of cheese and placing them artfully on a plate. It was all I could do to physically stop myself from grabbing the knife from his hand and cutting off a proper chunk of Cheddar.

'A good brownie is practically crack,' Evan agreed. 'Although crack is not delicious at all so that's kind of a dumb analogy.'

'You've done a lot of crack, have you?' I asked, chuckling at my own joke while keeping a very serious watch on the cheese preparation.

'No,' he replied casually. 'I wouldn't say a lot.'

I turned to stare at him, reminded of the fact I really didn't know anything about him at all.

Evan took one look at my face and burst out laughing. 'It was a joke, a bad joke, I've never done crack. I accidentally smoked opium once when I was younger but it did not go well and I never did it again and this is not something I usually tell someone the first time we meet so I don't know why I'm telling you now but could you please stop looking at me like that?'

I graciously accepted my woefully light sampling of cheese while Evan carefully studied his shoes and rubbed one finger against his forehead. 'You never did anything dumb when you were a kid?' he asked, blushing, as he stole a piece of blue cheese from my plate.

'Can't say I ever did crack or opium,' I replied, chowing down on the slice of goat's cheese, covering my mouth with my hand. 'But I did once drink four sugar-free Red Bulls in a row and my roommate had to take me to hospital because I thought I was having a heart attack. Turned out to be indigestion.'

'From the Red Bull?'

'No.' I chased the goat's cheese with a hunk of gouda. 'From the entire frozen pizza I ate after I drank the Red Bull. The doctor said I should have waited for it to fully defrost.'

'Wow,' he gasped with mock admiration. 'You were really hitting the hard stuff.'

'I admit it,' I replied, savouring the gouda as he plucked a grape from my plate. 'I'm a bit of a lightweight. I don't know, I prefer to be in control.'

'Does that apply to everything you do?' Evan asked, raising the grape to his lips and holding my gaze with his.

When some people are embarrassed, their cheeks turn pink, they might throw in an adorable titter, and the whole thing can be very charming. When I blush, my entire body goes beetroot red, my neck and my chest break out in an attractive rash and, if the other person is very lucky, I might even squeeze out a snort or two. This was a full neck rash, red face, double snort situation, but if Evan noticed, he was kind enough not to point and laugh, then run away.

'No personal questions,' I reminded him, filling my mouth with another piece of cheese.

'OK, Ms Francesca No-Last-Name, you're currently attending your first ever Crystal Ball.' Evan held an imaginary microphone in front of his mouth and then passed it to me. 'What do you want to do next?'

'What do I want to do?' It wasn't a question I was used to answering. I looked out of the window at the carnival below, the crystal Ferris wheel already turning and the unmistakable song from *It's A Small World* echoing through the windows. 'Can we go to the fair?'

'The carnival? Sure,' he replied. 'We can do whatever you want, Francesca's in charge. You ready?'

Nodding, I stuffed the last few bites of cheese into my chipmunk cheeks and gave the server a warning look. I would be back for the rest.

'I know we said no personal questions, but you've got to give me something. Purely for research purposes, you understand,' Evan said as we passed through the rear doors of the hotel and under a towering archway that declared our arrival at the Crystal Ball Carnival. 'If I'm going to make your evening unforgettable, I'm going to need some more info. Likes, dislikes, allergies, political allegiance, whether you have any strong feelings about the Red Sox. That kind of thing.'

'Is the Red Sox an American football team?' I asked, and his face relaxed into a huge smile.

'No, they are not,' he replied. 'But that was a helpful answer. So, I know you like cheese, being in control, and you know nothing about baseball. What else is there?'

I watched as someone who looked an awful lot like an actor from one of Stew's favourite superhero movies attempted to hook a crystal duck with a sparkly pole. On the back wall of the booth, dozens of little blue boxes tied with white ribbon hung from the prize wall, but we had already moved on by the time I realized they were from Tiffany.

'There's not much to know,' I said. 'I'm offensively normal.'

But he wasn't having any of it. 'Normal is subjective. What's normal to you might be totally fantastical to someone like me.'

'And vice versa,' I replied. strongly suspecting my weekly trip to Asda for the big shop would indeed be fantastical to someone like him. I eyed the next booth, where people were tossing basketballs for a chance to win a Rolex. 'Want to try?' I asked.

'Maybe later,' Evan said, steering me away as an extremely tall man wearing a lot of jewellery sent a basketball sailing through the hoop with a swish. 'My ego isn't strong enough to shoot hoops next to LeBron. Besides, I'm a Warriors guy.'

'I understood literally none of that, but OK,' I said as we walked up to a game of ring toss instead.

'Doesn't like basketball either, got it.' Evan picked up a stack of rings and handed me half of them. 'Without giving away any Googlable-specifics but I want to know, who is Francesca?'

I thought of all the different tests I'd taken over the years, all the horoscopes I'd read and the quizzes I'd done in the backs of magazines. I was a cool tone, ISFJ, type two Libra with Sagittarius rising. I was more Monica than Rachel without so much as a hint of Phoebe, and I was Team Edward all the way, although I *had* considered Team Jacob right up until he fell in love with a baby. But none of that answered Evan's question.

'After careful consideration, I have decided that answering would break the rules,' I said as I tossed my first ring and missed by a mile. 'Soz.'

'I'm not asking for your social security number, just a few helpful hints.' He took his stance, one foot in front of the other, knees slightly bent. He pulled his arm back slowly and released the ring. And missed. 'Fuck.'

'Competitive, then?' I said, only smirking slightly at his macho frustration. I chucked my second ring and watched it sail past every single peg.

'A little,' he admitted. 'I'll get it, that was just a warm-up.'

'What about you?' I asked as he wound up his arm, a deep crease forming between his eyebrows. 'I don't know anything about you other than you don't like heights, you don't like dickheads, and you have shattered childhood dreams of being an astronaut.'

'Did I say I'm not an astronaut?'

'Are you an astronaut?'

'No.'

'What are you then?'

He released his second ring and I held my breath as it hit the peg board, spinning around and trying to decide whether or not it would settle before falling straight to the floor.

'Fuck!' He planted his hands on his hips and looked up to the sky before gesturing for me to take my turn. 'I think job talk definitely counts as a personal question and I'd hate to break our own rules when we only just made them.'

'Oh,' I said, a realisation jumping up and giving me a short, sharp slap. 'I see.'

Evan raised one puzzled eyebrow.

'I thought the rules were for my benefit,' I said, lining up my last shot. 'But now I'm thinking maybe you're the one who has something to hide.'

I chucked my ring and watched with absolute delight as it landed right over one of the tallest pegs.

'We have a winner!' The male model manning the booth cheered loudly. 'The lady gets a prize. You can either pick something from the cabinet or bet your win against the gentleman's final throw and go for double or nothing.'

'Double or nothing,' I said confidently.

'You sure?' Evan replied. 'What if I miss?'

'I reckon I'll survive,' I told him, stepping to the side and gesturing grandly for him to take this throw as a small crowd began to gather. 'Go on, I have complete confidence in you.'

He stopped and stared at me, a strange expression on his face, and I felt an unexpected heat burn right through me.

'So that's what that feels like,' he muttered before taking off his jacket, rolling up his sleeves, and tossing the ring.

'Are we really going to carry this thing around all night?' Evan asked from behind the truly gargantuan teddy bear he was lugging around the carnival.

'Do you mean, are *you* going to have to carry it all night?' I asked happily. 'If you didn't want to carry it, you shouldn't have made the throw.'

'Of all the things you could have chosen,' he muttered, his voice muffled by a giant fluffy ear. 'You're sure you don't want to go back and trade it for something easier to carry, like, I don't know, *literally* anything?'

'I always wanted one of these,' I said as I skipped out ahead of him, grinning at the bear's idiotic face. It really was enormous. 'Well, a giant teddy bear or an A la Carte Kitchen. Did you have those in America? It was like a little play kitchen only for some reason you had to serve everyone jam roly-poly and baked beans.'

He made a face and stopped for a moment to hoist the bear up on to his hip. 'What's a jam roly-poly?'

'You poor, poor man,' I said, patting his hand. 'It's like you've never lived.'

'OK, I need a break. This guy needs to sit for a moment.'

Evan stopped right beside the big wheel, resting his elbow on top of the bear's head. I looked over at the ride as it towered above us, shining against the night sky, shrieks of happy laughter ringing out over the music that pumped from the speaker stack below. Evan propped the bear against a silver lamp post then propped himself up against the bear.

'Here,' I said, reaching across the bear's head to straighten Evan's skewed bow tie and as I looked up into his brown eyes, a thousand butterflies exploded into life where my stomach used to be.

'Your eyes are so interesting,' Evan said, gazing at me in the exact same way I was gazing at him, like he couldn't quite believe this was real.

'Interesting in that they should be studied, or interesting in that you'd like to pluck them out and put them in a life-size doll?' I asked, determined to ruin the moment.

'Why can't it be both?' he replied. 'Sorry, I should have clarified earlier, you don't have to worry, I'm *not* a serial killer.'

'Spoken like a true serial killer,' I pointed out.

'Nah.' Evan shook his head. 'I've seen all the documentaries. It seems way too complicated these days.'

'Well, that's true enough,' I agreed, picking a speck of dust off the bear's shiny black nose. 'It must have been so much easier before there were mobile phones and surveillance cameras everywhere. I suppose that's why you don't hear about it as much these days.'

'One of so many things lost to the digital age. The only problem is, what will we listen to when we run out of true crime podcasts?'

I considered the question thoughtfully. 'The podcasters are going to have to start committing the crimes,' I reasoned. 'They've studied enough crimes to know how to confuse the authorities for a while at least, and they need to keep their sponsors happy. It's only a matter of time before bodies start turning up inside Casper Mattress boxes.'

He grinned and rested his chin on top of the bear's head. 'You've thought too much about this.'

'I didn't say I wasn't a serial killer,' I said. 'Maybe you're the one who should be worried.'

'Oh,' he replied with starry eyes. 'Don't I know it.'

I spun away, pretending to be much more interested in the big wheel than I really was. The chat was even more dangerous than how good he looked in that suit. It wasn't fair for someone to be so good-looking, then turn out to be funny and quick as well. He could at least have had the decency to be dull. This was just rude.

When I turned back to Evan, he wasn't looking at me any more but staring at his phone instead. The screen throbbed with dozens of notifications, numbers in red circles hovering over every single app, I felt my left eye twitch at the state of it. I was morally opposed to people who left that many emails unread.

'Sorry,' he said, brushing his hair away from his face. 'I have to make a call. I'll be one moment.'

'No problem,' I said, taking over lead bear-propping responsibilities as he strode away with the phone pressed against his ear and a face like thunder.

As soon as he was out of sight, I felt the keen chill of the night air as though the temperature had suddenly dropped by ten degrees. There were inconspicuous heaters dotted around everywhere, but it was quite obvious the reason most people weren't worred about the cold was because they were extremely drunk. Cosying up to the bear, I watched a fresh batch of party-goers pile onto the Ferris wheel, squealing with delight as an attendant lowered the safety bar across their laps before they were swept off their feet. It looked like a normal fair, it smelled like a normal fair, and, aside from the fact they had an actual ride imported from actual Disneyland, it even sounded like a normal fair, but it really wasn't normal at all. A normal fair had goldfish in bags on the hook-a-duck stall, not Tiffany trinkets, and no one went on the waltzers in Chanel haute couture round my way.

Without Evan by my side I felt exposed. People didn't bat an eyelid at a happy, laughing couple, but it seemed as though everyone had time to check in on the woman shivering alone beside a giant teddy bear. Which was fair. But it wasn't until I saw a certain shock of blond curls heading in my direction that I began to panic.

'What do I do?' I asked the bear as I pressed myself up against him. But all he offered was a zen-like grin and middle-distance stare, the big fuzzy wanker.

Andrew stumbled onwards in my direction, occasion-ally stopping someone for a high five only to completely miss the other person's hand, and I cowered behind the bear, peeping out from under its armpit as he came closer. I was crouched down so low, I was little more than a big ball of blue tulle with a head poking out of the top when I heard someone loudly clearing their throat above me. It was an older couple I didn't recog-nize. He was tall and tuxedoed, a well-coiffed sweep of silver hair capping a slightly too tanned face, while she had the look of a hot mum, the one all the boys in the sixth form fancied.

'Hello?' I said politely, looking up at them from my hiding spot.

'Good evening,' the man said as his partner clung tightly to his arm. This conversation was clearly not her idea. 'Do you need some kind of help?'

'Quite possibly,' I muttered, sneaking a look underneath the bear's pit to see Andrew fighting his way to the front of the queue for the Ferris wheel. 'No, really, I'm fine. Just, you know, resting.'

'On the floor?'

'Really wanted to, um, connect with the earth,' I replied, patting the grass with one hand. 'I think it's important to stay grounded, especially at events like this.'

The woman looked at the man, he looked at her, then they both looked back at me with easy matching smiles, and I couldn't quite believe they'd bought it.

'I'm Aleister Vega,' the man said, squatting to hold out his hand. I saw Andrew being locked into his seat, then stood up to shake the proffered appendage. 'And this is my wife, Selina.'

'Nice to meet you,' I said, their clashing perfumes settling in the back of my throat, tacky and acidic. 'Francesca . . .' What was my fake last name again? 'Anderson. Francesca Anderson.'

'That's a gorgeous gown,' Selina said. 'It looks so charming on you.'

I couldn't quite work out where Aleister had cobbled together his accent, but Selina and her proportionally perfect face were American. She'd clearly had some work done, but it was excellent work and she looked beautiful and refreshed rather than overdone. Aleister's surgeon had not been so kind. The skin around his eyes had been tightened up just a little too much, giving him the permanent look of someone who had just found out Ryan Reynolds used to go out with Alanis Morrissette.

'We saw you with Evan and simply had to come over and introduce ourselves,' Selina said. 'We're very good friends of the family.'

'Oh, isn't that just wonderful?' I said, raising one hand to my neck as it began to burn. This was the perfect time for a panic rash. 'He had to take a phone call, but I'm sure he'll be back in a minute.'

'I've known him since he was born,' Aleister said, shaking his head as though he could barely believe it even though he had to be at least twice as old as Evan. 'Great kid, always on the move.'

'And such a catch,' Selina added with the knowing smile of a woman who knew nothing.

'I was very close with his mother,' Aleister said. 'We were on the board of a lot of the same charities. Tragic, to lose her so young, very sad. She was a wonderful woman.'

I squeezed the bear's paw tightly. Evan's mother was dead?

'And I've always felt maternal towards Evan myself,' Selina said, gazing up at the sky as though she expected a chorus of angels to appear and serenade her benefi-cence. 'That's why we wanted to introduce ourselves. We were just walking by and I said to Aleister, how long has it been since we saw Evan looking so happy?'

'How long since you've seen him looking unhappy?' I quipped.

'I don't think he's been himself since that fiasco of

an engagement,' Aleister replied gravely. 'But that only lasted, what, a week?'

'A month at most,' Selina guessed, 'and I heard she proposed to herself. Then he was seeing the model, wasn't he? The Russian girl?'

'I thought it was the actress,' he said. 'Or was it that girl from Australia? The one whose father owns all the opal mines?'

Selina coughed lightly and tugged on her husband's sleeve. I looked over my shoulder and saw Evan walking towards us.

'Selina, Aleister.' The three of them exchanged kisses as Evan resumed his easy stance by my side. 'You've met Francesca.'

'We have and what a joy she is,' the older man confirmed and I tried very hard not to be sick in my mouth. 'We were just on our way into the casino – won't you join us?'

Evan sucked the air in through his teeth and shook his head. 'We just left the casino,' he lied, and I looked up sharply. 'I'm sure we'll catch up with you later.'

'Absolutely, absolutely,' Aleister nodded. 'Have you seen your father yet?'

My ears prickled. Evan's dad was here?

'No.'

With one word, Aleister and Selina's smiles evaporated and an unpleasant tension filled the air.

'We'll see you later, Evan,' Selina said, pulling her husband away. 'Lovely to meet you . . . you.'

She'd forgotten my name and no one, including myself, seemed to think she needed to be reminded of it. I watched and waited, Evan standing stiffly beside me until they were out of hearing distance.

'They seem nice.'

'They're full of it,' he replied, the clouds clearing from his face as they disappeared from view. 'He just managed to weasel out of some tax scandal that almost bankrupted them, and she got busted a couple of years back for bribing a college to take their kid. Spent six weeks in jail for it. I'm surprised they were invited.'

The thought of Selina in the slammer was almost too much to bear. I'd seen a lot of TV shows about prison but I figured the place they sent rich people who bribed fancy colleges in America probably wasn't the same as the place they sent the women in gritty ITV dramas. More yoga, fewer shivs.

'Sooo,' I said, attempting too sound casual and promptly failing. 'Your dad's here?'

'He is,' Evan said, shifting his gaze up and over my head. 'But I'd rather not talk about my parents if that's OK.'

But it wasn't, not really. I knew something about him that he hadn't told me, and I couldn't say I liked it. Keeping our agreed secrets was one thing but this felt an awful lot like lying.

'I don't know if this fits in with the rules,' I said, chewing on my bottom lip between sentences, all I could do was level the playing field, 'but my mum passed away ten years ago.'

Evan found my eyes and I saw his soften. He knew I knew. 'It's been twenty-one years for me,' he replied. 'I was fifteen when she died.'

'I was twenty-two,' I said. He reached out for my hand and I let him take it.

'It was an aneurysm,' he said, scratching his chin and twisting his mouth into a grimace I was all too familiar with. 'It was quick. People seem to like it when I tell them that, like they don't have to feel as bad.'

'I'm sorry,' I replied. Not because it helped, but because it was just what you said. 'My mum had cancer. She knew something was wrong but she didn't tell me or go to the doctor until it was too late to do anything.'

'I'm sorry,' he said, not because it helped, but because it was just what you said.

'Really the worst club to be a member of.' I tried a smile and almost made it.

Evan placed his other hand on top of mine, making a Fran hand sandwich. 'Are you close with your dad?' he asked.

Staring down at the little stack of fingers and thumbs between us, I shook my head. 'No. They got divorced when I was little, he already had someone else and she got pregnant, so he left. My mum didn't really like me having anything to do with him or the baby. I know what happened isn't her fault, but it's still hard. We don't really have any sort of relationship, we're Facebook friends. That's about it.'

'Wouldn't you like to have a brother or sister?' he asked.

It was such a novel concept, I didn't know quite what to say.

'I – um – it would be . . .' I started to say, stuttering my reply. 'I couldn't before because it upset my mum, and Kim is so much younger than me, it always felt weird, but yes. I suppose in theory I would like to have a sister.'

'You sound surprised,' Evan said, holding my hand a little tighter than before.

'I am,' I admitted. 'It's not something I think about often. Are you close with your dad?'

He started to laugh but somewhere along the way it turned into a sigh. 'Would you believe me if I said it was complicated?' he asked.

Squeezing his hand, I nodded, eyes fixed on his.

'I would believe anything you told me.'

From this distance, I could see his eyes weren't just brown, they were more of a deep coffee colour with flecks of honey shifting in the light. His skin glowed, and there was the tiniest nick where he'd been careless with a razor on the left side of his jaw, and I imagined him shaving in the hotel bathroom, a towel wrapped around his waist, his bare chest reflected in the mirror. Hand in hand, face to face, our eyes locked together, I held my breath and the carnival melted away.

'You!'

A loud, angry voice sliced right through the moment and I turned to see Andrew Jergens and his curly blond hair struggling against the safety bar of the Ferris wheel, his fedora askew.

'Don't you move!'

'Let's get out of here,' I said, looking back at Evan as Andrew attempted to stand up in his seat. 'I can't watch this.'

'Really?' Evan replied. 'Because there's a good chance he might fall out if he keeps this up.'

'We should go back inside.' I nodded towards the hotel. 'There must be more to do in there.'

'A million things,' he confirmed. 'But what about the bear?'

I looked at the gargantuan stuffed toy and sighed. 'I think it would be cruel to make him live in captivity,' I decided. 'He's clearly a wild animal who wants to roam free.'

'He's wearing a top hat and a monocle,' Evan pointed out.

'A very suave, sophisticated wild animal.'

A few feet away and several more up, Andrew was still rattling the safety bar on his seat and wailing at the top of his voice, and I tensed when I saw several security guards making their way over to intervene.

'Come on,' I said, yanking Evan's arm. 'I'm ready for the next part of my adventure.'

And, I thought as we started back towards the hotel, ready to get as far away as possible from the security guards, Andrew and his questions about who invited me to the ball.

CHAPTER EIGHTEEN

'Your surprise is a fortune teller?'

'A tarot card reader,' Evan corrected as we arrived at our destination. 'She's supposed to be amazing.'

'I don't know. I don't believe in this stuff,' I said, hanging back in the doorway as he bounded into the tiny dark room, lit only by several golden orbs that swung in mid-air, hanging from invisible wires fastened to the ceiling. 'I've never done it before.'

'No big deal, I'll go first,' he said as he took a seat at an empty round table. 'If she's good, you go next. If she sucks, you don't have to do it at all. Anyway, we don't know enough about each other to know whether or not she's telling the truth. For all I know, you're the mysterious princess everyone's been talking about.'

'A mysterious princess who was running around the harbour this morning trying to buy orange San Pellegrino?'

'I've never met a princess before, I don't know what they do,' he said with a shrug. 'No, wait, I guess I have. Does it still count if I met her before she was a princess?'

I arched one eyebrow. 'Depends on what you mean by "met".'

Evan laughed as a blue silk curtain rustled and a short, dark-haired woman appeared in front of us, dressed exactly as though she had googled 'fortune teller' and ordered the first thing that came up on Amazon.

'Come in, come in, child,' she said, beckoning me inside before she took her seat opposite Evan. 'Don't you know it's rude to linger in doorways.'

'She stole that from *The Little Mermaid*,' I whispered as I slunk across the room and pulled out the chair beside Evan, 'and that does not fill me with great confidence.'

She took her seat and gave me a warning look. 'My name is Ethelinda.'

'Is it?'

'Francesca,' Evan shushed me with a smile on his face. 'I'm trying to listen to *Ethelinda*.'

'Tonight, I will read your past, present, and future,' she said, flashing her green eyes at me as she pushed a deck of cards towards Evan. She was totally wearing contact lenses. 'Shuffle.'

He picked them up and did as he was told, the cards passing easily between his hands.

'Any chance we can just do the future?' he asked as he placed them back down on the table. 'I'm very familiar with my past and my present.'

'It is the three card spread,' 'Ethelinda' replied. 'You cut the deck, draw three cards, and I will tell you what they say. You first, then her.'

'Rude,' I commented quietly, crossing my arms and legs at the same time.

'Are you wearing sneakers?' Evan asked.

I looked down to see my toe poking out from underneath my skirt and hurriedly tucked it back out of sight. 'No,' I lied. 'You just worry about your cards.'

'Try to hold a question in your heart while you shuffle,' Ethel directed. 'If you can focus on your question, the answer will come more easily.'

Evan was concentrating hard. The two little lines I'd seen at the ring toss reappeared between his eyebrows as he split the deck in two, his hand hovering in the air before he chose three cards, laying them out, face down on the table in front of him. Ethel turned over the first and the lights in the room flickered.

'Oh, come on,' I groaned.

'The Knight of Wands,' she cried, pushing the card towards us. 'This card represents something in your past. A time when you were filled with energy, passion, adventure, perhaps a little impulsiveness. Does it speak to you?'

'More like shouts,' he replied hesitantly. 'Passionate adventurer is the politest euphemism for me in my twenties ever.'

'It could speak to anyone though,' I said. 'It's a fairly general statement, you could read anything into it.'

'The cards work because you draw them with your energy,' Ethel said with no small amount of drama. She was very good at the performance part of the job, even if I wasn't having a bar of the rest of it. 'I can tell you their meaning, you are the only one who can know what that means to you.'

She turned over the second card.

'The Chariot?' Evan said. 'Am I getting a new car?'

'Reversed Chariot,' she corrected. 'Upright, it suggests control, success, action, but reversed, it tells us you are stuck. You have a lack of direction, a lack of self-discipline. You are in opposition with yourself.'

'Huh,' Evan scratched his head and gave a lopsided grin that didn't make it up to his eyes.

'It fits?' I asked.

'More than I'd like,' he answered.

'Final card,' Ethel said, tapping the table as she turned it over. 'This is your future as it stands today.'

'The Two of Cups,' he picked up the card and traced a finger around the two figures in the illustration, then held it up next to my face. 'Hey, she looks kind of like you.'

'Spitting image,' I said with a smile. 'Apart from the red hair and green eyes and the fact she's a drawing.'

'Two of Cups is a beautiful card.' Ethel looked happy as she scooped up the cards and shuffled them back into a pile. 'It tells us you will find a true love, mutual attraction, and unified feeling. It's the card most people want to see in their spread.'

'Convenient,' I muttered as she slapped the deck down in front of me. 'For someone being paid to read tarot cards to rich people at a fancy party.'

'Now you,' she ordered. 'Shuffle and cut.'

'I'm sorry,' I said, awkwardly flopping my hands around like dead fish. 'I don't mean to be rude, it's just that I've never really gone in for fate and destiny and telling the future. If it was that reliable, wouldn't we all be doing it all the time?'

'Do you eat sugar?' Ethel asked.

I thought of the half a Mars Bar still in my room and nodded.

'And do you drink alcohol?'

'Um, on occasion.'

'But you know both of those things are bad for you and you do them anyway?' she tapped the cards. 'The cards guide us to the truth we already know, this is all. They can't hurt you, they cannot reveal any dark secrets you are unaware of. If I could give you a book with your future written out on every page, most would choose to look away.'

'I think she's done this before,' Evan hissed in my ear.

'Think of a question, something you really want to know,' Ethel said. 'And we shall see.'

I picked up the cards and shuffled. Even if I did believe in any of this, what would I ask? Would things work out with Stew? What did my career hold in store? Would Terry's Chocolate Oranges still be a pound each in the supermarket when I got back, or should I have bought them when I saw them on offer last week?

Ethel snapped her fingers and we both jumped.

'Cut the cards,' she directed.

I couldn't tell if it was the spooky atmosphere, the stomach full of cheese, or sitting so close to Evan that I could feel his arm brushing against mine, but when I laid my three cards down on the table, my hands were trembling. Even though I tried to keep my mind blank, my questions about work and Stew kept tumbling over each other, trying to fight their way to the front.

'First card,' she said, turning it over to show a man in armour, brandishing his weapon. 'The Knight of Swords.'

'What does that mean?' I asked, rubbing at the finger where my mother's ring should have been.

'It tells me you are ambitious,' she replied without emotion. 'You have been very goal-oriented, very driven to succeed in whatever you do.'

So, the powers that be had decided work beat romance for me. Interesting.

'I wouldn't say that's in the past,' I said. 'I am those things.'

'Oh my god, maybe you *are* a serial killer,' Evan muttered.

'Shut up,' I replied.

'Or what?'

'Well, if I'm a serial killer, I'd have thought that was quite obvious,' I said, turning back to the cards. 'What now?'

'Let's see what you drew for your present,' Ethel said, and the glowing orbs shifted from gold to silver, casting the entire room in an ethereal light.

'Another knight?' I asked, turning over the centre card.

'The Knight of Pentacles.' She held up her hand and paused for maximum effect. '*Reversed.*'

Rolling my eyes, I nudged Evan in the ribs as he began to shake with silent laughter. 'And why do I get the feeling reversed isn't a good thing?'

'Most of us prefer to be in forward motion,' she explained. 'The reversed Knight of Pentacles is not a friendly card when paired with the Knight of Swords. You have the self-discipline to succeed but you're bored or perhaps you're stuck in a routine that does not inspire you, and continuing on this path, well, shall we turn over the third card and see if it will tell us what you do next?'

'We don't need to see the third card,' I said, standing abruptly and banging my head on one of the hanging lights. It shifted from silver to indigo, making the entire room look like the big purple one in a box of Quality Street. 'I think I'm going to go.'

'You are really so afraid of the future, you don't want to see what it says on a card that, according to you, means nothing?' Ethelinda asked with a smile that was, quite frankly, more than a little bit smug.

'Thank you, this was a fun game,' I told her as I made for the exit. 'I hope you have a lovely evening.'

'Francesca, wait,' Evan called as I swished through the silk curtains that stood in for a door and barrelled out into the hallway.

'What shall we do now?' I asked, eyes darting around the dimly lit corridor. 'Do you need another drink? Let's find a bar, I think I'm ready for one now.'

'You know that was kind of weird, right?' he replied, his forehead creasing with concern. 'They're only tarot cards, it's just for fun. Why are you freaking out?'

'I'm not freaking out,' I said, squeezing my bag tightly. 'I don't like that stuff, that's all. We decide what happens to us, no one else. I've got enough people telling me what to do without Ethelinda and her bullshit cards getting in on the act.'

He let out a low whistle. 'You weren't kidding when you said you like to be in control, huh?'

I looked down at the floor and waited until I was sure of what I wanted to say.

'If you have other friends you would rather hang out with tonight, I completely understand,' I said.

Even I was surprised by the coldness in my voice but not nearly as surprised as Evan.

'What are you talking about? Francesca, come on.'

But now I'd started, I couldn't stop.

'Well, you don't really know me, do you?' I replied. 'Maybe I'm really moody. Maybe I've just had enough.'

He looked confused and hurt and I hated myself for

it. 'Where is this coming from?' he asked, lowering his voice as a group of people pushed each other through the curtains to the tarot room. 'Ten minutes ago we were having fun. What happened?'

'I don't know what you think is going to happen tonight, but I really do have a boyfriend, a fiancé actually, so this isn't going anywhere,' I told him, mentally screaming at myself to shut up as I brought down all my walls, but it was too late for that. 'You ought to go and find someone who's available. I don't think you came here to not get off with someone, did you?'

'Is that what you really want?' he asked, catching my wrist in his hand. 'Is that what you really think?'

Say yes, ordered the voice in my head. *This has gone far enough*. Without a phone or a watch, I had no idea of the time, but it certainly wasn't getting any earlier, and I had to leave at the crack of dawn. Back to *The Songbird*, back to Sheffield, and back to Stew.

Back to my real life.

I pulled my hand away and nodded.

Slowly, Evan's arm fell back by his side and his features reset themselves into those of a stranger. 'Then maybe you'd rather check out the rest of the ball on your own,' he said, stuffing his hands in his pockets. 'If that's how you feel.'

'OK then,' I said quietly. 'That's what I'll do.'

'OK then,' he repeated, and with one last wounded smile, he turned around and walked away.

And then he was gone.

CHAPTER NINETEEN

Evan had been right about at least one thing.

Without someone who knew the lie of the land, it was impossible to find your way around the Crystal Ball. Miserable, mad at myself for sending him away, and furious at him for going when I told him to, I searched for a way out, stopping to ask the other guests as I came across them, but no one else seemed to know or care how they were ever going to make their own escape.

'Because it's only an escape if you're trapped,' I muttered to myself. 'And you're only trapped if you want to get out.'

Since losing Evan, I'd found a nail salon, a mini cinema, an ice rink, and a fully functioning tattoo parlour, but I could not find a way out to save my life. I had politely declined an offer to jump the queue at the tattoo parlour, not quite sure I wanted a permanent reminder of this night, but I had accepted a bag of popcorn from the cinema attendant. It was predictably delicious.

Opening an ornate silver door, I found myself in yet another room, even smaller than Ethelinda's, but what it lacked in square footage, it made up for in absolute ridiculousness. All four walls were covered from floor to ceiling in white roses, and it was packed with glass display cases full of jewels. Rings, necklaces, earrings, watches, and, because why the fuck not, two cases dedicated entirely to tiaras.

'Anything catch your eye?' a white gloved assistant asked from behind the closest counter.

'Yes,' I replied, forgetting why I'd opened the door in the first place. As someone who still couldn't walk past a Claire's Accessories without coming over all funny, it was almost too much for my magpie heart to handle. 'All of it.'

'Would you like to try something on,' he replied. 'Perhaps something to go with the lady's gown, maybe a sapphire?'

I found myself nodding and it could have been because of the beautiful jewellery, but I was fairly certain it had more to do with the kind look on the jeweller's face. Diamonds might be a girl's best friend, but I needed a friend far more than I needed a diamond.

'We have a lovely selection of headpieces that would look stunning with your gown,' the jeweller suggested as I surreptitiously dropped my empty popcorn bag into his bin. He opened up one of the cases and produced a black velvet tray holding several bejewelled tiaras. 'What do you think?'

'This one?' I said, pointing at the closest one.

'You have an excellent eye.' He held up the delicate silver-toned circle, curved to fit the crown of the head, and studded with diamonds and pearls. 'A platinum band with fourteen natural, saltwater pearls and five carats of white diamonds.'

He crossed from behind the counter and pushed it carefully into place, the band disappearing into my hair as he fastened it in with unseen clips, leaving the diamonds and pearls sparkling in the light as though they were part of me.

'Well, I don't hate this,' I said, staring in wonder at my reflection in the mirror. Maybe if I mortgaged the house, sold my car, maxed out mine *and* Stew's credit cards, and pledged the soul of my firstborn child, perhaps, perhaps then I'd have enough to give him a down payment.

'How about something in a choker, to set off the neckline of the dress?' the jeweller suggested.

Mirror Fran gazed back at me, all made up, perfect hair, perfect dress, and now with added diamonds. I looked as good as I could ever remember looking, like someone who belonged at the Crystal Ball, rather than a stalled thirty-two-year-old with no job prospects, who lived in a damp nana museum with someone who may or may not be shagging his ex-girlfriend. It was such a shame she wasn't real.

'How about a statement ring,' the jeweller said, eyeing my bare fingers. 'What do you think about this?'

He held up a knuckleduster of a ruby set in a giant hunk of gold that even Thanos would written off as a bit much.

'Do you have anything a bit more understated?' I asked.

'I know just the thing,' he said, reaching for a small black velvet tray at the back of the closest cabinet and pushing it across the counter towards me.

'Vintage Cartier,' he said with hushed reverence. 'One of my favourite pieces.'

It was a beautiful sapphire and diamond ring that looked delicate and strong at the same time. So far removed from my mum's plain wedding band or Nana Beryl's diamond flower engagement ring.

'Art Deco, platinum-mounted, claw-set sapphire with baguette-cut diamonds on the halo. A real forever piece, you must try it.'

But I couldn't.

'It really is stunning,' I said, holding my hands against my chest, away from the ring. 'But I can't.'

He was right, it was a forever piece, and seeing it brought my reality rushing back. This was not my forever. It wasn't even my tomorrow.

'At last,' a voice said as the door creaked open behind me. 'I've been looking for you.'

I spun around, hoping against hope to see Evan's dark hair and dark eyes, but instead I found a bleary-eyed mess of blond curls and crooked fedora glaring back at me and I was so disappointed I could taste it.

'Perfect timing,' I groaned as he stumbled into the room.

'*I said* I've been looking for you,' Andrew said, slurring his words. 'And here you are.'

'I haven't been hiding,' I replied, trying to work out how to get past him and out of the door without kicking him in the balls. Not that I wasn't keeping that option in my back pocket, just in case.

'Perhaps you should have been,' he replied with an unpleasant leer. 'Because I know your secret, I know who you are.'

The little room filled with sparkling jewels was far too small for the three of us.

'I know who you are,' he repeated gleefully. 'So you can stop lying.'

'No, you don't,' I replied, squeezing my cushion cover clutch.

'I think the lady would like to leave,' the jeweller offered, sidling around the counter to remove the necklace.

'No!' Andrew barked. 'She's not going anywhere until she admits it or I'm going to tell everyone.'

'Tell whoever you want,' I said. 'I'm done with the ball so it doesn't matter. Actually, it might get me out even quicker, I've still got no idea where the exit is. *Please* tell me, someone, I'm begging you.'

'You,' he replied, pointing at me with an unsteady finger, 'are the secret princess.'

He stood in the middle of the room, wobbling like the world's saddest Weeble with an angry, pathetic look on his face, and in spite of everything, I couldn't help but laugh.

'You think I'm a princess?' I reached up to the tiara. 'Thank you so much,' I said to the jeweller, who calmly accepted it back as I pulled it out of my hair.

'I know you are,' Andrew declared. 'No one's heard of you, no one recognizes you, there's no Francesca Anderson on the guest list, and no one else would dare speak to me the way you did earlier. No one ever has before.'

'Honestly, I find that very hard to believe,' I said, dancing around him to get closer to the exit. 'You must have met at least one woman?'

'Don't go!' he yelled as the jeweller pulled open the door and I darted outside. 'Your Royal Highness, wait!'

I heard the door slam shut, but I did not turn to look

back. With my head down, I marched up the corridor, determined to find my way back to my room.

The first time I saw the Crystal Ballroom, it took my breath away. This time, I was just relieved: it was the place I'd come in, it was the place I'd get out, the literal light at the end of the tunnel.

The music was louder and the lights were lower, the string quartet had been replaced by a DJ, and the dance floor was starting to see some really quite impressive business. All around the edges of the room, people were sitting at big circular tables, craning their necks to continue their conversations around the giant white rose centrepieces. Aerialists swung from silks, pouring champagne straight into people's empty glasses, and every sound I could hear was a happy one. I moved across the room, trying to memorize every moment. Every face was smiling, every voice was laughing, and for just one moment, I almost forgot how desperate I'd been to leave.

A few feet way, beside a woman in a silver leotard who was painting glitter tattoos on to people's faces, my eyes landed on a face I recognized. It was the woman I'd talked to in the toilets, the one who said she knew Evan. Only I couldn't help but notice she didn't look nearly as happy as she had before. She was twisting her hands, squeezing her fingers, and a slow, single tear cut a neat path through the makeup on her left cheek.

'Feel free to tell me to piss off,' I said, sidling over and pulling a tissue out of my cushion cover. 'But are you OK?'

She looked at me, then at my tissue, before reaching

a hand to her face and touching the tear in surprise. She hadn't even realized she was crying.

'Aw shit,' she muttered, turning her back on the party as she took the tissue and pressed it delicately to her face. 'I'm such a mess.'

'Not at all,' I said. 'You look amazing. I just noticed you didn't look especially happy, that's all.'

'You could say that,' she dabbed underneath her eyes without disturbing her perfect makeup, and then handed me back the used tissue. Huh. Not quite knowing what else to do, I took it, folded it up, and dropped it in a plant pot behind me.

'You don't happen to have a gun in that bag, do you?' she asked.

'Couldn't find one small enough,' I replied. 'Silly question, but are you OK?'

'My friend just posted an Instagram story of my boyfriend making out with some other woman.' She nodded at a group of people rubbing up against each other on the dance floor. 'He's the one in the white tux, and I'm pretty sure it was the girl in the red dress behind him.'

'Seriously, they were so clear about no phones,' I sighed, before I spotted fresh tears brewing in her eyes. 'I'm sorry, there's nothing I can say that's going to make this better. Are you sure you saw what you saw?'

She nodded glumly. 'I screengrabbed it. For evidence. Because I'm going to kill him.'

'Can you not psychologically destroy him instead?' I offered. 'Murder is very messy.'

'Yeah, and I don't want to ruin this dress.' She pulled herself upright and tossed her head, showering her shoulders with golden glitter from her hair. 'Fuck it,

244

you're right. I'm not going to let him ruin my night, this is the Crystal Ball, for Chrissakes. So what if he walked for Prada and has a masters in biochemistry from Cambridge?'

'Ten a penny,' I agreed. 'What do you do?'

'I'm CEO and founder of a magnetic false lash company and I invest in woman-founded start-ups that disrupt the beauty industry.'

'Right,' I replied, shuffling my trainer-clad feet beneath my skirt. 'Sounds fun.'

Her face transformed, the worn-down worries washing away to reveal a brilliant smile. 'I guess it's better that I found out what a dog he is sooner rather than later. I'm Orlander by the way.' She ran a finger under the corners of each eye, straightening out her eyeliner. 'You're the girl who *isn't* here with Evan.'

My shoulders sank at the mere mention of his name. 'I was only talking to him. And my name's Francesca.'

'You were *talking* to him?' Her eyes bugged out of her head as though I'd said something completely perverse. 'Wow. That is not what he's best known for.' She added a wink just in case I hadn't grasped her incredibly obvious hints. 'I'd better go.' She fluffed out her hair and reset her smile. 'Thanks for the pep talk.'

It was really more of a pep listen, but I still gave her a fist pump of solidarity and watched as she strode across the dance floor to confront the man in the white tux, suddenly struck with a memory from out of nowhere.

Instead of standing at the side of the dancefloor at the world's most exclusive party, I was reliving the exact moment I found out Stew had cheated on me. We were getting ready for bed, Stew in his boxers and me in the tattered old PJs I threw out the next day. His phone, charging on my bedside table because he'd lost his cable again, lit up with a photo of a woman I didn't recognize in a pose I did not care to see. I remembered it all so clearly. He saw my face, he read the text, then he apologized, made vague, remorseful noises, swore it was a one-time thing that would never happen again, and that was that.

I didn't say a single word.

Partly because I was so shocked, I didn't know what to say, and partly because I'd been waiting for him to cheat on me ever since we met. At least once a week, Mum had gone out of her way to tell me that all men lie and all men leave. I'd expected it of him. But Stew only proved Mum half right, He could have left, but he didn't, and at the time, I was so grateful.

When he should have begged my forgiveness, he acted as though he was doing me a favour, and I let him. Every day since, I'd been giving away tiny little pieces of myself just to hold on to what I had. But was it worth it? And what would happen when there were no more pieces left to give?

I could have packed a bag and walked out; instead I accepted his excuses, waited for Stew to fall asleep, then locked myself in the bathroom to sob my heart out. Orlander was already tearing White Tux Man a new one in front of an entire ballroom full of people. She wasn't ashamed. She didn't blame herself. She wasn't afraid.

With one last look around the ballroom, I smiled and tried to tie a bow around all my good memories of the ball, to keep them safe for Jess. It was time to make a graceful exit.

'There you are!'

With his tie hanging loose around his neck and his shirt poking out of his unzipped fly, Andrew splashed an entire glass of champagne in my general direction.

'Your majesty.'

My stomach lurched at the damp spot on my skirt as he stooped forward into a low bow before promptly toppling forward onto the floor, his face landing next to my feet. Dazed, he rolled up onto his hands and knees and stared at the broken glass, somehow still in his hand.

It was definitely time to leave.

'No!' he yelled from the floor as I turned around and walked away, searching for the gap in the wall panels where I'd snuck in. 'Stop, I want to talk to you.'

'No.'

'You must.'

'I'm not going to do what you tell me just because you own half of Facebook,' I replied as he attempted to stand up very, very slowly.

'Don't be ridiculous,' he slurred. 'I sold my shares in Facebook years ago.'

'Good for you,' I said, nervously noticing how many people had started to stare. 'But now I've really got to go.'

'I said stop!'

I winced at the unholy screech of a man who was not used to having to repeat himself all that often. Before I could make my escape, he was at my side.

'I'm sorry,' I said. 'But I've got somewhere else I need to be.'

'Where?'

'Literally anywhere.' Looking past Andrew along the edge of the room, I saw the wall hangings flutter as a

247

man in a waiter's uniform slipped into the ballroom. 'Please leave me alone,' I begged. 'I'm not the princess, I'm a thirty-two-year-old temp from Sheffield who really just wants to go back to her room.'

'Whoever you are,' he whispered, leaping in front of me as his glassy eyes misted over. 'I've been searching for you all my life.'

It all made sense now, it was a pheromone thing, I was irresistible to billionaires. It was the only logical explanation given I'd never exactly had to fight men off in the real world.

'Oh, you've got to be kidding me,' I groaned as he dropped awkwardly to one knee.

'You're a rebel, I love it,' Andrew said, his breath absolutely toxic. 'Marry me.'

He thrust out his arms and promptly fell over again.

Before he could find his way to his feet, I turned on my well-cushioned heel and took off at a sprint without a single care as to who might be watching. Let them watch, let them talk, let them take photos on their illegal phones, all I wanted was to get out of there. Andrew was still yelling when I reached the break in the curtains and, without looking back, I sliced through the fabric and hurled myself on to the other side.

It was pitch black, just like before, a slender shaft of light dancing up and down in the dark as the curtains fluttered closed behind me. Feeling my way around the darkness, I tried to remember my route through the storeroom, but not a single thing was in the same place I'd found it a few hours earlier. Everything had changed.

Moving slowly but purposefully across the floor I walked face first into something big, hard and invisible.

'Don't bleed on the dress, don't bleed on the dress,' I whispered with watery eyes, pinching my nose with one hand and feeling my way around the large, round obstacle with the other. Behind me, the curtains rustled and Andrew clattered across the room with a drunk man's interpretation of stealth.

'Hello? Princess?'

'Fuck off,' I whispered in response.

'I can hear you,' he sang, before he let out a high-pitched giggle. 'This is a fun game. Do you want me to come and find you?'

'No, I want you to go away,' I replied silently. The man would take breathing as a come on.

Still skirting around the giant round object, my hand found what felt like a handle, and the handle was attached to a door. For want of a better option, I opened it, climbed inside, and ducked down. The floor was covered in what felt like bits of shredded paper that rustled against my dress, and I held my breath, attempting to stay as still and silent as possible.

'Princess?' he called, so close I could smell him. Andrew's scent was not warm or spicy or expensive. He reeked, like someone who had drunk too much and possibly pissed on his own shoes.

'Excuse me, sir, you can't be in here.' A new voice cut through the darkness and a slice of blinding light illuminated the storeroom for just a second.

'I'm looking for someone, she came in here!' Andrew protested as his skittering footsteps moved further and further away from my hiding place.

'This area is off limits for safety reasons,' another voice said. 'We'll redirect your friend if we find them.'

'What do you think you're doing? I'm going, I'm going,

get your hands off me. Say, you chaps don't know anyone who's carrying, do you?'

The curtains flickered open again and Andrew's voice was gone. My shoulders sagged with relief as I pushed myself up on my knees. Now all I had to do was climb back out from my hiding spot in the dark without breaking my neck. Easier said than done. Clinging to the rounded walls, I felt for the door, but before I could make my escape, the entire thing moved.

'Be bloody careful!' One of the men who had turfed Andrew out of the storeroom bellowed below me. 'Are you even pulling on your side?'

'Are *you* pulling on *your* side?' replied the other. 'Because it doesn't feel like it. I don't remember it being this heavy earlier.'

'And I don't remember you being such a lazy bastard. When I say pull, pull.'

My hiding place shifted again, upwards this time, swirling around in the air and knocking me onto my backside. I braced myself, clambering on all fours as I rose onwards and upwards, swinging back and forth in the darkness.

'Hello?' I called, patting the walls for the door. Why was there no handle on the inside? What had I climbed into? This was not good. Not good at all. 'Can you hear me?'

But they couldn't. Outside, an orchestra was blasting a bold interpretation of 'Don't Stop' by Fleetwood Mac, the ambitious horn section drowning out my pitiful cries.

'Right, that's high enough. On the count of three, pull your lever. One . . . two . . .'

'Hello!' I shouted louder, scooping the shredded paper

out of the way to bang on the floor. 'Help! There's someone in here!'

But this wasn't a toilet cubicle besieged by drunk girls in a club, and the fact I didn't know what it was didn't help in the slightest. No one could hear me.

'THREE.'

The pod shot up twenty feet in the air then flew forwards, throwing me back against the wall and careening towards the curtains at breakneck speed.

CHAPTER TWENTY

'This is it!' I wailed as I zoomed towards my untimely death. 'This is the end!'

But it was not the end.

It was only the beginning of my complete and utter humiliation.

'Oh my god,' I gasped, peeking through my fingers as the reality of my situation slowly dawned on me. 'I should have let them throw me off the terrace.'

I was suspended above the ballroom in a transparent fibreglass 'crystal' ball, with confetti up to my ankles, sailing around the ballroom while the orchestra played below. The guests applauded, rapturously at first, but it soon petered out to a confused patter as those sober enough to catch on realized something was amiss. I looked down at the sea of puzzled faces below and tucked my skirts securely between my legs as confetti flew out of tiny slots drilled in the floor of the ball. Just because I was moments away from crashing out of the sky and falling to my certain death didn't mean everyone needed to see my knickers. Correction, Rachel's knickers.

The ball swung left and I lurched with it, my face pressed against the see-through side. Sitting at the bar, glass of whisky in front of him, was Evan. His eyes widened and his jaw dropped, and I waved weakly as I passed overhead.

It was impossible to know what would happen next, but I was fairly sure I wasn't going to like it. Was the ball going to explode? Crash to the ground? Were they expecting me to leap out like a stripper from a birthday cake? Because I was definitely not wearing the correct pants for that sort of thing and, truth be told, I did not have the moves.

Slowly but surely, the ball began to descend towards the floor as the orchestra went into overdrive and everyone in the ballroom began to cheer and yell and scream. I, for a none-too-brief moment, began to panic. Had I got myself in a Wicker Man situation? Were they going to drag me out and offer me up as a sacrifice to their god, Jeff Bezos? I couldn't decide which would be worse, being torn limb from limb by a bunch of maniacal billionaires or having to get out, stand up, and walk out of the room on my own two feet. At least a sacrificial death would be quick.

As the music and the screaming grew louder, I hung on to the edges of my crystal ball as it moved towards the stage. The floor was only a few feet away, but there would be no easy escape. There were people everywhere, I was completely surrounded. With the ball rocking from side to side, I attempted to kick open the side door. Maybe if I slithered to the ground like a very fancily dressed snake and attempted to roll all the way out of the ball, people would be so confused, they wouldn't try to stop me. But it was no use. I was still about ten feet off the floor.

And then, somehow, things got even worse.

A large central section of floor of the ball gave way and the rest of the confetti billowed out in a giant cloud of glittery excitement. People bloody loved confetti. The crowd went wild and, without warning, the ball dropped three feet in two seconds.

'Fuck!' I screamed, losing my footing and sliding towards the gaping hole in the floor. I clung on to the sides, my fingers slipping against the fibreglass and my feet already poking through the floor.

'Francesca!' Evan waved both arms from the side of the stage. 'What are you doing?'

'What does it look like I'm doing?' I shouted back over the music, a now very intense and string-heavy rendition of 'Dynamite' that I did not appreciate in the slightest.

The ball was still for a moment, hovering six or seven feet above the stage, and I realized it was now or never. I had to jump.

'Wait!' Evan yelled as I inched over the edge.

I looked up at the ceiling as the orchestra roared to a crescendo, and then the entire ballroom was filled with yet more sparkling confetti. Glitter canons exploded above my head and, out of the corner of my eye, I saw Evan climb onto the stage and hold his arms out underneath me. What had seemed somewhat possible a moment ago now looked like a terribly long way to fall.

'Jump!'

'I was going to,' I replied, trying to scramble back into the ball as it swung back and forth. 'But now I don't know if it's a very good idea!'

'You can do it,' he shouted. 'I'll catch you, I promise.'

With all the grace of a voted-out-in-week-one-*Strictly*-contestant, I let go of the crystal ball and fell through the air, into Evan's arms. Which could have been an incredibly romantic moment, had he not immediately crumpled to the ground like a soggy paper bag. I rolled off him and stared up at the crystal ball as it swung back and forth above us.

'That went better in my head,' Evan grunted, sitting up and patting himself down for injuries. As far as I could tell, the worst of my damage was to my pride.

'Do you think people saw?' I asked, still flat on my back beside him.

'You literally just fell out of a crystal ball in the sky,' he replied. 'Yes, I think they saw.'

'Please could you go and find Andrew and ask if he'd still like to throw me off the terrace?'

'Or,' Evan sat up and held out his hand, confetti still falling from the ceiling while people spun around in it like snow. 'We could dance.'

'Terrace it is,' I replied with determination.

'Come on,' he said, rolling over to the edge of the stage and hopping down to the floor. 'It'll be the best way to blend in.'

'Clearly, you've never seen me dance,' I said. 'I just want to get out of here.'

Nodding in agreement, he held out his hand to me and, as the falling confetti began to slow down and our cover thinned out, I slid over to the edge of the stage on my backside and let him help me down to the floor. My face burned as we were sucked into the crowd, my legs barely keeping me upright, but then he grabbed hold of my hand and I knew I would make it out in one piece.

*

We emerged onto the terrace, back where we started. It was practically deserted now, with everyone drawn into the ballroom by the shiny things falling from the sky.

'My whole plan for tonight was to get in, get out, keep a low profile, and eat as much as humanly possible,' I said, sinking into an empty seat at an abandoned table. 'I think it's safe to say I've failed.'

'Yes, but you've failed spectacularly,' Evan pointed out. 'And there's still so much more time to eat. It isn't even midnight yet.'

I still couldn't quite believe he was real, the full lips, the dark eyes, the wavy hair, but at the same time, I felt like I'd known him all my life. And, more importantly, I felt as though he knew me.

'I'm sorry about earlier,' I said. 'I didn't mean any of it.'

'I'm not going to pretend I understand what happened,' he said, taking the seat next to mine. 'But if you want to tell me, I'd like to try.'

'Actually, I'm lying.' I rolled my head back and rubbed my fingers against my temples. 'I meant all of it, I just didn't do a very good job of articulating it. I *do* have a boyfriend and I *don't* want you to waste your night on me when you could be, you know, enjoying yourself.'

Evan interlaced his fingers and clasped his hands together, sliding his forearms across the table. 'This might come as a shock but I don't have to get laid to have a good night.'

'Good to know,' I replied primly, eyes on the sky and not sure if I was more embarrassed or disappointed. 'I suppose the truth is I don't understand why you're wasting your time with me.'

256

'Because the moment I saw you standing on this terrace, I felt like my entire life had been leading to that moment?'

I dropped my head and saw a perfectly serious expression on his face.

'Oh,' I said. 'I see.'

He shrugged and smiled. 'You asked for the truth,' he said. 'Now can I ask you something?'

'Anything.'

'Who invited you to the Ball?'

It was a perfectly straightforward question that should have been very easy to answer.

'Um,' I fished around for an appropriate response, but came up with nothing but blanks. 'Well, I . . . you want to know who invited me?'

'You don't have an invitation,' he said, leaning forward across the table and lowering his voice. 'You are a gatecrasher.'

'Me? What a ridiculous thing to say!' I exclaimed, looking over my shoulder for the security guards that had to be on to me by now. 'I absolutely am not, I have an invitation. I was on the guest list. I was on, um, Clive Carden's guest list!'

He leaned back in his chair, shaking his head. 'I know that's not true.'

The jig was up.

'OK, I might not have been invited in the traditional sense,' I admitted, the relief of saying it out loud coursing through my veins. 'But I am a guest at the hotel. I'm supposed to be upstairs, in my room, out of the way.'

I gave my arms a brisk rub. Even with the heat lamps at full blast, it was officially cold now. Evan shrugged off his jacket and draped it over my shoulders. I accepted it silently, giving him a grateful glance as I wrapped it around my body, still warm, like a hug.

'I almost bailed on the whole thing.' He sounded confused and his eyes were a little dazed and I began to worry about a delayed concussion. 'Right up until the moment I left my room, I was pretty sure I was going to skip it. How crazy is that? We could have been under the same roof for an entire evening and never met.'

The thought of it took my breath away.

'Why didn't you want to come?' I asked. My senses were swimming in the faint traces of Evan's aftershave that lingered on his jacket and it was hard to concentrate. 'Everyone I've ever met seems convinced this is the greatest party in the history of the universe.'

He shifted in his chair, his body moving closer by an almost imperceptible degree. Imperceptible to anyone except me. 'To the rest of the world it is, but for me, it's kind of an obligation. And no one really enjoys doing something when they have to do it, right?'

'True enough,' I agreed. 'How is this an obligation?'

Evan turned his head towards me, that half-smile on his face again. 'Let's make a deal. I'll answer your question if you'll answer one of mine.'

'I just played a game of truth or dare and it went very badly,' I told him, shaking my head, 'I don't know if I'm ready for any more truths.'

'You can ask the first question?' he offered.

I sighed as I weighed up my options. It wasn't as though I didn't have questions I'd like answered but the thought of ruining my fantasy evening with something as silly as reality wasn't especially inviting. And yet, just as it always did, my curiosity trumped my common sense.

'Tell me why you had to come tonight?' I asked. 'What's the obligation?'

He breathed in, then exhaled through pursed lips, long and slow. 'It's a family thing,' he said. 'I don't get on so great with my family, but I'm the eldest and my attendance is expected.'

'You're the eldest?' I smiled at the thought of big brother Evan surrounded by mini mes.

'When Mom died, Dad got remarried pretty much right away,' he said with a nod. 'I think it was his way of avoiding the grief but it wasn't that simple for me. Before I had time to process any of it, I was trying to graduate high school with all these baby step-siblings running around.'

'That must have been tough,' I said gently. 'As if being a teenager isn't hard enough already.'

His eyebrows flickered upwards in agreement.

'It wasn't easy but my first stepmom was so much better than the second. And the third. The fourth one was OK.'

'How many have there been?' I asked as he laughed out loud at the look on my face.

'My dad is New York's version of Henry the Eighth,' Evan replied, his laughter turning slightly bitter. 'Only it goes died, divorced, annulled, divorced. I'm expecting a beheading announcement any day now.'

'Must make Christmas a bit awkward round your house,' I said, the weight of his phone and his wallet weighing down the pockets of his jacket as I pulled it around me to keep out the wind.

'I go away for Christmas. Far, far away. Usually right after the ball. Get through Thanksgiving, show up tonight, then disappear for a month. I'm not missed.'

259

I looked up and saw Evan's profile picked out in starlight. Our lives were very different, but maybe, as people, we were more similar than I'd thought possible.

'You're very easy to talk to, did you know that?' he said.

'It's been said,' I replied lightly. 'I don't know. I think a lot of people feel like they aren't being heard, so instead of really listening to what the other person is saying, they just wait for their turn to speak and continue the cycle. Life is so hard and we don't make it any easier on each other. That's my theory, anyway.'

'I have a theory on life too,' Evan said, unfastening one of his cufflinks and turning it over and over in his fingers. 'I think life is like a jigsaw puzzle.'

'Makes a change from a box of chocolates,' I said. 'Go on, wow me with your theory.'

One corner of his mouth turned up in a half-smile. 'Think about it. The puzzle starts out as one of those chunky, easy things with half a dozen pieces. Maybe Mom helps a little, but most of the time we can put it together all by ourselves and we're like, "Oh shit! It's a cow!" and everyone claps.'

'I definitely had that jigsaw,' I said, watching his fingers manipulate the silver cufflink. Or was it platinum? As if I'd know the difference. 'But I'm from Yorkshire, so no one clapped.'

Evan grinned and carried on with his theory.

'As we get older, the puzzle gets more complicated; it has more pieces, it's not so obvious what it's going to be when it's complete. Some people come into our lives and they help with the puzzle, they see parts we hadn't figured out yet, and other people come in and make it more complicated. They hide pieces from you or they mess up the parts you've already put together.'

'Maybe I should have been doing jigsaws instead of baking all that bloody banana bread,' I muttered, my stomach grumbling.

'What I'm trying to say,' Evan slipped the cufflink back into his shirt and flipped it closed, 'is that even when you think someone has totally fucked up your puzzle, once they're gone and you look at the mess they made, maybe you see something you missed before.'

He really had spent a lot of time thinking about this. Possibly too much time, it was hard to say.

'What if you're so used to helping someone with their jigsaw, you forget to work on your own?' I asked, sliding my hands inside the sleeves of his jacket.

Evan took my cold hands in his warm ones, both of us holding our breath as the heat from his skin seeped into mine. 'You have to move on from those people,' he said. 'Or you'll never find out what your finished puzzle is supposed to be.'

I looked up at the stars, wondering how many were still burning and how many had already imploded into nothingness. And I wondered how many people had sat in this same spot, looking up at the same sky, at the same stars. Then I looked at Evan, and I wondered what would happen if I kissed him.

'We should go,' he said, shooting out of his chair unexpectedly. 'Come on.'

'Why?' I asked as I followed his lead. 'Where?'

'I think the gentlemen by the door might be looking for you,' he replied, sliding his arm around me and steering me away from the main doors. Over my shoulder I saw three security guards with their telltale black suits and ties, speaking into hidden microphones and heading in our direction.

'Just keep walking,' Evan instructed without looking back. 'I know a place.'

I had to skip every third step to keep up with him until we stopped at the edge of the terrace, by a narrow gap between the balustrade and the wall. I peered over the edge and saw nothing.

'Do you trust me?' Evan asked, nodding down into the abyss.

'Absolutely not,' I answered. 'You've got to be kidding?'

'On the count of three,' he said with a grin. 'One, two, three.'

Then he jumped.

And so did I.

CHAPTER TWENTY-ONE

'Why would someone leave a pile of mattresses outside a hotel?' I asked as the air returned back to my lungs a long moment later. We were lying side by side, loud confused voices above us in the dark.

'They're not mattresses,' Evan said. 'They're crash mats. Every year they have acrobats perform on the terrace after the musical act, I watched them put them out this afternoon.'

A pale light from the lower level rooms of the hotel spilled out of narrow windows, casting a milky glow over everything and picking out the high points of his face, his nose, his chin, his sculpted lips. I raised my hands in front of me and found his chest, his heart beating beneath my palms. If I were to lean forward, just a couple of inches, our lips would be touching. Just the thought of it made me dizzy. Closing my eyes, I parted my lips and—

'They won't find us down here,' he declared, pulling away from me and bouncing off the crash mat onto his feet. 'You're safe for now.'

I stared after him for a moment before coming to my senses. What was I thinking?

'Big fan of acrobats?' I asked as I joined him on the grass, patting down my dress and checking the silver bow hadn't worked its way undone. The last thing I needed right now was to start flashing him.

'Not really. But last year I got so incredibly shitfaced, I fell off the edge of the terrace and that's how I discovered these were here.'

'So, what you're saying is, we like these crash mats,' I said, looking at them with new-found appreciation. 'Evan, that's terrifying.'

'And that's why I don't drink like that any more,' he said, as though it was nothing. 'Hey, you want to see something cool?'

I nodded, very much hoping the Crystal Ball committee had hired a secret jacket potato van and hidden it away in the undergrowth. I was starving.

'The ball takes over the whole bottom two floors of the hotel,' Evan explained as we made our way carefully through the grounds, my skirts swishing against the damp grass. The hotel on our right and huge, towering hedges blocked the view of whatever was on the left. 'Plus there's all the tents and marquees, and there's the carnival around the back, but this is my favourite part of the hotel.'

He led me through an archway cut into the hedge, so small, you wouldn't have seen it in the dark unless you knew where to look for it. On the other side was a clearing, lined by pretty flowering trees. They had sweeping leaves that brushed the top of a small gazebo, which looked out over the hills of Panarea before fading out into the ocean, sky and sea blending together and rolling out into infinity.

'It's beautiful,' I whispered, afraid to raise my voice and ruin the moment. 'How did you know it was here?'

'It's kind of a secret spot,' Evan replied. 'You can only get to it through the hotel kitchens.'

'Or by throwing yourself off the edge of the terrace,' I suggested.

It was so quiet, I could hear myself breathing, and so dark that when I looked up, there were more stars shining above me than I'd ever seen in my life.

I breathed in deeply. 'Wait, did you say kitchens?'

He nodded. 'Yeah, they're right behind us.'

My stomach complained again, loudly. 'Do you think it would be weird if we went in and made ourselves a sandwich?'

'Yes,' Evan replied, 'but I'm prepared to take that chance. Lemme go see what they have.'

'I can go,' I offered automatically.

But he was already jogging back towards the building. 'Stay there,' he called back. 'Check in on your puzzle.'

I watched him go until he disappeared completely, reeling from how close I'd come to kissing him two minutes earlier. Pulling a soft, grey blanket from a nearby pile, I settled onto a day bed and waited for someone to do something for me. Something else I wasn't used to. The bed was big and plush and hidden heaters sensed my presence, bathing the entire bed in a warm haze, and if it weren't for the fact I would eventually need a wee, there was a good chance I would have nailed my feet to the floor. I was in heaven.

Resting against a stack of cushions, I searched the sky for constellations I used to know, thinking about Evan's jigsaw theory. It was in my nature to help, I liked to be useful, but I also knew that solving other people's problems meant I didn't have to think about my own. I'd put years into Stew's jigsaw, while mine was still in the box, barely even looked at. I twisted the fringe on the edge of the blanket around my finger until it was so tight it hurt. There was a difference between being helpful and making yourself indispensable. The more I did for Stew, the more likely he was to stay. The more he relied on me, the fewer reasons he had to leave. A big fat tear ran down my cheek and I swiped it away in anger. I was killing myself to keep something because I was afraid to lose it, but I hadn't even stopped to think whether or not I really wanted it any more.

'I'm back!' Evan reappeared with an enormous tray full of food in his arms. 'They had a bunch of stuff, sandwiches, sliders, I got you more cheese, obviously, and shit, Francesca, what's wrong? What happened?'

He froze at the foot of the day bed, a look of genuine concern on his face.

'Nothing,' I insisted, rubbing my face and smiling manically. 'This looks fantastic.'

He set the tray down on the bottom of the bed and sat down next to me. 'You look like you just found out eating too much cheese could kill you. Which it can, but that's a problem for your future cardiologist, so what's wrong?'

'I was thinking about what you said,' I replied, reaching out for a hunk of artery-clogging Cheddar. 'About the jigsaws.'

'Francesca, no.' Evan retrieved a bottle of champagne from the tray and popped the cork without ceremony. He filled two plastic cups and I accepted mine without

266

protest. 'It's just a thing to say, I don't know what I'm talking about. Honestly, ask literally anyone here, they'll tell you that.'

I suspected Orlander and her friends might consider him an expert in at least one thing, but thinking about that would do nothing to help me in the moment.

'No, you were right,' I told him. 'And I've done it to myself, it's no one's fault but my own. You should be a psychologist or something.'

'Can I use you as a reference?' he asked. 'I'm hoping to finish my masters by the end of next year and it's not going to be easy to find clients.'

I spluttered into my cup, spraying champagne all over myself. Still too soon. 'That's what you do? You're a psychologist?'

He nodded. 'Almost. I figured I'd spent enough money on therapy over the last twenty years, it would actually work out cheaper if I went back to school and learned about this stuff myself,' he said. 'Working out why people do the things that they do is the most fascinating subject to me.'

Stuffing a macaron in my mouth, I carried on staring at him with wide eyes. Better to fill my mouth with food than words when I had no idea what to say.

'The idea that I might actually be able to help someone somewhere down the line is kind of appealing as well,' he added. 'Gotta try to work on that karmic balance, you know?'

'Not the job I would have guessed,' I admitted. 'But I like it for you.'

'What would you have guessed?'

'Racing car driver, super spy, or international playboy.'

'I will keep those in mind if the psychology thing

267

doesn't pan out,' he replied. 'I do have a lot of frequent flyer miles to use.'

'What did you do before this?' I asked. 'Before you went back to school, I mean.'

'Uh, I was a . . . ' He stopped, reset and started again. 'I worked for my dad's company.'

'Doing what?'

He leaned across the tray, picked up a brownie, and ate the whole thing in one bite. I sat, quietly waiting, while he chewed.

'It didn't bring out the best in me,' he said, washing down the mouthful with a sip of champagne. 'Took me far too long to realize the job was turning me into someone I didn't like very much.'

'Who?'

'My dad.'

He paused, scratched his chin, then sighed heavily. 'He's the American dream, according to most people. Started out with nothing, worked his way up, built an empire, and now he wants to know he can leave it in safe hands. But it's complicated. I don't think my hands are the safest.'

'You don't want the same things he wants?' I guessed.

'Oh, I absolutely want them, but I don't want to make the same sacrifices he has made to get them,' Evan said sadly. 'My dad made a lot of choices to get where he is today that I couldn't live with. Not easily at least. I know I only have the opportunities I do because he worked so hard to give them to me, but he talks like he wants a clone, not a son. It was always made very clear, I would go to college, join the business, and when he was satisfied that I could pick up where he left off, my dad would retire and hand the reins over to me.

But I've seen what it takes to do what he does, what kind of person you have to be behind closed doors, and I don't want it. I love my dad, but I don't want to be him. The thought that I might even be like him, deep down, it scares me.'

I rested my hand lightly on his leg as he shook his head. 'That makes sense to me. I loved my mum, but I'm terrified of turning into her.'

The moment the words were out of my mouth, I wanted to take them back. I clapped one hand over my mouth to stop anything else from slipping out.

'Do you want to tell me why?' he asked gently.

'Ever since she died, people always go on about how nice she was,' I said in a voice barely above a whisper. 'But I'm not sure that's how I would describe her.'

'People don't rush to insult the dead,' he replied.

'They didn't know her like I did. She definitely wasn't nice,' I said with a wry smile, knowing she would have hated to have been described that way. 'She was funny and clever and fiercely loyal. She worked harder than anyone I've ever met. But after my dad left, she was just . . .'

I trailed off for a moment and Evan waited patiently, still stroking my wrist, his full attention on me.

'She was bitter,' I said. 'Then she got ill and then she died. My mum wasn't a bad person, but she wasn't a happy person either. When people die, you want to be able to say they lived a good life, but what if it wasn't exactly a fairy tale? Sometimes I hear myself and I sound just like her and I am so scared of ending up bitter, alone and miserable, and not knowing how to change that.'

My chest sank as I exhaled, an impossible weight lifting from around my shoulders but somehow dragging me down at the same time. It was a release and a betrayal, something I'd never said out loud before. But if you couldn't tell the truth to a devastatingly handsome stranger you were never going to see ever again, who could you tell the truth to? A tear slid down my cheek and this time I didn't try to wipe it away.

'I hardly ever talk about her,' I said. 'I think about her all the time, but I never, ever talk about her. Am I crazy? Is that just me?'

Evan shook his head.

'People always avoid mentioning my mom, like they're afraid it might upset me when I would love to hear their stories about her. After my mom died, I was really angry. Like, smash up my dad's car, punch out a window, almost expelled from school angry. It took a long time and a lot of my dad's money to admit I was mad at her for leaving me. One of my therapists said that was why I was, uh, I think Ethelinda used the term "a passionate adventurer". I was so afraid of being left again, I didn't give anyone the opportunity. If you're not really there in the first place, how can they leave you?'

'Or maybe they'll stay if you give up everything to make them happy,' I said softly. 'Even if it makes you miserable.'

'Two sides of the same coin,' he said, placing his hand on top of mine. 'But we have choices, nothing is set in stone. You're not your mom, I'm not my dad. We've got to be brave enough to ask ourselves what we really want, then go after it.'

I could be brave.

I'd been brave when I called Vine & Walsh, when I told Stew I was taking the job, when I got on the train to London. Being brave meant changing things, and I was deeply afraid of change but what was worse, facing my fears or choosing unhappiness? I'd lived like this for so long, I'd got so good at it. And now someone was suggesting it didn't have to be that way.

'It's easy to make promises on a night like this,' I said, looking out over the sea. 'But things will be different when I wake up tomorrow and I have to go back to the real world.'

Evan reached up to my face and brushed the back of his hand against my cheek. Being brave had led me here and, whatever happened next, I knew I would never forget this night as long as I lived. His hand moved down and slipped inside the jacket I was still wearing, and my heart thudded so hard against my ribs, I felt sure he must be able to hear it. Just when I thought it might burst out of my chest, he pulled his phone out of the inside pocket of the tuxedo and pulled up a song, a soft ballad by one of my favourite singers, and held out his hand.

'Since it's your first Crystal Ball—'

'First and only,' I reminded him.

'*If* this is your first and only Crystal Ball,' he said, correcting us both, 'you have to dance. I'm afraid it's in the rules.'

'I really can't,' I said, not even sure I could stand up without melting away into a puddle. 'I've got a letter from my doctor somewhere. It's a medical condition, dangerously uncoordinated on the dance floor. If I even attempt to dance, you will get hurt.'

He pulled me up to my feet and rested my hands on

his shoulders. 'I'll take my chances,' he murmured in my ear. 'Just sway in time to the music.'

'It's the "in time to the music" part that's going to cause the problem,' I said, my body rigid in his arms. 'Don't do this to yourself.'

'Lucky for you, I'm a spectacular dancer,' Evan replied before dipping me so low I felt the strands of hair that had escaped my braid brushing the floor.

'And so modest too,' I gasped as he pulled me upright again. 'Please don't do that again, I really thought I was going to throw up.'

He smiled and rested his chin on the top of my head while I perched my fingers lightly on his shoulders before slipping my arms up to his neck. Our bodies softened into one another, each granting the other silent permission to move closer.

'What do you think would have happened if we'd met in the real world?' Evan's voice was low and husky and my whole body shuddered as his words tickled my ear. 'Like at a bar or a restaurant.'

'I don't think we go to the same bars and restaurants,' I said, eyes focused on the collar of his shirt, crisp, white and perfect. 'And even if we did, this is not my usual look. You probably wouldn't even notice me.'

Even as the words came out, they felt like a lie. I'd never felt more seen. And I would have found him if he was a needle in a haystack.

'Humour me. Let's say we met at a bar and I came over and said, "What's a nice girl like you doing in a place like this?"'

I lifted my chin so he could see my disgust. 'I'd say "Piss off, you American wanker". Surely you've got better chat than that?'

'Not a fan of the classics,' he laughed, cocking his head back. 'What if I said, "Hi, I think you're the most beautiful woman I've ever seen and I'd like to buy you a drink"?'

'Points for being direct,' I accepted grudgingly. 'But I'd probably just think you were leathered and once again, suggest you knob off. I know there are women who like strangers telling them they're beautiful but I'm not one of them.'

'Captivating, then.'

I shook my head. 'Captivating sounds like a perfume you can only buy in a gift set from Poundland.'

'You do not know how to take a compliment, do you?' he said, spinning me around so quickly that I barely felt my feet leave the floor.

'Once again, I am from Yorkshire,' I reminded him as I caught my breath. 'I know that might not mean anything to you, but the self-deprecation is real.'

'I think captivating is the perfect word for someone I haven't been able to stop thinking about ever since I first laid eyes on her. Even if she did try to kill me.'

'You were assaulted by a cat,' I reminded him. 'Which is really embarrassing when you think about it.'

Evan chuckled and pulled me back in as I pressed my face against the hollow of his neck, breathing him in.

'If we *did* meet in a bar,' I said, swaying dreamily from side to side. 'And I *didn't* tell you to piss off, what would happen next?'

'I'd ask if I could buy you a drink, which you would probably decline at first,' he replied. 'But your friends would encourage you because I'm so charming, and eventually you'd accept.'

'And then?'

'And then we'd talk for a while and I'd ask you to dance.'

'And I'd say yes, although mostly out of pity,' I said, my ears prickling as the song faded out and into another. 'But it would have to be going fairly well for me to agree to dance with you.'

'Oh yeah, things going pretty well at this point,' he agreed, pulling me even closer. 'Plus, I think we're both kind of drunk in this reality, and that really helps.'

'What happens after I agree to dance?' I asked as I realized I was keeping time with the beat of his heart instead of the music.

'We'd still be on the dancefloor, even though all our friends had left,' he said, barely moving at all. 'Because it felt so right having you in my arms, I didn't want to let you go.'

'I imagine we'd have to leave eventually,' I said, my own arms tightening around him. 'The staff probably want to go home.'

'Then I guess I'd have to make my move, because I wouldn't be able to live with myself if I didn't tell you how I'd been thinking about kissing you all night long.'

Evan tilted my face up towards his and, as his features blurred out of focus, my lips parted entirely of their own accord. His thumb grazed my bottom lip, just barely, and my entire body liquefied. The warmth of his breath, the scent of his skin. I curled my fingers into the hair that fell against his collar and took a deep breath in.

'And then?'

'And then I'd remember you have a boyfriend and respectfully excuse myself.' He pulled away from me and everything that was warm turned cold. 'I'm sorry. My life was a lot less complicated when I was an asshole,' he said as he stalked away, turning the music off on his phone.

'Please don't apologize,' I said, pressing my fingers against my tingling lips. 'You're right, I would not have felt good about myself tomorrow if . . .'

I didn't finish the sentence. I couldn't.

'I don't believe in love at first sight,' Evan said, keeping a safe distance between us. 'But I believe how I feel. This is something and, whatever it is, I don't want to ruin it with regret. Whether it's a beginning or an ending.'

There were only a few feet between us but the distance felt much further. Soon the night would be over and it would be time for me to leave. It wasn't just me going back to my life. Evan had to go back to his as well. Competitive, kind, funny Evan would go home to his complicated family and his masters degree, to his therapist, and the friends that flew each other out to parties in unsafe helicopters. He would be in New York, I would be in Sheffield, and with that realisation, everything changed.

'I have something for you,' he said, taking a seat on the edge of the day bed.

'What is it?' I asked, sitting down beside him. Nothing was going to happen between us now.

'Look in the inside left pocket,' he instructed. 'It's your future.'

I slid my hand inside the tuxedo jacket and found a stiff, glossy piece of card.

It was a tarot card.

'The Three of Cups,' I said. 'What does it mean?'

Evan opened the browser on his phone and searched. 'Upright, it means celebration, creativity and happy collaborations. Reversed, the Three of Cups can mean independence, going it alone, frustration or infidelity.'

He stumbled over the last word and I looked away.

'Was it the right way up or the wrong way up?'

'I don't know. I grabbed it from the table when you ran out, which I'm guessing I should not have done. That tarot reader has probably put a curse on me.'

'That tarot reader is probably appearing in panto in a regional theatre next week,' I told him. 'Thank you for this.'

'I guess it's up to you,' he said, giving me a friendly nudge with his shoulder. 'What do you think is in store for you in the future? Independence or happy creative collaborations?'

'We'll just have to wait and see.' I unzipped my cushion cover clutch and slid the card inside. If it was the only thing I took away with me from tonight, I wanted to keep it safe. 'Now what, Crystal Ball guide?'

He glanced at the dial of his beautiful watch. 'Almost midnight. The fireworks will be starting soon. We would have a great view if you want to stay here?'

'Let's do that,' I said, more than happy to leave the Ball behind. Reaching for the soft grey blankets, I shuffled back along the day bed, pulling them up over me as I went. After a moment's pause, Evan nodded and followed me up the bed. I pulled another blanket from the pile and tossed it over his long legs. 'Warm enough?'

'More than,' he replied, piling cushions behind us and draping an arm along the back of the bed. In the distance, I heard people cheering as a bell began to ring. On the twelfth chime, the whole sky exploded with a rainbow of fireworks. The sound echoed off the hills and the bright lights reflected in the water, turning Panarea into a sparkling, colourful snow globe.

Wherever she was, I hoped Juliette could see them. I rested my head on Evan's arm and smiled.

'What are you thinking about?' he asked.

'A friend,' I replied. 'And how much she would love this.'

'Maybe you can bring her next year,' he suggested. 'I could always pull some strings, try to get you in legit.'

'Never say never,' I said, cosying up under my blanket, but I knew I'd never be back here again.

For all the spectacle and grandeur of the Crystal Ball, I couldn't help but think this was the most magical moment of it all. Two strangers who might never have met, sitting together beneath a sky full of light. I marvelled at all the choices we must have made to bring us to this exact moment and I wondered where mine would take me next.

'Thank you for being my guide tonight,' I said as I pulled the blanket over my mouth to cover a yawn. 'Everyone was right, this is a night I will never forget.'

'Me either,' Evan said, resting his head against mine with a contented sigh. 'As long as I live.'

And just for one moment, everything was perfect.

CHAPTER TWENTY-TWO

When I opened my eyes, I had no idea where I was.

It was cold, it was dark, and my left arm was wedged underneath the body of a man that I was sure was not my fiancé. I rubbed at my eyes, all gummed up with mascara, and waited for my memory of the night before to come back. And it did, every single second of it. I remembered sitting down to watch the fireworks and pulling the blanket around me. I remembered resting my eyes for just a second. But how long ago was that? It was still dark out and the moon rested low in the sky, casting the clearing in its pale, milky glow. Twisting my neck to look at Evan, eyes closed, mouth slightly open, absolutely fast asleep, I swallowed hard. Between us, his phone sat on top of the blankets and I delicately tapped the screen to find out the time.

6.53 a.m.

'Fuck!'

I yanked my arm out from underneath his head like I was pulling off a plaster. He muttered something unintelligible, then pulled the blankets up over his head, barely moving and still fast asleep while adrenaline coursed through my veins. There were only seven minutes until my helicopter left for *The Songbird*, I had no idea how to find the helipad, and I was absolutely desperate for a wee.

'What do I do?' I whispered to a sleeping Evan, shaking my arm to get the feeling back.

But there was only one thing I could do.

Leave.

No matter how wonderful my night had been, it was always going to end this way, the same way every night ended. I woke up and the dream was over.

Without a sound, I reluctantly slipped my arms out of Evan's warm jacket. I wanted to wake him to say goodbye, but I couldn't. We'd shared too much, said too many things that were easy to say the night before but hard to admit the morning after.

Something small and dark fell out of his tux as I laid it gently on the bed. His wallet. It was lovely, of course, a soft black leather envelope that felt like butter against my fingers, either very expensive, very old, or both. One more reminder that we existed in completely different worlds. I picked it up from the floor and felt an unexpected rush. What if I took a peek inside? It was breaking the rules, but what did that matter now? I was leaving, I would never see him again, all I wanted was to know his last name. With cold, uncooperative fingers, I opened the wallet and found his driver's licence tucked inside a little pocket with a window, right in front. I rubbed at my eyes again, picking away flecks of mascara and eyeliner, holding it close to my nose until I could read the tiny letters and numbers. There it was, his date of birth, his New York address, his height, his eye colour, and his full name.

Clive Evan Carden II.

The wallet fell from my fingers, landing on the floor of the gazebo with a soft thud. Evan stirred and I grabbed my cushion cover clutch, backing slowly away across the grass, a light frost crunching under my feet until I reached the door to the hotel kitchens. With one last look, I opened the door, leaving Clive Carden's eldest son behind me.

'Bit overdressed for a Sunday?'

Lenny, a man who had risen swiftly up my Wouldn't Spit On You If You Were On Fire list, opened the door to the helicopter as the rotor blades slowly whirred to a stop above my head. He was grinning from ear-to-ear, hands held out towards me, as casual as you like.

It was not the correct approach to take.

I thanked the pilot profusely for reassuring me that I was not going to fall out for the entire duration of our flight, then slapped Lenny's hands away as he tried to help me out of the passenger seat.

'What?' he exclaimed, as I stumbled out of the cockpit and onto the almost-solid ground of *The Songbird*.

'What do you mean "what"?' I replied, ducking low as the helicopter took off above us. 'You left me, Lenny.'

'I didn't have any choice,' he protested with a pouty apology face I assumed worked wonders on women he hadn't callously abandoned on a Sicilian island. I was officially impervious to his powers. Every time I looked at him, all I wanted was to kick him square in the sack. 'The captain called, and we had to go. What was I supposed to do? You'd been gone for hours.'

'You're an arsehole,' I declared, stabbing him in the chest with my forefinger. 'I was gone five minutes and you could have come after me. You could have called, you could have left a message. You chose to leave.'

'Looks like you had an interesting time,' he replied as he followed me down the steps from the deck and inside the ship. 'Pretty sure that wasn't what you were wearing when you left.'

'When I was *abandoned*.'

I gave him such a glare, I was almost certain I heard his testicles pop back up inside him.

'You probably want to go back to your cabin and um, freshen up,' he muttered, hanging back until there was a safe distance of several feet between us. 'Is there anything I can do?'

'Yes, you can fuck off.' I jabbed the button to call the lift and it chimed softly, the doors sliding open right away. 'Do you think you can manage that yourself, or do you need to ask the captain for permission?'

'I'll give it my best shot,' he muttered as the doors slid shut on his pathetic face.

In the twenty seconds it took the lift to deliver me to my cabin, my Lenny-incurred wrath had melted away, leaving me a shadow of a shell of a human being, and when the doors pinged open, I was practically on my knees. All I wanted was a shower, a clean pair of my own pants, and bed. Whatever came after that, I would deal with it.

I was outside my cabin, one hand on the door handle and just moments away from the greatest wee of my life when I noticed the door to Juliette's cabin was slightly ajar.

'Not my problem,' I said out loud. I wasn't her assistant any more, after all.

But why was the door open?

'This is officially the last of your nine lives,' I muttered, and with an extremely heavy sigh, rapped on the woodwork, waited for a moment, then let myself into the cabin.

'Hello?' I called into the seemingly empty room. 'Juliette?'

It was a mess. The covers had been kicked off the bed, there were clothes all over the floor, and empty bottles everywhere. The sliding doors to the terrace were wide open and the curtains blew into the room, slapping at me like a drunk girl being forced into an Uber. I was attempting to yank them shut, wrestling the heavy fabric into the rose-gold tie-backs, when I spotted two legs hanging over the edge of the terrace. Long, slender legs, the tips of their toes just barely making contact with the deck.

'Juliette!' I screamed, tossing my bag on the floor and bolting outside. 'Juliette, no!'

I'd never moved so fast in my life. Diving across the deck, I grabbed her legs and hoisted her back onto the terrace, clutching her tightly as my chest heaved with panting breaths.

'It's not that bad,' I wailed. 'Nothing's that bad.'

'What are you talking about?' Juliette replied, wriggling out of my vice-like grip and staring at me like she'd seen a ghost. 'I was watching dolphins playing off the side of the yacht. Didn't you see them from the helicopter?'

'No,' I said, regaining my composure and my rage as she sat there, staring at me and laughing. 'I did not see any dolphins from the helicopter.'

'It was amazing.' She hopped to her feet and adjusted her grey marled jogging bottoms and the matching cropped sweatshirt that showed off a strip of soft, smooth tummy. 'There were four of them, right there, swimming at the side of us. I love dolphins, I know it's very Nineties kid of me, but they're just so cool.' I lay on the deck in thousands of dollars of couture and stared up at the sky. 'What did you think I was doing?'

'You know what? Never mind,' I said, rolling onto my side, pushing up to my knees and forcing myself back to my feet. 'You're OK, I'm going to go back to my room.'

She picked up a strawberry and popped it in her mouth.

'Aren't you a bit overdressed for a Sunday?' she asked.

'Lenny already beat you to that one,' I replied, drained.

'You're not going to tell me why you just stormed in here, wearing a ballgown?'

'Are you going to tell me why you bailed on the Crystal Ball and left me on Panarea?'

Juliette pursed her lips and looked down, checking her nails. Her manicure had not held up well in my absence. Every nail was bitten down to the quick.

'Fine,' I said, a wave of exhaustion carrying me back insider. 'That's fine, I don't really care anyway.'

She followed me across the deck and slammed the door to the terrace shut behind her. 'What do you mean you don't care?' she asked. 'Aren't you supposed to be my assistant?'

'I was,' I replied. 'But I'm not any more.'

With my head held high, I walked back across the room, and retrieved my bag from the floor. There would be no tears until I was safely in my cabin, under the running shower and blasting Taylor Swift from my phone. If nothing else, I had to get the dress off. Whatever magic spell Rachel cast to make it fit was wearing off fast and I was about to Hulk out of the thing at any second.

'Wait a minute, did you go to the ball?'

I turned to see her staring at me with her hands on her hips.

'No, I just thought it would be fun to sleep in a corset,' I replied, twisting my arms around my back and clawing at the fastening that kept the dress crushingly tight around my ribcage. Even when I sucked all the air out of my lungs, it was impossible. Rachel must have been a lot stronger than she looked. Juliette clucked her tongue and crossed the room, knocking my hands out of the way.

'Breathe in,' she ordered.

I did as I was told and, as she unhooked the catch and pulled down the concealed zip, I exhaled fully for the first time in about fourteen hours. No wonder I'd fallen for Evan so hard and fast, my brain had been starved of oxygen for more than half a day.

'I can't believe you went to the ball,' Juliette said, almost smiling.

'And I can't believe you didn't,' I said as my organs reacquainted themselves with each other. 'I also can't believe you sent me out to buy you a drink and then left me on the bloody island on my own.'

'Clearly you managed all right,' she replied, utterly dismissive. 'How did you get in?'

'Never mind how I got in, what happened to you?' Now that my blood was circulating all the way around my body instead of just changing direction when it arrived at my waist, I found I had just enough energy to be pissed off. 'Are you even going to apologize?'

From the look on her face, I couldn't work out if she was shocked, furious, or had just wet herself. 'I wasn't planning on it,' she said. 'I didn't do anything to you, I don't have anything to apologize for.'

'Wow.' I clutched my half-open dress to my body, my blood boiling. 'Just wow.'

She stared daggers across the room, but it didn't matter. I was furious.

'You were incredibly rude to me yesterday morning,' I said, pinning my dress in place with my armpits and counting off her offences on my fingers. 'Then you randomly decided you didn't want to perform at the ball even though that's why you were here in the first place. *Then* you decided to leave me behind when you could have just as easily waited for me to come back. No one attempted to get in touch with me to make sure I was OK. Did you even speak to Sarah? Did you even know whether or not I made it to the hotel, or did you think I was just hanging around the Panarea docks all night for a laugh? Because it's not funny to me, Juliette, it's my job. It's my *life*. Sarah isn't going to give me a glowing reference, is she? No, she isn't, and I don't blame her. I'll be lucky to even get a part-time job on the reception at the vet's now.'

'Honestly, Fran,' Juliette dropped backwards onto her bed, 'I don't know if you mean to, but you're coming off a little bit entitled.'

'Oh my god.' I pressed a hand against my forehead to check whether or not my head was about to explode.

'*I'm* coming off entitled? You were booked to perform at a charity ball and you didn't bother to show up.' I enunciated each word clearly to make sure she was following along. 'Your hangover couldn't have been that bad. Please tell me there was a good reason and it isn't just because you're an actual monster.'

'You need to calm down or you're going to have some sort of episode,' she said with a yawn. 'Are you hungry? Let's get Chef to make something obscene. I'm thinking Nutella pancakes and a bottle of tequila.'

It was all too much. Everyone had been right, even shithead Lenny. She was a rude, arrogant user and I'd let myself be taken in for the same reason I let Stew walk all over me: I needed to feel needed.

'I don't think so,' I said. 'If you require anything between now and the time we dock, you should ask Lenny. I'm not your assistant and I'm not your friend, you've made that quite clear.'

And before she could protest, I marched out of the room, let myself into my cabin, and locked the door behind me.

I couldn't say how long I was in the shower but by the time I emerged into my cabin, the sun was high in the sky, my entire body was wrinkled and my phone had cycled all the way through the 'Bittersweet Swifties' Spotify playlist three times. It felt so strange to be back on the yacht, like the ball had been a dream inside a dream. Had I been inceptioned? I'd only seen that film once and I fell asleep before the end, but I was fairly sure I'd got the gist of it. I scanned the room for any obvious signs of my subconscious or Joseph Gordon-Levitt. Perched on the edge of the bed, wrapped in a robe, I opened my cushion cover clutch and pulled out the tarot card Evan had rescued from Ethelinda. Flipping it over, I noticed there was writing on the back that hadn't been there before, a name and a phone number scrawled in thick black Sharpie.

Evan's name and Evan's phone number.

'I am not going to cry,' I whispered with determination even though I was quite clearly already crying. There had to be something in the sea air that was making me overly emotional and I didn't care for it at all. The sooner I was back on dry land, the better.

A gentle knocking at my door distracted me long enough to wipe away my tears and tuck the card back in my now officially stolen cushion cover.

'Fran?' Juliette called through the door. 'Fran, will you open the door please?'

'No,' I called back, not moving from the bed.

'Please open the door,' she whined. 'I've come to say I'm sorry.'

'First time for everything,' I grunted, sliding off the bed, squinting through the peephole to see her standing with her hands clasped in front of her, a picture of contrition. 'Thanks,' I said through the door. 'Bye.'

'I brought you a present,' she said, waving a bottle of something in front of her, 'and if you don't let me in I'll be forced to sing until you do, and as I'm sure you know, I didn't perform last night, which means my voice is fully rested and I could go on for ages.'

Grudgingly, I opened the door and snatched the bottle out of her hand before she could open it.

'No to this,' I said, placing it on the console table next to the door, out of her reach.

'Someone *is* in a bad mood,' she said, prancing across

the room barefoot and inspecting my suite. 'OK. The Ball. Tell me everything.'

'Didn't you come to apologize?' I reminded her, arms folded in front of me.

With a theatrical sigh, Juliette walked across the room and pulled my gown down from its hanger. I was hoping hanging it up would magically return it to its unworn state but it turned out positive thoughts didn't get champagne stains out of silk. 'This is beautiful, I never would have chosen it. I'm so glad you did.'

'Still not an apology.' I took the hanger from her and draped the gown over the back of the settee.

'I couldn't face it,' she announced as she sat herself in one of my armchairs and looked out of the window. 'Things have been rough lately and playing private parties for rich people is the absolute worst. You'd think it would be fun, no pressure, smaller crowds, but it's so much worse than anything else. They don't care about the actual show, it doesn't mean anything to them. Most people just stand in the back talking, or else they stand at the front demanding their favourite songs, like a jukebox. I woke up, I felt like shit, and I didn't want to go. And now I feel worse than ever.'

'Because it was for charity?' I guessed.

'No, because I was a dickhead to you,' she muttered, resting her chin in her hand and her elbow on the arm of the chair. 'The Crystal Ball committee doesn't care, no one's asking for a refund because I didn't show up. Christ, it was probably a bonus, fresh gossip to go with their $50,000 tickets. I bet they were talking all kinds of shit about me.'

She didn't need to know how right she was. I sat down in the chair opposite, making sure my robe was securely closed. Accidentally flashing her wasn't going to make either of us feel any better.

'I got dumped.' She pulled her feet up onto the chair and wrapped her arms around her shins. 'I was seeing someone, I thought it was the real thing, then she dumped me. No word of warning, nothing. She just left.'

'When did this happen?' I asked.

'Eleven days ago,' she replied, checking the time on the clock by my bed. 'Eleven days, fourteen hours and about fifteen minutes, give or take.'

'That's why you cancelled? Why didn't you tell me?'

'Because I thought I could power through and be a professional,' she said with a sad shrug. 'Then I woke up yesterday morning and she'd texted me to say one of her friends had got hold of some of our "private photos" and there was nothing she could do about it. I took it out on you, and I took it out on the Crystal Ball.'

I had no idea what to say and so, I listened.

'I know we've all done shit things after a break-up, but I cannot believe she showed our photos to her friends,' Juliette groaned. 'The idea of standing on a stage and grinning like an idiot, when half the world was probably looking at those pictures, I just couldn't do it. And Clive Carden, the wanker in charge, he's the worst of them. Raising money for charity one minute and publishing nudes in his shitty tabloids the next. Men like him think they can do anything they like and no one will ever hold them accountable. The worst part is, they're right.'

Poor Evan, I thought. My dad was an arsehole but he was a common or garden arsehole. He wasn't out there

289

publishing naked photos of people and ruining their lives.

'The photos are out,' I told her with an apologetic grimace. 'You should know.'

A flicker of something crossed her face but she didn't move.

'Did you see them?' she asked.

Not wanting to say the words out loud, I nodded, and her shoulders slumped, defeated.

'Well, that's that, then,' she said. 'I'm sorry I was so rude yesterday, I've forgotten how to behave with real people. When everyone agrees with you all the time, you start thinking you're always right. Ronnie used to call me on it all the time.'

'Ronnie was your ex?' I asked as she coiled her hair into a bun on the top of her head and nodded. 'How did you meet? I know you said dating was difficult.'

Juliette linked her fingers behind her head and looked up at the ceiling, smiling sadly. 'She was my assistant.'

'Ah,' I said, putting two and two together and coming up with something that looked suspiciously like a four.

'Just so you know, that's not something I make a habit of,' she said. 'I'm not like some creepy old man, trying it on with the help. She started working for me in April and by May, we were together. It was mad, just an instant connection, like I'd known her all my life. As soon as things changed, I suggested I get another assistant, but she said having someone else around would only get in the way and that people would start talking about us and she didn't want that. Then I found out her mates had been selling stories to the press all summer. We fired everyone trying to work out who was leaking stuff. When there was no one else left, Sarah confronted her and that was it. Boom, she was gone. And boom, it was over.'

'That's why you needed someone to start in such a hurry?'

'Yep.' She dipped her head down and twisted it from side to side, massaging the back of her neck. 'Sarah thought you would be a good replacement because you're not in the industry. Less likely to try to shaft me. And she made a point of telling me you were engaged so I suppose she meant literally and figuratively.'

'And I would never shaft you, professionally *or* personally,' I promised, giving her a reassuring shoulder squeeze. 'I know you're rich and gorgeous and everything, but you are far too high maintenance. So not my type.'

Juliette choked out a laugh and made an agreeing noise in the back of her throat.

'I genuinely am sorry,' she said. 'For treating you like a rent-a-friend then being so rude and leaving you behind. None of it was your fault.'

She placed her hand on top of mine and I let her. It didn't feel like she was taking advantage of me, it felt like she was truly sorry.

'Apology accepted,' I said.

'We make a good team,' she declared, giving my hand a quick and decisive pat. 'Any chance you'd reconsider the assistant job? I think we'd have fun. We'd get to hang out, go to cool places. I can get a private tour of Disneyland any day of the week, they even let me use the secret tunnels. What do you think?'

This was it. This was my chance to get out. Working for Juliette would take me all over the world, introduce me to all kinds of people. Events like the Crystal Ball

291

would be ten a penny and every day would be glamorous and exciting and full of adventure. Maybe it wasn't exactly what I wanted to do with my career and sure, I'd have to deal with more than my fair share of Aleisters and Andrews, but wouldn't that be worth it? To escape?

All I had to do was say yes.

'I'm sorry but no,' I said, wincing as her face fell.

I couldn't do it. Jumping into something that wasn't right for me was the worst kind of running away, and I'd already said yes to someone when I wasn't certain, and that had not gone well at all.

'Your assistant isn't someone to have fun with,' I explained. 'Your assistant is someone who works for you. What you're talking about is a friend.'

'Huh.' Juliette sat up, cross-legged, and pulled a face. 'You know, I've been meaning to get one of those. What do you reckon?'

'It's not as easy a job as people make it out to be,' I warned. 'You have to be brutally honest with each other.'

'Down with that,' she confirmed.

'And always support the other person.'

'Even when I think they're being a dick?'

'Especially when you think they're being a dick.'

'Is there any upside at all?' she asked. 'Because I'm not sure there's anything in this for me.'

'Well, you do get some stuff out of it,' I said thoughtfully. 'They have to support you when you're being a dick as well, remember. And it's nice to have someone you can trust, to talk to when you're going through difficult stuff, and celebrate with when things are going well. Also worth noting a friend would probably be quite interested to know more about those secret tunnels at Disneyland.'

'In that case,' Juliette took a deep breath in, then exhaled steadily, 'Fran, would you like to be my friend?'

'How about a trial period?' I suggested. 'Option to extend after ninety days if you're not too much of an arsehole?'

'I believe those terms are acceptable,' she said gravely before clapping her hands together. 'Now, that's business taken care of, I was deadly serious about those pancakes. Can I call Chef?'

'I don't know,' I replied. 'Can you?'

She clipped me around the back of the head and she reached for the phone. 'Some friend you are.'

'Shut up and order those pancakes,' I ordered, the very idea of food giving me life. 'And don't make me regret this.'

'Oh, I almost certainly will,' she called as I headed towards the wardrobe to find some clothes. 'But I promise I'll do my best.'

And in my heart of hearts, I believed her.

CHAPTER TWENTY-THREE

Just like me, London wasn't quite sure what to with itself when I arrived back on Tuesday morning. The last two days on *The Songbird* had been completely wonderful, but even as I lounged in the hot tub with my new pal, I knew I was only delaying the inevitable. Juliette and I had been on a total friendship binge – eating (mostly me), drinking (mostly her), watching all our favourite 90s films in the cinema, staying up late to discuss every last little thought that crossed our minds and generally torturing Lenny – but I knew the real world was only time away. After putting her on a private jet to Los Angeles for a recording session, I boarded my own economy flight back to London and came down to earth with a literal bump. Very messy landing from the pilot.

With no Bentley waiting for me outside the airport, I took the tube back into town and my suitcase lagged behind me like a temperamental toddler as I fought the flow of human traffic streaming over London Bridge. I'd always loved these big city landmarks – striding through town made me feel like I was living in my own TV show, Westminster on one side of me, Tower Bridge on the other – but today I didn't know how to feel. A sad side effect of not having felt much of anything for far too long. I was dreading seeing Stew, I missed Juliette already and try as I might, I couldn't stop thinking about Evan. So much of my life was suddenly up in the air and the uncertainty of it all ate away at my bones.

'Should have stuck around for that last tarot card,' I mumbled, burying my face in the upturned hood of my parka to protect my ears from a bitter November wind.

The glossy red door of Sarah's office seemed to have an invisible forcefield all around it, repelling me as I walked down the alleyway. Was there anything in my contract that said I had to return my phone and all the borrowed clothes in person? Maybe I could leave them all on the doorstep and ring the bell in a very high stakes game of knock-a-door-run? No. This was one of those things that had to be done, whether we liked it or not, and it just wouldn't sit right with me if I didn't do it in person. Plus, there was still a sliver of a chance I could talk Sarah into giving me a good reference. Juliette was alive and mostly well, and I *had* delivered her to the jet in one piece. Admittedly, I'd completely failed to get her to the Crystal Ball, but who wanted to split hairs?

I knocked on the shiny wood and waited.

And waited.

And waited.

Was she even there? I checked the time on my phone, re-read her terse email confirming the drop off and knocked again.

'I'm coming!' yelled a voice on the other side of the

door, followed by the clatter of footsteps and locks clunking and clanking into place. 'Yes?'

Sarah was a mess.

Her glasses were covered in smudges and behind the lenses, her mascara was most certainly not where it was supposed to be. What had once presumably been a tidy ballerina bun had devolved into an out-of-control top knot and there were at least three different phones ringing in the office.

'Oh, hi,' I said, remarkably less concerned about the fact I was wearing mismatched socks than I had been twenty seconds earlier. 'I'm here to drop off—'

'Yes, fine, put it over there,' she replied, leaving the door open and rushing back to her desk. The entire office was in a state of disarray, pizza boxes and take-away salad containers stacked up in one corner, a bin overflowing with giant cardboard coffee cups and piles of unopened post covering the floor. I wasn't sure where 'over there' was but I did know I wasn't about to leave a phone, a laptop and all my beautiful clothes in the middle of this disaster area.

'I can take them upstairs, it's no problem,' I said as she slid back behind her desk and began punching at the keyboard. 'Or drop the clothes off at the cleaners?'

'The clothes?' Sarah looked up at me, blinking behind her dirty glasses. 'Oh, the clothes. You don't have to return the clothes. Keep them. Call it a bonus.'

That should have been my cue to turn tail and leave, but underneath the stale smell of leftovers and too much coffee was the distinct aroma of panic and my former, super-assistant self just could not leave her alone in this state.

'Are you OK?' I asked, already knowing what her answer would be.

'Yes,' she replied instantaneously. 'Of course I am.'

'Of course you are,' I agreed. I rested my bag on top of my suitcase by the door and took off my coat as I surveyed the disaster zone. Sarah pushed her glasses on top of her head as I picked up a box of bin bags that had somehow made it into the office but not yet been used, and began loading in all the empty food boxes and coffee cups.

'What are you doing?' she asked as I tried not to retch at the rancid remains of what had once been an egg salad sandwich.

'Tidying,' I replied, tying the bag shut and starting another. 'Helping.'

She looked puzzled.

'Why?'

'Because it looks like you could use a hand.'

'But I sacked you?'

'You did,' I agreed with a grimace as I dumped the bin bag outside the front door. Even London's bravest and most foolhardy rats would give that one a wide berth. 'Should I stop?'

She watched me warily, as though I might flip at any second, pull a baseball bat out of my pocket and go the full Harley Quinn on her office, but then all three phones began to ring again at exactly the same moment and her attention went elsewhere.

'No,' Sarah said, reaching for a gold iPhone first. 'Thank you. Carry on.'

Having reached an accord, I found a safe enough spot on the floor and began sorting through the post, an endless stream of packages, bills, letters that looked important and junk mail that was clearly tosh. Helping out wasn't entirely brought on by the goodness of my own heart – I was much happier sat on the floor of Sarah's office opening council tax demands and *Reader's Digest* offers than I would be waiting at Kings Cross for a train headed home – but as I felt the familiar thrill of being useful run through me, I wondered if there was a chance for me as an assistant yet. While she made call after call after call, I slipped into my favourite role, answering the other phones, taking messages and putting people on hold, making a priority pile of the important post, and generally tidying up until it looked something like the office I'd walked into six days earlier. I was upstairs, straightening out the flat and making tea when Sarah finally put down all three phones long enough to take a breath.

'Milk? Sugar?' I asked as she sank onto one of the stools pushed up against the kitchen counter, like someone had let all the air out of her.

'Normally neither,' she replied. 'But both. Lots of both.'

I poured her an oversized mug, made my own regular cup and sat down across from her, waiting until she'd taken her first sip to speak.

'So, long day?'

I was rewarded with one of her rare smiles, her eyes doing most of the work. She looked so exhausted, her mouth barely moved. I checked my watch, I saw that it wasn't even noon.

'Running Juliette's career is not a glamorous pursuit,' she replied. 'I've got the Crystal Ball Committee lawyers threatening to sue Juliette and Juliette's lawyers trying to work out if there's a lawsuit to be brought against Ronnie, all while I attempt to manage madam herself. I could clone myself ten times and still not have enough hours in the day.'

'That sounds like a lot to deal with,' I commented without passing judgement.

'That's because it is.' She pulled the pins out of her top knot and let her hair fall around her shoulders before scooping it back up and tethering it down more tightly. 'If we hadn't sacked every single person who worked for her over the last six months we might not be in this mess, and right now none of the decent publicists want to touch her, which only leaves the vultures and the hacks and, quite frankly, I don't trust any of them.'

I held up my forefinger, stood up and returned to the kitchen, opening and closing cupboards until I found what I was looking for.

'Here,' I said, presenting her with an entire packet of chocolate Hobnobs. Every good office had one. 'Juliette told me about all the Ronnie stuff, sounds like she had everyone fooled.'

Sarah cleaned her glasses on the hem of her white cotton shirt.

'She told you about Ronnie?'

I nodded. No need to elaborate.

'You know, she left me a voicemail the night before the ball saying you were the best assistant she'd ever had, which she has never done before. Although she also sounded extremely drunk which was something of a concern.'

'She might have had a couple,' I muttered into my mug.

'We need to rebuild the team with people we can trust,' Sarah said. 'She trusts you. I know this last week didn't go exactly according to plan but would you consider trying again?'

An hour earlier, I'd walked into the office expecting

nothing more than a complete bollocking, so a job offer was a very welcome surprise, but I knew I only wanted to say yes because I knew it would make Juliette and Sarah happy.

Which meant it would have to be a no because it wouldn't make me happy.

'Juliette actually already asked me, and I declined,' I replied. She looked shocked at my candour as she scarfed down another biscuit. 'Sorry, but I'm not cut out for the celebrity PA gig. I always thought there was no assistant job I couldn't do but it turns out there are assistant jobs I don't *want* to do.'

'That's a shame,' she said, not sounding entirely surprised. 'Aside from the getting-left-behind-on-the-island part, you really did seem very well suited to it. Not very many people want to take on the behind-the-scenes jobs, they all want the glory. Knowing someone with their head on their shoulders was keeping an eye on her would have been one less thing on my plate.'

And then a thought occurred to me.

'What if I was *your* assistant?' I suggested. 'Working for Juliette isn't a good fit for me but I could do a bloody good job for you.'

Sarah brushed some biscuit crumbs off her lap and pursed her lips. 'Keep talking.'

'I can take all the admin off your hands, all the annoying little things you shouldn't really be dealing with, and anything else you need me to do; I really do pick up new tasks incredibly quickly. I bet there are a million things I could help with.' I pulled forward to the edge of my seat, my hands moving excitedly in front of my face. The idea was coming to life in front of me and unlike the thought of working for Juliette, this felt right. 'I know some brilliant recruitment firms who could fill the rest of the jobs – I've handled hiring before so I'm totally happy to handle all of that – and if I took some of the shit off your plate, you might have time to do your actual job.'

She picked up a third biscuit and broke it in half as she considered my proposal.

'I haven't had an assistant in years,' she said eventually. 'I don't like having someone buzzing around all the time.'

'I could work remotely!' I replied, getting more and more giddy by the second. 'A virtual assistant is just as efficient as an IRL person, if not more so. I just wouldn't be here to make tea every day, that's all.'

'This *is* a good cup of tea,' Sarah said thoughtfully, swirling the liquid in her mug.

'You're probably not leaving it to steep long enough,' I said. 'Most people rush their tea. If you had an assistant, you wouldn't have to.'

Biting down on the inside of my cheek, I waited for her to consider my proposal and reached down for the third finger of my right hand to twist my mum's wedding band. But the ring was still in my wallet, along with my engagement ring. I'd completely forgotten to put them back on.

'I'll need a couple of days to think about this,' she said. 'I'm just not sure.'

I couldn't imagine a world where Sarah Pierce wasn't sure about anything, but I kept my opinions to myself.

'Completely understand but I really do think we'd be a good fit,' I replied, not quite ready to give up. 'I might not be very good at babysitting a celebrity but I'm a killer when it comes to pivot tables and presentations.

No one runs an expense report like me. I mean, have you ever seen anyone this excited about spreadsheets? Give me a week's trial and I'll show you I can give you back hours of your day.'

'And what's in it for you?' Sarah asked, reasonably suspicious.

'A job,' I answered truthfully. 'And the chance to support and learn from someone at the top of her game.'

A reluctant smile found its way onto her face because truly, flattery will get you everywhere, especially when you mean it. I returned the smile as I realized perhaps there was still a chance for me to be just like Sarah when I grew up.

'I'll think about it and get back to you,' she said, sliding off the stool and pulling back her shoulders. 'Right now, I have to call Clive fucking Carden, apologize profusely and offer to make an obscene donation to the Crystal Ball Committee on Juliette's behalf. She won't be happy, she *hates* Carden.'

I flinched at the mention of the 'C' word. It was too strange that he was Evan's father, that he was anyone's father. It seemed to me that those kinds of people were only supposed to exist in boardrooms and in newspaper print, not at home, clipping their toenails or flicking through Netflix. And what was the point in having all that money and all that power when no one, not even your own family, actually liked you? I couldn't help but think it must be a bit shit to be Clive Carden.

Sarah tucked her shirttails into the waist of her trousers and straightened her glasses, looking more and more like herself by the second. The panic was gone from her eyes and all I could smell now was a lingering trace of very expensive perfume.

'Thank you for your help today,' she said, following me around the winding spiral staircase and gazing around the newly tidied office as though she was seeing it for the first time. 'I might actually get a couple of hours of sleep tonight.'

'If I was your assistant, I would guarantee you a minimum of five hours, every night,' I replied. I placed my borrowed laptop and phone on the edge of her desk before pulling the strap of my bag over my head, ready to leave.

'What are you doing?' she asked.

'These are yours,' I explained, giving them a tender pat. 'The Juliette bible said to bring them back. Did you want them left on *The Songbird*?'

'No,' she said, settling back in behind her desk. 'But if you're going to be my assistant, I imagine you'll need them.'

'Really?' I asked, picking up the laptop and clutching it to my chest. 'I thought you wanted to think about it?'

'I've thought about it. We'll start with a one-week trial period. How soon can you begin?'

It took every ounce of self-restraint in my body not to say 'right away'. This time, I wanted to do everything right. This was a job, not my reason for existing. I would set boundaries, I would respect my own needs, I would prove to myself that it was possible to be a brilliant assistant without being a complete martyr.

'Thursday,' I said confidently. 'I can start on Thursday.'

'Then I'll speak to you on Thursday,' she said, turning back to her computer. 'Thank you, Fran.'

I popped up the handle of my suitcase, looking doubt-fully at the full-to-bursting black shell. 'And you're *sure* I can keep the clothes?'

'I'll speak to you on Thursday, Fran,' she said again, two deep furrows appearing between her eyebrows as she stared at her screen.

'Right you are. I'll just let myself out,' I said, opening the door and kicking the suitcase onto the street with a heart full of joy.

CHAPTER TWENTY-FOUR

By the time I got home to Sheffield, it was raining cats, dogs and any other domestic animal you cared to mention. Just crossing the street from the train station to catch my bus was enough to soak right through my supposedly waterproof coat, and by the time I got to the house, my hair was plastered to my head and what was left of my makeup looked like it had been applied by a drunk toddler. And not a very talented one at that.

I was still buzzing from my meeting with Sarah, thrilled at the prospect of my new job, but the closer I got to Nana Beryl's house, the further away it seemed to slip, the reality of the Stew Situation coming into full focus. I'd spent a long time trying to decide what I wanted to say to him, Juliette and I had discussed it endlessly, but now I was here on the doorstep, all my prepared speeches slipped away.

Stew looked up from the television while I stood dripping in the doorway, slipping off my sodden shoes.

'Oh. You're home.'

Taking off my coat and hanging it on the end of the

stairs, I crossed the living room to close the curtains. When the streetlights came on, the curtains were closed, a concept he had never been able to grasp. Or rather, he hadn't needed to because I had always been there to do it for him.

'There's a shepherd's pie in the oven,' he said, turning his eyes back to the TV. 'Mum brought it round yesterday but there's still some left if you're hungry.'

'Thanks,' I said. 'Sounds good.'

The photos above the settee smiled down at me the same way they always did, but in the time I'd been gone, they'd changed somehow, like each one was a full stop rather than a reminder of what had been and could be again.

'Stew,' I said. 'Can you turn the TV off for a minute?'

'Fran, no.' He didn't even look at me. 'I've been up since half five and I'm knackered. Can we not get into it right now? You've just walked through the door, for Christ's sake. Have a minute.'

I sat in the chair nearest the door and wrung my hands together, hunching over my damp knees while Stew kept his very steady gaze on the television. It would have been easier to go upstairs, change out of my wet clothes, eat some shepherd's pie and deal with all of this tomorrow. Or at the weekend. Or five years from now.

'Sorry, I need to talk to you,' I said, forcing out each word, one after the other. If I didn't speak now, I never would. I reached for the remote control to turn off the TV and Stew blinked at the screen as it turned black, his jaw set so tight I was worried he might crack a tooth.

'Talk about what?'

'Us,' I replied, my heels bouncing up and down on his nana's carpet.

'What about us?' he asked. 'What exactly is there to talk about?'

It was a classic Stew Bingham avoidance tactic. Ignore a problem until someone else bought it up, then blame them for its existence; it was the relationship equivalent of 'whoever smelt it, dealt it'. No wonder men were so good at gaslighting, we'd been teaching them how to do it from birth.

But not this time.

'We've got to talk about what's going on.' I forced myself to meet his eyes across the room, but his face was cold and stiff and I had to look away. 'I don't think we're very happy and I don't think we've been happy for a while.'

His phone lit up on the arm of the settee. He glanced at the screen, turned it over then glared back at me. 'Oh, have *we* not been happy? Please don't put words in my mouth.'

'OK, you're right, *I'm* not happy.' I swallowed the lump that was forming in my throat, determined to say my piece. 'I thought it was just a phase, but it's been like this for a long time and I don't think it can get better unless we talk about it.'

Stew looked down at the floor, suddenly very interested in his slippers, and I sat and waited for him to speak, listening to the sounds of the living room. The rain beating against the window, the washing machine churning in the kitchen, the thermostat clicking into action and the whoosh of the central heating that followed right behind. Familiar sounds that used to be comforting but now felt like threats.

'What do you want me to say?' Stew said. 'Couples fight. Then they apologize and move on.'

I rubbed a finger under my eye, attempting to dislodge some of the smeared mascara and failing miserably. 'I don't want you to apologize—'

'I'm not the one who should be apologizing!' he yelled, standing so abruptly, three pink velvet cushions fell to the floor. I picked up the one that landed near my foot and cuddled it close to me. 'I'm not the one who fucked off to London on a whim without even discussing it first. You disappear for days, waltz back in and you want me to apologize to you?'

'It was a job, not a jolly,' I replied, as Stew booted the other cushion across the room. 'And I tried to discuss it with you but as I recall, you didn't seem that interested.'

'Because I didn't want you to go,' he roared, swirling his arms around like one of those weird inflatable things they kept outside car dealerships. 'I didn't want you running off to London, chasing your old life, because that's what's making you unhappy. Living in the past. I'm not a photographer any more and you're not some fancy executive assistant. This is where we live, this is who we are, why can't you accept that? This is your lot, Fran, why can't you settle for what you've got?'

I looked up at him from the armchair, my mouth hanging open in shock.

'You can't be serious?' I replied. 'Because that's the most depressing thing I've ever heard anyone say in my entire life.'

He slapped away the empty air with a frustrated grunt. 'Look at what you've got, a home, a family, me. Why isn't that enough?'

'Because it's not really my home and it's not really my family,' I said, forcing the words out slowly and clearly. 'And you say I've got you, but do you even really want me?'

Stew's mouth collapsed in on itself, lips turning inwards as he considered the question.

'You're being ridiculous. I proposed, didn't I?' he replied, but some of the force was gone from his voice. 'Where exactly were you this week, Fran? What is going on? How have you been gone five days and come back a completely different person?'

'I have changed,' I agreed, letting go of the cushion and placing it behind me on the chair. 'But not in the last five days. It just took getting away for a bit to see how much I've changed. And you have too, that's how life works. We're not the same people we were twelve years ago, and honestly, it would be weird if we were. But we're supposed to change and grow together and that's not happening, is it?'

'I don't understand you any more,' he muttered, flopping backwards onto the settee as though someone had just pulled their hand out of a sock puppet. 'I never know what you're thinking and I am not a mind reader. You are very hard to talk to, Fran, very hard.'

Smiling sadly, I shook my head, watching while he gnawed on his thumbnail.

'I'm not a bad person for wanting something else from life,' I said, even though I wasn't sure I believed it myself in that moment.

'Say what you mean, you want something more,' Stew corrected bitterly. 'Something better.'

I looked around the living room and couldn't see a single trace of myself anywhere. 'No,' I said. 'That's not fair. This is an amazing life for someone but that someone isn't me. I've been trying really hard to fit in but I've been a square peg in a round hole for a very long time.'

He huffed a loud grunt of frustration and gave the third cushion a final solid kick. I watched as it skidded all the way out of the room, bumping to a halt against the legs of the kitchen table as Stew sat back down on the settee.

'This is shit,' he declared, solid words that came out rough around the edges. 'I'm not doing it. I'm tired, you've just walked in the door, you're not making sense. You go and have a bath, we'll both get some sleep, and then talk about it tomorrow.'

Treading lightly across the room, as if afraid to make footprints that proved I'd been there at all, I sat down next to him. 'There's no point putting this off until tomorrow,' I said. 'It's not going to make it any easier.'

'Nothing happened with Bryony if that's what all this is about.' He wiped away a single angry tear and pulled his hand away from mine. 'I went to fix her sink and she said why don't you come over for tea and I was mad at you so I did, but that was all it was, tea.'

My heart ached as his tears began to fall freely. I hadn't seen him cry since his nan's funeral and for a moment I considered taking it all back, doing as he'd asked and pretending this conversation had never happened. But what good would that do now?

'It's not about Bryony, it's about us,' I said, wanting to squeeze his hand and make it better, but it didn't feel right to touch him now. 'All I know is, you've been my best friend for so long, and I don't want to make my best friend miserable, but I don't want to be miserable any more either.'

'I asked you to marry me,' he said in a hollow voice. 'You said yes.'

I pulled my wallet out of my pocket and opened up the little pocket inside, taking out the diamond engagement ring. His shoulders sagged at the sight of it, at the realisation it wasn't on my finger. He hadn't noticed until now.

'Why?' I held it between my thumb and forefinger, studying it properly for the first time in ages. It really was a pretty ring but it wasn't what I would have chosen for myself. Stew hadn't even chosen it, it was just available and convenient, like me. 'What made you propose?'

'Because I thought it would fix things,' he replied, drawn and defeated. 'I know you've never forgiven me for what I did but I thought if I asked you to marry me, you could get over it and be happy.'

'I did forgive you,' I said. 'The problem was I never forgave myself.'

He looked at me, confused. 'That doesn't make any sense.'

'I know,' I said, because he was right, it didn't. 'Are you happy, Stew?'

He drew his shoulders up to his ears, then, slowly, shook his head and pressed his palms against his face, shoulders shaking with the force of his sobs.

Just like that, it was over. After all the years I'd spent panicking about what would happen if I lost him, I'd ended up giving him away.

I remembered the flush of confusion and relief I'd felt when he slid the ring onto my finger in front of all his friends and family three years ago, and as I pressed it into his palm and folded his hand closed around the sparkling diamonds, something similar washed over me. I'd done the hard thing. I'd been brave.

'I'm sorry,' he whispered, rubbing his face with the back of his hand. 'I do love you.'

'And I love you too,' I replied. 'I think that's why this feels so bloody horrible.'

He sniffed loudly and folded me into his arms for one last hug. 'I really thought things would get better.'

'So did I,' I said, squeezing him tightly as I said goodbye. 'And now I think they will.'

CHAPTER TWENTY-FIVE

The next day, Jess whirled through the door of the café, removing her winter layers as she settled in her seat.

'I've only got half an hour for lunch,' she declared as she unfurled her scarf from around her neck. 'Tell me everything. Who did you meet? Who did you see? What did you eat? Shock me.'

'Me and Stew broke up,' I replied.

She froze, holding her bright pink earmuffs inches away from her ears.

'Congratulations, I'm officially shocked,' she replied, mouth agape. 'Fran, are you all right?'

'Yeah, I think so.' I pushed the coffee and muffin I'd ordered for her across the table. 'I'm mostly relieved.'

'I thought you might open with which celebrities you talked to in the toilets but this is big news.' Jess shuffled around the table and settled into the seat beside mine, giving me a tight sideways hug. 'What happened? I mean, I'm so sorry.'

I passed her two sugar packets which she immediately

tore open and dumped into her coffee. 'Don't be, it's definitely for the best.'

'Have you been practising that?'

'Yes,' I admitted, tucking a freshly washed chunk of hair behind my ear only for it to immediately spring back out. The Sheffield frizz was real. 'But I think it's true. Things haven't been good between us for a while but I still can't quite believe it's over.'

Jess pulled a spare hair elastic off her wrist and handed it to me without a word. 'Should I ask how Stew's taking it? I'm assuming he didn't initiate things.'

'He seems OK but he also left before I woke up this morning,' I said, pulling my damp hair back into a ponytail. 'There was a sort-of fight, obviously, then a bit of crying and then it was done. If I'm being honest, it was mostly just weird. I thought there would be more shouting and slamming doors, but once it was done, he heated me up some shepherd's pie, we watched telly for a bit, then went to bed. Separate beds,' I added before she could ask. 'I don't think it's entirely sunk in yet.'

'These respectful, conscious uncouplings are the worst,' she said as she tucked into her muffin. 'You need a lot more rage for a clean break, a good slanging match, maybe smash a few plates. Breaking up is much easier when you really hate the other person, but I'm proud of you and you know I'm here if you need anything at all.'

I nabbed a crumb of muffin from her plate before she could devour the whole thing. 'Since you're offering, I might need some help flat hunting? Last night I slept in the spare room but I'm going to have to find some-where to live sooner rather than later. Slightly terrified of living on my own but if you can do it…'

'Well then, problem solved,' Jess replied, looking delighted. 'Neither of us has to live on our own. Come and stay with me.'

'Oh, no, I couldn't.'

She raised her eyebrows at me over the rim of her coffee cup. 'Was it fun sleeping in the spare room with your ex next door?'

'Not especially.'

'And do you think it'll be more fun or less fun a week from now?'

'Less fun?'

'And how long do you think you'll be able to stay civil with each other, living under the same roof while you're mid-breakup?'

'I can have my stuff over at yours by teatime,' I replied. I was so, so relieved and more than a little bit excited. 'And I promise I won't outstay my welcome. Thank you.'

She knocked the side of her head gently against mine and smiled. 'You'll stay as long as you need. No one's moving at this time of year and I'm not going to turn you out onto the streets at Christmas, am I?'

'I won't hold you to that until you've lived with me for a couple of days,' I said with a genuine grin. 'What if I'm a nightmare housemate?'

'Yeah, I can imagine what kind of nightmare you are.' Jess pressed her hand against her forehead in mock horror. 'Oh no, Fran cleaned out all the cupboards and is silently listening to ASMR videos in her room again. How will I ever cope?'

'I have been known to leave washing in the machine overnight,' I confessed and she pretended to fall off her chair. 'Honestly, Jess, you're amazing.'

'Right, fine, it's all settled, enough's enough,' she said, the Yorkshire in her coming out to put a stop to any display of excessive sentimentality. 'Now, perhaps you can explain how you went from popping down to London for a temp job to ending up on a yacht on your way to the Crystal Ball, then came home and dumped your fiancé inside a week? What happened?'

I inched further away from the cold window, pulling the sleeves of my sweatshirt over my hands. The radiators were most certainly not working in the café today. 'It's a long story,' I said, not sure where to start.

'I'm not going anywhere,' Jess replied, picking up her coffee and taking a sip, and I had genuinely never been more appreciative for another human being than I was in that moment.

'So, I left for London last Thursday morning and—'

Before I could finish my sentence, Jess whacked me across the chest and pointed at something out the window. 'Sorry to interrupt but have a look at that,' she gasped as I gingerly rubbed my right boob. 'There is a *man* over the road, and he is *not* from around here.'

'Please tell me he hasn't got curly blond hair and a fedora?' I said, my chest seized with terror.

'I said man, not twat,' she replied. '*Look* at him. Do you think he's lost?'

Across the road, a tall, dark-haired man climbed out of a shiny black Range Rover and when he turned around to face the café, I almost fell out of my chair. Our eyes met through the window, his face breaking into a huge grin as mine went completely blank.

'Evan?' I gasped.

'Evan?' Jess asked.

'Evan,' I confirmed, standing as he walked into the

café. 'Is this really happening or am I having a psychotic break?'

'Francesca!' His whole face lit up and I knew this was real. I remembered that smile. It was the same one I'd seen when I first saw him on the terrace at the ball. 'I can't believe you're here.'

'This is where I always am,' I replied as Jess repeatedly kicked at my shins under the table. 'I can't believe *you're* here.'

He stood a few feet away, a look of complete accomplishment on his face while I silently admonished myself for choosing to dress like a children's television presenter from 1984 that morning.

'Hello, Evan, I'm Jess.' She stood up and took his hand in hers, pumping it up and down enthusiastically. 'Now, I'm going to pop up to the counter while you two do whatever this is. Can I get you anything?'

'No, thank you,' Evan replied, remembering his manners. 'Nice to meet you, Jess.'

'And you,' she said, shoving her entire fist into her mouth as she walked away before mouthing 'he's so hot' and fanning herself with her hands.

He was still stood beside the table, beaming at me in a tailored grey overcoat and black leather gloves, looking every inch the polished New Yorker. Which might have been fine in a coffee shop in Manhattan but in a cosy café in Sheffield, he stood out like a sore but beautifully dressed thumb. I busily straightened up the faded red dinosaur sweatshirt I'd chucked on when I woke up and pulled my hair out of its ponytail before putting it right back up again.

'What are you doing here?' I asked.

'Can I sit?' he replied.

'Yes, of course,' I said, watching as he attempted to origami his legs into a package small enough to fit under the low table. 'What are you doing here?'

'Didn't have anything else to do.'

Over by the counter, Jess was still staring at him and, I realized when I took a look around the café, so was everyone else. But Evan only had eyes for me. He was looking at me as though he couldn't quite believe I was real, as though he was the one who had the right to be surprised.

'All right, *how* are you here?' I said, starting a new line of questioning. 'How did you find me? Are you Batman?'

'I *wish*,' he replied, eyes bugging out of his head as took off his gloves and peeled off the grey coat to reveal a gorgeous charcoal jumper underneath. 'Although it would be a lot of pressure. What if you're in the bathroom when the Bat Signal goes up? How do you explain to Commissioner Gordon you didn't stop a crime because you were, you know, taking care of personal business?'

'It always seemed inefficient to me,' I agreed. 'Can they not just text him like normal people?'

We smiled at each other and I felt my heart thudding underneath my dinosaur jumper. Seeing him here was like seeing a dog in school. It didn't belong there, you had no idea how it had got inside in the first place, but for a brief moment, it was the most exciting thing that had ever happened to you.

'I took my life in my hands and went back to the grocery store on the harbour,' he said, picking a packet of sugar out of the basket on the table and flicking it lightly, his fingers just inches away from mine. I wrapped my hands around my mug to keep them at a safe distance. 'Thankfully, the girl behind the counter remembered you.'

'You don't say?' My eyes bored into my coffee cup and I wondered if there was enough left for someone to drown in, if they were properly motivated to try.

'She still had the piece of paper with your name and number, which was pretty much the most expensive thing for sale in the whole store.'

'She made you pay for my phone number? That girl's a hustler,' I replied with a whistle. 'She should be running the entire country, let alone a supermarket on the harbour.'

'I know, I should introduce her to my dad,' he agreed and I couldn't stop myself from flinching at the reminder of exactly who his father was. 'I tried to call you, but it said the line was disconnected so I did a little non-Batman detective work with your name and number, found out where you lived and this all sounded very romantic in my head but, is it me or is it coming off a a little stalker-ish now I'm here?'

'There's a shade of it,' I said even though I couldn't stop smiling. 'But we're in broad daylight in a public place so I think you're all right. How did you know I'd be here?'

'This part is a happy accident,' Evan replied. 'I stopped to get coffee on my way to your place and there you were.'

The effort he had gone to stunned me into silence. Once upon a time, I had asked Stew to stop off on his way home to get me some Nurofen for my period pains but instead he gave me two loose pills he found in the bottom of his bag because the supermarket car park

319

'looked busy' and he was 'fairly certain' they were ibuprofen. Eight hours later when I finally stopped screaming and trying to hurl myself out of the window because I was convinced I could fly, we came to the conclusion they were not.

'Wow,' I exhaled. 'Is that a glass slipper in your pocket or are you just pleased to see me?'

'Oh, I am *extremely* pleased to see you,' he said in a low, rough voice.

He put the sugar packet back in the basket and moved his hands so close to mine, I could feel the warmth from his skin. I held my breath as Evan extended his forefinger, brushing it lightly against my thumb, then rested on the back of my hand. Just one finger holding on to me. The night of the ball flashed through my mind, the moonlight on his face, my head on his chest, the way his body felt pressed against mine as we danced.

'When I woke up and you were gone, I thought I must have imagined you,' he said, in a voice so soft and tender it was just for me. 'I needed to know you were real.'

'I'm real,' I confirmed. 'And so are you.'

He pinched himself and nodded. 'More or less.'

'And your dad is Clive Carden,' I said gently as I pulled my hand away from his.

'Looks like I'm not the only one who did some detective work,' Evan ducked his head and let his dark hair fall in front of his face. 'Yeah, he is.'

'This is all so mad, Evan,' I said, inhaling sharply and huffing out a confused sigh. 'I can't get my head around the fact you're here.'

He looked up at me with a rakish grin. 'Is there any chance mad means romantic in Britain?'

'No,' I said, coming dangerously close to my senses.

'Mad. It sounds mad. What kind of person goes to all this trouble just to find someone they met at a party?'

Evan reached across the table and placed his hands on either side of my face. My cheeks flamed, my heart stopped, and my body melted from the inside out.

'The kind of person who hasn't been able to stop thinking about you since the moment he laid eyes on you,' he said, thumbs caressing my cheeks. 'The kind of person who has done a million dumb things and is absolutely certain this is not one of them. This is a grand romantic gesture, Francesca, they're extremely common in books and movies, you can google it.'

'Can't,' I replied, still staring into his eyes. 'Haven't got a phone.'

'Then let me show you.'

He leaned across the table, pulling me towards him, my eyes sliding shut, but the moment before our lips touched, I stopped and yanked myself backwards.

'I'm sorry,' I said, my hands shooting up to his shoulders, holding him at a literal arm's length. 'I can't, this is just too much.'

Across the room, I heard Jess howl in horror as Evan pulled back into his chair. 'Um, OK,' he said, combing his hair away from his flushed face. 'That's not entirely how I imagined that going, but OK.'

'It's not that I'm not blown away, I am,' I told him as my heart sank in my chest. I knew I was ruining the most romantic thing anyone had ever done for me, but I also knew I had to. 'Panarea, the ball, you showing up here, now, out of the blue, it's all amazing. But it feels like a fairy tale and I have to live in the real world. We have very different lives, things like this don't happen to people like me.'

Evan shook his head gently and looked at me with liquid eyes.

'Francesca,' he said, reaching across the table. 'It's happening to someone like you right now.'

'Oh, for fuck's sake, kiss him!' Jess yelled from across the room. 'I'm dying over here.'

'Thank you!' Evan called back, pointing over his shoulder. 'I like her.'

'I have been single for exactly sixteen hours,' I said, doing my very best to ignore Jess and everyone else in the café, who was openly staring at us like we were a live action episode of *EastEnders*. 'I can't jump on the back of your white horse and ride off into the sunset. I need to be brave, remember? You said that. I don't need you to save me, I need to save myself.'

The café was so quiet you could have heard a pin drop.

Evan looked at me with quiet awe and a longing I could hardly bear.

'There are two things I want to say,' he began as he cleared his throat. 'The first one is, I'm not here to save you, I'm here to thank you. Meeting you reminded me things don't have to stay the same just because that's the way they've always been. I got to be a brand-new person for you, and I liked that guy.'

'I liked him too,' I replied truthfully. 'What's the second?'

He rested one elbow on the table and propped his chin up on his fist. 'You said you're single?'

I couldn't not smile.

'I get it, I've done the work, I know it's not easy. Whatever you need from me, you got it,' he said. 'What can I do?'

'Give me time?' I said, my words loaded with the kind of hope I hadn't felt in so long. 'I will never forget that night and I will never forget today—'

'—but now isn't the right time,' he finished for me.

I nodded and pursed my lips tightly at the collective sigh of everyone in the café.

Evan leaned across the table and placed a light kiss on my cheek before shuffling out of his too-low chair and slipping his arms back into his coat.

'Will you call me when it is?' he asked.

'If you want me to,' I promised. 'But I don't know when it'll be.'

'Doesn't matter,' he replied, leaning down to plant another soft kiss on my cheek. 'It's not like I could ever forget you.'

He turned and walked out of the café, crossed the street and climbed back into the black Range Rover. I held my hands against my cheeks, half wanting him to turn around and run back inside to me, half willing him to drive away before I chased him down, pinned him to the floor and did something no one should do to another human being outside the post office at midday on a Wednesday.

'Fran?'

Jess was in his seat before the door could close behind him.

'That was Evan,' I said, still half in a daze as he shut the car door, started the engine and drove away without looking back. 'I met him at the ball.'

'That's it, I'm cancelling my meetings,' she said, placing a chocolate brownie in front of me with an impatient, expectant look. 'We have *a lot* to talk about.'

I picked up a knife and sliced the brownie in half,

sliding the plate into the middle of the table with a grateful smile. I'd been crazy to think losing Stew meant I'd be on my own. I might not have a million friends or a big family to turn to, but I had someone who saw me for who I was and loved me because of it, not in spite of it.

That was more than enough for me.

CHAPTER TWENTY-SIX

'Fran, wake up!'

'I'm awake, I'm awake,' I exclaimed, sitting bolt upright and looking all around for the fire. 'What's wrong?'

'Nothing's wrong.' Jess poked her head around my bedroom door and grinned. 'It's Christmas!'

The clock on my bedside table said it was seven o'clock, altogether too early to be awake on Christmas Day when there were no kids involved. Except there was a child involved, her name was Jess and she was thirty-five and a quarter years old.

'Get your arse downstairs, I'm making tea,' she called as she galloped down the stairs. 'It's time for presents!'

If I'd learned nothing else in the month we'd spent living together, I knew there was no point trying to go back to sleep once Jess was awake. She was a tornado in the mornings, grinding her coffee beans, singing in the shower, thundering down the stairs with the force of a small stampede, and since I'd never met anyone quite as excited about Christmas as she was, I really should have expected this. The tree went up on the first and the perfectly wrapped presents started to appear the very next day. Most were labelled 'to Jess, from Jess' but they still looked pretty under the tree. Other than the early wake up calls, living together was fun. We settled into an easy rhythm right away, shopping together, cooking for one another when we could, and going through enough wine for the owner of the local off-licence to invest in a holiday home in Tuscany. He assured us the timing was entirely coincidental, but I wasn't convinced.

My eyes wandered around my room as they did every morning when I woke up, still mildly surprised not to be in Stew's house. My bed took up most of the space by design (and I had taken to starfishing right in the middle of it), but there was still room for a wardrobe, a soft pink chair that was not even slightly comfortable but looked great and my desk, tucked under the window, neatly stacked with all my to-do tasks for Sarah. Work was going well. As I'd predicted, the two of us were a good, long-distance fit and, slowly but surely, she was giving me more responsibilities, letting me take on more interesting tasks. I'd even started to think that perhaps I'd like to move into management one day. Only, not for Juliette. I wasn't that much of a masochist.

A token bit of tinsel was draped around a small, square picture frame that hung on the wall, directly opposite my bed to mollify my landlady, and inside the frame was my tarot card from the ball, mounted upright.

The Three of Cups, celebration, creativity and happy collaborations.

So far, so good.

*

'Remind me why I'm awake at this ungodly hour,' I said, yawning as I wandered into the living room clutching my phone. Jess clanged around in the kitchen, cupboard doors opening and closing as she whirled around me.

'I found a Christmas present waiting for you on the doorstep,' she replied. 'I didn't want to leave it out there to freeze.'

'Jess, I told you, a dog is for life, not for Christmas,' I said, settling cross-legged in front of our absolutely massive tree. Yes, we were drinking when we ordered it. No, we hadn't checked the height of her ceilings before it arrived.

'Who are you calling a dog?' Kim, my dark-haired, mini-me of a stepsister, walked into the room carrying an enormous gift bag. 'Nice PJs.'

'Kim!' I exclaimed, scrambling to my feet and meeting her hug head on. 'I didn't think you were coming over until later. Is everything all right? It's so early!'

'Oh, yeah,' she looked away briefly, her cheeks turning the same colour as the end of her frosty nose. 'Dad had a kitchen crisis. His oven conked out so they're bringing lunch over to mine. I wanted to give you your present before I'm elbow deep in giblets.'

'Right,' I nodded, hands on hips. 'Of course.'

One of the first things I did after moving into Jess's house, was call Kim. The more I thought about it, missing out on a sister because our father was an arse and my mum wouldn't have liked it seemed really stupid. I couldn't live my life for other people any more, whether they were still here or not. She'd jumped at the chance to build bridges and after one boozy brunch that turned into an early dinner, unplanned cocktails and eventually a sleepover, we'd been more or less joined at the hip.

'Here, I hope you like it.' Kim handed me the gift bag as she loosened her scarf. 'It was the last one.'

Inside the bag was an enormous neon-orange, zebra print onesie. Jess walked in the room, sipping from a cup of coffee, saw the onesie, spluttered into her mug, turned around and walked back out again.

'Like it? I said, holding it up against myself. 'I love it!'

It was at least two sizes too big and felt so flammable, I was afraid to sneeze in case it exploded in my face. No one wanted to spend Christmas in hospital.

'It's been such a cold winter, I wanted to get you something to keep you cosy,' she explained, clapping her hands with glee. 'I saw it and I thought, I bet Fran would love that.'

'And I do!' I lied, reminding myself that my sister had only just turned twenty-two and while neon-orange zebra print wasn't necessarily my signature print, it was a very sweet and thoughtful gift. 'Here, let me get yours.' Crawling underneath the Christmas tree, I rooted through all of Jess's gifts to self, looking for the little cashmere jumper I'd seen her mooning over in Whistles.

'I know you have your dinner plans all sorted,' she said, clearing her throat as though she was about to deliver a well-rehearsed speech. 'But there's going to be loads of food at mine if you and Jess want to eat with us? Save yourself all that cooking?'

Slowly, I backed out from under the tree, pine needles in my top knot, pyjama bottoms riding down as I went.

'Thank you,' I said, handing her a carefully wrapped parcel and yanking up my trousers. 'I do appreciate the offer, but I think I'm going to stick with dinner here.'

As happy as I was to have my sister in my life, I was not ready to rush into a happy family Christmas with our dad. He'd never shown any interest in being there for me before and I couldn't help but feel that the baby steps he'd made in the last couple of weeks, a Facebook friend request and a brief, awkward conversation at her birthday party, were for Kim's benefit rather than mine. I didn't know if we'd ever have a real relationship and if we didn't, that was OK. Not everyone got to have a great dad. A fantastic sister was more than I'd ever hoped for. I was happy.

'OK, if you're sure.' Kim tore into her gift without trying to force the issue. She dropped the paper where she stood and held up a soft grey cashmere jumper, studded with tiny crystals from top to bottom.

'Fran, thank you! It's gorgeous!'

It really was. My mouth curved into a wistful smile as she moved it to and fro to make the crystals sparkle. Another little magpie.

'Everything still on for New Year's?' she asked, wrapping the jumper back in its paper.

'Absolutely,' I confirmed. 'Train tickets are booked, hotel is all sorted, our names are on the list.'

'I can't believe I'm going to see Juliette perform in person,' Kim gushed. 'Do you think I'll get to meet her?'

'I'm sure of it,' I replied, pleased that my new job had such great benefits. I'd convinced my new pal to put on a special invite-only gig to remind her why she did the thing she did. Just two hundred of her biggest fans, no Crystal Ball-attendees allowed. Well, except for me.

'I'd better get back home,' she said, reaching out for another hug. 'Mum and Dad will be banging my door down any minute. The turkey has to be in the oven by eight or Christmas is cancelled. Merry Christmas, Fran.'

'Merry Christmas, Kim,' I replied, squeezing her tightly and feeling so glad to have her in my life.

'What now?'

'What do you mean, "what now"?'

I lifted my head and saw Jess staring at me from the other settee, her reindeer antler headband set at a precarious but admittedly fetching angle. It was only half past eleven and we'd already watched *Home Alone*, *The Snowman* and *Miracle on 34th Street*, finished all the Quality Street her grandma had sent us, and polished off a Terry's Chocolate Orange. The turkey was in the oven but the thought of eating again any time soon made me feel sick to my chocolate-filled stomach.

'What shall we watch now?' Jess clarified as I refreshed my inbox. '*Love, Actually* or punish ourselves with *Last Christmas*?'

'Whatever you want,' I replied absently. 'Up to you.'

No new messages.

I placed the phone down on the floor and twisted my new ring around and around on the middle finger of my right hand. It was a thin rose-gold band, set with absolutely minuscule diamonds. Hardly an heirloom piece but it was mine, bought for me, by me. Mum's wedding band was safely put away in my jewellery box and Nana Beryl's engagement ring was where it always should have been, with Stew's older sister, Mandy.

'You know, you've been staring at that thing all day,' Jess said, treading lightly. 'Expecting any messages?'

'Nope,' I replied as she rolled onto her back and grabbed the remote control, scanning through the

330

channels far too quickly for anyone but her to see what was actually on. 'Do you fancy a walk?'

'I don't think so,' she scoffed, adjusting her antlers. 'It's brass monkeys out there. Ooh, look, *Vicar of Dibley* Christmas special.'

'Come on, just down to the park and back. You'll feel better for it.'

'I'll feel better for another cup of tea and a bag of Quavers. Put the kettle on if you're going past the kitchen?'

'Someone ought to study your insides,' I muttered as I left the room to get dressed, or at least replace my pyjama bottoms with a non-holey pair of jogging bottoms. 'It's a miracle to me how you're even still alive.'

'Iron constitution, I get it from my grandad,' she called after me. 'And you can bring the biscuits while you're up.'

Baby, it was cold outside.

Even in my hat, scarf, mittens, earmuffs and biggest coat, I was still shivering as I tottered down the street towards the park. Sheffield's hills offered beautiful views and the kind of cardio conditioning Peloton could only dream of, but between the months of November and March, they were an absolute death trap. The frost was so thick, I half expected to find a woolly mammoth frozen instead of the central reservation on Psalter Lane, but if you could overlook the fact I was moments away from skidding down the hill to my death, it really did cast a magical kind of Christmas glow over the city. The streets were so quiet, it felt as though everyone had agreed to save this moment just for me.

It was fair to say I'd been worried. Christmas was always when I missed Mum the most and the thought of getting through the festive season without the distraction of Stew and his family was enough for me to buy up all the two-for-one bottles of Baileys at Asda three times in a month. We had been in touch since I'd moved – a few texts, the odd awkward phone call – but he already felt like someone I used to know instead of my Stew. And not that it mattered, but rumours about him and Bryony were already circulating, ever since they sat together at the pub quiz the Wednesday before last. When Jess broke the news, I was surprised to discover I didn't care nearly as much as I thought I might. I wanted him to be happy. Preferably with anyone else on earth, but if it had to be her, I could find it in myself to wish them luck. Luck and a painful, embarrassing but ultimately treatable sexually transmitted infection.

Overall, I was pretty proud of myself. I had a job I loved, a roof over my head, and even though my ex was almost certainly already banging someone else, I hadn't burned down his house. I was doing so well. Mum would have been proud.

But there was still one thing that kept me awake at night.

Evan Carden.

It was an infatuation the likes of which I hadn't experienced since the dawn of the Hemsworth era. I'd given myself all the logical pep talks but nothing changed; every night when I put myself to bed, I tossed and turned, remembering how it felt to be in his arms. I hadn't lied to Jess when I said I wasn't expecting a text, but I was hoping for one because late last night, when she was tucked up in bed watching *A Muppet Christmas Carol*, I was texting Evan.

Hope you're having a perfect Christmas, Fran x

Hours went into the drafting of my message and that was the best I could come up with. I'd typed and deleted 'love, Fran' so many times I would need physiotherapy on my thumb come the New Year, but in the end, I came down on the side of no love and one kiss. Not too desperate, casual enough, but there was an opportunity to start a conversation if he wanted to.

Prising off my mittens, the bitter sting of the cold air burning my fingers, I checked my sent messages again. He'd had thirteen hours to respond. Even with the time difference of wherever he was, there was no way he hadn't seen it now. The message was marked as sent, seen, and read. The only notification that wasn't available on an iPhone was 'rejected' and surely that was in the works for the next operating system.

'I still think I did the right thing, sending him away,' I told the tiny robin redbreast that bounced along the low stone wall beside me, much less concerned about falling on his arse than I. 'Granted, I haven't read a single self-help book in my life, but they all say it's never a good idea to bounce from one relationship to another. Rebounds never last. Real life is not a fairy tale.'

He cocked his head to one side and looked back at me with bright black eyes, confirming I was certainly no Cinderella.

'So glad we agree,' I said as I crossed the road to the Botanical Gardens, the little bird fluttering on ahead of me, watching me plant one foot carefully in front of the other. My plan was to spend the rest of the day snout deep in a bottle of Bailey's, not nursing a broken ankle at A&E.

'I just can't stop thinking about him,' I sighed, taking a seat on a bench just inside the gates. 'I know it's stupid, I *feel* stupid, but I don't know how to make it stop.'

The new Fran, the single, happy Fran who had her career on track, a wonderful sister and a fabulous best friend, didn't need a man to be happy. That was an unequivocal fact. Ending things with Stew had shown me I was stronger, confirmed I was better off by myself than wasting my life with the wrong person, but somehow, that knowledge only made things worse. I wasn't interested in dating, I'd declined the apps, the set-ups, all the friends-of friends that already had been thrust my way. This wasn't a case of glomming on to the next boy-shaped thing that came along and I meant what I said, I really didn't *need* a man.

But I wanted Evan.

The robin swooped into a flock of little birds, all of them fighting over what looked like an entire loaf of breadcrumbs and as they all flapped and hopped and pecked around each other, I couldn't work out which was my robin any more.

Resting my elbows on my knees, I cupped my face in my mittens and pouted, phone resting on my knee. Christmas made everyone extra melancholy, that's all it was. How many people had sent texts they would regret in the last twenty-four hours? Thousands of people. Hundreds of thousands. Half of all humans with a phone, I expected. He probably wasn't even as wonderful as I remembered. He was probably rude to waiters and didn't tip very well. For all I knew, he was one of those men who turned his underwear inside out instead of doing a load of washing.

Even so, the memory of our evening together haunted me in the best way and I couldn't quite shake Jess's advice as it nagged away at me, in the back of my mind. We don't wait for things to happen, we make them happen. How was this any different? There was only one sure-fire way to deal with this situation and that was to do something about it.

And then it hit me. What if I went to New York? Men weren't the only ones who could show up out the blue with their grand romantic gestures. The idea took hold fast and before I knew it, I was looking up flights and hotels and tapping Evan's address into Google Maps. One of the reasons I was such a good assistant was because I remembered everything, names, faces, phone numbers, how many sugars you wanted in your tea, and Evan's address had been burned into my memory since the moment I saw his driver's licence. 22 Mercer Street, New York, New York.

I could do this. I could be my own fairy godmother.

My whole body hummed with purpose as I pulled on my mittens and stood up, waving goodbye to the flock of tiny birds, still fighting over their Christmas dinner. I didn't want to be a princess who lived in a castle and danced around at balls in glass slippers. I liked the real world too much, and glass slippers sounded like a sliced Achilles tendon waiting to happen, but that didn't mean I couldn't work a little bit of magic now and then.

CHAPTER TWENTY-SEVEN

'Jess!' I shouted, slipping off my trainers at the back door. 'You were right, it's bloody freezing out there. Seriously, it's so cold it's frozen the actual wee in my actual bladder.'

The central heating hit hard and my hair frizzed around my face, crackling with static as I peeled off my hat and my earmuffs, and I unwound my scarf as I scooted into the living room, spooling the heavy grey wool around my arms, excited to tell my friend about my plan.

'Just as well because otherwise I would have wet myself. Anyway, I need your help. I've decided I'm going to go to New York and find Evan and – oh my god.'

The scarf, the hat, the earmuffs and mittens all fell to the floor.

There was no need to go to New York to find Evan because Evan wasn't in New York.

He was standing in my living room.

'Oh, there you are,' Jess said, casual as you like. 'I was just about to text to say we've got a visitor.'

'That would have been nice,' I replied as she peeled herself from the settee, a steaming mug of something that smelled suspiciously boozy in her hands.

'It's half whisky, you're welcome,' she whispered, handing it to me before leaving us alone.

I took a deep drink of her Irish coffee. It was more than half whisky.

'Hello,' I said.

'Hi,' Evan said. 'I got your text.' He held up his phone as evidence. 'And I was going to message you back but I was pretty close by and I thought, it's Christmas, why not stop in and say hi?'

'How close?'

'Paris.'

'Just down the road then,' I replied and took another glug of coffee.

He was wearing the same grey coat he'd worn the last time I'd seen him and his brown eyes twinkled with the reflection of our tree's fairy lights. His dark hair was a little longer and he looked as though he hadn't shaved in a couple of days. There were dark circles under his eyes, and I couldn't stop myself wondering if he'd been losing sleep for the same reason as me.

'Hey, did you know everything in this country is completely closed today?' he asked with a lopsided smile. 'Even Starbucks.'

'Well, yes,' I replied, catching sight of myself in the mirror above the sofa and immediately wishing I could go and get changed or put on some mascara or jump out of a window. 'It's Christmas.'

'It's not super convenient.'

'Not if you're an American billionaire who wants a

337

coffee,' I agreed. 'But we normal folk manage for one day. Here.'

I held out the mug and he took it, drank it dry then handed it back without a word.

'Sheffield is *not* New York,' he said with a choked cough, as though that fact might be news to anyone on earth. 'And by the way, I'm not a billionaire.'

I raised an eyebrow. My online stalking said otherwise.

'My dad is,' he corrected.

'My mistake. You're still very rich though?'

'Oh, yes,' Evan confirmed with a shrug. 'But don't let that put you off.'

'I'll try,' I promised weakly.

'That's all anyone can ask.'

He gave me a look that somehow made me forget I was wearing jogging bottoms and my pyjama top underneath my coat, and I had to reach out for the doorframe to steady myself.

'Sounds like I saved you a trip,' he said, stood right in front of the tree while I hovered in my own doorway. 'This is the worst time to go to New York. Too many tourists and the weather is terrible, plus the airlines are totally gonna gouge you for flights.'

Obviously, I'd spent the entire walk back planning my trip and it had quickly become clear as to why you never saw grand romantic gestures from the other end on TV or in the movies. Someone doing something epic for the person they loved was so overwhelmingly wonderful, you let yourself be swept along in the adventure without having to worry about the logistics. There was nothing sexy or romantic about logistics. No one wanted to see their hero toggling between flight options to find anything under a grand any more than they wanted to see some perfectionist fiancé screaming at his rehearsing flashmob until his second cousin locked herself in the toilet, sobbing.

'The flights did look quite expensive,' I admitted. 'And, you know it would have been a bit of a downer if I'd got all the way there then found out you were here.'

'And is it OK that I'm here?' he asked. 'When I got your text I figured…'

'It's more than OK,' I replied in a whisper, very much wishing I had more Irish coffee. 'It's very, very OK.'

My heart soared as he smiled and reached inside his coat to pull out a silver envelope from the inside pocket. 'I got you something,' he said. 'It didn't feel right to show up on Christmas Day without a gift.'

He held up the envelope and I saw a name written on the front in very fancy handwriting. Francesca Anderson.

'What is it?' I asked.

'In America, it's traditional to open presents, that's how you find out what's inside,' Evan replied, handing it over. He sat down on the floor in front of the tree and crossed his long legs, patting the floor beside him. Reluctantly letting go of the doorframe, I sat down beside him, close enough to smell his aftershave, that same spicy, warm scent, and I realized I was shaking.

Inside the envelope was a stiff piece of card, heavy and thick and coated in some sort of iridescent varnish that made it hard to read. At the top, was a small engraving of a crystal ball and underneath that, the details of an all-expenses paid, luxury shopping trip to New York. First class flights, five-star hotels, private chauffeur and, most importantly to me and my stomach, all meals included.

I looked up at him in disbelief.

'What is this?'

'Guess who won the auction at the Crystal Ball?' he replied, waggling his eyebrows up and down. 'Congratulations.'

'Evan, it's too much,' I said as I tried to jam the card and my feelings back inside the envelope. 'I can't accept this.'

He pressed his lips together in a small smile. 'Yes, you can. The auction was for charity and I bid with my dad's credit card, so if you refuse it, that would pretty much make you the reverse Robin Hood. Isn't he from around here?'

'Only if you're American,' I replied before eyeing him doubtfully. 'I thought the Crystal Ball committee raised money for homeless charities?'

'Entirely possible,' he said. 'If I'm being honest, I don't know what they raise money for. The ball has always been more about getting wasted and smoking in the bathroom with Jennifer Lawrence for me.'

'I KNEW IT,' Jess yelled from the kitchen.

'Please ignore her,' I instructed. 'It's not easy, I know, but give it your best shot.'

'Only if you agree to accept this,' he said. 'I mean, it has your name on it.'

'Actually, it doesn't,' I laughed, tracing a fingernail over the 'Anderson' on the envelope, overwhelmed by the feeling of allowing someone to do something nice for me. First, Rachel taking care of me at the hotel, then Jess giving me a home, and now this. If they weren't all careful, I was going to get used to it. 'Thank you,' I said, nodding to myself before meeting his eyes. 'I wish I had something to give you.'

'The way I see it, the trip is a gift for both of us,' Evan smiled. 'You get to visit New York and I get to see you again. If you want to see me, that is, I didn't mean. . . you're not obligated in any way, there aren't strings attached to the trip. New York's pretty big, it's very unlikely we would run into each other if you—'

Without thinking, I placed a finger against his lips to cut him off mid-flow. He had waited until I let him know I was ready. He had travelled all this way to see me. He had done something incredibly thoughtful and kind. And, in a true Christmas miracle, he was just as ridiculously attractive as I remembered.

'I would love to come and visit you in New York,' I said, rising up on my knees and brushing his hair out of his face. It was so silky, it fell right back in front of his eyes and I had to try very hard to focus on the moment instead of asking what kind of shampoo he used. 'You know, I think I might have a gift for you after all.'

Resting my hands on his thighs, I leaned in until I could feel his breath warm against my lips and I kissed him.

It was almost impossible for something you'd dreamed about for so long to live up to your expectations, even orange Twirls weren't *that* good, but kissing Evan Carden was the most overwhelming, heart-stopping experience of my entire life. Every dream, every fantasy, every impossible scenario I'd spent the last few weeks cooking up in my mind, none of them even came close to the way it felt when my lips met his. The books, the songs, the movies, none of them could have described it fully and it wasn't their fault, words just couldn't do it justice. Everything stopped and sped up at the same time, the room spinning around us even as time stood still.

I felt Evan's mouth smiling against mine, his hands against my cheeks, warm palms cupping cool skin and I wrapped my arms around his neck to pull him closer. I'd waited long enough. His hands moved into my hair, pulling it lightly away from my face, and I gasped, shivers running all the way down my spine as my mouth opened to his, body to body, heart to heart, all tangled up in front of the tree.

'In answer to your text, I'm having a perfect Christmas *now*,' Evan said as we broke apart, my lips already aching and swollen. 'You wouldn't believe how much time I've spent thinking about this.'

'I would believe anything you told me,' I replied, combing my hand through his hair then pulling him back in for another kiss.

And even though it felt like a happy ending,

I knew in my heart,

it was just

the beginning.

ACKNOWLEDGEMENTS

As ever, I owe this entire book (and let's be frank, so much more) to my agent, Rowan Lawton. You're the best agent, cheerleader and friend I could ask for. I'm so proud that you choose to work with me.

This year more than ever, you only have a book in your hands because of the grace, tenacity and editorial wizardry of Lynne Drew. Lynne, I've said it a thousand* times, I cannot imagine doing this without you. Thank you, thank you, thank you. More thanks to Sophie Burks and Lucy Stewart for keeping me on the straight and narrow, to Felicity Denham for continuing to be the actual best (verified fact), to Hannah O'Brien, Rachel Quin and Maddy Marshall for your tireless hard work and putting up with my constant stream of theoretical nonsense, to my copyeditor, Charlotte Webb, and to Holly MacDonald, Isabel Coburn, Alice Gomer and everyone else at HarperCollins – THANK YOU. I will inevitably miss off a thousand* people who deserve

---

* seventeen and counting. Which is practically a thousand.

individual appreciation, but whether you're in sales, marketing, publicity, production, legal, art, design, customer service, logistics or anywhere else in the entire company, please take it from this recovering Hammersmith-ite, your contribution to this process does not go unnoticed or unappreciated.

And thank you to all at The Soho Agency, especially Isabelle Wilson, for all your continued support. I'm very proud to be part of your team.

To all my book-world friends, thank you so much for everything. I don't know if anyone has mentioned the Trying Times TM & © 2020 but honestly, without you to bitch, moan, laugh, cry, commiserate and sulk with, I'm not sure I would be writing this now. Mhairi McFarlane, Lia Louis, Kevin Dickson, Paige Toon, Giovanna Fletcher, Louise Pentland, Marian Keyes, Kwana Jackson, Sarra Manning, Lauren Ho, Sally Thorne, Helly Acton, Jane Fallon, Lucy Vine, Claire Frost, Rosie Walsh, Gillian McAllister, Holly Seddon, Holly Bourne, Rowan Coleman, Julie Cohen, Isabelle Broom, Andrea Bartz and heaps of other people I'm forgetting in this moment for understanding and supporting and being generally brilliant. Whether it was a brief Tweet, the odd DM or a deep dive into the cultural impact of the work of Taylor Swift (you know who you are), I am SO APPRECIATIVE OF YOU.

As ever, I'm only able to do this because I am propped up by my friends and family at all times: Jeff, Bobby, Lesley & Walter White, Della Bolat, Julian Burrell, Kevin Dickson, Louise Doyle, Philippa Drewer, Emma Gunavardhna, Tal Harris & Kasia Kowalcyzk, Emma Ingram, Hal Lublin, Danielle Radford and of course, Terri White, all more than earned their money on this one. Pals, your cheques are in the post. A million more of you are cursing my name right now. Sorry, I've been writing this for ages and I'm shit, as you know.

There is still part of me that can't quite believe this book exists. It was written and edited through one of the most challenging years on record and this time not just for me but for all of us, and so I say this with a full heart, if you're holding it in your hands right now, this book was written for you. I usually reject anything that sounds like an Instagram wellness slogan immediately and without question but this one I believe whole-heartedly – we didn't come this far to only come this far. Work out what you want and get after it, time is ticking.

ABOUT THE AUTHOR

Lindsey Kelk has never worked on a yacht, but she did work as a sales assistant, a publicist, a silver service waitress and a children's book editor before moving to New York to become a full-time writer. Now living in LA, alongside writing she co-hosts the award-winning beauty podcast, *Full Coverage*, and the professional wrestling podcast, *Tights and Fights*.

For the latest on new books, tours and events, sign up to Lindsey's newsletter at www.lindseykelk.com and follow her on social media @LindseyKelk.